GET A FREE BOOK

Check out Hangfire, the next Cutter Grogan thriller

Check out Tightrope, the next Zeb Carter thriller

Join Ty Patterson's group of readers, on Facebook

ALSO BY TY PATTERSON

Most recent first

Cutter Grogan Series (Zeb Carter Universe)

Two books in the series and counting

Zeb Carter Series

Eight books in the series and counting

Zeb Carter Short Stories

Three books and counting

Warriors Series (Zeb Carter Universe)

Twelve books in the series

Gemini Series (Zeb Carter Universe)

Four thrillers in the series

Warriors Series Shorts (Zeb Carter Universe)

Six novellas in the series

Cade Stryker Series

Two military sci-fi thrillers

ACKNOWLEDGMENTS

They say it takes a village to produce a book. In my case, many continents have been involved. Sure, an author's job is a solitary one, but writing is just one part of putting out a book.

My beta readers, who are around the world, are my first responders. I owe a debt of gratitude to them for putting into shape all the words I write.

They are:

Dori Barrett, Laura Rachwalik, Jobins MJ, Simon Alphonso, Maria Stine, Steve Panza, Ann Finn, Don Waterman, Kimber Krahn, Robin Eide Steffensen, Blanca Nichols, Loz Yeung, Charlie Carrick, Martin Pingere, Terrill Carpenter, Kathryn Defranc, Dave Davis, Mike Duncan, Donna Young Hartridge, Shadine Mccallen, Shell Levy, Wanona Koeppler, Marion McNulty Hulse, Gerry Kenny, Rob Fox, Dan Gherasim, Toni Osborne, Theresa Ann Kari, JoAnn Cates Lewis, Cathie M Jones, Debbie McNally, Sylvia Foster, Beth Perry, Mike Davis, Pat Barling, Mary Kauffman, John Spiller, Dave Campbell, Mark Campbell, Cathy Silveira, Franca Parente, Jan Fisher, Nancy Schmit, Claire Forgacs, Pete Bennett, Eric Blackburn, Margaret

Harvey, Jim Lambert, Jimmy Smith, Suzanne Mickelson, Brad Werths, Allan Coulton, Paula Artlip, Pat Ellis, Linda Collins, Tricia Cullerton, Alun Humphreys, Jennifer Anderson, Manie Kilian, Larry Kahhan, Tania Reed, Debbie McNally, Heather Tudgey, Gary Bristol, Lyn Fox. Hannah Lewis and Gary Rounds.

Donna Rich, my proofreader, and Doreen Martens, my editor, have been invaluable in polishing the book.

Lastly, a special thanks to Debbie Gallant, Tom Gallant, Michelle Rose Dunn and Cheri Gerhardt, who have supported me since the beginning.

DEDICATIONS

To my wife and son for their sacrifices in supporting me

Tip the world over on its side and everything loose will land in Los Angeles.
— Frank Lloyd Wright

'That's far enough,' the bearded man snapped.

Cutter stopped in the clearing and raised his hands as wide as he could.

'I'm alone.'

'Do you have the money?'

'What do you think I'm carrying in this?' he retorted. He dropped the heavy gym bag to his feet and massaged his fingers.

'Piotr, count it.'

'Not so fast,' Cutter warned the gangbanger. 'Where's the girl?'

The thug nodded at another heavy, who disappeared into the darkness and returned with a teenage girl. Her eyes were wide with fright, her mouth taped, and her hands bound behind her.

'Amy?' Cutter recognized her from her photographs. 'This will be over soon. I'll take you to your mom and dad.'

She nodded rapidly and sobbed in relief.

'Count it,' he told the leader of the kidnapping gang, at whose shoulder jerk two gunmen came forward with counting machines. They opened the bag and placed the bundles of used notes on their trays. For long moments, there was nothing but the sound of the whirring devices and the girl's dry heaves.

'Three million,' one shooter announced.

'Just as we agreed. Let the girl go.'

'I think not,' the leader smirked. 'We have the money, the girl. You're alone. We'll kill you here.' He hefted his AR-15. 'It's a remote part of the Catskills. No one will hear a few shots. It'll take days or weeks for your body to be discovered.'

'You think you'll get away?'

'We know we'll escape. It's not the first time we've taken the money and run off with the girls. Who'll stop us?'

Cutter clamped his lips tight as his rage flared.

ABRAHAM ZINOV, A RUSSIAN GANGSTER, HAD MADE A successful business of kidnapping the children of millionaires and escaping with the ransom money. In most instances, the victims weren't seen again.

He was wanted by the FBI and by every law enforcement agency in the country, yet he had evaded capture.

Amy Sorkin was his latest victim. He had grabbed the eighteen-year-old as she was emerging from her upscale private school in Brooklyn Heights. He had sent the ransom demand to her father, Travis Sorkin, a multimillionaire hedge-fund owner, and Sorkin had contacted Cutter.

'No cops,' the distraught father had insisted. 'I know how it's gone down before. More than half of the kids are still missing.'

'You need to trust the FBI and the NYPD. I'm by myself. I'll—'

'No!' the dad had yelled. 'I'll pay. Three million is nothing. I would give away thirty, everything I have, to get back Amy. Take it to them and get my daughter back.'

Cutter tried his best to convince the parent, but his arguments fell on deaf ears.

'You cannot go to the cops either,' Sorkin told him. 'You've got to promise.'

Cutter had given his word and agreed to go to the drop-off in the Catskills.

'YOU THINK I'M ALONE?'

'That trick won't work,' Zinov boasted. 'We followed you when you entered the forest. We've searched you. No phone, no tracker. You're surrounded by thirteen men. Yeah, I think you're alone. You're bluffing, and you'll die.'

Amy screamed when he raised his gun.

Her shriek turned to a startled gasp when the gangbanger holding her fell to the ground as his head exploded.

Cutter dived to his left and grabbed his left shoe as the rattle of guns burst the silence.

'POLICE. GIVE YOURSELF UP,' a loud-hailer announced.

Zinov grabbed the girl and fired wildly into the dark.

Cutter scrambled away as the kidnapper turned on him. He tore the bottom of his shoe away and removed the composite-made, 3D-printed gun and took aim.

He didn't flinch when a bullet smacked into the ground next to his face, spraying him with dirt and leaves.

'I'LL SHOOT HER,' Zinov yelled as his men disappeared into the woods. He crouched behind Amy, holding her hostage.

Cutter could see the side of his face, was aware of voices and shouts as cops captured the escaping gang, and then he saw nothing but the gangbanger's forehead beyond the sight of his gun.

'No, you won't,' he whispered and fired.

'I TOLD YOU, NO COPS,' TRAVIS SORKIN SAID AS HE HUGGED his daughter tight.

They were at the FBI's perimeter half a mile from the scene of the drop-off. The father's face was streaked with tears and lines of worry.

'I gave you an order,' he bellowed.

'I didn't go to the cops, sir,' Cutter replied.

He hadn't. He had confided in Zeb, who had alerted the Feds, who had worked with him to set up the trap. An ingestible GPS tracker, which he had swallowed, had enabled the federal agents to track him down. The ceramic gun was his own improvisation.

'How did they know?'

'Dad!' his daughter caught his lapels and shook him. 'I'm safe. Alive. Mr. Grogan got me out. Isn't that the important thing?'

Her father burst into sobs at that and blindly reached out and squeezed Cutter's shoulder.

'YOU DIDN'T HAVE TO SHOOT HIM,' PEYTON QUINDICA, FBI Special Agent in Charge, chided, frowning at him.

'I didn't have to,' he agreed sarcastically. 'I could have let him shoot Amy and me.'

'We would have taken him down.'

'I couldn't risk it.'

'I told you not to be a hero.'

'I was trying to stay alive and keep Amy safe.'

She grinned wryly as she shook her head. 'We'll need that.' She gestured at his gun. 'That escapes the detectors?'

'Yeah, it's made of a composite material that the NSA is testing. I wouldn't be alive otherwise.'

'You'll keep that to yourself?'

He searched her eyes under the glare of spotlights and nodded. *If that gets out, every terrorist and criminal in the country will be printing guns.*

He grinned as his eyes searched the area over her shoulder. 'I'm half-expecting to see Difiore.'

Gina Difiore, Detective First Grade with the NYPD, the FBI agent's partner. He had come across them in a previous assignment, and the initial antagonistic relationship had turned into a kind of friendship.

Sort of, he told himself.

Cutter called himself a Fixer, someone who helped those whom the system couldn't. The detective considered him to be a vigilante and treated him with disdain.

'This is an FBI operation,' Quindica said, smiling. 'We aren't joined at the hip.'

'She knows I was involved in this?'

'Yeah. She said the world would be a better place if I let you get shot.'

'Sounds like her.' He high-fived Quindica and went to his SUV.

Leaned back wearily when his phone rang.

'Yeah?' he asked. *That's a West Coast number.*

'Is this Cutter Grogan?'

'That's me.'

'Mr. Grogan, I'm Diego Cruz, detective with the LAPD.'

'What's this about?'

'I've got bad news. Arnedra Jones and her sister were killed in a gang shooting.'

T he five-and-a-half-hour flight from JFK to LAX the next day passed in a blur.

Cutter had wrapped the takedown with Quindica the previous night and had driven numbly to his apartment on Lafayette Avenue in the city. He had packed, booked a flight to Los Angeles, then gone to his office to tidy it up and close it down for the time he would be away.

ARNEDRA AND HE RAN THE FIXING BUSINESS—WHICH IS WHAT they called it—as equal business partners. They were close friends, as well.

They helped people whom the system couldn't or wouldn't help. Kidnap cases the cops had effectively given up on. Kids who had fallen in with gangs.

People often came to them instead of going to the law because of the reputation they had earned. The police, and Feds too, referred their cold cases to Cutter and Arnedra.

They had become known nationwide when Cutter took down a white supremacist gang that was looking to influence the presidential elections.

He was the field operative; she managed the business—a distribution of work that took best advantage of their skills.

Cutter was a former Delta Forces operative whose military file was filled with redactions. Afghanistan, Iraq, Somalia, Europe, Croatia, Iran, Pakistan, Indonesia—he had been to hotspots all over the world, in covert operations that would never be known to the wider world. He had spent a few years as a mercenary as well, at a time when he had lost himself.

Arnedra had run a PI business with her husband and was in the process of winding it down following his death when Cutter rescued her from a mugging in Central Park. That brought the two of them together.

The soldier-for-hire business had been very lucrative. Those earnings and smart investments had left him flush with funds.

He convinced her to restart the business but with a different focus—helping those in need—and bought into half of it.

She helped me heal after Riley's death, he thought bitterly as he looked out the window of the aircraft while it cut through blue skies and fleecy clouds. Riley Grogan, his wife, who had died in Turkey when his past resurfaced.

The traveler next to him tried to make small talk. Gave up when Cutter's monosyllabic answers and negative vibe let him know conversation wasn't welcome. An air hostess tried to flirt with him. His six-foot-one frame, dark, styled hair and intense green eyes caught the eye of many women, but he wasn't interested.

Cutter brooded and mourned for his partner as the packed aluminum tube traversed the curve of the earth.

'If you need any help ...' the air hostess's cheeks dimpled in a smile as he was leaving.

'I won't, but thanks,' he said, forcing a smile in return. She wasn't to blame for how he was feeling. He strode through the terminal and donned his shades when he stepped out into the August late-afternoon heat.

He flagged a cab and gave the driver an East Hollywood address. Looked blindly out the window as blue skies and buildings merged and became a liquid line of construction, residences and commercial buildings as the cab sped through the traffic.

It circled the edge of downtown LA and dumped him half an hour later on North Heliotrope Drive.

A line of single and multifamily residences on one side, some kind of low-slung office building on the other.

The house he wanted was in front of him. A chest-high concrete wall running around it, separating it from the residences on either side. A ficus on the sidewalk just outside the wrought-iron gate threw a large shadow, offering respite from the heat.

The gate squeaked when he opened it. A middle-aged woman peered over the wall and checked him out as he walked up the concrete path set into the lush lawn of the front yard. Four palm trees and several flowering plants dotted the garden. Ms. Neighbor continued watching him when he climbed the porch, inserted his key in the door and entered the still house.

Vienna McDonald, Arnedra's elder sister, lived alone. No spouse or partner. She had never married and had taken her mother's second name. Her passion for working with nonprofits had taken her around the world. Her last overseas job had been with the United Nations in Kenya, and then she had returned to the States to train as a paramedic. The Los Angeles Fire Department's Emergency Medical Services Bureau had recruited her immediately, and the city had been her home for over a decade.

Arnedra helped her buy this home, Cutter mused as he checked out the cool interiors of the house. Warm colors, soft carpet, pictures and awards in the living room, two couches that showed signs of use, a TV screen in a corner.

He picked up a photograph from a chest of drawers and inspected it: Arnedra and Vienna in happier times, their smiles brilliant white in contrast to their darker skin. His lips turned up involuntarily at their joy. He wandered around the house, inspecting the kitchen, dining room and the backyard, in which was another exquisitely maintained garden. He went up the stairs to the three bedrooms.

Nothing in any room other than personal belongings, clothing, suitcases, books. No clue why they had been killed.

Still, he searched every room. Checked out floors and walls to see if there were any hidden compartments or crevices in which drugs, guns or money could be stashed.

All he found were photographs and journals and letters from loved ones. Bank statements and forgotten receipts and bills.

They were all that remained of a life lived fully.

3

'I'm a family friend, ma'am,' Cutter told Ms. Neighbor, who was still watching when he went out. 'Arnedra, Vienna's sister, was my business partner in New York. We were close. I met Vienna a few times when she came to visit.'

'You heard about it?' the suspicion in her eyes faded when he showed her a photograph on his phone, of him with the sisters at a diner in New York.

'Yes, ma'am. Got a call from the cops yesterday.'

The Catskills shootout had been less than twenty-four hours ago, but it felt like an eternity.

'Vienna was so happy,' the neighbor said, then introduced herself as Naysha Sutton, a city worker. 'We got along together like a house on fire. I was right there when she moved in. Trayvon, Alisha and Jonas, my kids and husband, we helped her settle in. We barbecued together, had parties in our backyards ...' Her lips quivered. She sniffled and angrily brushed her tears away.

'No,' she said, reading his question. 'She wasn't into drugs. None of that for her. The cops came round today, in the morning, and I told them the same thing. Vienna didn't have enemies.

Heck, even her former boyfriends, she was on good terms with them.'

'You met Arnedra, ma'am? When she arrived here?'

'Yeah, many times before as well. I liked her.' Her teary eyes widened. 'You're Cutter Grogan?'

'Yes, ma'am.'

'Holy sh—' She cut herself off quickly. 'We saw you on TV a few times. You were responsible for that gang takedown.'

'It wasn't just me, ma'am. Arnedra was involved in it as well. FBI, NYPD, several agencies. I played a small role. The media, they blew it up, you know how they are.'

Naysha Sutton waved his self-deprecation away and urged him to her house. Over coffee and cookies, she plied him with questions, and when her husband, son and daughter joined, the gathering turned into dinner and weepy reminiscing about Vienna.

It was eleven pm when Cutter left them, knowing nothing more of why the sisters had been killed, or by whom. The cops had given the Suttons the same bland message that Diego Cruz the detective had given him: that the women had been murdered in a gang attack.

I've got friends at the LAPD, he thought, gazing at the trail of a passenger aircraft as it flew high above him in the night sky.

No. There was another house he wanted to check out.

The kill site.

❦ 4 ❧

Cutter took a cab to Beverly Hills, the upscale neighborhood populated by high-fliers and shot-callers in the movie business.

The driver sized him up in the rearview mirror, taking in his Tee tucked into jeans, sneakers, and the backpack over his shoulder.

'You a model?'

'Nope,' he replied curtly, hoping his brusque answer would be enough to silence the man's curiosity.

'It's my first night in a cab,' the man confided. 'I had to take this job when my startup collapsed. My first time driving to Beverly Hills, too.'

LA was like that. It was the West Coast's answer to New York. A magnet that drew people from all over the country and the world. Many of them fleeing the colder eastern cities, pursuing a dream of making it big in the film or glamor industry. Or the burgeoning tech one.

They went down quiet streets noticeably different from Vienna McDonald's in East Hollywood. Larger trees on the sidewalk, all of them neatly trimmed. Well-lit roads, high concrete walls, behind which the tops of houses were sometimes visible through foliage.

He got the driver to drop him off at Tower Grove and walked up Beverly Grove Drive. A steep, curving street that rose up the hill, dotted with exclusive residences. A Porsche slid past and illuminated him briefly. A Ferrari growled and slowed. Its driver window lowered and a blonde eyed him speculatively and then sped away.

Not many walk here. She must be wondering if I'm a hobo. Or part of a home invasion crew. His lips twisted sardonically.

The air turned cooler and the city's sounds fell away as he went higher, until he came to a hairpin bend—and there it was.

The murder house.

An open garage, which was empty. A rolling metal gate, which was closed. Police tape across the front. Lights inside the house, but no sound of any occupants, no cruisers in sight.

Cutter noted the camera and shrugged.

So what if someone was monitoring the house? He vaulted nimbly over the barrier and stepped onto the driveway. The front was as large as a tennis court, with a garden and several fountains that were still. Plants and flowers withering from neglect. Only the lights suggested that someone was attending to the house.

He went up to the door. Locked.

Went down the side of the house and climbed inside through a window that was partly open. A large room that smelled of dead air. He turned on the flashlight on his phone and navigated through the darkness. Some kind of reception room, a hallway beyond, another large room. Kitchen, which seemed to be equipped with every modern convenience, a dining room whose black surfaces gleamed in the night. More rooms that he checked out carefully, and then another living room with floor-to-ceiling windows and doors, one of which slid back noiselessly and opened to a patio.

Cutter crouched over the two blobs of darkness on the

concrete. Dried blood from Vienna and Arnedra's bodies. Police markings on the floor that showed where they had lain. He took a deep breath and got to his feet. Went to the patio and looked out at the vastness of Los Angeles laid out before him.

The house was perched on the side of the hill, with just a sturdy glass wall separating it from the steep drop. He took in the conglomeration of lights and yellow glow that stood out from the surrounding dimness that wasn't LA.

The Tongva, the original indigenous occupants of the land, had been driven out by settlers from Mexico, Sonora, Franciscan priests and Spanish colonizers, in a centuries-old cycle repeated around the world.

How Los Angeles came to be called the City of Angels was a matter of some dispute, but the name obviously had a nice ring to it and had stuck.

He checked out the darkness of the neighboring hill, where a few lights twinkled. More houses, higher up, discreetly hidden by nature and artful construction.

Cutter turned his back on LA's sprawl and looked again at the dark splotches on the concrete. The numbness left him, replaced by rage and fury that consumed him until all he could see was darkness. As the earth rotated and revolved, those, too, faded, until he was left with cold detachment and a simple resolve.

Screw the cops. He was going to find out who the killers were.

He was The Fixer. He would deliver his justice.

And that was when the house's lights suddenly turned on and a voice yelled.

'RAISE YOUR HANDS. STEP AWAY FROM THE WALL.'

5

Cutter lifted his hands and took a couple of steps towards the patio door. Two men in civilian clothes pointed their guns at him. Behind them, a line of patrol cops with their weapons similarly trained.

He cursed himself for his negligence. *I was facing the house. I should have seen them coming.*

'Are you armed?' the cop on the left barked. He was dark-haired, with silver in his long sideburns that caught the lights.

'Nope.'

'What's in your backpack?' his companion—lean face, watchful eyes—asked.

Cutter tossed his bag at them, at which they jerked sideways and tightened their grips on their guns.

'HEY!' the first speaker yelled. 'YOU WANT TO GET KILLED?'

'Diego,' the second cop hissed, 'that's Grogan.'

Diego's eyes flickered over Cutter. The anger on his face diminished.

'That right?'

'Yeah.'

'You're alone?'

'There's something else you should know.'

He turned at the tone in the detective's voice and looked at him sharply.

The cop hesitated and then thrust his chin forward at a nod from Matteo. 'Both the women were tortured before they were shot.'

'Tell him everything,' the lead detective growled.

'And sexually assaulted,' Cruz added.

⚜ 6 ⚜

For a moment Cutter thought he hadn't heard correctly. 'Tortured and raped?' he repeated.

'Their nails were pulled out, there were cuts on their bellies, chests and thighs.' Cruz looked away from his burning stare. 'And yes, sexually attacked.'

Cutter looked up when he heard the throbbing of a chopper and then realized the sound was coming from inside him. It was the pounding of his blood, loud in his ears as the banked fury burst and filled him.

'Are you all right?' Cruz's voice came distantly.

'GROGAN?' Matteo called out loudly.

'Yeah,' he mumbled and forced himself to unclench his fists. He sucked lungfuls of air until the pulsing faded and the night and the light breeze returned.

'Semen?' he swallowed. 'Hair, skin, DNA?'

'None of the former.' The lead cop sighed. 'We're working on the second.'

'Both of them?'

'Yeah, both were assaulted.'

I asked Arnedra to come to LA. I told her she would be safe from that supremacist gang, he thought bitterly.

'Come down tomorrow, to headquarters.' Matteo glanced at his watch. 'We'll brief you fully.'

'How did you get here?' Cruz asked him.

'Cab,' Cutter forced himself to reply normally.

'We'll give you a ride. Where are you staying?'

'Vienna's house. East Hollywood.'

He got into the back of Matteo's unmarked car, while Cruz got into the front. The lead detective rolled down his window and instructed the patrol cops to secure the house.

Cutter didn't break the silence until they were nearing their destination.

'How did you know I was there?'

'Patrol car in a neighbor's driveway.' Cruz met his eyes in the rearview mirror. 'We've been keeping watch to see if any bangers return.'

'Did they?'

'You're the only one who turned up.'

He climbed out when the car rolled to a stop on North Heliotrope. Pocketed Matteo's card, which the detective handed over, and thanked the cops.

'Yeah, I'll be down tomorrow,' he told them and turned to the gate.

He waited until their tail lights disappeared behind a turn and pulled out his cell.

One am. He'll be awake.

'Chad?' he asked when a voice answered.

'Yeah, you know what time it—Cutter? That you?'

'I'm in town. I need some gear.'

'And you think the middle of the night is the best time for it?' Chad groused, though there was no rancor in his voice. 'All right,' he continued when Cutter didn't respond. 'Come on over.'

CHAD LIU: ARMORER TO COVERT OPERATIVES, THOSE WHO HAD to gear up by themselves when they were deep undercover.

Former Delta who ran a gun range in Culver City. Outfitting trusted friends was a side gig that had required him to modify his home and convert the garage into a secure weapons storage. He was well-connected to the cops, many of whom bought their backup weapons from Chad, and that, along with largely selling licensed weapons, had helped him stay clean.

He crushed Cutter in a bear hug and didn't stop beaming as he escorted his visitor into the house.

'Sandra?'

'She's sleeping. Livia and Jeff, too. An earthquake could hit LA and they wouldn't wake. Besides,' he added, pointing to the concrete ceiling in the living room, 'I've soundproofed the house. Nothing can be heard in the bedroom.'

He went to a bar and pulled out two glasses. Splashed alcohol into one and then stopped.

'You've taken up drinking?'

'Juice.'

'You're an insult to Delta,' he grumbled. Nevertheless, he went to the kitchen and returned with a carton of orange juice, filled Cutter's glass and handed it over.

'Remember the time in Afghanistan when Duke thought that goat was Taliban?' Chad started.

It was three am by the time they finished reminiscing.

'You didn't come to LA just to gear up.' The armorer's eyes narrowed. 'What have you gotten yourself into?'

His eyes turned flinty when Cutter broke it down for him. 'Gangs,' he spat. 'They're everywhere. I heard that on the news … didn't think it would bring *you* here.' He got to his feet and beckoned his guest with a finger. Led him through the kitchen, to a side door and into the armory.

'I built out the back and created this room.' He jerked his head to indicate the front wall. 'Beyond that is my garage. This, here, is secure. Fingerprint scan, iris, all that. Only Sandra and I have access.'

Guns, all of them collectors' items, lay beneath a glass

mafia, are into financial fraud, real estate scams and cyber-crime. That last business is their fastest growing. The gang has a team of hackers that produces deep fake porn videos and blackmails celebrities. They send phishing emails, penetrate bank accounts ... you name it, they do it.'

'We'll bring in some of Janikyan's men, too, and him.' Matteo threw his toothpick into a trashbin and inserted a new one in his mouth. 'If we find him.' He got to his feet, signaling the meeting was over. 'We told you all this out of courtesy. We know your reputation and what you did in New York. This isn't your turf. Stay out of our investigation. You've got enough on your plate. Funerals for—'

'DNA on their bodies?' Cutter interrupted him. 'Did you find who it belonged to?'

'No one in our system. LDIS, CODIS, no hits.'

LDIS, Local DNA Index System, CODIS, the FBI's Combined DNA Index System.

'Can I see the surveillance video from the neighboring houses?'

'Nothing much there.' Matteo nodded at Estrada, who connected his laptop to a projector, logged into the system and threw up a black screen on the wall. 'We spliced the different clips into one,' he explained as a view of the street came up. 'That's just after the hairpin bend. No cameras before it.'

Three SUVs rushed past, all of them dark, and disappeared out of the frame in a flash. 'This is the cleaned-up version,' the cop narrated when another video played in slo-mo. 'The same three rides appeared, shadows distinguishable inside, and then they were out of sight.

'We worked out the models of those vehicles.' The BHPD detective turned off the projector. 'Two Toyota Highlanders, and one of them is a Toyota RAV. Those are the most popular SUVs in the country. We haven't been able to narrow down those rides any further. Sorry.' The cop shrugged his shoulders. 'Don't have better news for you.'

'What about their phones, their bags?'

'Their bags were at the scene. Their wallets, credit cards, everything seemed intact. We identified them from their driver's licenses. No phones, however.'

'The shooters took them.'

'That's what we believe. The cells are offline. Probably destroyed. We contacted their network providers and got a list of calls. Nothing that stood out. Each other's numbers, a few local stores, a theater, restaurants. We placed their devices on Beverly Hills Grove Drive about an hour before time of death. Last position was up the drive. They didn't ping the towers after that.'

'Their killers turned them off?'

'Possibly, but there's network reception to consider as well. It's sketchy in the hills.'

'How did they get there?'

'Vienna McDonald's car is missing. We suspect she drove, but we haven't found it. It's a Mazda, again a common make.'

'We called various bodyshops.' Matteo's toothpick bobbed in his mouth. 'None of them got any such vehicle in the last forty-eight hours.'

Cutter sat grimly in silence and then got to his feet.

'No interference from you.' Matteo shook his hand. 'Are we clear?'

'Of course,' Cutter lied smoothly and followed Cruz to the lobby.

HE STEPPED OUT OF THE FUTURISTIC-LOOKING LAPD headquarters on First Street. Searched for a food truck, didn't find one, but spotted the LA Times building just behind. *Times Mirror Square, that'll have eating places.* He ordered two large servings of nachos and found a bench in the lobby of the Times building. Checked his watch, pulled out his cell and dialed a number.

demographic was prominent. *No bangers sporting guns or tattoos.* That would be bad for business.

He walked around the bar. It fronted both the main streets, and to its rear was an unnamed alley that ran a long way down to the intersection with Lexington Avenue. A tall iron fence at the rear that closed off the backyard of the bar. That could be a delivery entrance. As he watched, the back door opened. A splash of light and music spilled into the quiet alley and a man emerged. Chef, taking a breather. The man fumbled in his pockets, came out with a cigarette, lit it, inhaled and blew out with a sigh.

Cutter ghosted around the alley, noting the two cameras at the back, and joined the line of entrants at the front.

The interior was warm, dark curtains hanging from the ceiling to muffle the sounds of the pounding beat. A Prohibition-style bar to his left, at which were stools and a crush of people. A stretch of dining tables spaced out to his right. At the far end was a small stage with a keyboard, a drum set and speakers. No performers on it.

He went to the bar and ordered his drink. Found an empty table and settled in to watch. Drew out his phone and scrolled on it occasionally, as if he were reading it.

The restrooms were behind a curtained partition to his eleven-o'clock. After an hour, he went down the passage and checked them out. Beyond them was the kitchen and a passage that opened around the bar for the servers to bring food through.

No gangbangers in sight.

They came at twelve am.

Four of them, with a distinctive gang swagger. Loose shirts, tattooed arms, low-riding jeans, baseball caps at an angle, and jewelry.

He thought they looked familiar, looked similar to some of the members' photographs that Matteo and Cruz had shown him.

One of them yelled raucously at the bartender, who waved and gestured at the stage.

None of them is Covarra or Salazar. Is that where they're going to sit?

That's where the heavies arranged themselves. They brought out a folding table from the back of the elevated area, a couch and two chairs, and sprawled on it like they owned the place. A server brought over drinks and two bowls of nachos. They dipped into their food and swigged from their bottles, ignoring the rest of the patrons.

Need to confirm who they are. The cops had shown him several images, and he could be mistaken in recognizing them.

Cutter got his chance half an hour later.

One of the men got to his feet, pulled up his Tee and scratched his belly. The butt of a waist-tucked gun was visible even at this distance. He belched and stumbled toward the bathroom.

He was washing his face when Cutter joined him at the line of sinks. He stumbled and crashed into the man. Got hold of his Tee and yanked down hard, making it look like he was regaining his balance.

There it was. The tattoo on the neck that identified LA Street Front thugs. A man lying on a sidewalk.

'S'rry, bud,' Cutter slurred and let go of the hood, who cursed and knocked his hand away.

Cutter raised his palms in a peace gesture and went to the last sink, where he washed up and staggered out. He returned to the bar, paid up and went out quickly.

Brought his Land Cruiser to the front of the bar, where he parked illegally and made to look like he was arguing on the phone.

The bangers came out at two am. Laughing, backslapping and high-fiving. Bathroom Man leered at a couple of women who were leaving too. They stiffened but made no comment and hurried away, which amused the thugs even more.

Cutter fired up his ride and followed them at a distance. Watched them climb into an SUV that was parked in a neighboring house's drive and fell behind them when they hit the Hollywood Freeway. They went southeast, through downtown, where they exited at the East LA Interchange and entered Boyle Heights.

Dense neighborhood. Public housing projects. Multiple gangs in the area, where often one side of a street belonged to one outfit, the other to another. All of them in perpetual conflict with one another. Tagging, firebombing, drive-by shooting, racial harassment—this locality had seen it all.

Crime had reduced in recent years, the graffiti had disappeared in many places, but the bangers were there. Hispanic crews clashed with black outfits. Several white supremacy gangs had emerged as well.

It was worse before. At one time, bullets had replaced hope. He knew this, because he had spent several months undercover in Los Angeles, infiltrating a violent gang that had links to terrorism. One of the redacted missions in his military file.

He slowed further when the SUV's tail lights flared and it came to a stop. Bathroom Man climbed out and spoke through the window at his crew. He fist-bumped them and approached a house as the vehicle departed.

Cutter drove down the street. Oregon Street. Single-family homes. Trash bins on the sidewalk. A kid's bicycle leaning against a lamp post. Lines of cars parked on the street. A few houses were lit from within, but most were dark and there was no street traffic other than his ride.

The dim glow of the city bathed the neighborhood as he parked several houses away and walked back to Bathroom Man's house.

A spiked metal fence, a small gate, a chipped concrete walkway, a lawn that was once green but now was dirt and dead plants. Several plastic bags, fast-food containers littered near the wall.

Looks like a one- or two-bedroom house.

He had to question the banger, find out where Covarra and his deputy hung out. He jumped over the fence and crouched low as he went to the nearest window.

Living room. A couch. Bathroom Man on it, idly thumbing a remote, surfing channels on TV. Alone. He went down the side of the house. A dark window. Could be a bedroom. He came up against the rear fence and a pile of trash that he dared not navigate. *Any sound will alert him.*

He had returned to the front to check out the other side of the house when the scream stopped him.

❦ 9 ❦

C utter dropped lower, almost hugging the ground as the shriek pierced the night.

'No! Please. I—'

'BEER!' Bathroom Man's voice was unmistakable. 'I TOLD YOU TO STOCK IT. WHY DIDN'T YOU—'

The sound of flesh being smacked.

Cutter looked at the neighboring houses to the left and right. No lights came on. Not across the street, either. *They're probably used to it.*

He crab-walked to the living room window and risked a glance. Bathroom Man was on his feet. Left hand grabbing the long hair of a dark-skinned woman, who was cowering in fear. As he watched, the banger slapped her across the face and punched her belly.

She screamed again. 'I'm sorry, Moe. Don't hit me. Not there. The baby—'

'BABY? DID I ASK YOU TO GET KNOCKED UP? DID I WANT THAT?'

He slapped her again, a heavy blow that rocked her head to the side. 'I BET IT'S NOT MINE. WHOSE IS IT? WHO'RE YOU—'

The scene registered and was translated to a command by Cutter's brain, which fired electrical impulses to his muscle, turning him from stationary to liquid, flowing movement as he exploded into action.

He broke the window's glass with his elbow and dived inside the house. Rolled once and got to his feet and faced Bathroom Man, who gaped at his sudden entrance.

'Who're you, dude' he blinked.

His face lit up in recognition.

'YOU! IN THE BATHROOM!' He yanked the woman's hair hard and brought her to the front. 'SHE BANGING YOU? You seeing him on the side?' He snarled at her.

She moaned. Her cry turned into a choking sob when he punched her hard in the belly.

'Stop.' Cutter didn't recognize his own low voice. He was still. That familiar feeling of being at a distance, as if observing himself, came over him. 'Leave her alone.'

'Oh, yeah, homie? You'd want that, wouldn't you? You been seeing her when I was away?' His fist cocked. His eyes turned mean.

'I DON'T KNOW HIM,' the woman screamed and shrank when he turned on her. 'I swear, Moe, he's a stranger. I don't know where he came from.'

Cutter took her in fully. Tall. Swollen eyes, bruises on her face. Cracked lips. Blood on her white Tee from the cuts on her face. The roundness of her belly that he could now see. Her eyes were dark with tears.

'I don't know him,' she repeated brokenly.

'She's telling the truth. Let her go.'

'SHE'S MINE!' Moe yelled.

He raised his hand to deliver another blow when the door opened and his crew entered.

🎴 10 🎴

The three men who had been with Moe at the bar. They swaggered in, grinning menacingly, and cut off his escape routes.

Cutter to the right in the living room, the new arrivals to his four-o'clock. Moe and his girlfriend in front of him, just over ten feet away.

The front door slammed as one of the hoods kicked it shut.

'Wassup, Moe?' he grinned wickedly, his thumbs tucked in his waist. 'You 'splainin' the rules to your woman?'

'Dime,' said a second hood, whose lips curled as he bobbed his head at the first speaker, 'suspected we were being followed. We tracked back and sure enough, this dawg's here. Who's he?'

'Brae's banging him,' Moe said bitterly. He jerked her hair hard. Made her whimper and stumble. Straightened her with another savage pull.

'Who's the homie? Looks familiar.'

'He was at the Blue Goose,' the banger raged. 'He mad-dogged me in the bathroom. I could feel his eyes even when I left.'

'Who are you, dawg? You with the 13? Crips? Kings?'

Cutter didn't reply. He had assessed attack vectors instantly. Flight wasn't an option anymore. He was outnumbered four to one. Moe wasn't a threat—for now, he was occupied with his girl-friend. But the three hoods were.

He was at a disadvantage, since they were behind him and he would have to turn to take them on. They were bunched too close, though, and they believed they had him trapped. None of them had drawn weapons, either.

I can come out of this.

'Dawg? Homie? Dude?' Dime snapped his fingers to get Cutter's attention.

He still didn't reply. He watched Brae, who was staring back at him, her head twisted at a painful angle from the grip Moe had on her.

She's saying something.

Her lips moved.

She's praying.

No. That wasn't it. Her eyes were desperate.

He ignored the bangers for a moment and let himself *feel* her fear and desperation, and that, along with the movement of her mouth, did it for him.

Save me. Please.

He read her lips again to be sure.

No doubt about it. She was pleading for his help.

'HEY!' Dime yelled. 'YOU DEAF? WHO'RE YOU WITH?'

'I'm my own gang,' Cutter said, smiling. Nope, that didn't strike fear in the hoods. He had to come up with better lines. He turned to face them, keeping Moe at nine o'clock. 'She's telling the truth. I don't know her, either. It's the first time I've seen her.'

'His own gang! You hear that, Dime? We've got a smartass here. Drop him!' the third hood hissed. 'Moe, you seen him before?'

'Nah. Homie's a stranger. Don't believe him. Brae's got something going with him. Doncha, babe—'

'Last chance.' He had to give them that opportunity. 'Let her go.'

❧ 11 ❧

Dime's eyes narrowed at his confidence. 'Look at him. Dawg's surrounded by us. But the way he talks, he thinks he holds the cards,' he spoke wonderingly.

'He's alone,' Third Man growled. 'We checked out the outside. The other cars. I say, drop him.'

'We will.' Dime's eyes gleamed. 'But not before we have some fun. We need to know which barrio he's from. Hold him, Gusto.' He drew out a long blade.

Gusto, Third Man, stepped forward eagerly.

A mistake, since for a brief moment his body covered Dime and Second Man.

It was the last mistake he would ever make.

Cutter's hand flashed to his waist and came out with his Glock. It bucked as his first round caught the approaching banger plumb in the face. He dived backwards and double-tapped Second Man in the chest.

Dime yelled in anger and threw the knife at him. It flew, slammed into the wall above Cutter's head, and clattered to the floor. The hood clawed at his waist, came out with a gun and fell back when red splotches blossomed on his upper body.

Cutter rolled desperately as Moe roared in fury, flinging Brae away and charging at Cutter.

Can't shoot. Need him alive.

He kicked out and caught the rushing man in the belly, which sent him sprawling. The hood cursed and swore. Got to his knees and lunged across, his fist swinging.

Cutter blocked the first blow, took the second to his chest, winced at the punch fueled by blind fury. He deflected the next incoming fist, trapped Moe's wrist, and broke it. Followed that up with a throat jab that turned the hood's shriek into a gasp. But the hitter wasn't finished. He headbutted Cutter, who twisted away just in time but caught the blow on his cheek.

Enough!

He caught the man's throat in a vise-like grip, powered up with his upper body, and flung him away with all his strength.

Moe slammed into the wall and fell facedown. His hand tapped again limply on the floor as his body shuddered.

What?

Cutter crawled forward carefully, wary of a ruse. Swore at himself when he felt the thug's broken neck. That crash against the wall ... that did it. That was not the only killing blow, however. He sucked his breath sharply when he turned the body over and found Dime's knife stuck in his belly.

He got to his feet and checked out the remaining hoods.

Dime's eyes were flickering when he bent over the thug. 'Where's Covarra?' he asked urgently. 'Snake?'

The hood looked at him blankly and the light left his eyes. Cutter checked out the other bangers. Dead. He went to the window and looked out cautiously. Still, no lights. No sounds of any cruisers, either.

'Sir.' He whipped around at the sound of Brae's trembling voice.

Forgot all about her.

'I'll do anything for you,' she pleaded. 'Please get me out of here.'

He studied her: tall, willowy frame, neat features, long hair that she had straightened.

'I don't have money.' She licked her lips and thrust her body at him. 'We can go to the bedroom,' she whispered.

Shame flooded him when her meaning registered. 'Ma'am,' he replied thickly, his face red, 'that's ... no.' He gave up and looked away. Cursed himself savagely. *Why did I check her out so openly?* He had gotten himself under control when he looked back at her. 'I was checking to see if you could walk. How badly are you hurt?'

'I can move.' She took a step forward, clutched her belly and grimaced.

He was at her side in an instant. He held her hand and led her to the couch. Helped her sit.

'Stay here,' he said. 'Where's your room?'

She pointed weakly down the hallway.

Got to leave soon. Those shots wouldn't have gone unnoticed. Moe and Dime's buddies might come looking.

Calling the cops wasn't an option. *They might arrest me. Matteo and Cruz will assume I'm on a vengeance run.*

Which was true.

Brae's room. Small bed. Curtains on the window. Nothing else. No photographs, jewelry, nothing personal.

He went through the closet in her room and brought out a suitcase. Swiftly packed any clothing he could find, shoes, under-garments. Found her purse on her dresser. It was empty. He removed a thick bunch of bills from his wallet and stuffed them inside. *Phone?* He looked around but couldn't find one. He checked beneath the pillows, mattress and bed but couldn't find it, nor did he spot any cash.

'Where's your phone?' he asked her when he returned to the living room.

'I don't have one.' She twisted her hands. 'Moe controlled my life. He gave me money for groceries. I cooked for him and his friends whenever they arrived. I slept with him. He owned me.' She looked at the dead man bitterly.

She didn't go into shock. Most people would have, at the shooting.

'Moe and Dime,' she said, reading his thoughts, 'they brought captives here. They killed two of them right where you're standing. I've seen them do ... things to their prisoners.' She shuddered.

'I'll take you to the cops. They will help. You can tell them what happened. That some stranger burst in and killed all of them.'

'No.' She shrank. 'The gang's got their informers everywhere. Their men will kill me.'

'The LAPD will protect you.'

'No.' Her hands came together in a begging gesture. 'Please. You don't know them like I do. They have officers on their side.'

Cutter studied her as his mind raced. Dirty cops. It wasn't a surprise. Every police department had them.

'I didn't know the Street Front was that big ... to have its snitches.'

'That's what everyone thinks. They are more dangerous than anyone knows.'

His head cocked up when he heard the distant wail of a siren. He moved swiftly to the wall and turned off the light. Draped a shawl around her shoulders, caught her elbow and suitcase in the other hand, helped her to the door.

He opened it cautiously and checked the street. Nothing but the yellow glow of the city. The siren had faded. He hurried her down the walkway to the sidewalk. Nudged her into his Land Cruiser and fired it up as soon as she was seated.

'You got any place to go? Somewhere safe?'

'I've got a sister in Texas. I'm not close to her. If you can take me to any women's shelter, I'll look after myself.'

He nodded. He knew just the place.

He drove aimlessly, checking his mirrors to see if he had any tails. *Dime spotted me when I was shadowing them. That was careless of me.*

'Amarillo, that's where I'm from," she said, opening up after a while. 'Came to LA to be a model. Found a few gigs. Partied with other girls. Started taking drugs. To relax. Moe turned up at one of the events. I found out later that's how the Street Front got users. They threw these parties for models, for people on the edges of the movie industry. One thing led to another, I moved in with him. By the time I realized he was a gangster, I was in too deep,' she said bitterly. 'I cleaned up, kicked my habit, but he had power over me.'

Cutter drove into Downtown LA when he was sure there was no pursuit. Past the Fashion District, north towards City Hall. He broke off to enter West First Street and stopped in front of a red-brick building nestled between two tall office buildings.

He called a number. 'Judith? It's me. Cut—' He caught himself before he mentioned his name. *No need for Brae to know it.*

He grinned and held his phone away when a voice squawked angrily.

'Yeah, I'm outside,' he told her and hung up.

Judith Lintock, wrapped in a colorful dressing gown, her grey hair flowing around her head like a halo, her dark skin glowing in the street lights, bustled out of the building.

'You know what time it is?' She scowled at him. No hesitation, no questioning looks at his disguise. She had recognized his voice, and that was enough for her to place him.

'I knew you would be awake.'

She hugged him and kissed his cheeks and sized up Brae. 'She needs shelter?'

'If you'll have her. Brae, meet Judith Lintock, director of the Lintock Foundation. She runs this women's shelter. She owns it. You'll be safe here.'

'Honey.' His friend shushed him quiet. 'Whatever your story is, whether you're running away from a husband, boyfriend, your folks, a drug habit … none of that matters. My center, it was my daddy's, is for women. We have retired cops for security. I have the mayor on speed dial. No one will touch you.'

Cutter chuckled when Brae looked at her and then him, in wonder. 'It's true. Judith's shelter is the safest place you can be.'

'I don't have money.' She dropped her eyes to the ground.

'Did I ask about that?' The director placed her hands on her hips. 'Money! Pshaw!' She straightened when she took in the rounded belly. 'You got any luggage? Let's go inside, where it's warmer.'

Cutter brought out her suitcase and followed them inside the building.

'You *will* be safe,' he told Brae when she looked at him uncertainly. 'This is a well-regarded shelter. Look it up on the internet when you have time. You can trust Judith. She will do everything in her power to help you make a new life.'

'I don't know how to thank you. I don't even know your name.'

He caught his friend's eyes when he saw she was going to utter it and shook his head imperceptibly.

'Judith's got my number,' he replied. 'Call me if you need anything.'

She hesitated at the elevator and returned to him while Judith remained in the elevator car.

'I heard you ask about Covarra. You're looking for him?' she searched his eyes.

'Yeah.'

'Why?'

'I have some business with him.'

'I should have asked you before ... which gang are you with?'

'None.'

'Are you a cop? Some kind of undercover Fed?'

'No.'

She nodded as if he had confirmed something she had suspected.

'Snake and Fuse—that's Salazar—they're bad.'

'I know.'

'They're worse than Moe and Dime. You should leave them

alone.' When Cutter remained silent, she added: 'You won't, will you.'

'I need to talk to them.'

She licked her lips. 'Covarra's got a place in East LA.' She gave him an address. 'I heard Moe and Dime talking about it. Heavy security. Cops don't know about it. You can't take them on.' She looked at him pleadingly. 'They will kill you.'

He didn't tell her that many terrorists and cartel bosses had said just that.

'Make a new life here,' he told her instead. 'Judith will help you.'

He waited in the lobby while his friend took her upstairs.

'What's her story, and what's with your getup?' Judith said when she returned half an hour later, bearing two cups of steaming tea. She handed one to Cutter, planted herself on a couch and patted the seat beside her.

He did her bidding and sipped gratefully at the beverage. 'Her boyfriend was with the LA Street Front.'

'Was?'

'Yeah.'

She listened silently when he broke it down for her swiftly. Squeezed his forearm when he told her about Arnedra and Vienna.

'You can't go to the cops,' she guessed.

'Correct.'

'You should leave it to them. I don't know those two, Matteo and Cruz, but if Terry rates them highly—'

'He does.'

'Then they're good. I trust Terry's judgment.'

Judith knew most of his friends. She threw welcome parties whenever he was in town and over time had gotten to know everyone he was close to.

'You won't give up, will you?'

'No. Arnedra came into my life when I needed structure, something to focus on. She was like you. She brightened—'

She brushed his compliments away with a rude sound. 'I won't tell her your name. I'll arrange for her to have some funds—'

'No need. I left enough bills in her purse.'

'She won't need them, in any case. Not here.'

Her father had made it big in the oil industry and after exiting his businesses had turned to philanthropy. He had bought the shelter's building outright and had turned it into one of the most trusted safe-houses for vulnerable women in the country.

Judith, his only child, had taken over from him after his death and had improved on his legacy. Her work had drawn attention and won her numerous awards, not just in the city but nationwide. Cutter had come across her in one of his previous missions and had been floored by her warmth. The two of them had gotten along right from the start and she became part of his family.

'Stay safe. I'd better not hear about you on TV.' She hugged him again as he was leaving. She caressed his cheeks and peered into his glasses.

'It's an improvement.'

'What is?' he asked and walked right into her trap.

'Your new look,' she chortled.

Everyone had to be a joker.

❧ 12 ❧

'I need your help.' Cutter turned on his cell phone's speaker and placed it beside him.

He was at his screen in the Sycamore Avenue house at ten am.

He had gone to Chuck's bodyshop after leaving the Lintock Foundation and there he had disposed of his Glock and clothing. He had slept on his return and, after waking up, decided to reach out for assistance.

'Took you long enough.' He could practically hear Beth Petersen's smirk.

He did hear the sound of flesh striking flesh and pictured her high-fiving her sister.

As if on cue, Meghan's voice in the background announced: 'That's ten bucks you owe me.'

'You bet on me?'

'Sure as hell we did. Easy money.' The elder twin snickered.

He sighed. *I'm surrounded by women to whom I'm easy picking,* he groused to himself.

'What do you need?' Beth asked him.

'That program you have—'

'Werner. It's got a name.'

'Yeah, that. Can I get access to it? That way I can research myself without troubling you every time.'

'You can handle a computer, Cutter? Since when?'

'I know my way around,' he replied stoutly and ignored their derisive laughter. He knew what he was asking. The twins, Zeb Carter and five other operatives were his friends. They worked with the Agency, a covert intelligence outfit that took out terrorists, international criminal gangs, and various threats to security. Every mission was clandestine. Its boss reported to the president. Werner was its intelligence backbone.

They'll have to security-clear me to allow access.

'Done.' Beth surprised him with her prompt reply.

'What?'

'Hold up, we're calling you.'

A video call window popped up on his screen that he accepted. The younger sister waved at him when they appeared.

'No bruises on your face.' Meghan surveyed him. 'You haven't taken on any thugs?'

'Give him time,' Beth chided her. 'He's been there just four days.'

'He's slacking.'

'I'm right here,' he reminded them. He was sure they knew about the four bangers he had killed. *They track my phone and would have followed the news.* The twins would have put two and two together, but they wouldn't pass up an opportunity to rib him.

'You find us funny?' Meghan snapped at his smile.

'I wouldn't dare,' he mumbled and threw up his hands in surrender.

'Click on that link,' she ordered as a message came up in his chat bubble.

She guided him through the login and security protocol. 'Facial and voice recognition,' she explained. 'That will grant you access. If you were with us, the Agency, you would need fingerprint recognition.'

'What about your missions, however?'

'You won't see any of those, hotshot.' Meghan smirked. 'Those are behind more security than you can think of. You can use Werner for all its capabilities and even search its databases, but nothing more. Now, what were you looking for?'

She shook her head when he gave them Covarra's address.

'Nope, search for it yourself. That's the address bar. Go on, enter it. Werner doesn't bite.'

The house came up in a map view, along with its building plans.

'How—'

'You wouldn't understand,' she told him. 'Those plans ... you can't rely on them. They are what got filed with the authorities. The residents could have modified the house.'

'You can't get those?'

'We could try. Hack into architecture firms, but that will take time and you will require more knowledge of how Werner works.'

'Whose house is that?' Beth interrupted.

'Francisco Covarra, leader of the LA Street Front.'

'That's a vicious gang.' Beth traded glances with her sister. 'He killed Arnedra and Vienna?'

'Don't know. I'll have to ask them.'

'You need help, buddy?' Bwana came up behind them, tall, dark, biceps flexing as he crossed his arms. 'Give us a call.'

'He wants to *ask* them, Bwana.' Meghan chuckled. 'Not burn down the city.'

'I need to hide my phone's movement. Cops might want to track it to see where I've been.'

'Easiest way is to leave your phone in the house. Clone it with another and take that other one with you. Use burners. You were Special Ops,' she said in irritation, 'you should know all this.'

'Yes, ma'am,' he admitted ruefully.

'We'll show your phone's been around in the city,' Beth

Davidian *Associates* was etched in white on the mirrored glass door of the ground-floor office on Western Avenue in Little Armenia.

Cutter parked his Land Cruiser in a vacant space and watched the office for several minutes. No foot traffic. He broke open a packet of hard candies and inserted one in his mouth. He climbed out and donned his shades against the three pm sun that beat down mercilessly, reflecting off the building he was heading to.

OFFICES ON THE TOP FLOOR, SIGNBOARDS FOR LAW FIRMS, accountants, therapists stuck to the dark windows. Ground level was a row of stores—convenience, liquor, massage parlor—and the real estate broker.

A bell tinkled when he pushed open the door and entered a small hallway. To his right was a reception desk, but no one was behind it. Brochures of the properties the broker was selling, a smiling photograph of the man himself, Arek Davidian, and his profile. If his achievements were to be believed, he had single-handedly rescued the property market from going bust.

'Coming,' a voice called out from inside.

Cutter waited, scanned the ceiling for cameras ... and spotted one just above the door jamb.

Arek Davidian came out of an office, a wide smile splitting his face. He was deeply tanned, with dark hair gelled in a smart style, brown eyes, white teeth that flashed, and an outstretched hand as he approached.

'You're alone?'

'Yes, sir,' the broker beamed. 'Personalized service, low costs, that's how I operate—'

Cutter grabbed him by his shirt and shoved him back. Backhanded him with a lazy slap that sent Davidian staggering backwards.

'Hey! You!' the broker shouted. He recovered and held one arm up to fend off a blow while he searched for his phone with the other. He brought out the device and was dialing for help when Cutter punched him in the belly.

Davidian wheezed and gasped as he doubled over and dropped his phone. Tears leaked out of his eyes. His lips worked, but before he could utter a word, Cutter hauled him up.

'That your office?' he snarled, gesturing at the one the man had come out of.

'Yes—'

He dragged him down the hallway and threw him across the wooden desk and onto the leather chair.

The broker collapsed in a heap and moaned. A telephone fell to the floor, followed by several folders.

'WHO ARE YOU?' The broker dabbed at his split lips and yelled at Cutter in fear and anger. 'WHAT DO YOU WANT?'

'Where's Panig Janikyan?'

'WHO?'

He leaned across and slapped the broker again. 'Panig Janikyan,' he repeated, 'the Armenian Bros leader.'

'I DON'T KNOW.'

He shrank when Cutter made a threatening move.

'I SWEAR. I DON'T KNOW HIM.'

'You don't know that gang?'

'NO! I've heard of them, but I've got nothing to do with them. I'M A BROKER.' His fury burst through his fear. 'WHY WOULD I WORK WITH THEM?'

Cutter dropped into a visitor's chair and gestured at Davidian to take his seat.

'How badly are you hurt?'

'I DON'T KNOW, DUDE!' the man shouted. 'MY CHEEK'S BROKEN—'

'It's not. Your lip's split. It will heal. Your dignity is hurt, nothing more. How would you like to experience real pain? Slowly?'

'What are you talking about?' Davidian whispered, his eyes wide. He dabbed at his mouth with a paper towel and shuddered when he saw the blood on it. 'Who are you? Why are you doing this?'

'You called Vienna McDonald several times. About selling her house.'

'Vienna—'

'East Hollywood. North Heliotrope Drive.'

'Ms. McDonald! Yes, I know her. She sent you?' He straightened angrily.

'How could she? She's dead. Killed a few nights back. Along with her sister.'

Arek Davidian collapsed in front of his eyes. His shoulders sagged. His face turned pale.

'Dead?' he asked hoarsely and reached out blindly for a glass of water.

Cutter thrust it at him and watched as the broker drank hastily. Several drops ran down his chin. He returned the glass to the table and wiped his mouth with a paper towel. Appeared to compose himself, and when he spoke, his voice was calmer.

'I didn't know,' he said.

'It was all over the news.'

'I don't watch it. Fires, politics, that's all they seem to cover. My business is hard enough without getting stressed out over events not in my control.'

He's telling the truth. No reason for him to lie.

'She and her sister were killed in Beverly Hills. Cops suspect it was a gang shooting.'

'What's that got to do with me?'

'Armenian Bros operate in this area—'

'And you thought I'm Armenian, so I must be a gangster?' the broker fired back.

'Yeah,' Cutter replied bluntly. 'Or you have gang connections.'

'I don't. I run a clean business. Of course, I've heard of that gang. Who hasn't? And that Janikyan? I don't know him, I've never met him in my life.'

'You were trying to get Vienna and her neighbor to sell their houses.'

'That's my business. They've been there a long while. Their houses have appreciated significantly. There's a lot of demand for residences in that area. Dude,' he said scornfully, 'do you know anything about real estate?'

'Other than people live in houses, nope.'

He stared at Cutter, uncertain if his visitor was joking.

'Shooting our clients,' he said sarcastically, 'that would be great for business, wouldn't it?'

'What would happen to the value of those properties? Where the owners were killed?'

'They would drop, dumbass, which would mean less commission for me.'

'Not if the Armenian Bros were the buyers. They would love to get the properties cheaply, or for nothing.'

'Read my lips,' the broker said savagely. 'I. Have. Nothing. To. Do. With. The. Gang. I'm gonna sue you. You'll regret coming to my office. What's your name? Where do you live? What interest do you have in—'

'Good luck with that,' Cutter told him and strode out of the office.

He drove away from the building quickly and went to a fast-food joint, where he ordered food and sat at an umbrella-covered bench.

That was a dead end. He chewed thoughtfully as he considered Davidian's interrogation. He felt guilty about roughing up the broker and decided to make up for it. *I'll go back when he's calmed down. Apologize.*

He froze mid-bite.

He had to get to Vienna's house immediately. He would get near-certain proof there that Davidian was telling the truth.

❧ 14 ❧

The car rolled up in the evening, when Cutter was sitting on Vienna's porch. Drinking tea, watching the world go by, observing the two men climb out and walk up the walkway.

I was expecting Armenian Bros hitters.

He had been in his disguise when he roughed up Davidian, but if the broker was involved with the gang, Janikyan would have sent heavies to check out who was at Vienna's house. That was the only link to the attacker.

Cops showed up instead. That means Davidian wasn't lying. He could cross the man off his list of possible suspects.

Matteo stood at the steps and surveyed the house. He cocked his head at Naysha Sutton, who was checking them out over the garden wall. She disappeared when he bobbed his head at her in greeting. Cruz had his hands jammed in his pockets, whistling tunelessly.

'What will happen to this place?' the LAPD detective asked around his ever-present toothpick.

'Dunno.' Cutter shrugged. 'I'm meeting Vienna's lawyer tomorrow. Looks like she made a will.'

'You collected the bodies?' The gel on Cruz's hair caught the evening light and shone.

'Tomorrow as well.'

'You'll arrange a funeral?'

'Dunno. Arnedra never wanted one. Vienna ... I'll have to see what's in her will.'

They aren't here to talk about the burials and properties. He suspected what they were after but didn't hurry them. He had a warm beverage, the evening was getting cooler, he had time.

Cruz brought it up.

'You met Arek Davidian today?'

Cutter made a show of frowning heavily. 'Davidian ...?' he trailed off. 'Name rings a bell—'

'He's a real estate broker in East Hollywood.'

'Got him. Naysha gave me his card. He had been calling Vienna, asking her to sell.'

'He was assaulted today by someone who looks like you.'

'Me?' Cutter wore an innocent look, as if he wouldn't hurt a fly. 'I haven't met him. I was planning to call him but didn't get around to it. He gave a description?'

'He filed a complaint. That came to us because of ...' Cruz jerked his head at the house to make the connection obvious. 'Attacker is a tall male, your build.'

'Must be a few hundred thousand men in LA who match that description.'

'There's only one who would be asking Davidian about his calls to Vienna,' Matteo growled.

'I've never been to his place.'

'Where were you today?'

'Around. Here, at my Sycamore Avenue place—'

'You aren't staying here?'

'Nope.' He gave the address of his house. 'Here.' He tossed them his cell phone. 'Location tracking is turned on. See for yourself.'

Matteo caught the device deftly and swiped through screens

as Cruz watched over his shoulder.

'You got any witnesses?'

'Nope. This dude attacked the broker? He must have left hair, skin—'

'Nothing.' The BHPD cop's lips thinned. 'He seemed to be prepared.'

'Back up a moment.' Cutter sat up straight. 'You said this person matched my build. You've got security camera footage. What did he look like?

'Nothing like me, right?' he chortled when the cops remained quiet.

'You could have been in a disguise,' Matteo said impassively.

'He sound like me?'

'No audio. Video only.'

Cutter had enough. It was time for the outraged citizen act. 'Search my vehicle, that's the Land Cruiser on the street, search my house, this place … arrest me if you find anything, otherwise leave me alone.'

My ride. They made no mention of a Toyota. Maybe Davidian's building didn't have cameras in the parking lot.

'We've warned you before,' Matteo threatened. 'Don't interfere in our investigation.'

'Yeah, you told me. You going to arrest me?'

The LAPD detective glowered at him for a moment and turned away furiously. Cruz, not to be outdone, shot a hostile look and followed his partner down the walkway.

Cutter couldn't help grinning at their erect backs and angry steps as they left. He made a mental note to thank the twins for whatever they had done to make his phone look like it had traveled around the city. *They must have dummied it, got the fake phone's signal to bounce various towers.*

He went inside the house and washed his cup. His eyes lingered on the photograph of the two sisters in the kitchen.

Back down from his investigation?

Like hell he would.

15

Three am.

Cutter was in a different disguise. Grey-haired wig. Hefty build due to the extra padding beneath his upper clothing. Crooked teeth and brown contacts.

He had a different ride, too. He had bought two more SUVs, a Tahoe and a Durango, both of them used, black and unstriking in their looks.

He was in the Chevy, which sported fake license plates, parked behind a truck down the street from Covarra's house.

At three-thirty am, he launched the drone from the vehicle. It was a custom-built UAV that Chad supplied to very few customers. Stealth paint to minimize its radar footprint, infrared cameras, thermal imaging, and extra-long flight time. It had a mechanical claw at the bottom to lift or drop light equipment.

It came with its own screen, split to have finger-touch controls at one side and the camera feed on the other.

Cutter navigated it high in the air and familiarized himself with its controls before flying it to the house. He had used such drones before, but the one Chad had given him was new to him. Nevertheless, flight controls were similar and he soon got the hang of it.

A different guard at the front. This one was more alert than the one he had seen during the daytime. The sentry had a weapon by his side and patrolled the front of the gate in a routine.

Another guard at the back alley, similarly outfitted.

Cutter nosed the drone over the front yard. Fountains. Lights in the well-maintained garden. A concrete driveway to the door, where there was another guard on a chair. He flew over the house, noted the AC equipment and the water tank on its roof, and went to the back. Another garden. A swimming pool. A line of tall trees at the compound wall that gave the house its privacy. Two more guards.

He turned on the thermal imaging and counted the shapes inside the house.

The two men in those bedrooms could be Covarra and Salazar. The smaller figures beside them seemed to be women. Four more men on the ground floor, spread out in the living room and at the back exit. A woman in a separate room to the side of the house. Was she a guard? A doctor? A masseuse? He shook his head. There was no point in guessing.

Eight guards, nine if he counted the solitary woman in that room. Covarra's and Salazar's girlfriends could be in the gang too. That meant thirteen hostiles, if he included all of them.

I can't take them all.

He would have to find a way to draw the leader and his deputy out.

RUSS MEEHAN, OF MEEHAN AND BROTHERS, A FAMILY-RUN law firm in East Hollywood, had a finely maintained mustache. He was in his seventies but moved in a spritely way and had a trim build, a full head of silvery hair. The stache was waxed, trimmed, and highlighted his intelligent-looking face.

'Vienna and I went back several years,' the attorney reminisced over his coffee.

tightly. Vienna had wished her ashes to be with her sister's. Arnedra had wanted hers to be scattered in the Hudson. Therefore, Cutter would be carrying both jars back to New York.

When it's over, he thought grimly.

And when he spotted the figure waiting outside, on the crematorium lawn, he knew it had become more complicated.

'LISA.' CUTTER GREETED LAPD'S CHIEF OF POLICE.

She's in uniform. This is not a social call.

No Matteo or Cruz, just her.

The crematorium was on Santa Monica Boulevard, an oasis of green in the snarl of the city. In the distance he could see her official vehicle parked on the street, its flashers blinking, her driver lounging against it, watching them.

'Cutter,' she acknowledged with a head bob and pointed at a bench. 'You got a few minutes?'

The way she said it, it wasn't a request.

'I saw your interviews.' She removed her shades and swept back her hair.

'You couldn't have missed me. I'm the best thing to happen to TV the last few months.'

She remained impassive.

Cops were like that. Inside, they hollered with laughter at his lines. Outside, they were stoic, like nothing fazed them.

'You need to stop.'

'Everyone seems to be saying that. This is LA, right? Where everything is possible.'

Her green eyes continued to regard him expressionlessly. A stray curl of graying brown hair escaped from the rest of her styling and waved and danced in the breeze. *She's aged well*, he thought as he considered her. The fine lines around her mouth and eyes added to her presence, gave her heft and weight. A passing couple eyed her in her uniform, recognized her with a double-take and whispered to each other as they walked away.

'Vance and Diego are good cops. They will find out who killed Arnedra. What they're working on is big. You mean well, but the way you go about—'

'I've heard that before.'

'You'll stand down?'

'I'll think about it.'

I won't.

Her eyes bored into him as if she could read what he was thinking.

'If my task force's case falls apart because of your interference, I'll kneecap you.'

She loved him. She just had a different way of showing it.

She rose from the bench and headed to her ride without a word. Waved a gloved hand at him when he called out, 'Tell Jerry I said hi.'

Jerry Dade, her husband, a man who had a ready laugh and quick wit, the perfect foil for his wife.

No dinner invite this time.

Previous visits to LA had always included several visits to her home and at least one gathering with Chad, Terry and Lisa and their families.

He understood her position.

I would've done the same if I was LAPD's chief.

He sat there with the two urns as the city went about its business around him.

The sun went down and painted the sky orange. Another group of mourners came to the crematorium, and he watched as some of them wept silently.

He had done some of his crying at Meehan's. His grief was still there, though, and he knew from past experience that it wouldn't ever go away.

Bearing the weight of it would get easier, however.

Easy. That reminded him.

Covarra and Salazar didn't know about him. Not yet. They would.

❧ 16 ❧

'**S**ir.' Lisa Dade addressed Bart Jamison, Director of the Federal Bureau of Investigation, who was on a big screen in her office, on a video call. 'I'm onboard. You'll get no pushback from the LAPD.'

'Great.' He smiled. 'You have my A-team,' he said, nodding at the visitors in her office. 'They've done this before.'

'I heard about that, sir.' She hung up after a few pleasantries and turned to her guests.

'We're ready to rock ... boss.' Special Agent in Charge Peyton Quindica grinned at her.

'None of that, here.' She chuckled. 'You know our backstory?'

'Peyton doesn't stop talking about it.' NYPD Detective First Grade Gina Difiore rolled her eyes. '82nd Airborne, Afghanistan, you were her captain.'

'I was lucky to have her.'

'And, she you, ma'am.'

'Lisa,' the LAPD chief said, waving away the formal address. 'When we are alone. Fill me in on how this came about? Jamison gave me the broad outline, but I want the deets.'

'Peyton had been investigating white supremacists, I was

looking into racial crimes. Our cases merged and the commish, Rolando—'

'I know him, good man.'

'Yeah, he and Jamison created a joint task force with wide powers. I got assigned to it, worked with Peyton—'

'She's modest,' Quindica interrupted. 'We wouldn't have achieved what we did without her.'

'I gathered that,' Dade said drily. 'Weren't you New York's SAC?'

'I still am,' the FBI agent said with a grin. 'However, my boss has created this new role for me: countrywide oversight.'

'Congratulations.' The LAPD chief meant it. She knew how hard it was for women to come up the ranks in male-dominated law-enforcement agencies. To overcome the casual sexism, what passed for banter in the locker rooms.

'LAPD's the next police force we are focusing on.' Difiore broke through her musing.

'You're still NYPD?'

'Yeah, assigned to the FBI until Peyton's had enough of me.'

'I'm proud to have you,' Dade sighed, 'but let's not underestimate what you're taking on. We have about nine thousand officers and three thousand civilians.' She sighed again. 'Will we have some supremacists among us? Heck, yeah. Will they collude with criminals? I don't know.'

'Which is why we are here.'

'I've assigned you a floor, the one below this one. Work stations, whatever you need.'

'We've got our own staff. They're—'

'Trusted. I know. I get it. I told Jamison there would be no pushback from me, no hostility, no turf wars. I mean it. You get any of that from my people, come to me. However, I think you'll still need a few people here to help you.'

'Yeah.'

'I'll get my best detective to work with you. I trust him—' Dade broke and frowned heavily. 'Let me ask him.'

'Vance.' she spoke into her phone. 'Can you come to my office?'

'Vance Matteo,' she introduced the detective to her visitors. 'He's with GND, has the best clearance rate in the department. Not only that, he's been with the LAPD for over fifteen years. He knows just about everyone, how we work, our culture. He's also heading a joint task force with BHPD, investigating criminal gangs in Los Angeles and Beverly Hills.'

'That's Peyton Quindica, SAC with the FBI; that's Gina Difiore, detective with the NYPD. She's working with Quindica, however. On a joint task force.'

'Task force?'

'Yeah. To look into white supremacy and nationalism in the country's largest police forces. You heard what went down in New York. We are next in their investigation. Which reminds me ... I was thinking of assigning you to work with them. However, aren't you leading that task force with BHPD?'

'Yes, ma'am, but I can work with Quindica and Difiore too.'

'I want your full attention on that one,' Dade barked.

'You'll get that, ma'am. Cruz and Estrada are on that task force as well. Both of them are good cops. Way I see it, I won't be needed full time here, with the FBI's task force, will I?'

'Nope,' Quindica assured him. 'We will need your insights, guidance, but we can work to your schedule.'

'Ma'am, I'd love to help them.'

'This has to remain confidential. Not even Cruz or Estrada should know.'

'Yes, ma'am.'

'I've assigned them the lower floor. Get them set up, their own access, you know how it works. I need a few more minutes with them.'

'Yes, ma'am.'

She turned to Quindica and Difiore when Matteo had left.

'You need to know something,' the NYPD cop said before she could start.

'Yeah?'

'Peyton and I ... we are in a relationship.'

Dade smiled. 'I figured that from your body language, both of yours. Why did you think you had to mention it?'

'We're professionals. It won't be a problem—'

'Gina, stop. I appreciate your telling me, but it doesn't change anything for me. Your relationship, that's your business. You're great cops and we are here to clean up my department, are we clear?'

'Yes, ma'am—'

'Call me by my first—'

'Yes, ma'am, you told us, but we prefer it this way. We'll be informal outside the office.'

'I told you she'd react like that.' Quindica grinned at her partner.

'Enough of that,' Dade interrupted them. 'Cutter's in town.'

'Yeah.' Difiore's smile disappeared as she leaned forward. 'Peyton told me all about it.'

'Vance's task force is investigating that killing. I met him yesterday, told him to stand down and let us do our jobs.'

'He won't.'

'I know. But I think he's smart enough to not screw up an LAPD investigation. In any case, his presence has nothing to do with your task force.'

'Let's hope so,' Difiore growled. 'Cutter Grogan is a man who can fight with his own shadow.'

'WHAT WAS THAT ABOUT?' CRUZ LOOKED UP WHEN MATTEO entered their office.

'Boss needs my help with something else.'

'You're leaving the task force?'

The detective closed the door to their glassed-in office and checked that no one was watching them through the windows.

The sensitivity of the task force had won them their own space, which they shared with Estrada. Who hadn't arrived yet.

'This can't leave you. No one else should know about it,' he told his partner sternly.

'You know how I am with secrets.' Cruz zipped his lips with his fingers.

'I am advising an FBI task force that's looking into white nationalists in the LAPD. It won't be full time. Our gang task force takes priority. It's a good move for us. They might find something that could be useful for us here.'

Cruz nodded, satisfied. 'Nothing on that shooting in Boyle Heights. No one saw anything, no one heard anything.'

'That's the way it usually is.' Matteo picked up his mug and sipped his coffee. Made a face when he found it had gone cold. 'CIs?'

'Nothing from any snitches.'

'Moe, Dime and two others, right?'

'Yeah, the dead bangers. Moe and Dime were senior foot soldiers in the Street Front.'

Matteo got to his feet, yawned and stretched. He rocked on his heels as he closed his eyes and thought rapidly. 'No progress on those AR-15s. You think it could be the Armenian Bros retaliating?'

'Only one way of knowing.'

'Yeah, talk to our informers and see what they say.'

✣ 17 ✣

You couldn't just walk into the Street Front's hideout and ask to see Covarra. He didn't run a medical clinic where walk-ins were allowed. Those who went to see him often required healthcare services, however.

I'll have to find a way to get him out of that house, Cutter mused as he sat at his screen and logged into Werner. His search led him to his first stop.

Isaiah 'Issa' Limon was lounging against his ride at the far end of the LAX-it lot, from where travelers picked up their cabs or app services rides. It was next to Terminal One of Los Angeles International Airport, a new development to reduce traffic congestion at the airport.

'Off duty,' the driver said, waving Cutter away as he approached.

That's a joint he's hiding between his fingers.

'I don't want a ride,' he told the tall African-American. 'You want to make some easy money?'

Limon snorted. 'No such thing, dude.'

'This one is. It pays thirty grand. Ten, up front, balance on completion.'

The figure got his attention. He stuffed his phone away and straightened against his vehicle as he studied the speaker, who was in a new disguise.

Brown wig, long sideburns, crooked teeth, a scar on his forehead. A look could either be forgettable or memorable. Cutter had gone for the latter. Middle-aged spread at his belly, nothing special about his clothing, shades that concealed the dark contacts in his eyes.

'For doing what?'

'Driving a car.'

'I do that already. This babe,' Limon patted his ride, which had seen better days. 'Don't need your money or the sweat. I bet there's some criminal activity involved.'

'Yeah. You'll need to crash into a car.'

'Nope. Not—'

'You're a convicted felon. You did time for possession and dealing. You got your driver's license and signed up for this ride share outfit using a fake address and Social Security number.' There were no secrets from Werner. 'You're still dealing. You sell weed to your passengers. On top of that, you're behind on your alimony payments. I can make one call to the cops and get you back in prison. Thirty grand for doing what you do every day or ... you know the alternative.'

'Who are you, dude?' Limon scowled at him. 'How do you know that? Are you a cop? A Fed? Is this a setup?'

'How I know is not important. Search me.' Cutter spread his hands wide. 'No wire on me. You'll find a driver's license in my wallet. That's fake, as false as yours. You'll find one grand in my pocket, which is yours. You can keep it as a sign of good faith on my part. But I need to know right now. Are you in or do you want to be a guest of the state?'

'Just what's this about?' Limon asked suspiciously. 'No killing, kidnapping, drugs, nothing of that sort. I'm trying to stay clean.'

'By dealing on the side.'

'I've got costs!'

'Are you in or out? I can find someone else while you spend time with the LAPD.'

'What's this about?'

'You don't need to know. Your crash will not kill anyone.'

'You can't guarantee that.'

'Nope. But if you're wearing a disguise, your car's untraceable, there'll be no blowback on you.'

'I can't use this ride.'

'I'll get you one.'

'Just who are you, dude?' Limon repeated. 'Are you from some gang?'

Cutter peeled off a bunch of bills and counted them. 'One grand.' He handed them to the driver, who took them readily. 'Nine grand, right here, right now, if you agree.'

'Tell me what I gotta do.' The driver slipped the cash into his pocket.

Gotcha!

THE SECOND DRIVER WAS HANGING OUT ON HOLLYWOOD Boulevard, discreetly dealing to tourists from his ride-hailing vehicle.

'You could go to prison for that.' Cutter climbed into the backseat after the 'customer' had left. 'What was that? Coke? Oxy?'

'HEY!' Ruben Garrido whirled on him in anger. 'ARE YOU A COP?'

'If I was, you'd already be cuffed.'

'THEN, GET OUT.'

'You want to make thirty grand?'

The driver took less time to be persuaded than Limon.

. . .

Cutter took both of them, separately, to car dealers and bought them used rides of their choice. He paid with a credit card that had a dummy address on it, linked to an account that had sufficient funds in it.

He gave them two earpieces and taught them how to operate them and then gave them wigs, cheek pads, false noses and gloves.

'Hang around East Hubbard Street,' he told them. 'I'll tell you which vehicle to smash.'

'You sure this will work?' Limon asked him doubtfully.

'All you gotta do is ram your car and run away.'

They could do that. Besides, thirty thousand dollars was a very persuasive amount.

Cutter removed his disguise and returned to Chuck's. The bodyshop also sold customized bikes to enthusiasts, and one half of the dealership was a glass-enclosed showroom.

'I didn't know you were a rider.' Chuck came out and joined him as he surveyed a Ducati Panigale. 'That's one heck of a machine.'

'Yeah,' he agreed. *But I don't want a memorable ride.* He wanted something more familiar and moved to a Kawasaki Ninja H2R.

'That's fast and powerful. Three hundred and ten horses in that engine. That's standard. I modded it to three-fifty.'

I want a quick getaway.

There were other bikes at Chuck's. Hondas, Triumphs, Suzukis; he checked all of them out but kept returning to the Ninja. *I've ridden those. I know how they handle.*

'Off the books sale?' he asked his friend.

'Always.'

'You still do those gun rack mods? For an HK?'

'Yeah. Side of the tank. You planning on something?'

'Buying this bike.'

❧ 18 ❧

Cutter chose to attack just after noon. He figured Covarra and Salazar, having nothing to do but hide in their house, would have a big meal and follow it up with a siesta.

That would slow their responses. He hoped it would lower the guard of their men, too.

'You're in place?' he called Limon.

'Dude, stop asking me that,' the driver snapped in his earpiece. 'I've been hanging out here all morning. This beard's itchy. I'm sweating under this jacket.'

'Your Ford's got air conditioning. You checked it out yourself when we bought it yesterday.'

'It's not cool enough—'

'Stay alert,' he cut in before Limon resumed his complaining.

'Ruben?' he switched frequency and called Garrido. 'Estas listo?' he asked in Spanish. *Are you ready?*

'Si,' the driver replied and hung up. A man of few words.

Cutter checked the mirrors of his Durango. He was on Hubbard too, parked well away from the gangbangers' hideout. The Ninja was parked on the street behind him. Traffic passed him without slowing. An elderly couple pushed a shopping cart on the sidewalk; a mom walked home with her daughter.

He lifted the drone from the passenger seat and inspected it. Two stun grenades in the claws, which he could operate remotely. Both of them gave a louder bang than standard equipment. That was Chad's doing.

He checked himself out. His sideburns disguise. Gloves on his hands. Black leather riding jacket. His armor beneath it. Zipper down partway, for easy access to his kydex-holstered Glock. Another Glock strapped to his back. That would take longer to draw, however, since he would have to reach behind, thrust his hand down the back of his neck.

The HK was strapped to the side of his bike, covered with a leather flap that was Velcroed to the tank. A quick pull and twist and it would come free. He had practiced the maneuver several times until he had gotten the draw down to a couple of seconds.

Explosives, stun and tear-gas grenades in pockets down the side of his combat trousers, spare magazines and the Benchmade.

He waited until the clock turned to two pm, checked his mirrors again and launched the drone through the window.

He got out quickly and locked the Durango. Hustled to the Ninja and fired it up as he strapped the control screen to the top of its tank. He buckled the helmet and idled as the UAV flew over Hubbard, its feed coming on the screen.

He nosed forward as he navigated the craft and slid behind a parked Mazda when he came within eyesight distance of the residence's gate.

Two guards. A similar number at the back alley.

The killing at Moe's must have gotten Covarra to beef up his security. Sentries patrolled the front and back gardens, and the thermal imaging from inside the house told him there were thirteen hostiles in total, three of whom seemed to be women.

Same as from my recon run.

'Any moment now,' he called Limon and Garrido. 'Get closer to the Hubbard and South Sadler intersection. Be ready to travel either way.'

He waited for their confirmation and, at two-forty-five pm, let loose the first stun grenade.

19

The blast was audible even where he was, at a distance from the house.

On screen, the guards reacted predictably. Some fell to the ground, others clutched their eyes or ears. Those at the front and rear gates rushed inside.

He dropped the second grenade just outside the front door and kept the drone in hover mode as he revved the Ninja.

Counted down to himself as he watched orange-yellow figures in the house burst into action. A garage door opened. A vehicle nosed out.

'SOUTH SADLER AVENUE,' he instructed his drivers.

His Ninja surged ahead, responding smoothly to his throttle command.

The first Land Rover exited the back alley and approached Sadler.

Left, or right? Left would take it to Whittier Boulevard, right would go to East Sixth.

The vehicle went right, just as two more Land Rovers followed it out.

'THREE LAND ROVERS. BLACK,' he yelled at Limon.

'TAKE OUT THE FIRST ONE BEFORE IT REACHES SIXTH.'

'TAKE OUT THE LAST ROVER,' he instructed Garrido and watched the screen for one last moment to check that no other vehicles emerged from the house.

He pressed *Self-Detonate* on the screen, and the feed went blank as the drone exploded.

He took the turn and joined Sadler. Spotted Garrido's Camry and raced past him, a dark figure on a black bike, easily powering past slower-moving vehicles.

The first Land Rover, which was Ruben's target, was two vehicles away. He slipped between the two rides and waved a hand in acknowledgement when they made room for him. Just because he was on a deadly mission was no reason not to be polite.

The car ahead of him carried just its driver. Through its rear and front windows, he had a clear view of the SUV and could see shadows moving inside, despite its darkened rear window.

Three vehicles in the bangers' convoy. It wasn't the presidential cavalcade, where an entire group of vehicles could be a dummy move while the Commander-in-Chief rode in a different convoy.

Covarra and Salazar will be in the middle vehicle. He could see it as it sped through the traffic. In the distance, traffic lights on East Sixth, strung out in the sky.

'NOW!' he ordered both men.

He watched as Garrido overtook him. Ignored the angry honks from behind as his slowing down forced other vehicles to follow suit.

The Camry was driven expertly as it sped up and crashed full-on into the back of the Land Rover and kept going; the force of the impact drove the bigger vehicle onto the sidewalk, where it smashed into a lamp post and stalled.

Cutter didn't turn to watch. He could see Garrido jump out of his vehicle and run, and then the crash was behind him. The middle vehicle slowed. He could see figures moving inside violently. Hands waving.

Wait. Let Limon make his move.

The LAX driver acted before his thought finished.

There was a commotion ahead. Tail lights turned red. Squeals of brakes and shouts that he could hear even through his helmet and the rushing of air.

Covarra's ride slowed and stopped.

The driver's door opened.

A Hispanic-looking man jumped out.

Which gave Cutter the opening he wanted.

≈ 20 ≈

T he Ninja glided as smoothly as a snake as it cut past the ride in front and approached the SUV.

The driver heard it approaching and half-turned.

His mouth opened to yell a warning shout when Cutter shot him in the right shoulder and followed that with a round to his chest.

He sprang off the bike and let it crash to the ground. A large stride to the SUV, whose front door was open, moving with liquid ease, a tall, dark-clad figure filled with lethal intent and deadly capability as drivers around him honked, several vehicles swerved around and passed, while a few stopped to unload their occupants, who watched in horror.

Cutter paid them no attention. He was in his zone as details registered automatically.

Driver door open. A passenger, recovering swiftly from shock, reaching for a rifle between his legs. Two men in the backseat. Covarra and Salazar. Their mouths open, eyes narrowing.

He shot the passenger in the shoulder and threw a tear-gas grenade into the vehicle. Slammed the door shut and kicked the passenger door back when Salazar tried to escape. He shot into

85

the vehicle's base deliberately and ran behind the rear and caught Covarra just as he fell out of the vehicle, coughing, tears streaming down his face.

'Why did you kill Arnedra and Vienna?' he hissed coldly as he jammed his Glock against the man's neck. Time was running out. Cops could show up any moment. The hitters from the other Land Rovers would approach.

He shook the gang boss hard when Covarra raised his face uncomprehendingly.

'THOSE WOMEN IN THAT BEVERLY HILLS HOUSE. WHY DID YOU KILL THEM? WHO RAPED THEM? WHO PULLED THE TRIGGER?'

He repeated it in Spanish and pressed his gun tighter against Covarra's neck.

'Who ... they ...' the Street Front leader flailed with his arms as he drew gulps of air. 'I ... didn't—'

'YOU HAD A SHOOTOUT WITH SOME OTHER GANG. YOU LEFT THEM THERE.'

'WHICH WOMEN?' Covarra roared back as he regained his strength. 'YOU!' He stabbed a finger at Cutter's chest. 'DO YOU KNOW WHO I AM? I WILL HUNT YOU DOWN—'

He broke off with a shriek when his finger was twisted in a merciless grip and snapped.

Cutter turned him around and used him as a shield to walk back to his bike. Spotted the approaching bangers. Shot at their feet, making them dive away. Someone screamed. Rubber burned and engines whined as vehicles came to sudden stops.

Cutter didn't stop moving. He lashed out at the Land Rover's door, which was opening. It slammed back and caught Salazar in the face.

He sent Covarra crashing against the vehicle, upturned his bike in a flash and climbed on it.

He threw a phone at the bangers' boss. 'CALL ME,' he ordered. 'I WANT THE KILLERS AND THE RAPISTS.

AND IF YOU ORDERED THEIR DEATHS, I WILL COME FOR YOU.'

He revved and the Ninja shot past the Land Rover. The first convoy vehicle to his left, Limon's Ford, buckled into its rear. Shattered windows and steam. Ugly skid marks on the road.

Movement!

Two hitters came around the front, their guns raised. Cutter straightened his gun arm and fired in a continuous stream at them, jammed his gun down his jacket when they fell behind him, and weaved through the crowd of vehicles at the front.

He swerved momentarily when something slammed into his back with the force of a tree trunk. His armor had taken one of the hitter's shots. He recovered his balance, and then he was away, hanging a left on East Sixth, taking a right at Margaret Avenue, and then opening up the throttle.

Cops will have been called. They'll have choke points.

He had prepared for that. He took turns at dizzying speed, cutting illegally through red lights and racing until he wheeled into the parking lot of an enormous self-storage center in East Los Angeles.

A truck at the far end, permanently broken down, was his destination. No other vehicles nearby, since the parking spaces were inconveniently located. He knew the security cameras didn't work. He had jammed them with an EMP blast before heading to Hubbard.

He parked behind the vehicle, removed the HK in its leather case, and slung it across his shoulder. Cracked the drone's screen with his feet and tossed the largest pieces onto the bike.

He reached beneath the truck and grabbed a can of lighter fluid he had stowed there. Sprayed it liberally over the Ninja and set it alight.

He hustled to the Tahoe he had parked in front of the truck and dumped his helmet and jacket in its trunk. The HK went into the passenger foot well. Nine minutes after attacking Covarra, he was driving out of East LA.

He switched cars on Wilshire, where he had parked his Land Cruiser. He drove it out and headed to Lake Hollywood Drive, parked, and hiked up the Burbank Peak Trail with just a backpack and his Glock.

He cut away from the tourist hiking paths and took a lesser known track to climb up to a spot he knew from his previous visits. Underneath the overhang of a tree, near the crumbling cliff face.

Santa Monica Mountains spread out, views of Burbank and Hollywood, and the orange sky over LA above.

He stayed there until it went dark and lit a fire. He changed into a spare set of clothes and burned his attack outfit and disguise until they turned to ash. Gathered and blew them over the cliff.

He ate a cold dinner and thought back to the attack.

Had he left any traces of himself?

The Durango was still on Hubbard. *I'll recover that later.* It was untraceable in any case.

He was sure the cops couldn't place him at the scene. His cell phone would show he was elsewhere. *Covarra won't go to the LAPD. He's wanted by them. There's no way he'll turn to the cops.*

The gang leader's expression stayed with him, however.

He was surprised when I asked him about the killing.

He considered that as he chewed slowly and the night turned colder.

Was it possible that the LA Street Front wasn't involved?

Does it matter? he thought savagely. *If I can find out who triggered it, I can track back to the killer and the shot-caller. Their gun was at the scene. Find who triggered it, and I'll get to the killer.*

He wrapped up the remains of his dinner, scattered dirt over his tracks and ghosted down the mountain.

He could have killed Covarra and Salazar, but that hadn't been his objective. He wanted confessions and the perpetrators. He had always known grabbing the gang boss would be impossible to carry off in the street. Hence the attack the way he had staged it.

His face turned grim, hard, as he recalled Cruz's words, what Vienna and Arnedra had undergone. He was one man, and chances were high he would get killed.

Not before I get some answers, he vowed. *I won't let up. I will keep coming until Covarra uses that phone and calls me.*

21

'ONE MAN!' A vein in Covarra's forehead stood out as he yelled at those assembled in front of him. 'ONE MAN ON A BIKE. HE GOT THIS CLOSE,' he held up his left thumb and forefinger, which was bandaged. 'TO KILLING ME. HE BROKE MY FINGER. YOU HAD AR-15s, AKs, GHOST GUNS, ROCKET LAUNCHERS—AND YOU LET HIM GET AWAY.'

'Those crashes left us out of it for some time, Snake,' a hitter replied, without raising his eyes from the floor.

'YOU WERE OUT OF IT? YOU DIDN'T THINK ABOUT ME AND FUSE?'

'There was traffic. Too many cars. We couldn't have escaped if we had opened fire. He was on a bike. He had that advantage.'

Covarra stared at the thug in rage and, with a curse, drew a nine-mil gun from his pocket and shot him in the chest, triggering until his magazine emptied. Salazar grabbed his gun and snatched it away and made soft, soothing noises in his ear.

'Go,' the deputy ordered the remaining guards. 'Take Cisco's body away. Dispose of it. Felix,' he looked at a senior hitter. 'Send people back to Hubbard and Sadler. Question everyone in the neighborhood. Carefully. Someone must have seen this shooter arrive.'

'Cops are all over the place. They've been there since yesterday.'

'We've got our own men in several houses on Hubbard. Their families might have noticed something. Go!'

'He could have killed us.' He turned to the leader when they were alone in their Central Alameda house. It was another gang hideout, with security similar to the one on Hubbard—with one major difference. Bangers were on the street, in cars, watching every passing vehicle suspiciously.

'I am aware of that,' Covarra snapped. He brought out the phone the attacker had tossed at him and inspected it. 'It has one number on it. His, I'm sure.'

'Those women ...' Salazar frowned thoughtfully. 'It was all over the news.'

'I remember. It didn't strike me just then.'

'Why did he think we're responsible?'

'Why don't you find out?' Covarra snarled at Salazar. 'We have contacts in the LAPD. Is there something they know? What's the situation with Moe, Dime and the others? Who killed them? WHY ARE YOU STILL HERE? GO FIND SOMETHING. FIND THIS SHOOTER!'

Salazar left the room quickly and breathed easier when he was in the hallway. Covarra's rages were legendary. He could go into brutal killing mode for no reason when he was in this kind of a mood. The deputy was a stone-cold killer himself, but even he had no wish to be around Covarra when he'd worked himself into this state.

He went to a bedroom and slapped the rump of a woman, who giggled. He gestured at her with his finger and, when she left, he called a number.

'I need to know everything about those killings in Beverly Hills. Yeah, those women,' he told a police captain. 'No,' he said menacingly. 'I don't want excuses. I want information. We pay you well enough for this.'

He hung up and went to search for Felix, who was climbing into a vehicle packed with other hitters. 'Go to Sixth Street as well. Question people there. He went down that way.'

'It won't be easy,' the heavy said, glancing at the house. 'What does Snake think we should do? Go door to door and say we're from the Street Front, and hey, did you see who that shooter was?'

Salazar grinned at him and clapped him on the shoulder. 'I'm sure you'll find a way.'

He beckoned at a driver and gave him Moe's address on Oregon Street. He had to inspect the dead banger's house himself.

COVARRA WATCHED THE ACTIVITY FROM AN UPPER FLOOR bedroom. His rage had subsided, leaving him bitter. His gang was one of the deadliest in the city. Even the larger, more established ones respected his outfit's boundaries. Only the Armenian Bros went up against him.

Could he be Janikyan's man? Why would he bother about two women?

He had a back channel into the rival gang. 'Toros,' he said on a call to the Armenian street dealer. 'It's me. Was your gang involved in a shooting in Beverly Hills?'

'I know,' he snapped when the man squawked in reply, 'it's not your territory. Why don't you find out?'

He threw the phone to the bed, lay down on it and stared at the ceiling. Fury washed over him again. He was Francisco Covarra. His hitters and enemies called him Snake because of his deadly killing nature. And here he was, hiding in South LA because of one motorcycle rider. One man.

He would find that man. He would kill him slowly. He might even drink his blood.

22

Difiore knocked briefly on Lisa Dade's door and promptly opened it, but stopped so abruptly that Quindica bumped into her from behind.

The police chief stood behind her desk, arms akimbo. Facing her were Matteo, Cruz and a third police officer she didn't recognize.

'We'll come back,' she said hastily and made to close the door, but Dade made a beckoning gesture.

'Come in,' the chief growled. 'You might as well sit through this. You're security-cleared. You know Vance. Meet his task force deputies: Diego Cruz, LAPD, and that's Gus Estrada from the BHPD. Joint task force. Gus, Diego, that's Peyton Quindica, FBI SAC, and Gina Difiore, NYPD, but seconded to Gina. They're helping me with something.'

Difiore took a seat to the side of the office and was joined by her partner. *She didn't mention our investigation.* Which meant Matteo's deputies were in the dark.

'You're telling me,' Dade carried on as if there had been no interruption, 'a motorcycle rider can attack a convoy, in broad daylight, in my city and get away with it?'

'He wasn't acting alone, boss.' Cruz shifted uneasily in his chair. 'Those two cars, those drivers were likely working with him.'

'You got nothing from those vehicles. Two men bought them, paid with a credit card that has a false address to it. Facial rec can't identify those men. Who are they? The remains of the drone ... you can't trace where it's from. That rider was after Covarra. There are videos all over the internet. Chances are good that Salazar was in that vehicle, too.'

'Covarra.' She leaned over the desk and drilled Matteo with her green eyes. 'LA Street Front's boss. Guy we've been hunting for months. We thought he and Salazar were in Mexico. They were here all along, in that house on Hubbard. Why didn't we know about it?'

Difiore expected the detective to offer explanations. He nodded instead and got to his feet. His deputies took his cue and rose with him.

'We messed up,' he acknowledged. 'We'll do better.'

'Do that,' Dade ordered, 'before this rider turns this city into his personal battleground. This isn't another banger. The gear he used, the moves he made, Mystery Rider is one smart operator.'

She settled back into her chair with a sigh and gazed broodingly into the distance. Picked up her phone and told her assistant to hold her calls. 'Yeah, I know the mayor wants to talk to me. I'll call him when I'm done.'

'You've seen the news?' She beckoned at her visitors to occupy the chairs Matteo's team had occupied.

'Yes, ma'am,' Quindica answered drily as she took the seat next to Difiore. 'We could hardly miss it. The videos are on repeat on TV and all over the internet.'

'Who took them?'

'Many people,' the police chief said, addressing Difiore. 'Bystanders, passengers in cars that had stopped—heck, there's one clip from a bedroom window. From one of the houses at the side.'

'That rider knew what he was doing.'

'He was a professional,' the SAC agreed. 'No wasted movements. Taking out those outriding cars was a genius move.'

'He spared Covarra, which means he wants something from the man.'

'He threw something at him.'

'A phone.' Dade turned her screen to face them and played a clip that had been sharpened by LAPD's technicians. 'And here,' she forwarded the video and resumed playing, 'looks like Rider got a round in his back. See the way he swerves.'

'He was wearing armor,' Difiore exclaimed.

'We found his bike.' Dade smiled mirthlessly at their surprise. 'We kept it off the news. No clues there. Burned in a parking lot. He's gone. A ghost.' She sighed and waved in the air as if to brush away the shooting. 'You didn't come here to discuss that.'

'No, ma'am,' Difiore replied. 'Matteo was with the sheriff's department previously?'

'Yeah, he was a deputy there. He was responsible for bringing down a deputy gang in Compton.'

Her visitors nodded at that. The Los Angeles Sheriff's Department was suspected to have several deputy gangs at various stations who harassed prisoners, planted evidence, turned a blind eye to some crimes, jacked up arrest rates and even killed suspects.

Those suspicions had turned to facts when Matteo had come forward with evidence on the Blue Brothers, a deputy gang that operated at his station, and his testimony and evidence had led to the arrests of several officers.

Matteo had become a celebrity for his actions and had gone on several talk shows but had also received several anonymous death threats.

He quit the sheriff's department and applied to join the LAPD, where he had excelled and risen up the ranks.

'What about him?' the police chief asked her visitors.

'He's good.' Difiore grinned. 'We are impressed with his

knowledge, the way he goes about his investigations, his file-keeping.'

'Yeah.' Dade lowered her voice. 'This doesn't leave the room … he could be Chief of Detectives if he continues in this manner.' She glanced at her watch. 'I've got to call the mayor. What was it you wanted to talk about?'

'It's about that attack on Sadler. Those videos.'

'What about them?' the police chief's voice sharpened. 'You have something? Why didn't you say so when Vance was here?'

'There's one man in the city who has the motivation to go after Covarra. And the skills to carry out that attack. You know him.'

Dade half rose and gripped the desk. 'Cutter,' she breathed softly. They had an unspoken agreement that they would refer to him by his first name only when it was just the three of them.

'Yes, ma'am. We all know why he's hanging around LA. He could have returned to New York by now. Nope, he's still here because he wants to find the perps. He knows Street Front's involved in some way.'

'You know what he's capable of,' Quindica chimed in. 'You've known him longer than we have.'

'I warned him myself,' the chief replied. 'But he isn't breaking any laws.'

'Until that attack,' Difiore reminded her.

'I'll tell Vance. He might already have Cutter as a suspect.'

'I doubt it. We spoke to him yesterday evening and he made no mention of our friend.'

Dade made to pick up her phone and paused. 'Isn't he your friend?'

'He is,' Quindica nodded.

'And yours?' The chief directed that at the NYPD detective.

'Gina and Cutter have a complicated relationship.' the FBI SAC said, smirking. 'She likes him but will never admit it.'

'He's a loose cannon, a vigilante,' the detective growled.

'He could face a long prison term if he's arrested,' the chief said.

'He's your friend, too, ma'am,' Difiore told her bluntly. 'I think the three of us think the same way. Cutter's close to all of us but gets no special privileges because of that.'

'I'll get Vance to investigate him.'

'Matteo won't get anywhere.'

'Vance is good.'

'Yes, ma'am.' Difiore got to her feet and started to leave the chief's office with Quindica in tow. 'But Cutter ... Vance Matteo will have never come across anyone like him.'

❧ 23 ❧

The subject of their discussion was at the Lintock Foundation, in the lobby watching the TV as he waited for Brae to come down.

'That's something,' a visitor chuckled as the video of the Sadler attack came up. 'That rider ...' he whistled in admiration.

I was lucky to get away without any injuries. Those hitters took a long time to recover; otherwise they could have picked me off.

There had been no calls or messages from Covarra.

He won't make contact so quickly. He'll be hunting me.

Which was why he was at the Foundation.

He looked up as Judith brought down Brae, who smiled broadly at him.

'Judith said I should call you Friend. That right? Surely you have a name?'

'Friend will do.' He grinned. *That was smart of Judith not to give away my identity.* He was in the same disguise he had used when rescuing her. 'How are you doing?'

'This place is great,' she gushed and launched into how her rehabilitation was going.

'You saw that?' He gestured at the TV when she finished. 'Someone attacked Covarra.'

She shuddered. 'It's all I could think of when I heard about it. But Judith assured me no one will suspect I am here. I'm registered under a false name, and my date of check-in is a week before when we actually arrived. She tells me the security here is the best. No one can break in, cops patrol past here continually.'

'She's right.'

'How can I thank you?' Her eyes filled as she clutched his hand.

He felt awkward and glared at Judith when she snickered softly at his discomfort. 'Anyone would have helped you.'

'No.' Brae shook her head decisively. 'That's not true.' Her eyes widened suddenly. 'Are the cops looking for you?' she whispered, 'for Moe, Dime and the others?'

'I can handle myself.'

'I won't tell anyone,' she murmured, leaning closer. 'Is that why you came? You don't need to worry. I haven't even told Judith.'

'If the cops do question you, tell them everything. That I,' he gestured at himself, 'helped you and brought you here.'

'Won't they—oh.' She broke off. 'That's a disguise. That's why Judith won't speak your name.'

'Covarra,' he said, dodging her comments, 'do you know what other hideouts he's got?'

She glanced at him for a long while and then at the TV. She licked her lips as the video played and gripped his forearm tightly. 'Moe and Dime, they controlled two neighborhoods in East LA. I don't know anything much beyond that. Covarra's house on Hubbard, the address I told you, the one that got hit.' There was a knowing look in her eyes. 'That's what I overheard when they were talking. I never met Snake or Fuse.'

'Do you remember anything else? Where else the gang has places? They must stock their drugs, money, in many places."

She frowned and bit her lips as she gazed into the distance.

'Moe took me once on a drive,' she said slowly. 'In East LA.

Verona Street. He looked at a house and laughed. Said Fuse's name was enough to remember that address.'

'Salazar Park?' Cutter knew the area. 'The house was near it?'

'Yeah.' Brae nodded. 'It was on a corner, I remember that much. He said it was valuable. I laughed, said every house in LA was expensive. He shook his head, started to speak, but changed the subject.'

He waited and let the silence build until she shook her head. 'That's all I remember,' she said apologetically.

'Any other places?'

'No.'

An address would have been better, but he would take what she had given. It was a starting point.

Judith took Brae's seat when she had left and gave Cutter a piercing look. 'I'm not stupid,' she informed him. 'I can put two and two together. From what's on TV, what she said and what she didn't say.'

'It's better you don't ask—'

'I won't. I've heard of the Street Front. I fully expect you to show up on the news. Either as arrested or dead.'

His friends never failed to cheer him up.

He had an address, however.

Nope, he corrected himself. *A street and a park. He could narrow it from there.*

❧ 24 ❧

'I reached out to a police captain I know,' Salazar briefed Covarra that evening. 'A task force is investigating the killing at Moe's and also that rider. He doesn't have access.'

'Toros from the Armenian Bros called me.' The Street Front boss nodded and said bitterly, 'He doesn't know anything about those women. He's not senior enough.'

'We can set up a meeting with Janikyan, in a safe place, and ask him.'

'You think he'll tell the truth?' the leader burst out. 'He's been encroaching on our territory. He's hit our warehouses several times. He's tried to attack me. No. We are not meeting him.' He paced the room as he thought aloud. 'How did that rider know where we were? Only our top lieutenants were aware of that Hubbard Street house. You vetted the guards personally—'

'Are you accusing me of—'

'No, you fool. Don't you think I would have killed you if I knew you were a traitor? Moe!' He waggled his finger in front of Salazar's face. 'He and Dime knew of that house. Their killer could be the rider.'

'You could just call that number and find out what he wants.'

'No! I need to know more. What is he after? Why does he suspect us? And,' his voice rose, 'I AM FRANCISCO COVARRA. I AM LEADER OF THE STREET FRONT.' Veins stood out on his forehead as he yelled. 'NO ONE IS GOING TO DICTATE ANYTHING TO ME. UNDERSTOOD?'

'Yes, Snake.'

Covarra resumed pacing, placated by Salazar's muted answer. He turned at the wall and stopped suddenly.

'Didn't Moe have a woman?'

'Yes, boss, but she's missing.'

'Find out if anyone else knows her. She might have gone to friends or family. She'll know who that killer is.'

He fumed when the deputy left. Why was it that he had to do all the thinking? Fuse was his friend, his deputy, but there were times when the man was slow to grasp or comprehend.

He looked up when his deputy returned with a shout and gleaming eyes.

'You found that rider so quickly?' Covarra spat at him.

'No, Snake. But we're looking in the wrong places and asking the wrong questions.'

'You're not making sense.'

'That man was asking why we killed those women. He must have some close relationship with them.'

Covarra stared at him. 'Yes,' he whispered, 'call our police captain. Find out where the women were staying. Whether they had families—'

'I did. One woman lived in East Hollywood. The other was her sister, visiting. No kids, no other family. But,' his voice rose in excitement, 'some man from New York collected the bodies. A close friend.'

'Where's he staying?'

'At their house.'

Covarra rubbed his fingers together as if he could feel the man's neck in his hands.

'Send people. Bring him.'

25

Cutter went to Hubbard and recovered his Durango, which showed no signs of having been searched by the cops. He drove past Covarra's house, which still had a sizable police presence, took Eastman Avenue and hung a right on Whittier Boulevard.

The late evening was spectacular, with streaks of orange in the sky. Dark clouds roiled in the distance, hanging heavy, and for a moment he thought they were smoke from California's fires.

Nope, he shook his head. *Nearest one is Bobcat, in the Angeles National Forest.* The county's fire department was battling it, not close yet, but every resident of the city was aware of the burning devastation and cast their eyes to the sky frequently, as if expecting to see smoke and flames.

He put the disaster out of his mind and drove through the city towards his destination.

SALAZAR PARK WAS A LARGE RECREATION AREA ON WHITTIER Boulevard. It had open spaces with play equipment, tennis and basketball courts, and an indoor center for various activities.

He circled it once. Whittier, Ditmar Avenue, Dennison Street, Alma Avenue and back to Whittier. No bangers that he could spot.

He drove down Verona and checked out the various houses on each side. Didn't spot anyone who looked like hoods. He went all the way to Eastman Avenue and returned, slowing down on his second pass.

Brae said the house was on a corner and near the park. That could be either of the two houses on the two sides of the street. One had a wooden fence, a large tree on the corner of its front yard, pale walls and a flat roof. No garage that he could see, or driveway. There was an old Toyota parked on the street in front of it. The residence had a forbidding air.

The one opposite was more cheerful-looking. Chain-link fence, front yard with a child's tricycle on it and a slide, potted plants and a drive that had a wooden gate.

Cutter parked his Durango behind the Toyota and got out and stretched. He crossed the street to Salazar Park, found an empty bench and began his recon.

LIGHTS TURNED ON IN BOTH HOUSES WHILE HE BOUGHT A vegetarian burger from a food truck. A man came to the Toyota from the house with the wood fence. He reached into its trunk, brought out a grocery bag and went inside. Cutter snapped photographs discreetly with his phone and turned his attention to the other house, which also showed activity. The man looked like he was in his sixties. Would bangers be that old?

A young man came out into the yard of the other house, picked up the tricycle and took it inside. *He fits the profile. Looks Hispanic.* Did he have a family? Was he a single parent? Or did he live alone and have some child visiting him during the day?

Cutter grunted as he got to his feet and made a show of trudging back to his Durango. He was still in the transparent-

They picked the lock easily. That didn't surprise him, since Vienna didn't have security of any kind and her doors were old-style, with out-of-date locks. *They'll check this floor, one or two will go up to check the bedrooms.*

He had his armor, he had his Glock and several spare magazines, and he had his fury.

Cutter stepped onto the porch, took a long stride to the door, crouched and snapped a quick look. No one visible.

He snuck inside and was straightening when a figure came out of the kitchen, looked at the ceiling and called out softly, 'He's not here. He must be up—' He broke off and yelled loudly. 'HE'S HERE.'

Cutter shot him before the hood could raise his rifle, a double tap to his chest just as he heard movement upstairs and loud exclamations.

He lunged forward, caught the falling man, kicked away his gun and was hauling him up when he felt the breath of air against his neck, and then he knew why the hoods had come up so blatantly.

They had more people on the street.

Who had come up from behind in an ambush.

❧ 28 ❧

Cutter dived to the side, but not before he caught a wicked blow to his shoulder.

That wasn't a shot! They want me alive, he thought dimly as he fell, turned and fired blindly.

Three more shapes, one of whom had hit him and who took one of his rounds and shrieked, and then the living room exploded in sound as the other two hoods opened fire, joined by the men who hurried from upstairs.

Cutter wasn't in the living room, however. He had rolled to the kitchen immediately on landing. He crashed through the rear door and ran the other way, around the back of the longer side of the rear wall, jumping over flower pots and plants, racing to come up to the front from its left.

He threw himself down at the crunch of a footstep. A hood loomed around the side and shot at him. The bullet whizzed over his head, but before he could shoot again, Cutter dove at his feet and brought him down and clubbed him with his gun until the hitter went still.

'Julio!' a voice called from the front.

He peered around the corner of the house and saw four men

hustling down the driveway, one of them hobbling as fast as he could.

He fired at them, cursed when he missed and ducked back when a barrage of shots slammed into the wall. Felt movement behind him and rolled desperately to a side as Julio reared on his elbow and brought his gun up.

Cutter triggered as fast as he could in the shooter's direction as dirt and stone chips flew into his face and a slug smashed into his chest.

He crawled forward cautiously when the hitter groaned and fell back. Cutter snatched his rifle away, ready to fire, but it wasn't necessary. The shooter was dead.

He slithered to the corner and swore loud and long when he saw the drive was empty. He raced across the lawn and leapt over the wall and landed on the sidewalk, ready to fire.

All he saw were the tail lights of the hoods' car, fading into the distance.

The cops arrived by the time he made it back to the front door.

❧ 29 ❧

Cutter checked the thug at the kitchen doorway, the first man he had shot. Dead.

He threw himself into a chair and wiped his sweat.

'Throw down your gun,' Matteo ordered as he came up the driveway, flanked by Cruz, Estrada and several officers, all of them with weapons trained on him. Police snipers were at the wall at the front, alert for any hostile activity. Lights had turned on in several neighboring houses, their residents awakened by the shooting. He thought he saw Naysha's head bob over their common wall, but realized he could be mistaken, since the police had trained their lights on him.

'You have any more weapons?' Matteo picked his Glock by the barrel, between thumb and forefinger, and dropped it into the plastic baggie Cruz held open.

'Not on me.'

'What happened here?'

He told them briefly, while several officers fanned through the house and around it and confirmed his count of two dead.

'Who were they?' Estrada returned from the inside of the house and joined Matteo and Cruz.

'I didn't stop to ask. I heard the escaping thugs call out a

'Accusing Cutter of killing Vienna and Arnedra ... that's disgusting.'

'Ma'am, we didn't—'

'Do you know why no one trusts LAPD? This is why.'

Cutter concealed his grin as Naysha Sutton steamrollered onwards, speaking over Matteo, her anger bludgeoning him and the rest of the cops into awkward silence.

'And,' she signed off with a flourish of her finger, 'we've got security cameras. Two of those look over Vienna's house. You can take a copy of the recording. You'll see Cutter acted in self-defense. Just so you know,' her voice rose in triumph, 'they are still recording. They would have gotten what happened just now. Get this, we've got those fancy kinds that don't have just video but audio, too. in high definition. Everything you've said and done is on tape.'

The cops had no comeback to that.

❧ 30 ❧

C utter went to the LAPD's headquarters during the day and repeated his statement to Matteo and Cruz, who acted as if the previous night's confrontation hadn't happened.

He was heading out of the building when he felt eyes on him. Looked up to see Lisa Dade watching him from inside an open elevator. She didn't smile, didn't approach him; all he saw before the door closed was her inscrutable expression.

Looks like I'm a suspect. She figures that biker was me.

It wasn't a surprise to him. *They know I'm not just an idle spectator. They don't have anything more than suspicion. No evidence.*

He knew he was playing a dangerous game. *What choice do I have? They haven't made any progress in their investigations.*

'Grogan's statement checks out. The neighbor's security cameras had a good view of the outside of the house. They showed the thugs entering the house. He acted to protect himself.'

Matteo, the speaker, Cruz and Estrada in Lisa Dade's office.

Difiore and Quindica in side chairs, in what was fast becoming a usual configuration for their daily briefing.

'I saw it myself,' Dade said coldly. 'Everything. I'm more interested in your conduct. We set high standards here. I didn't see you stick to those at Grogan's. I am disappointed. Diego,' she lashed out at Cruz, 'what were you thinking when you said that?'

'It's an ongoing investigation, ma'am. Everyone is a suspect. Grogan, too—'

'Tell me you didn't check him out. Matteo?'

'Yes, ma'am. He's clean. No connection to the sisters' killings. Diego was just riling him, to see if he would say something inadvertently, implicate himself in the Sadler Avenue attack.'

'LAPD will play by the book. We will stick to the rules. We will not resort to underhanded tactics, not under my watch. Is. That. Clear?' she glared at them.

'Yes, ma'am,' the officers chorused.

The harsh lines on her face softened. 'Are you okay?' she asked Cruz.

'Yes, ma'am.' He let a rueful smile slip. 'Grogan hits hard.'

'Any idea who those hoods were?'

'Street Front ink on the dead men, ma'am,' Matteo responded. 'They don't match any of the thugs we have on file, so we haven't been able to identify them. They had nothing in their pockets. No one's come forward to claim the bodies. We've circulated all their photographs to our informants. So far, no bites.'

'Why were they there?'

'Our theory is that Grogan was that bike rider. Covarra connected him to the house and sent those men. However, we don't have any proof. If they weren't Covarra's men, they could be just about anyone. A home invasion crew, like Grogan said.'

Dade gave no indication that she had had a conversation about the rider with Difiore and Quindica. 'You don't believe that?'

'No, ma'am.'

'I've read your report. That drone in Covarra's house had no markings; serial number was filed off. Control screen crushed beyond recognition. Some of the brass at the Sadler Avenue shooting were nine mil. No connection to any guns in our system. Those drivers and cars and the bike ... you've got zilch.'

'Yes, ma'am,' Matteo replied. 'But we still think Grogan's good for that attack. Nothing else makes sense.'

'You've got someone following him?'

'Yes, ma'am.'

'He'll make them.'

'My people are good, ma'am. They'll put a tracker on his vehicle.'

'You don't know who you're up against.'

'Chief.' Estrada straightened his legs. 'Grogan is taking on one of the most dangerous gangs in Los Angeles. He's alone. This will end in one of only two ways. The Street Front kills him or we arrest him.'

'Cutter Grogan is the most dangerous man I know, and I have known several. He'll make our officers and evade them.'

'Which will prove that he's got something to hide.'

'No.' Dade cracked a tired smile. 'It'll just show that he doesn't like to be followed. And, he doesn't. Believe me. I know him.'

'We have some experience with him,' Difiore said, breaking the short silence. 'We agree with the chief. If I was Francisco Covarra and I knew about Grogan, I would be fearful.'

The BHPD detective ignored her intervention. 'You sound as if you admire him, chief.'

'I like him; he's a friend. I'm sure you know that. But if he breaks the law—'

'He has. We just need to prove it.'

'Get evidence and bring him in. You won't find me stopping you. But don't lose sight of your task force. It's not solely about Grogan.'

. . .

CUTTER WAS IN EL ABAJENO, A MEXICAN HOLE-IN-THE-WALL joint in Del Rey that he had discovered several years ago.

He chewed on his vegetarian tostada and soaked in the atmosphere in the small restaurant. Yellow walls with brick arches. Brown tiles. Wooden tables with ceramic inlays. Photographs on the wall. Light music in the background, and warmth and cheer.

He closed his eyes in bliss as he swallowed and washed down the food with a sip of his juice.

When he opened them, Difiore and Quindica were in front of him.

He gaped in amazement. Blinked. Nope, they were not figments of his imagination.

'You? Here?' he blurted.

'Yeah,' Difiore said expressionlessly.

'You missed me,' he chortled. 'You missed me so much you followed me from New York.'

'We didn't miss you,' she snarled, grabbed a chair and plopped herself in it.

'I know what it's like.' He patted her hand. 'That empty feeling inside you when your best friend goes missing. She must have been hard to live with.' He addressed Quindica sympathetically.

Difiore jabbed his hand with a fork. 'You're not my best friend.'

He grinned and winked when he caught the FBI agent hiding a smile.

'What can I do for you, didn't-miss-best-friend-but-followed-him-across-the-country, Detective Gina Difiore?'

'Don't use my first name.'

'You gave me permission. Back in New York.'

'That was then.'

Difiore was like that. She put on this tough, uncaring, hostile front, but inside she was soft as jelly.

'How did you find me?'

'We're cops,' she snorted.

He caught her eyeing the menu on the blackboards hung over the counter. 'Everything is good,' he announced. 'I can vouch for the dishes.'

'You're a vegetarian. What would you know?'

'I've brought friends here.'

He waved his hand to signal the server, who took their order and disappeared. He looked at them expectantly when they were alone, but neither of his visitors broke the silence.

Quindica checked out the restaurant with curious eyes while Difiore continued to gaze at him with flat eyes. Like a lizard eyeing its prey.

'Don't talk,' she barked when he made to speak.

Their food arrived just then, which saved him a reply.

They ate in silence and, from their expressions, he could see it was as he had advertised.

'That was good,' the detective admitted grudgingly and glared at him when he fist-pumped.

'Cutter.' Quindica wiped her lips with a paper towel. 'Go back to New York. Drop whatever you're doing.'

'I'm enjoying the company of my friends, that's what I am doing.'

'Don't. Act. Innocent.' Difiore punctuated her words with finger jabs in the air. 'You're that bike rider.'

'I don't know what you're talking about, and I don't see how it's your business.'

'We're working with the LAPD,' Quindica explained. 'Similar scope and investigation to what we did with the NYPD. Rolando released Gina and assigned her to my task force.'

'You're investigating those killings? Matteo and Lisa didn't mention the FBI's involvement.'

'No. That's Matteo's. You know what we look into. But we're read into the gang investigations.'

'You're here officially?'

'No.'

'Grogan.' there was something in Difiore's eyes that he couldn't place. 'We told Matteo that the rider could be you. You're a suspect.'

He speared a remaining piece of tostada and ate it. Looked at her with his game face in place. 'I saw that clip on the news. That man was good, wasn't he?'

'Did you hear what I said? The cops think you're good for that shooting.'

'That's not news to me. Matteo accused me of that last night. He's even got cops trailing me. I lost them on the way here.' He shook his head in disappointment. 'I thought LAPD had better officers. I made those two easily.'

'You're out and about because they don't have any proof.'

'Are you going to be my snitch, Difiore? You'll tell me if Matteo finds anything?'

Her eyes blazed at that. 'Walk away,' she said in a low voice.

'I can't,' he said, deliberately misconstruing her words. 'I haven't ordered dessert yet.'

She swore softly and got to her feet. Reached into her back pocket, drew out her wallet and flung several bills on the table. She walked out of the restaurant without another word.

Quindica lingered for a moment and eyed him speculatively. 'You're not going to back off.'

'I told you, I'm going for the pastries—'

She cut him off with a hand wave, thought of saying something, changed her mind and went out.

Cutter watched them leave bleakly and wondered if he had lost them as friends.

I hope not.

He waved his hand for the server and placed his order.

There was no way he was going to miss El Abajeno's sweet treats.

'HE WON'T STOP,' QUINDICA SAID AS SHE SETTLED IN THEIR car and buckled up.

'Is that what he told you?' Difiore fired up the engine and rolled out of their parking space.

'No, he pretended we were talking about food.'

The detective's hands tightened on the wheel as she came to a red light and slowed to a stop.

'He won't back down. He won't stand by. He'll keep doing his thing regardless of Matteo's investigation.'

'Until Covarra, or whoever the killers are, are dead,' Quindica agreed.

'Or he is.'

Neither said a word after that until they reached head-quarters.

'Hey, Matteo,' Difiore greeted the detective as he emerged from an office. 'Those cops who were shadowing Grogan—'

'They lost him.'

'He was at El Abajeno's half an hour ago. He might still be there if your men hustle.'

Matteo stared at her as he reached for his phone automatically. 'How do you know?'

'We were having our lunch there when we spotted him.'

'What are you doing?' Quindica hissed at her when they were alone.

'Enjoying myself,' said the detective, her eyes dancing. 'We have premium seats to the Cutter Grogan show.'

❧ 31 ❧

Cutter picked up the cops when he was on the Santa Monica Freeway.

Same dudes, same unmarked Chrysler, three cars behind. They're wearing shades this time, as if it's a disguise.

I bet Difiore told Matteo where I was. He grinned sardonically as he kept going and took the exit to the Harbor Freeway. He headed to the LA Convention Center and drove aimlessly through its immense parking lot; sure enough, the Chrysler followed him.

The cops hadn't done anything wrong. They had alternated between shadowing him and overtaking him and always kept several vehicles behind or in the front. However, Cutter was a battle-hardened veteran who had lived undercover in terrorist country. His inner radar had pinged and, after several counter-surveillance maneuvers, he had spotted the cops.

He needed to shake them again, however.

Chad's stowed the weapons in Union Station. Can't let the cops see me collecting them.

He exited the conference venue and drove into downtown LA, making random turns, entering and exiting streets for no reason. He parked at a bay near Grand Central Market and hopped out of his vehicle. Made a show of speaking loudly in his cell phone and gesticulating furiously. He went inside and joined hundreds of shoppers. Browsed at several stalls and, at the food section, barged into a crowd of tourists and lost his followers.

He hurried out on Third Street and sprinted to Office Depot on Second Street, where he had parked the Tahoe.

The cops would exit the market and keep eyes on his Land Cruiser.

He chuckled and drove to Union Station, to the Amtrak lockers. Brought up the ticket on his cell phone that Chad had sent. Showed it to the attendant at the luggage storage place, who disappeared and returned with a gym bag.

'That's heavy,' he grunted.

'Yeah, skiing equipment.'

Cutter returned to his Tahoe and dumped it in its cargo space. Unzipped it swiftly and whistled in admiration when he saw the gear his friend had packed. C4 explosives, several detonators, spare Glocks, knives, magazines, more drones and equipment.

This is more than I need. He made a mental note to top up Chad's bank account with an additional payment.

He drove to his house on Sycamore, checked it out to make sure there was no police surveillance, and entered it. He returned with more gear and drove to East LA, where he checked into a motel under a fake identity and stayed there until evening fell.

He drove out when it got dark and found a parking space on Dittmar Avenue. He changed into the older-person disguise inside his vehicle, settled into the driver's seat and brought out a book to read.

CUTTER MADE HIS MOVE AT THREE AM, WHILE THE CITY slumbered.

He brought out the drone and flew it high over the street.

The first recon was over the house with the wooden fence. Thermal imaging was clear. Two figures in a bedroom. One had the size of the older man, the other was smaller. *His wife or partner.*

Would they be Street Front thugs?

Doubtful. Criminal gangs didn't recruit from that age group.

He navigated the drone to the second house and smiled coldly in the dark when he saw the shapes of four men. Two of them were in the living room, one each in two bedrooms.

He frowned when he recalled the tricycle. He checked his screen again. No children, no women.

He leaned back and thought it over. If Brae had been right, then either one of those houses were Street Front's. Judging by the occupants, the chain-link fence was the more likely one.

That kids' bike could be fake. To present a false image.

He inspected the house again. Two exits. One, a driveway that opened into Dittmar; the other, the one he had spotted two nights ago, the entrance from Verona Street. A living room facing that street, while the two bedrooms were next to the driveway. A garage that showed no signs of occupancy.

He checked out the neighboring residences. The one behind the target house was smaller. A family of four. The house next to it on Dittmar had three occupants, a couple and a child. More families in the next two.

Cutter was parked in front of the fourth house from the target one, on Dittmar. *All of them have bigger plots, bigger backyards, than that one.*

There was only one way to be sure if those four men were bangers.

🏵 32 🏵

Cutter left the Tahoe and slow-walked down Dittmar. An occasional passing car, street lights that glowed orange in the night, no one else on the sidewalk.

He turned right on Verona and checked out several parked cars. He smashed the windows of three of them with the butt of his Glock, raced across Dittmar and threw himself down on the patch of grass in front of Salazar Park.

He brought up his night-vision goggles and trained them on Verona as the car alarms rang shrilly in the night.

The old man came to the door of the wooden-fence house on the left. He was in pajamas and peered into the darkness. Shook his head and went back inside. *Nope, not a banger. He wasn't armed.*

Lights turned on in more houses, and their residents came out. Voices rose as the car owners discovered the state of their vehicles. Cutter ignored them.

He was observing the chain-link fence house, where a door had opened and two men had emerged. Both of them bearded, standing close together, neither venturing into the street.

It was what they were carrying that interested him. AR-15s, by the looks of the rifles.

He had his answer.

He returned to his vehicle when all the residents disappeared back into the houses. Launched the drone again, and it looked like the figures in the living room were the ones who had ventured out. The ones from the bedroom hadn't moved.

Cutter changed into combat trousers and a dark vest that went over his armor. Drew a jacket around him and strapped his HK to his back, put his Glock in its holster, and stuffed tear gas and stun grenades into his pocket. He drew thin gloves over his hands and checked that his disguise was intact.

The drone had another hour of flight time on it, after which it would return to its launch location.

Enough time for him to execute his attack.

He got out of the Tahoe and went down Dittmar again and went to the first car on Verona. Crouched and attached a remote-operated explosive to its chassis.

He returned to Dittmar and went down the driveway of the house he had parked in front of. Ignored the security cameras. *They'll record an elderly-looking man.*

He vaulted over the fence and landed in the neighbor's back garden. The third house from the bangers'. A motion-activated light came on as he darted silently on the soft grass and climbed over the next fence and dropped onto the concrete yard of the neighboring house.

A dog barked from inside. He swore and hustled to the six-foot-high wooden barrier, beyond which was the target residence.

Looked once at the glass doors of the house that held the barking animal. No lights had come on yet. He hoped that would continue. All he needed was a few more minutes.

He brought up the drone's screen. No change to the status of the occupants. The same two men in the front room overlooking Verona, the others in their bedrooms. *They're probably on some kind of guard detail, taking turns in pairs.*

He detonated the explosive, which exploded with a dull but

audible *whump*. The car lit up his screen with a bright flare as it burst into flames.

Several moments passed, and then lights turned on in several houses.

The two bangers in the living room moved. They went to the door and left the house to inspect the burning car.

The men in the bedroom got up and went out as well. However, one of them waited in the living room, peering through the window, while the other came to the door at the driveway, opened it and stood in it.

Dog barking from the house to his left. A banger just across the fence. Two others outside the house on Verona. A fourth inside the residence. Many people up and down the street, judging by the voices coming to him.

It was time to attack.

33

C utter glanced at the screen one last time to check the locations of the hitters. *All of them are armed.* The one at the driveway door, however, looked relaxed. *He hasn't seen any threat from that side.*

He attached the screen to his vest with Velcro strips and zipped his jacket over it. Removed a balaclava mask and put it over his head. Adjusted it over his eyes so that the transparent glasses were visible. He often used disguises to not just mask his real look but also to give something to be remembered.

He took three steps back, ran over his move in his mind, and sprinted.

With two long strides, he reached the fence. Planted his left foot high on it and vaulted it easily, with his left hand for balance.

The banger was looking right at him, his face scrunched together. *Dog! He's annoyed by its barking.* That expression changed to surprise and then alarm as Cutter landed smoothly on the balls of his feet.

He lunged forward in a smooth, animal motion, as if the night parted for him. He swatted the rising rifle away easily, but retained his hold on it long enough to control the sideways movement so that it didn't slam into the door jamb.

His Benchmade cut through the air and slid into the banger's chest with ease as his momentum and the force of his jab got the blade to pierce skin and flesh and muscles. His left hand left the rifle and crushed the hood's lips to muffle his warning shout. It turned to a groan when the knife retreated and jabbed several times in a blur of motion.

Cutter laid him down gently, retrieved his AR-15 and entered the house. He rested the rifle on the floor and, crouching low, moved fast inside the residence. Kitchen, dining room, and ahead, the living room. Sounds from the street. Angry and alarmed voices that had drowned out the sounds of his attack.

The banger was against the window, watching cautiously through a chink in the curtain. He stiffened suddenly, as if alerted by a reflection in the window, and threw himself to the side.

Cutter was anticipating the move. He dove at the hitter, grunted when the rifle's hard edge slammed into his side, and then he was on top of the hood, who was punching furiously, trying to regain control of the AR-15.

Can't let him shoot. That will alert the neighborhood. It was why he had opted for the Benchmade. He head-butted the banger savagely. Brought down the handle of his Benchmade on the hood's forehead and was raising his hand for another blow when the scrape of a foot alerted him.

He grabbed the banger with one hand, turned on his back, getting the thug to roll on top of him, and shoved the hood away with all his strength at the two men who had entered the living room through the driveway door.

They circled the house and came that way. Must have spotted their dead friend but didn't shoot. They want me alive.

The man he had attacked slid on the floor and made one banger stumble. Cutter powered off the floor with his left hand and struck Staggering Banger in the belly with his blade.

Extracted it in a blur of motion and wrapped his left arm around the man's neck and sent both of them heaving into the fourth hood, who was jumping away to get clear for a shot.

The three of them fell in a tangle of bodies, their weapons clattering to the floor. Cutter, on top, slashed indiscriminately with his knife until he saw the terror-stricken eyes of Fourth Hood.

'Don't talk. Don't move,' he whispered, 'or I'll cut your neck and let you bleed to death.'

The man nodded dumbly.

He eased up cautiously, his knife held at the ready, and rolled Staggering Man over. The thug was beyond help. Blood frothed in his mouth as he lay on his back, staring at the ceiling.

He snapped a glance at Window Hood, who was still alive and, as he watched, lunged for a rifle. Cutter skipped a step with his right foot and pole-axed the man with a wicked kick that dropped him to the floor.

'What's your name?' he asked Fourth Hood.

He raised his Benchmade menacingly when the thug didn't respond initially.

'Ernesto.' The hood licked his lips.

'Get up.'

He watched alertly as the banger stood up.

'Your friend in the driveway—'

'He's dead! You killed him.'

'You should have shot me, you had the chance.'

'Snake wanted you alive—'

He cut himself off abruptly.

'Shut the front door. If you shout, you're dead.'

The banger followed his orders without resistance. He tied and gagged Window Hood and dragged Driveway Banger inside the house and closed the rear door.

'Sit.' Cutter pointed to a chair at the window. 'Snake wanted me alive ... who does he think I am?'

Ernesto stared at him defiantly for several moments and looked away.

No time for polite questioning, and with that thought, Cutter thrust his blade deep into the banger's thigh and jammed his left hand over the man's mouth to muffle his shriek.

'I asked you a question,' he grated, then removed his hand to let the man answer.

'I ... DON'T ... KNOW ... SNAKE ... TOLD ... US ... TO ... BE ... ALERT ... FOR ... WHOEVER ... COMES ... AND ... TAKE ... HIM ... ALIVE.'

Cutter knifed him in the shoulder and winced when Ernesto bit his palm in agony.

'IT'S ... TRUE ...' the banger cried.

'Why are you here? What's in this house?'

The hood looked away.

'OXY!' he shrieked when Cutter grabbed his neck and thrust the blade at his eye.

'Where?'

'Kitchen counter. Storage under it.'

Cutter looked at him in surprise and backtracked cautiously towards the sink. He reached behind him, felt for a door knob on the counter door and opened it. Snatched a glance and whistled in surprise at the cardboard box filled with baggies.

The counter was L-shaped, with several doors beneath its ceramic surface. He opened them all and found one more box.

He sensed Ernesto's move before he heard it. He ducked away without looking back, caught the rushing man by his neck and slammed his face on the countertop.

Ernesto howled in pain. His second scream turned into a choking gasp when Cutter punched him in the belly.

'You give me no choice.' He thrust the banger into a chair and tied his wrists with cable ties. He secured Ernesto's legs to the chair with rope he found in the kitchen.

He moved the dining table out of the way and brought out

the cardboard boxes and placed them on the floor. He removed one packet and hefted it in his hand.

Mexican Oxy—he recognized the blue pills. Fentanyl that was cooked in laboratories south of the border and distributed by the cartels.

The synthetic drug was fast replacing heroin in the illegal drug trade. *Each pill sells for ten to twenty dollars on the street*, he mused as he inspected one baggie. He recalled Matteo's briefing on the Street Front, which felt like it had happened years ago. *Covarra's linked to the Juarez Cartel. That's where he gets his supply.* The number of baggies suggested the house had close to a million dollars' worth of narcotics.

'This is your store?' he asked the banger. 'Where do you keep the drugs for distributing?'

Ernesto tried to stay defiant but dropped his head and nodded when Cutter moved menacingly. 'Si,' he mumbled.

'Street Front's a big gang.' Cutter scratched his cheek as he paced the kitchen. 'This can't be the only warehouse you've got.' He grabbed Ernesto's hair and yanked his head up. 'Where are the others?'

'I DON'T KNOW,' the banger shrieked. 'I WATCH OVER THIS ONE ONLY.'

'Of course, you know,' he scoffed. 'You're guarding this amount of drugs, which means Covarra trusts you. You're part of his inner circle. You'll know where the other places are. A gang like yours doesn't rely on just one stock point.' He inspected his Benchmade, twisted it this way and that, to make light shine off its metal.

He surged forward suddenly towards his captive, the knife's point held high.

Ernesto screamed and fell to the floor as he reared back with his legs.

'STOP!' He pleaded. 'BOYLE HEIGHTS. FOREST AVENUE.'

'That's where another store is?'

'SI, SI, THAT'S THE ONLY ONE I KNOW.'

Cutter hauled him up and slashed the blade across the front of his chest, a thin cut that oozed blood immediately.

The banger looked down in horror and then up. His mouth worked for several moments before sound emerged. 'I DON'T KNOW OTHER PLACES. I SWEAR,' he howled. 'THAT'S THE ONLY ONE.'

'Is that the same size as this one?'

'BIGGER. MORE GUARDS.'

'How many?'

'I DON'T KNOW. I WENT THERE ONLY TWICE.'

Cutter sized him up. The banger was sweating, bloody, and his face was tear-streaked. The desperation in his voice was unmistakable.

He's telling the truth.

'Where is Covarra?'

'I DON'T KNOW. I GET ORDERS FROM FUSE, NOT FROM HIM. I DON'T MEET HIM.'

'Where's Salazar?'

'I DON'T KNOW. I SWEAR. HE CALLS ME.'

Cutter searched the hood's pockets and found his cell phone. Checked the call log and found several incoming ones. *Number withheld.*

That didn't surprise him. The Street Front hadn't become one of the foremost gangs in the city for nothing. *They probably use burners and proxies for their calls.*

He tossed the phone back at the hood and searched the kitchen and the utility room and then went to the garage, where he found a can of kerosene. He doused it liberally over the packets and, as Ernesto watched wide-eyed, set them on fire.

'Tell Covarra to call me,' he said with a grin and disappeared into the night.

34

Francisco 'Snake' Covarra watched Ernesto with lizard-like eyes as Salazar interrogated the banger.

They had a protocol. The guards at each store had to check in every hour with their lieutenants. If no call occurred, the gang sent thugs to the location to check it out.

Ernesto and his people hadn't checked in the previous night. However, before that information came up the chain to Salazar, a hood had alerted him about a burning car on Verona. The deputy had immediately dispatched several bangers, who arrived at the house and discovered the scene.

They hustled Ernesto away before the cops arrived, leaving the dead bangers behind.

It was a gang rule. Those who died in attacks were left on the street for the dogs to urinate on and the birds to peck at, until the cops or the city authorities took away their bodies. Covarra had no use for those who failed. He took good care of their families, however.

'Was he the bike rider?'

'I don't know, boss,' Ernesto groaned when he shook his head. 'He was wearing a mask. He seemed to be the same size, but I can't be sure.' He leaned forward in his chair, wincing from his wounds. A gang doctor had cleaned his wounds, bandaged them, pronounced that he would live and given him pain killers.

His face brightened when a memory struck him. 'He was wearing glasses. Did that rider have them?'

All the bangers in the room turned to Salazar and Covarra.

'How would I know?' the gang leader snarled at them. 'He was wearing a helmet. Did this man speak English?'

'Si, boss. Spanish also. No accent.'

'It must be the same man,' the deputy told his leader. 'Who else would know about the phone?'

'HOW DID HE KNOW ABOUT THAT PLACE?' Covarra thundered.

No one dared to reply.

'Fuse,' Covarra asked silkily, 'do you think we have a snitch?'

'No.' The deputy shook his head. 'If we had one, why attack that place? He could have gone after the bigger one in Boyle Heights.'

'The snitch might not know that place.'

'We don't have leaks. I vet our senior soldiers myself.'

'THEN HOW—'

'It must be Moe's woman. He and Dime knew everything. That fool must have told her something in bed.'

'WHY HAVEN'T YOU FOUND HER BY NOW?'

'She's disappeared, boss.'

Covarra moved so fast that Salazar was caught unaware. The Street Front boss grabbed his friend by his shirt, whipped out a knife from his pocket and thrust it at his chin.

'Fuse, how long have we been friends?'

'Since childhood, Snake,' the deputy gasped.

'What do I keep telling you?'

'That you won't hesitate to kill me if I let you down.'

'Then, don't.' He shoved Salazar away roughly. 'Find her. Bring her to me.'

'I know where he will go.'

Covarra turned slowly toward the speaker, Ernesto.

'You know?' he asked softly. 'How?'

'He tortured me, boss. He made me give up the Forest Avenue place. I think he'll go there.'

The gang leader played with his knife as the room went still. He crouched in front of the banger as the man licked his lips.

'You told him?'

'I tried to resist, boss,' Ernesto stammered. 'That's how I got these wounds.'

'There were four of you in that house. All of you were armed. He was alone. He attacked you with a knife, not even a gun. Do you know what I do to those who fail me?'

The hitter broke into a sweat.

Covarra smiled suddenly and patted him on the shoulder. 'I won't kill you, Ernesto. You are the only person who saw him up close.'

'Fuse.' He got to his feet. 'How many men do we have at Forest Avenue?'

'Ten.'

'Double them.'

'That house isn't big enough, boss. That many people will get noticed.'

'Have them on the street, in that case. We want to welcome our friend.'

When he was alone again, Covarra brooded. He felt trapped, his back to the wall. The loss of the fentanyl would hurt. He had negotiated credit terms with the Juarez Cartel, but they still had to be paid. Sure, he could make up for the loss but it would take time, and the Mexican outfit wasn't known for its understanding.

His eyes fell on the phone on the night table, the device the rider had thrust at him. His hand reached for it involuntarily, but with immense effort he stopped himself.

No. He would not give in. He would not call the stranger. He,

Francisco 'Snake' Covarra, was one of the deadliest men in Los Angeles. Reaching out to that attacker would be a sign of weakness.

'FUSE!' he roared. 'Let's inspect that house,' he ordered when his friend came running.

'Boyle Heights?'

'No, you fool. The one on Verona. I want to see how that man got inside.'

'Ernesto told us.'

'I. WANT. TO. SEE. WITH. MY. OWN. EYES.'

'YOU'RE SURE GROGAN DIDN'T LEAVE HIS SYCAMORE HOUSE?' Dade asked Matteo after the detective had finished briefing her on the Verona Street attack.

'We had a patrol car watching it all night,' Cruz replied before his partner could. 'His Land Cruiser was in the driveway. His phone showed no movement.'

'Did they see him?'

'No, ma'am.'

'Does he have any other vehicles?'

'Not that we have found.'

She looked out of the window, to the City Hall tower in the distance. Blinding white in the sunlight, standing proud and tall. Atop it was the Lindbergh Beacon, installed in honor of Charles Lindbergh after his solo trans-Atlantic flight. It was lit on special occasions, casting its beam into the night, making the building stand out.

My city, she thought. *Cutter's turned it into his personal battle-ground.* She was convinced he was carrying out deliberate attacks on the Street Front, but wouldn't admit it to Matteo and his team. Sure, they thought he was the perp too, but she wasn't going to throw her weight behind their suspicions. *Let them prove it.*

She had spun the incidents to the media as gang warfare and

given the same message to the mayor. They bought it—and why wouldn't they? Bangers wiping out each other was good news for the city. The Beverly Hills case was still open, however, and the press was increasingly questioning the LAPD on the investigation.

'No progress on Vienna McDonald and Arnedra Jones?' she asked Matteo, though she knew the answer.

'No, ma'am.'

'What about those killings in Boyle Heights? Those hitters were Street Front thugs, weren't they?'

'We found nothing there, ma'am. No prints, no casings, no DNA. Rumor on the street is it was either an Armenian Bros hit or some other rival gang.'

'Why hasn't Street Front retaliated, if that's the case?'

'Covarra's occupied with this rider.'

'I hope there will come a day when you bring me some good news, Vance,' she said bitingly and dismissed him and his team.

Stay, she made a discreet gesture to Quindica and Difiore, when they made to rise as well.

'Do you have anything good?' she demanded when they were alone.

'Depends on what you mean by that,' the FBI SAC said cautiously. 'If you mean, have we got proof that some of your cops are white nationalists, nope.'

'But?'

'But we've detected a pattern,' Difiore chimed in. She turned on her screen and presented it to the police chief. 'We compared the gang arrests for the last five years, and the findings are interesting. Hispanic, black, white, Armenian gangs, we looked at them all. All of their bangers, lieutenants, and in many cases their shot-callers, were arrested.'

'What am I looking at here?' Dade frowned at the colored graphs.

'The seniority of those captured. White gangs had the least

number of shot-callers arrested. Most of those taken in were low-level soldiers.'

The police chief blinked as she took it in. 'It's sketchy,' she said finally. 'There could be any number of reasons why that data is what it is.'

'Yes, and that's why we haven't come to any conclusion. We're digging into it.'

'What does your gut say?' she asked when the detective shut down her screen.

'You have rogue cops. Either acting independently or in a gang.'

Dade played with a glass paperweight on her desk, glanced at her watch and took a phone out of her purse.

'Meet me at the usual,' she commanded.

'Come,' she said as she got to her feet and beckoned to her visitors.

'Where to?'

The police chief didn't say anything until they were in the elevator, just the three of them.

'I've got my own rogue cop.'

❧ 35 ❧

Difiore looked at Quindica, who shrugged when Dade didn't say another word.

They followed the police chief out of the head-quarters and down First Street. A brisk walk two blocks down to the Japanese Village Plaza, a shopping mall.

It was crowded with visitors, and their slow going was compounded by Dade's window-shopping.

The NYPD detective frowned at the chief's behavior. *That's so unlike her. She doesn't go to malls during her working hours.*

She was about to ask a question when realization struck.

She's checking for tails!

She turned to her partner, who smirked at her. 'I figured it out a while ago. You're slow on the uptake.'

'Smartass,' Difiore hissed and put on her game face when Dade looked at them inscrutably.

They went down narrow alleys, checked out bonsai stores and Japanese sweets, until the chief took them to a tea shop and sat at a table.

Difiore ordered a matcha soft-serve ice cream while the chief and Quindica went for the green tea. 'I need my calories,' she defended herself when they looked at her quizzically.

'Why are we here, Chief?' she asked when their orders arrived. 'Why the secrecy?'

She frowned when Dade looked over at a neighboring table, at a man who was sipping his beverage by himself.

'Join us.'

The stranger bobbed his head at them and dragged his chair over.

'This is Matt Lasko,' she introduced him. 'LAPD's worst detective. He's been on several disciplinary charges, has been suspended a couple of times, reinstated when Internal Affairs cleared him. He's been accused of being a racist, a white supremacist ... the list goes on. He's my undercover cop.'

Difiore studied the man curiously. Blond hair in a buzz cut. He was in plain clothes, a short-sleeved blue shirt loose over his jeans. Tattoos on his forearms that he didn't have to conceal, since he seemed to be off-duty.

'Matt was a deputy in the LASD,' Dade explained. 'Not just that ...' She trailed off and jerked her shoulder at Lasko. 'Why don't you take over?'

'I was with the Blue Brothers,' the cop declared. A small smile tugged his lips at the shock on Difiore and Quindica's faces. 'I went with that deputy gang, even committed some crimes, but all along, I was feeding information to Matteo.'

'You were responsible for busting that gang?' the detective exclaimed.

'Nope, that was him. My information helped, but he had other sources, evidence. The credit's all his.'

'I don't understand. Your name wasn't mentioned in any of the press releases or investigation reports. She and I,' Difiore said, nodding at Quindica, 'we went through all the files—'

'That was at my request.'

Difiore looked at him and then at Dade. 'I'm lost.'

'Me, too,' Quindica chimed in.

Lasko looked at the police chief, who smiled and squeezed his forearm gently.

That's ... affectionate! Difiore straightened in surprise. *What's their relationship?*

'Matt is my godson. His mom, Nancy, and I were good friends. We met in college, stayed in touch over the years. She and Doug, her husband, settled in Dallas. I was there for his christening.'

'My folks were racists,' Lasko said bluntly. His blue eyes lingered on Difiore and Quindica, to assess their reaction. 'They were hostile to immigrants, anyone who wasn't white. I grew up in that kind of environment and ended up believing all that ...' He swallowed a swear word and grinned. 'I spent a couple of summers with Lisa when I was in my late teens. She helped me work out how wrong I was. I moved to LA, did odd jobs, and then joined the LASD. Reached out to her when I found out about the Blue Brothers. She asked me to come forward with evidence. I told her I could do better by joining them. I heard rumors of Matteo's investigation. I started feeding him information.'

'How come you weren't arrested?'

'That was her doing.' Lasko pointed a drinking straw at Dade. 'My involvement with that gang isn't on record anywhere.'

'I used my juice.' The chief shrugged. 'I kept his name out and got him to join the LAPD. He's a good cop. He's become a detective on his own merit.'

'Those suspensions, those disciplinary charges, they're all an act!'

'The behavior is an act, sure.' Lasko grinned. 'But the repercussions are real.'

'I bounced him from department to department, hoping he could find LAPD's equivalent of the Blue Brothers.'

'I couldn't. Matteo—'

'Yeah, how did that happen? If the chief says you're the worst detective, how did you end up on his team?'

'He found out who I was. There was one call I made to him where I didn't disguise my voice. He placed me from that.'

'One tape was all it took for him?'

'Nah! He checked out my background, reached out to deputies in the LASD, those who would still talk to him, questioned me ... more like an interrogation.' He smiled, remembering. 'I admitted I was his snitch.'

'You said there was no record of your involvement ... what about those deputies, however? They know about you.'

'They won't talk. No one wants any association with the Blue Brothers. They only spoke to Matteo because he promised them confidentiality.'

'Does he know about you and the chief?'

'Nope. Nor does he know I was her inside person as I went from department to department. I played up my folks' background. Hinted that I was into that ideology.'

'You're close to them? Your folks?'

'They died several years ago. Car crash. A semi plowed into them when they were on the highway. Multiple-vehicle collision.'

'I'm sorry.'

'No need to be. It was a long time ago. We had drifted apart by then.'

'What have you found? In the department?' Quindica finished her green tea and placed the cup back on the table.

'No proof of any outfit like that deputies gang.'

Difiore narrowed her eyes at his choice of words. 'No proof?'

'Yeah. I'm sure such gangs, or at least rogue officers, exist. They're smart, however, which is why I haven't picked up anything. Sure, there's locker room talk, but I've got no evidence. Nothing actionable that I can take to the chief.'

'These two,' Dade said, nodding at Difiore and Quindica, 'have a theory.'

Lasko nodded when the detective broke it down for him. 'It doesn't surprise me. A police department the size of the LAPD is bound to have corrupt officers. All we've got to do is keep digging.'

. . .

'YOU DIDN'T INTRODUCE US,' DIFIORE ASKED DADE ON THEIR return.

'I'm sure he's heard of you. The entire department would know by now that there's an NYPD detective and a Fed who have their own team. They'll figure out some kind of investigation is under way. I don't want Matt to be seen in your presence. He reports to me only. I'll pass on anything he finds.'

Difiore nodded. *It's better that way. We don't want to be seen with cops either, unless it's in formal settings.*

'He's playing a dangerous game.'

'It's his choice,' Dade sighed. 'He's a great cop. As good as Vance. That act he puts on ... he didn't need to. But he's got this ...' She searched for words. 'This drive inside him. As if he wants to make up for his folks' beliefs, or his own initial thinking.'

'That's ridiculous!' Quindica exclaimed.

'That's what I've told him. But he's determined.' She threw her hands up in exasperation.

'He's part of Matteo's task force?'

'Yeah.'

'He can help us.'

'That's what I figured. You'll have your inside asset. A racist cop working for you.'

❧ 36 ❧

Cutter licked his ice cream as he bobbed to a tune on his headset. He waved his tattooed arms and his Hawaiian shirt fluttered in the breeze as he sang aloud in Salazar Park in full view of passersby and vehicular traffic. His hair was styled with blond streaks, and a fashionable beard covered his chin.

His eyes were watchful behind his shades. The house he had attacked the previous night was just across the street. Police tape around it, cruisers parked on Dittmar as well as Verona. A few white-coated technicians leaned against a van and ate their lunches hastily.

No sign of any bangers. I've been here all morning.

'Thank you, ma'am.' he said, bowing elaborately to a woman who complimented him on his singing. That could be an alternate career path for him if the Fixing business collapsed.

He went to a food truck and had just placed his order for a bowl of chili and nachos when his skin prickled. He turned around slowly, nodding his head, mouthing the lyrics, and spotted them.

Quindica and Difiore, leaning against the side of their

unmarked car, parked on Dittmar, just in front of the bench he had occupied during his recon.

He turned his gaze away swiftly, took his bowl and went deeper into the park.

Why are they here?

He brought out his phone and checked his calls. Nothing from either of them. A message from Russ Meehan that he had to sign a few papers. It could wait.

He had finished his food when it came to him.

They're here for the same reason I am. They're checking out whether I return.

The difference was, he was hoping Covarra would show up. He wanted to see how well-protected the bangers' boss would be.

Cutter took cover behind a palm tree and observed them carefully. They made no move to cross the street and go to the house; they kept waiting, speaking occasionally to each other.

A grin tugged his lips as he imagined what Difiore would be thinking. *I bet she's telling Peyton, we should have shot him in New York.*

The detective looked around searchingly as if she felt the weight of his gaze, scanned the park, shrugged and said something to Quindica. The SAC nodded, and the two of them got into the car and drove away.

The man he was waiting for arrived at six pm.

Cutter had changed his disguise by then. He was still sporting the fake tattoos, but the bright shirt had been replaced with a businesslike one, and the hair was shaped differently.

He looked up from the book he was reading when he felt a vibration in the air.

A Hummer slowed to a crawl as it came up Dittmar and started turning onto Verona. The rear passenger window was open a crack—and there was Francisco Covarra.

The Street Front boss looked out arrogantly through his shades until a shadow beside him pointed at the house.

Why's he parading in plain sight? LAPD's got an arrest warrant for him.

It came to him when the Hummer returned for a second pass.

He thinks I might be here, too. He wants me to see he isn't hiding. That I didn't hurt his gang.

It was posturing, but it fit the profile in the gangster's file.

Cutter counted the shadows he could see in the vehicle. *Six men, and that car behind it seems to be a gang vehicle, too.*

He couldn't pull off another bike stunt again. He would have to try another way to get to Covarra.

Which left him with just one option.

The house on Forest Avenue.

❧ 37 ❧

Cutter slowed as he approached Vienna's house. *Now, mine,* he thought to himself, but it was hard to get used to. He would have to decide what to do with it, but that could wait.

His eyes sharpened when he spotted the two SUVs parked in front of the gate. He got out of the Durango and went up either of the walkway. A man sat on the porch, drinking from a bottle of water. Dark hair cut short. Clean-shaven face. Brown eyes that he could see no expression in as he got closer. Lean, wiry, a short-sleeved shirt that hung loose over his blue jeans. Eight men ranged around him, all of them hard-faced and, judging by the bulges at their waists, armed.

Who's this?

He was unarmed; his Glock was in his SUV. He had no armor, since he was still in the plain shirt that he had changed into at the park.

'You're trespassing,' he said shortly as he climbed the steps and leaned against a pillar.

The man in the chair was obviously the boss. *I can reach him, grab him by the throat and use him as a shield.* He was confident he could execute the move before the guards could shoot.

'I come peacefully,' Bossman smiled, his brilliant white teeth contrasting with his deep tan.

His accent isn't American.

'Who are you?'

'You don't know me?' His eyebrows drew together in astonishment. 'I heard you were asking a real estate broker about me. I am Panig Janikyan.'

Cutter put on his game face. Didn't let his surprise show. *What does he want?*

'Yeah. I'm no longer looking for you,' he replied flatly. 'But you're here. Why?'

'I was curious to see who was bringing up my name. You might have heard some people call me Pain. I don't know why. I'm just a businessman. No one has any reason to be frightened of me. Anyhow.' He got to his feet and smiled again. 'I just wanted to see who you were.'

'Davidian works for you.'

'Who? That broker? No, no, you misunderstand what this is about. He has no connection to me. I wanted to check you out. No other reason.'

'Do you go to people's houses whenever they mention your name?'

Janikyan gave him a surprised look. 'Of course, if I hear they are violent. I have my reputation to protect. I need to know why they are talking about me.'

'Your reputation! You run a criminal gang. You brought your goons with you just to look me up. No wonder people talk about you.'

The Armenian took no offense. He laughed and waved airily. 'I've heard that, too. I buy and sell properties, I import and export, I make investments; all of that is legitimate. My rivals spread these rumors about me, and they have stuck. You know how people are ... they like to think the worst of others.'

'You saw me. Get going.' Cutter pointed at the gate. 'Take your thugs with you.'

'Sure, Mr. Grogan.' Janikyan smiled politely. 'I am sorry for your loss. I heard you were close to these women.'

He's done his research. He wants me to know that.

'Did you think I was in some way responsible for their deaths? Is that why you asked the broker?'

'If you know who I am, you must have connected the dots already. What do you think?'

'I don't kill people, Mr. Grogan.'

Cutter almost believed him.

Janikyan climbed down the steps and went out to the gate, waving as he did so. His men formed a protective ring around him, several of them walking backwards, alert for any move.

Cutter was impressed despite himself. *These heavies aren't like the Street Front bangers. They're good. They haven't left any inch of him exposed.*

He waited till his visitors climbed into their vehicles and drove away. Dropped into the chair that Janikyan had vacated and thought back to what had happened.

It made no sense. Why had the Armenian come? Nothing indicated that the Bros were involved in any killing.

Did he come to size me up? If so, why? Maybe what he said was true. He heard about my conversation with Davidian and wanted to see me for himself.

It was when he was showering that two thoughts struck him.

One was that Panig Janikyan was one of the most dangerous men he had come across. He had been in control, utterly confident, hadn't made any threats, and yet, Cutter had sensed the man was capable of inflicting tremendous violence.

The other thought made him frown.

Janikyan didn't say he had no involvement in Vienna and Arnedra's killing.

❧ 38 ❧

Cutter came out of the bathroom with a towel around his waist. Still frowning, thinking of his visitor.

Do I add him as a suspect? Do I go after him, too?

He dressed in his armor with a Tee over the top and tucked into his jeans, and fastened a belt around his waist. Applied the cheek pads and the false nose and put on the transparent glasses. Fastened the shoulder holster and inserted his Glock in it. Shrugged into his lightweight jacket. *LAPD doesn't know who the two gangs were that night.* They knew about the rifle, nothing more.

No, he would stick to his plan. Find the rifle's shooter and go up the chain. Which meant he had to carry out his next move without getting killed.

HE TOOK A CAB TO A CHILDREN'S HOSPITAL IN BOYLE HEIGHTS and watched from the back window. No tails. There had been no shadowing the previous night, either. *Looks like the cops have given up following me.*

He paid the driver and waited till the vehicle turned a corner.

Walked through the building's parking lot, past anxious, hurrying parents, injured kids, paramedics and ambulances.

He went to the rear of the building, where the deliveries arrived. Spotted a line of ambulances parked against a wall. *Their drivers are off-duty.*

He checked each of them and got lucky with the third one. Its door opened and its keys were dangling from the rearview mirror. A paramedic's coveralls were hanging from a hook in the cab.

He checked that there was no one around him, grabbed the uniform and went to the rear of the vehicle. Under its cover, he dressed in the coveralls. He tried the zip and left it partly open to allow for fast access to his gun.

He climbed into the driver's seat, fired up the ambulance and rolled out of the hospital.

Forest Avenue was a residential street in Boyle Heights. Single-family homes, quiet roads, a few palm trees on the sidewalks, electric cables strung high on posts. Nothing to distinguish it from the thousands of family neighborhoods in the country. Nothing to show that the house on the corner of Forest and Malabar Street was a Street Front stash for drugs.

Nothing, except the men sitting in several cars on the street.

Cutter spotted them immediately. *They aren't hiding. They're making their presence felt. Deterrence.*

Looks like Ernesto's told Covarra that he confessed.

He counted ten men on the street, all of them alone in their vehicles. Three of them on Forest, two on Malabar.

The house was a two-story one. Painted light brown. Lightly sloping roof, on which were two skylights. Chest-high fence around it. Brick pillars with iron railings running between them. A rolling metal gate on Forest Avenue that opened to a short driveway, in which were parked a Mazda and a Beemer. White entrance door facing that street. Lights turned up inside the residence.

Cutter drove to the end of Malabar, turned around and returned.

Yeah, there were two more upward-facing windows on the rear slope of the roof. A getaway gate on that street as well. An escape route. It looked like Street Front took over corner houses that had such exits, or built them on acquiring the properties.

Ten men on the street. Ernesto didn't know how many would be inside. Covarra will expect me to hit the house. He'll have flooded it with hitters. Will he move the drugs?

He debated that with himself as he parked and checked his phone. *Covarra's got an ego. He doesn't like to back down. Another gang leader would have called me by now and suckered me into a trap. He doesn't work like that. He won't move the drugs. They'll be there, inside.*

But he couldn't enter the house.

There was no way he could take on that many shooters.

He frowned as he checked out the house from a distance. *I can't pass up on this house. I have nothing else on Covarra. I've got to keep pressure on him—wait, what's that?*

It was a crane that had caught his attention. On a construction plot at the far end of Malabar. He had seen it but hadn't given it any thought.

He turned his ambulance and drove back to the construction site. The developer seemed to have acquired three houses and was in the process of demolishing them to build something larger.

That boom is fifty feet high. Looks over all the houses in the neighborhood. It's got to be telescopic, since the cab is at ground level.

He brought up a maps app on his phone and checked out distances. Calculated that the top of the boom was about three hundred and ninety feet from the target house. That residence was taller than surrounding houses.

A smile twisted his lips as he fired up the ambulance and

headed back to the children's hospital. Made a spare key before parking the vehicle in its bay.

He had his ride, means of entry as well as exfil.

39

'Anything?' Covarra growled at Salazar.

'No, Snake. We've got men at the house. No one came near it yesterday.'

'That man will not give up. He will have checked out the house.'

'Snake,' his deputy said patiently. 'We've got ten men on the street, like you ordered. They rotate in shifts and have been watching for cars, trucks, any vehicle that drives on Forest and Malabar. Almost every car has been local, from one of the neighbors. No strange vehicle slowed down. No one got out and took pictures.'

'We shouldn't underestimate him.'

'We aren't. We have ten more men inside.'

'He can launch tear gas grenades from a distance. That's how he got us at Hubbard. We thought it was a big attack coming; that's why we escaped. If we had stayed inside, nothing would have happened,' Covarra ranted angrily.

'Our men have masks. They are prepared. Relax.'

'DON'T TELL ME TO RELAX,' he roared and glared at a hitter who popped his head into the bedroom. He took a deep breath when the heavy disappeared. 'This man is smart. He is determined. He—'

'He can't get inside that house,' his deputy interrupted. 'And he can't attack from outside.'

Covarra nodded, unconvinced. 'We have that other house as well, don't we? On Forest Avenue, diagonally opposite, across the intersection with Malabar.'

'Yeah, Snake. It's empty—'

'I know that. I wanted a backup.'

'You want us to move the drugs there?'

'No. Our stock is too large. It might get noticed. I don't want our people to show themselves.'

'Moving our stash is the safest—'

'NO! THIS MAN IS NOT GOING TO DICTATE HOW WE WORK.'

'What do you suggest then, Snake?'

Covarra's smile was cold. 'Put a sniper in that empty house.'

40

'Y ou want what?' Chad looked up from his food.
'Zip lines, rollers and incendiary grenades,' Cutter repeated.

'Jeez.' His friend looked around him. No one in El Abajeno was paying them any attention. Everyone was focused on their lunch and on the conversation with their dining partners. 'You planning to start a war?'

'If I have to.'

'No.' His friend raised his palm. 'Don't tell me anything more. I'm following the news. I can put together the pieces. I can guess what you're doing.'

'I wasn't planning to. Can you provide that gear?'

'That?' Chad snorted. 'I could get you an aircraft carrier if you wanted—' He squinted his eyes. 'You don't need one, do you?'

'Nope. Nor do I want an Abrams tank or anything of that sort. Just what I asked. And yeah, more drones.'

'I got a payment in my offshore bank,' Chad said suspiciously. 'From some company I've never heard of. Was that you?'

'There's not enough love in the world,' Cutter told his friend solemnly, 'that you should turn it down when you get it.'

He got a curse in return.

HE LINGERED WHEN HIS FRIEND HAD LEFT AND CALLED
Meghan.

'Can you get access to the LAPD's system?'

He bit his lip as soon as the words were out.

I shouldn't have led with that.

He got a long silence, and then the younger sister spoke.

'He's old. He's forgetting what I said.'

They said they can do just about anything, he groaned inwardly.

'Senility.' There was a smirk in Beth's voice. 'It comes to
everyone, though it seems to have hit him earlier.'

'What do you want, Cutter?' Meghan asked him.

'What's LAPD got on Vienna and Arnedra's investigation?'

'Hang on.'

'Nothing much,' she said after a while. 'The detectives have
made contact with snitches, who got no information.'

'They still think Street Front is responsible?'

'The gang's a suspect. They've made contact with the
Mexican federal police to get a list of Covarra's known contacts,
safe houses in LA. No reply so far.'

'Armenian Bros? Is that gang a suspect, too?'

'Matteo got some intel from an informant who denied the
gang's involvement. Street Front's their main suspect.'

'You want to know what they have on you?' Beth chortled.
'Tell him, sis.'

'They suspect you were that rider.' There was a smile in the
elder sister's voice. 'They've made no progress with that drone or
the bike, however. They're still looking for those two drivers.
That was smart, Cutter. That was a move we would have pulled
off.'

'It wasn't me—'

'Save it,' she scoffed. 'We're on a secure line. Your secrets are
safe with us.'

'Can you show me how you got that? Getting into their system?'

'Nope,' she said flatly. 'You don't need to add hacker to the list of your criminal activities.'

I'm not one, he wanted to retort, but she was right. He had crossed the line when he had carried out the attack on Sadler Avenue.

He thanked them and hung up. Went to his ride and drove back to his house on Sycamore.

He brought out his Glock in its stillness, broke it down and cleaned it. The sisters had confirmed what he had guessed: that Matteo's task force hadn't made much progress. *There would have been arrests by now if they had, reported in the media.* As for his being a suspect, that wasn't a surprise either.

He assembled the Glock and sighted it against the blank wall. Went to the bedroom and came out with all his gear and dumped it into his SUV.

He wouldn't be returning to the house again. It was no longer safe.

LAPD will be issuing a warrant for me. Any day.

Cutter drove to an auto dismantler in Huntington Park when it was evening. The owner, Wyatt—big, burly, his body stretching his coveralls— was well known in the shadowy world of deep-black operators. He provided rides or disposed of vehicles on a no-questions-asked basis. For a hefty fee, of course.

His face flowed with perspiration when Cutter entered the cavernous garage half the size of an aircraft hangar.

'At the back.' Wyatt wiped his brow on his sleeve and grinned, his teeth contrasting sharply against his dark skin. 'Been a long time.'

'Yeah, I've been busy, here and there.'

'Kicking ass?'

More like getting mine kicked.

'Something like that.'

'It's a Peugeot,' the owner yelled. 'Red. Windscreen's shattered. You can't miss it.'

Cutter waved and winced when Wyatt started his grinder and applied it to a car's frame.

He went past neatly stacked shelves, car parts wrapped in plastic, labeled and ready for sale in the after-market. The back of the warehouse was the receiving area, where wrecked cars were taken in and disassembled, their components labeled either for scrap or resale.

He spotted the French vehicle immediately and popped its trunk. Zipped open the large camping bag and whistled softly at the array of contents. Chad had gone above and beyond in fulfilling his shopping list. Zip cords, grappling hooks, drones, more tear gas and stun grenades, and there were the ANM14 thermite grenades, bubble-wrapped and good to go. He picked one up and inspected it. Military grade, used to destroy tanks, buildings, just anything they were thrown at. *These are timed to explode after a few seconds' delay.* Which was what he wanted. Don't want to be anywhere near them when they detonate.

He checked the rest of the equipment, then spotted the folded note inserted between the cable coils.

He unfolded it and grinned when he recognized Chad's scrawl. *Nothing's traceable.*

He burned it with a lighter and returned to the front of the garage.

'Wyatt?' he yelled over the grinder. 'I need to bring my vehicle to the back. Load some stuff in it.'

'Go ahead,' the owner replied without looking up.

'I need plates.'

The owner turned off the machine, removed his safety glasses and wiped his mouth. 'Plates?' he thumbed toward the wall where a small mountain of them lay. 'Help yourself. All of them, clean.'

Cutter peeled off several bills from his stash and handed them over.

Half an hour later he was driving the Durango out of the neighborhood.

HE CHECKED INTO A MOTEL NEAR HOLLENBECK PARK AND rested. At twelve am, he drove to the children's hospital and waited until its backyard was clear of people traffic. He ghosted inside and fist-pumped mentally when he spotted the ambulance. In the same parking space, with the same uniform hanging off a hook as the previous night.

He unlocked it with his key, changed into the EMT's coveralls, fired it up and rolled out of the hospital.

He went to the street where he had parked the Durango and transferred its contents to his new ride.

Checked himself in the mirror one last time. Disguise was good. Face was darkened with paint. He had his gear.

It was time to hit Covarra.

⚜ 42 ⚜

Eduardo 'Sight' Aponte yawned lustily as he lay on the roof of the house on Forest Avenue. He scratched his butt, ran his fingers through his hair and sighted through the nightscope.

The Street Front house was across the street from him. He could see down both Forest and Malabar from his vantage point.

He didn't know why Fuse wanted him on this roof. There were ten men down there, more in the street. *No one's going to attack us*, he grouched to himself.

He was the Street Front's best sniper, which was why he had been given his nickname. With his Remington MSR, he was a deadly shot and his best kill had been at three hundred yards. He knew that distance was average, but heck, he was in a drug gang. They didn't go for sniping.

Even this, he grumbled, *isn't for me.* But Fuse said Snake wanted a sniper, and he was the only one Street Front had.

He checked the scope again and pulled out his phone. He could while away the time by messaging his girlfriend. He smiled in the dark as he pictured her shapely curves, and cursed Fuse again. He could be with her instead of lying on a roof.

· · ·

CUTTER PARKED THE AMBULANCE AT THE MOUTH OF MALABAR, just off Evergreen Avenue. Ahead of him, towards his left, the crane rose in the sky. A red warning light on top of it flashed periodically. He climbed out of the vehicle and did a recon.

The first run was with his drone, which identified several security cameras around the site. He put them out of commission with an EMP blast. He checked the thermal imaging. No guards. *Why do they need it? No one's going to steal that heavy machinery.*

He returned the UAV to the ambulance and headed to the site on foot. There was tape around it, wooden barricades that he could easily navigate. The ground was uneven, with soft soil and deep holes, being prepared for a new foundation.

The machine lay in the center of a freshly dug clearing. Tram-track wheels, yellow frame, at the front of which was the cab. The boom rose above it, at a steep angle in the sky.

He climbed up to the cab and inspected the long arm. The crane was of the older variety, with the boom being a metal framework within which its arm could be extended or retracted. Enough bars and angled slats for him to hold.

He returned to the ambulance and extracted the coils of zip cable and slung them around his shoulder. Fastened them to his chest with belts to keep them from slipping away. Reached into the bag and extracted a canvas belt that he wrapped around his waist. He attached the hooks and grappling gun to it and Velcro-ed them tight to prevent them from falling off or making any noise.

The thermite and tear-gas grenades went into his pockets. *Can't reach for my Glock. Not easily. No room for the HK, either.*

He shrugged. That was a risk he would have to take.

He returned to the crane, conscious of the weight he was carrying. Started climbing without a second thought.

Self-doubt was an operator's enemy. He wouldn't allow himself to question his actions.

The going was slow. A thin breeze rocked the boom, which

creaked as it swayed in the night. He had hardly reached one-third of its length before he broke out into a sweat. His Mechanix tactical gloves retained their grip, however, as he clutched at the boom's laddered surface and hauled himself up.

The neighborhood grew smaller as he went up. Ambient lighting was good enough for him to get a satellite view of surrounding houses, their yards, cars, the boundary fences.

He paused for breath at the halfway level and wiped the perspiration from his face.

Good thing I'm good with heights, he grunted to himself.

The swaying of the boom was more intense as he reached its end. It grew narrower as well. *Do I need to reach the hook?*

He gripped the frame with his thighs as he considered it. The long arm was over sixty-five feet long. He had about ten more to go. *It'll be difficult to maneuver at the small end.*

He decided he had gone high enough.

Cutter uncoiled the longer zip cable with difficulty, attached a hook at one end and fastened it to the boom. He squeezed his thighs harder when he slid an inch, and swore at himself.

I didn't do all this to fall to my death, he told himself irritably. Grinned when he imagined the look of satisfaction on Difiore's face at his precarious position. *She'd love it.*

He removed the grappling gun carefully and attached the free end of the cable to it. The launch device was a military-grade piece of equipment that wasn't available in any commercial store anywhere. It was a pneumatic line launcher powered by close to five thousand pounds per square inch of air pressure. The grapnel was a titanium and steel composition that stuck to walls, roofs and wooden surfaces.

He had trusted his life to similar gear.

He hadn't ever launched it at a tiled roof before.

There's always a first time.

He made sure the length of cable was loose, took aim at a point near the skylight, and fired.

There was no dramatic noise. Nothing but a sharp sound that

got lost in the night's sounds. No screen music played out, like it did in the movies. Just the pounding of his heart and his breathing. Both of which were steady.

The hissing and uncoiling of the cable stopped as the grapnel landed on the roof. He hauled up the slack and coiled it up around the boom as tightly as he could and reattached the hook to its frame.

Too far for me to make out if the hook's stuck firm.

He waited for several moments for lights to go up in the house, to hear sounds of alarm.

None came.

That window might be an attic room. No one's there, likely. Or, the sound hasn't registered on its occupants.

He tried the cable with his gloved hands. It felt taut enough. No slippage when he applied all the force he could.

Cutter holstered the grapple gun, made sure the second cable and the rest of his gear was secure. Inserted a pulley into the zip line and let his body swing out into the night.

৩ৎ 43 ২ৎ

Average zip line speeds in recreational uses are thirty miles an hour.

Cutter decided to go slower and applied his gloved palm to the cable as a braking mechanism. *Don't want to slam against the roof and alert them.*

Fifteen seconds to travel four hundred feet, roughly parallel to Malabar Street, starting high over rooftops and dropping low as he drew closer to the target residence.

He let go of the cable and jammed it against the roof, bent his elbow to absorb his momentum and brought his body flush against the roof.

SIGHT SNACKED ON A PROTEIN BAR AS HE CHECKED HIS SCOPE, idly. No movement. He returned to his cell phone, and his breath hitched when he checked out the photograph his girlfriend had sent him. Whoa! What was that she was wearing? He cursed Snake and Fuse loudly. He could have been with her instead of lying on a cold roof with his gun.

· · ·

CUTTER STRAINED HIS EARS TO HEAR ANY MOVEMENT. LOOKED down at the walls of the house and the windows to see if any shadows emerged. He let out his breath when no one appeared.

He could hear the faint sounds of voices from within. *House is packed with people. Not all of them will be asleep.* He reached out with his left hand and felt the skylight. Yeah, he could break its glass.

First, however, the escape cable.

He twisted on the pulley and drew out the grapple gun. Inserted a second hook in it and let it dangle from his waist while he uncoiled the spare cable and fixed one end to the grapnel embedded in the roof. No give when he tugged firmly on it. *Its claws have sunk into the roof's frame.*

He finished setting up the cable and raised the gun to aim at the target house—the fourth from the bangers' house. Its roof was at a lower level, which was why he had chosen it. That, and the alley at its back, which would be his escape route.

The cable flew with a hiss when he triggered and tautened when the hook struck and held on the exit house. No lights turned on there, either.

He wrapped the slack of the cable around the embedded grapnel and tugged sharply again. It held.

He took a deep breath and released it. And again, to center himself in the night to prepare for his next move, which had to be flawless for him to escape.

Cutter extracted the Glock and smashed its butt on the skylight, shattering the glass. Returned the weapon to its holster, then removed the first thermite bomb and tossed it inside the house.

Doesn't matter if it's an attic. It will burn and the flames will spread. Threw two more for good measure and swiftly transferred his pulley to the escape roof and kicked off.

He went four feet and slowed himself. Dangled in the air while he twisted to look down at the lower window of the house. *Can I reach that?*

Conscious of time ticking by, he lobbed another incendiary grenade at the target window. It bounced off the wall and landed in the yard. *No matter. It'll explode there, too.* He threw another grenade and that one missed, too. The third landed squarely on the window, broke through its glass and disappeared inside the house.

He lobbed all but one of remaining thermite bombs and swung his body into motion to escape. By the time he had crossed the boundary wall, the Street Front house was glowing orange and the shouts of its residents were audible in the quiet night.

The shouts alerted Sight, who reluctantly drew his eyes away from his phone. His jaw dropped when he saw the burning house.

How did that happen? He hadn't seen anyone go in.

He put his eye to the scope and watched in horror as flames exploded from the windows and several hoods came running out.

Wait. What was that behind?

He stared in disbelief. Was that ... yeah, it was! A dark figure on some kind of cable who was escaping away from the house, above the yards of the houses.

SON OF A—Sight clamped his lips firmly and went into sniper mode. He relaxed his body and, at the lower end of his respiratory cycle, triggered.

His teeth bared in a grin when the man jerked but didn't fall.

Some kind of armor.

Sight didn't go for a head shot. He wasn't that good a shooter. He fired at the man's legs and pumped his fist when the stranger dropped out of sight.

He got to his feet and reached for his phone.

He dialed a number and then stopped himself.

This was his chance. If he could capture this person, all by himself, Fuse and Snake would reward him. He would get the promotion he wanted. Boss of a neighborhood cell.

He erased the number and called another one.

'Armando?' he asked sharply. 'Are you okay?

'NO!' He cut his friend off. 'STOP TALKING. I KNOW WHAT HAPPENED. I KNOW WHO DID IT AND WHERE HE IS. Come to Malabar. BY YOURSELF. YOU AND I CAN CAPTURE HIM.'

❧ 44 ❧

Cutter almost lost his grip on the pulley when he felt the first blow on his back. Before he could comprehend what had happened, something smashed into his left thigh and sent him falling into the backyard of the house.

He rolled instinctively to absorb the impact of the twenty-foot fall.

Someone shot me!

His armor had saved him from the first round, but the second had found the fleshy part of his thigh.

He grimaced when he felt the stickiness on his leg and traced the wound gingerly. It burned, but it seemed like it was a flesh wound. *Got to move!*

He winced and got to his feet. Thanked his luck that the residents of the house hadn't woken up. Tested his leg, gritted his teeth against the searing pain and hobbled to the fence. He hauled himself up clumsily and fell over it into the garden of the third house, on whose roof his cable had landed.

He groaned and got to his feet. *That rear wall leads to the alley —I can get away from there.*

He took two steps, just as a dog started barking.

. . .

'HE FLEW OVER THE HOUSES ON A CABLE,' SIGHT WHISPERED to Armando as the two men ran down Malabar, guns in their hands. A neighbor came out, woken by the blaze and the commotion from the Street Front house. Took one look at them and disappeared inside hastily.

'Cable?'

'Yes. I shot him. If we get him, just you and me, we'll be rewarded.'

'But how did he—'

'Stop talking,' the sniper snarled. 'I'll explain everything later.' He drew up in front of a house three doors away from the burning building. 'He fell in the backyard,' he whispered.

He was about to go down the driveway when a dog started barking in the neighboring house.

'HE'S IN THAT ONE!' Sight hissed loudly and raced to the next yard.

CUTTER HUSTLED TO THE WALL AS FAST AS HE COULD, CURSING, sweating. He got his palms on the fence. Had wrapped his fingers on its top when the backyard door slid open and a light came on.

'WHO ARE YOU?'

He turned cautiously to check if the speaker had a gun.

An old woman in her robe. Her husband behind her, holding the leash of their pet, which was straining, barking, at the stranger's intrusion.

No weapon in their hands.

'I mean no harm,' he replied. 'I'm going—'

Something crashed at the front of the house.

The couple turned at the sound. The woman screamed, the man yelled, and before Cutter could react, two hoods appeared. Both of them armed, one of them with what looked like a Remington, the other, a handgun.

'THERE HE IS!'

'GET OUT OF MY HOUSE!' the elder man roared. 'YOU HAVE NO RIGHT—'

He fell when Handgun Man slashed him across the face with his weapon. His wife shrieked and rushed to his aid. The dog yelped when a boot struck its ribs and resumed barking as it leapt around, trying to attack, but hindered by its leash.

The throbbing in Cutter's leg faded as the animal in him took over.

Twenty-five feet from where he was, to the back door, where the hoods were.

'YOU!' Sniper ordered. 'COME HERE. SLOWLY. DON'T REACH FOR A WEAPON.'

'Please don't hurt us. Please. We don't know who he is. We—'

The woman's pleading turned into another scream when Handgun Man slapped her. The force of the blow felled her to her knees, and her husband joined her. They cowered in fear as they held each other, blood streaming down from cuts on their faces. The man reached out to his dog, which climbed into his arms and kept yapping at the strangers.

'Let them go,' Cutter told the hoods softly.

'You hear that, Armando?' Sniper laughed. 'See how calm he is? He is *telling* us, not asking, as if—'

Cutter wasn't conscious of his draw. One moment he was heading to the back door, the next, his Glock was bucking in his hand.

His first shot caught Sniper in his chest. The second was a dollar bill apart from the first, and the third was in his face.

Armando gasped as his partner fell. The hood's eyes widened. He had thought he and his friend had the upper hand. He yelled and had just brought up his gun when Cutter shot him twice.

'Please ...' the woman sobbed as she turned blindly to him. 'Don't kill us. Please—'

'I won't, ma'am. MA'AM!' He shook her gently and stood as unthreateningly as he could as she and her husband focused on him.

'I'm not here to kill you. I was looking to get away when they shot me and I fell. Tell the cops everything that happened. What happened, how I arrived. Don't—'

'You need to get away.' She grabbed his hand as sirens wailed in the distance. 'Go. Leave us.'

'You're hurt, ma'am. You and your husband. You need—'

'GO!' she insisted fiercely. Her grey eyes burned into his. 'You don't need to jump over the fence. There's a door that opens into the alley. Go down it, between the houses. You'll get to Boulder Street. Jim's got an old car there. A Ford. Keys are in the glove box. It's so old no one will steal it. It works and there's gas in the tank. Take it.'

'Ma'am—'

'Son,' her husband interrupted. Blood streamed down his face and had colored his shirt to a dark red. He was smiling, however. 'When Em orders, no one protests. Do it.'

'Why?' Cutter shook his head dazedly. 'Why are you helping me?'

'Why did you save us?'

HE LOPED OUT INTO THE ALLEY, HIS HEAD BOWED. HE KNEW he looked conspicuous in his EMT uniform, with his gear over his back, his face darkened with paint and sweat.

The neighborhood was awake, alive with the sounds of cruisers and fire trucks and the voices of residents. No one was in the alley, however, and when he peered cautiously into Boulder Street, it wasn't busy. *All attention is on the burning house and perhaps that couple's house.*

Jim's Ford was easy to spot. It was in a sorry state, with its peeling paint, dust and grime-laden windscreen and nearly bald tires. The engine turned smoothly, however, when he tried it.

Cutter rolled out without drawing any attention, turned left on Evergreen Avenue and went down to the intersection with Malabar. He parked between two cars and got out cautiously.

Straightened his walk as smoothly as he could, as he bit his lips against the burning pain.

He turned the corner and breathed a sigh of relief. Police vehicles and fire trucks at the far end of Malabar, where the house was burning. Two cop cars in front of Jim and Em's house. No one was near his ambulance.

He went to it, opened the rear door, lobbed his last thermite grenade inside, then returned to his getaway vehicle and drove down Evergreen.

He was a block away when he heard the escalation in sirens and knew the ambulance was on fire.

He had *escaped*. He was alive. The Street Front's house was destroyed.

It doesn't even matter if there were no drugs in it. Covarra's got the message. His business isn't safe as long as I am around.

45

Cutter gritted his teeth as his thigh reminded him he had been shot. He hoped it was no more than a flesh wound, that it wouldn't hinder him.

He drove out of East LA, skirted downtown and, when he was in the central part, reached for his phone and sent a text message.

It's Cutter. I'm coming.

On La Cienega Boulevard, with just the radio to keep him company, he heard a journalist breathlessly reporting that Boyle Heights was under attack.

He shook his head and grinned mirthlessly at the exaggeration. Entered Beverly Hills, drove to Foothill Road and approached a black metal gate, which rolled back. He drove down a concrete driveway and parked in front of a large triple garage. Got out of his vehicle and limped to its side, where a man stood.

'I was hoping you were dead.' The man sized him up.

Cutter had fans all over the world.

'Good to see you, too,' he growled and winced when his leg complained as he climbed the single step and followed the man inside.

Yevgeny Kozlov had been a doctor in Moscow, but he wasn't the kind any random citizen could go to for their ailments. He worked in GRU, the secretive military intelligence agency that carried out covert attacks all over the world. The agency was widely believed to be behind election manipulation in the Western world, hacking on an industrial scale, and assassinations.

Kozlov had walked into the US Embassy in Moscow on a spring morning and turned himself in. He had given up intel on active Russian agents in the US, Germany and UK and had been immediately flown to the US, where he had been further debriefed and rehabilitated under a new identity.

The Russian had established himself as a cosmetic surgeon of repute and was on speed-dial on every A-lister's phone.

'That's recent,' the doctor commented as he cut the EMT uniform's legs and inspected the wound.

'Would I come to you if it weren't?'

'Of all the gin joints in the world, you had to pick mine.' Kozlov cleaned Cutter's thigh as he paraphrased. 'You want the good news or the bad news?' He went to a chest of drawers and brought out a bottle of vodka. Poured a generous shot into a glass and offered it to Cutter, who shook his head.

'I don't drink. Have you forgotten?'

'I wish I never remembered anything about you.' The doctor emptied the glass in one swallow and donned his gloves.

'You're going to operate on me after that drink?'

'That's how it's done in Moscow.'

'We're in LA.'

'Be my guest.' Kozlov gestured expansively. 'Find someone else who will treat you no-questions-asked.'

Cutter gave up. He had yet to work out why everyone in his life was stubborn, headstrong, and got great pleasure from yanking his chain.

He lay down on the bed and then remembered and propped himself up on an elbow. 'What's the good and bad news?'

'Ah, that.' The Russian picked up gleaming instruments. 'It's not serious. The bullet grazed the side of your thigh, took out a chunk of flesh, but you won't die. You don't even need complicated surgery.'

'What's the bad news, in that case?' Cutter eyed him suspiciously.

'It's going to hurt,' and with that Kozlov jabbed him right on the wound.

'YOU PASSED OUT,' THE DOCTOR SAID UNSYMPATHETICALLY when Cutter came to. 'For maybe fifteen minutes.'

'That's what happens when you torture someone.'

'Torture, droog? That was not even close. I should know. I worked in the GRU, in case you were forgetting.'

Droog. Friend. That's who Kozlov was to him, despite his attitude.

It was Cutter who had escorted him from Moscow to the States, and during the flight and in the subsequent months, they had developed a close friendship. Cutter was at his side when Kozlov heard from Moscow that his parents had been arrested in retaliation for his defection. He held the Russian when they heard the news that his folks had died after being tortured. He had been best man when the defector had married Marta, another Russian émigré, a psychiatrist.

Kozlov cleaned up and bandaged his thigh. Washed his hands in the sink and cocked his head at Cutter, who was inspecting what remained of the EMT coveralls.

'I guess I have to provide you with some clothing,' he sighed. He went to a dresser and returned with a clean Tee and a pair of jeans.

'They're mine. They should fit. We're the same size.'

'Neat place,' Cutter commented after he had put on the clothes.

'Yeah.' Kozlov had developed an American accent as he

established his business. 'Marta would have killed me if I started seeing patients in the house. Turning the garage into my surgery was the obvious choice. I didn't need it anyway.'

'How is she? The kids?'

'She misses you. No,' he replied quickly when Cutter looked up. 'She doesn't know you're here. Vasily's in New York, working in a law firm, while Taty's at Princeton.'

Cutter smiled absently at the pride in Kozlov's voice and tested his leg by pacing the room. It throbbed dully, but he could move.

'Painkiller will wear off in a few hours. There are more in that baggie. Take them regularly. I've written a prescription too, in case you need more.'

Cutter inspected the medicines and pocketed them. Reached for his wallet and got his hand slapped.

'Don't,' Kozlov told him roughly. 'You should rest for a few days. Let your leg heal.'

I can't.

'You won't, will you? What have you gotten yourself into this time? I thought you were in New York. Marta was proud when you came up on TV. She told all her friends how close we were.'

'It's better you don't know.'

Kozlov nodded, as if he had been expecting just that response.

'You'll have to erase your security camera footage.'

'This isn't the first time you or other operators have turned up in the middle of the night. I know what to do.'

Cutter grinned and squeezed his shoulder. Went to the door when the Russian turned off the inside lights and slipped out.

'Try not to get killed,' his friend told him in a low voice when he climbed into his car.

He drove away on that upbeat note, and in the coolness of Beverly Hills worked out his next moves.

I can't go back to Sycamore Avenue or Vienna's house. Cops will be watching those places.

He was confident there was nothing to link him to the burning house or the ambulance. However, LAPD already suspected him. *I don't have an alibi. They'll find the burner phones if they search hard enough.*

They wouldn't find his arms caches because he had stashed them in various locations all over the city.

What of Covarra? Will this attack be enough for him to call me?

He would have to find other places to hit if the shot-caller didn't respond. Which would be a challenge, since he didn't know any others.

His hands tightened on the wheel as he drove through the night.

I won't give up, he vowed. But his words felt hollow, even to himself. All the Street Front boss had to do was stay silent, and that would leave Cutter with nothing and nowhere to go.

He drove to Pacific Palisades, an upmarket neighborhood on the west side of the city, and checked into a hotel.

The thought came to him just as he dropped off to sleep.

I can ask Janikyan. He might know where Covarra's warehouses are.

❧ 46 ❧

Difiore watched as Matteo briefed Dade in her office. It was more crowded than usual. Cruz and Estrada were present, along with more cops from the task force. Lasko, seated at the back, hadn't acknowledged her or Quindica when he entered the office.

It's a show of force from Matteo. He knows the chief will be furious at what happened last night. He's brought so many of his team to demonstrate they're working hard.

'We arrested three bangers in that house, ma'am. There were ten inside, and ten more outside—'

'Three out of twenty,' Dade interrupted him coldly.

'Yes, ma'am. The rest of them got away. Their entire stash burned down. These hoods say there was close to one-and-a-half mil worth of product. Mexican Oxy, mostly, some meth. Our technicians are still on site—'

'Tell me something new, Vance.'

'Ma'am. That house went up at two am. Firefighters got it under control by about three am. No other houses were affected, thankfully. We were able to enter the house only at five; by then it had cooled down sufficiently. That's just six hours ago, ma'am. We need time—'

'You realize whoever is doing this, attacking Covarra, is several steps ahead of us?'

'That's the way it is with any crime, ma'am. We'll get him.'

'You sound very confident about that.'

'He'll trip up, ma'am. He'll make a mistake.'

'Break it down again for me.'

Difiore tuned out when Matteo went through the sequence of events. She and Quindica had visited the scene early in the morning and had gotten a report from Estrada.

'No one saw this attacker,' the chief summarized when the lead detective had finished. 'He blasted the cameras at the building site, zipped down, threw ANM14s inside the house, got away, burned down the ambulance he stole and disappeared into the night.'

Her icy look froze Matteo when he attempted to speak.

Lasko wasn't deterred, however. 'Correction, ma'am. There were twenty-one bangers in or around the house. We got three, Mystery Man got two: Eduardo Aponte and Armando Dengra. The first was the sniper—'

'Lasko.' Dade cut him off sharply. If a voice could freeze, the cop would have turned to ice. 'You think I haven't read the reports or listened to Vance?'

'No, ma'am,' the detective mumbled as his face turned red in embarrassment.

'That couple.' The chief regarded him silently for a moment and then turned to Matteo. 'I want to talk to them. Make it happen.'

FRANCISCO COVARRA WAS IN ANOTHER SAFE HOUSE IN EAST Hollywood. Salazar with him, along with the sixteen bangers who had fled from Forest Avenue.

'I don't pay you to run away from fire,' the gang leader said venomously as he eyed the men. 'You should have gone inside the house and captured this man.'

'It was burning—'

The shot-caller snarled and pounced on the speaker. A blade appeared in his hand as if by magic and he plunged it repeatedly into the man's chest until Salazar grabbed him and pulled him away.

Covarra didn't resist. His chest heaved as he watched the thug writhe and moan on the floor and die. His face, when he raised it, was cold and hard.

'Go,' he said, pointing a finger. 'Spread out in the city. Find out who did this and where he is.'

'They won't find anything,' Salazar told him when the men left. 'We know who did this. Call him—'

He broke away when the gang leader looked at him viciously. He changed tack. 'I called Santangel, our captain in the LAPD—'

'I know who he is.'

Salazar swallowed. It was difficult to have a conversation with his friend when he was in such a mood. 'He told me the attacker used military equipment. Thermite grenades, he called it. They burn anything down. He used a zip line to land on the roof. From the crane on the building site—'

'I don't need to know that. DO YOU KNOW HOW MUCH PRODUCT WE HAVE LOST IN THOSE TWO ATTACKS? ALMOST THREE MILLION DOLLARS. HOW ARE WE GOING TO MAKE THAT UP?'

Covarra pounded his friend's chest with his fists and then broke away, panting.

'Fuse,' he snarled. 'Don't tell me how that man attacked. Tell me how we can get him.'

'There is only one way. Call him.'

47

'Why are we with her?' Difiore mouthed at her partner as they accompanied Lisa Dade to her official vehicle.

Quindica shrugged and climbed into the rear seat while the police chief sat next to her driver.

'I need to get away,' the LAPD boss said wearily. 'Keep me company.'

'Yes, ma'am. You think the couple will tell us anything more than they told Matteo?' Difiore glanced back through the rear window and spotted the lead detective following them in their car.

'I hope so. When they see us in person.'

Jim and Emily Curiel. The NYPD detective brought up Matteo's report on her phone. Retired. He had been a building construction inspector, employed by the city, while she had been a school teacher.

'Salt-of-the-earth kind of people,' Difiore guessed, speaking softly so only her partner could hear. 'One daughter, who works in tech in San Francisco, no other children. They've been in LA all their lives.'

'You think we'll get nothing from them?' Quindica whispered.

'Yeah.'

'You heard what the chief said. Look at her. She's stretched tight.'

Difiore nodded. Dade's neck was rigid with tension, tendons taut against her skin. A pulse fluttered visibly in her forehead whenever she looked at them.

'Understandable. Her city hasn't experienced these kinds of attacks in a long while.'

They broke off when the vehicle slowed to a stop in front of the Curiels' residence.

A patrol cop who was leaning against a cruiser snapped to attention.

'They're inside, Chief,' he told Dade at her questioning look. 'I informed them you would be coming.'

'Thank you, Terry. You did great.'

That's one reason she's got most of the cops' loyalty, Difiore thought as she observed Dade at work. *She calls them by name, makes them feel important, can relate to them. She goes to bat for them.*

'Waste of time,' Matteo grunted when he joined them. 'They aren't going to tell the chief anything more than what they told me.'

Difiore made no comment and trailed behind Quindica as they went into the house.

THE LIVING ROOM WAS COZY, WITH WARM COLORS. A MUTED-red throw on the floor. A well-used couch in front of a fireplace, which the elderly couple occupied, family photographs and paintings on the mantelpiece and walls. A home on which love and care had been lavished.

Dade introduced herself and her companions, made small talk to make the Curiels feel comfortable. She noted the small bandages on their foreheads and, despite her warm words, the wariness in their eyes.

'You've met Vance,' she said, smiling at them. 'He's our best detective. He'll find who is responsible for burning that house. He'll—'

'That place deserved to be destroyed,' Emily Curiel interrupted her fiercely. 'It was used by that gang. Entire neighborhood knew about it. What did the cops do? Nothing.'

'Ma'am, you know we can't act unless we suspect—'

'Jim, you remember when LAPD raided it?'

'Yeah, last year. They arrested a few men, some cop came on TV and said they had cleaned up the neighborhood. But the gang returned as if nothing had happened.'

This will be tough, Dade sighed internally.

'How are your wounds healing?'

'They're fine. Superficial cuts,' Jim Curiel growled. 'Ma'am, I have to ask, why are you here? We told him everything that happened.' He jerked his chin at Matteo. 'We held nothing back.'

'You don't remember anything else? About that man who shot those two—'

'He saved us.' Emily Curiel glared at her. 'He could have run away. There was enough time for him to escape when those thugs broke inside.'

'Yes, ma'am. Did he say anything that you remember? He's our prime suspect—'

'He should get a medal for what he did. Cleaned out that place and took out two gangsters.'

'Ma'am.' Difiore came to Dade's rescue. 'Did he look like this?' She showed them Grogan's photograph on her screen.

'Him! No. We described him to this cop.' It was the wife's turn to jerk her head in Matteo's direction. 'He was wearing glasses, he had a heavier build. He didn't have green eyes.'

'Brown or black.' Jim Curiel nodded his head. 'Neither of us were in a state to observe him closely.'

Difiore wasn't done. She scrolled swiftly on her phone, turned the screen towards the couple and played a video. Ellen Ronning, a prominent TV journalist, interviewing Grogan in New York. 'Did he sound like this?'

Emily Curiel's lips thinned in anger. 'We told you he didn't look like this man. Why do you keep showing—'

'Mrs. Curiel,' Dade interrupted gently. 'That attacker—'

'He didn't raise his hand or his gun on us.'

'No,' Jim Curiel echoed. 'In fact, he was unarmed when we saw him. He reached for his gun only when those thugs broke in. He rescued us from them.'

'Sir,' the chief said patiently, 'he could have been in a disguise. That's why Detective Difiore is playing that tape. Perhaps you could recognize his voice.'

The couple listened intently and then shook their heads. 'He didn't sound like that. That man's voice was deeper, harsher,' the wife said. 'No, he isn't that person in the interview.'

'Did he say anything about a vehicle? Where he was going to?'

'He took Jim's Ford.'

Matteo leaned forward urgently. 'Ma'am.' He addressed them sharply. 'You didn't tell us that. You said he went through the back gate.'

'We are old,' she snapped back. 'You think our memories are like yours, young man?'

Dade couldn't help smiling at Emily Curiel's stinging reply. She broke into a grin when Jim Curiel winked at her slyly. Her troubles—the mayor demanding hourly updates, the media camped outside the headquarters, the investigations that were going nowhere—suddenly seemed distant. *I like them,* she thought. *What did Gina say about them? Salt of the earth? She's right.*

'The key was hanging there.' She pointed to a hook near the door to the backyard. 'He took it, asked where the vehicle was and went away.'

'You remember the license plate, ma'am?'

Jim Curiel snorted. 'It's our car. Of course, we do.' He recited it to the detective, who made a hurried phone call and put his phone away.

'Where was it parked?'

'On Boulder Street.'

'Why there?'

'We run out of parking on this street quickly. There are always spaces on Boulder. And no,' he said firmly when Matteo made to question him again. 'This man didn't say where he was going. He didn't tell us his name. He didn't leave anything behind.'

A dog trotted into the room, sniffed the visitors and climbed into Emily Curiel's lap, its tail wagging furiously.

'We wouldn't even have known he was passing through our yard if Oscar hadn't woken us up.'

'Ma'am.' Dade stroked the pet, who licked her palm. 'Did Oscar attack him?'

'No. He was on a leash. But those thugs—' Her eyes hardened. 'One of them kicked him. He deserved to die just for that.'

DIFIORE LED THE WAY OUT OF THE CURIELS' HOUSE, DONNED her shades and waited with Quindica while Matteo and the chief thanked the couple.

'That was smart thinking,' the task force lead complimented her as they headed back to their vehicles, 'showing them Grogan's photograph and video.'

'It came to nothing.'

'Investigations are like rolling a boulder uphill.' He shrugged, waved to the chief and drove away.

'Vance will find the Ford dumped somewhere,' Dade said after a while, as her driver took them back to the office. 'Probably burned, and even if isn't, it will be clean.'

'Yes, ma'am,' Difiore agreed.

'You know.' The chief turned around to face them. Her eyes

were distant, her expression remote. 'I've never had to arrest a friend.'

She's referring to Grogan.

'It could be anyone, ma'am,' Quindica said softly. 'Another gang attacking the Street Front. Heck, Covarra doesn't lack enemies.'

'It isn't anyone. His gang and Armenian Bros have been sniping at each other for years. That's the most brutal rivalry in town. None of the previous attacks had this kind of precision. They were street brawls, drive-by shootouts, killings in a bar. These attacks,' she said as her green eyes regained focus, 'they are military-style. Planned to the smallest detail, executed perfectly. And the gear,' she paused, laughing mirthlessly, 'no banger would even think of using such equipment.'

Difiore squeezed Quindica's thigh in warning when her partner went to speak. *Let her talk.*

'But, Cutter, I've seen him work. This has his signature. He can disguise his appearance, his voice, he can use ghost weapons ... but it's him.'

She straightened and pulled out her phone. 'Vance,' she ordered the detective, 'meet me at the office. We're fifteen minutes away.'

DIFIORE AND QUINDICA FOLLOWED HER SILENTLY WHEN THEY reached the LAPD headquarters. They took their cue from the chief, who ignored the assembled reporters' questions and didn't look at the TV cameras.

Up through the elevator and to her office, where Matteo, Cruz and Estrada were waiting.

'We found the Ford, ma'am. Burned out, in a parking lot in West Hollywood. Forensics team is going over it right now, but I'm not hopeful.'

Difiore watched the chief straighten files on her desk. Adjusted a paperweight and placed it neatly on a stack of papers.

'Where's Grogan?' Her eyes were flinty when she raised them.

'He's gone, ma'am. He's not at the two addresses we have for him. He's not answering his phone. It shows he's at the Sycamore place, but its empty.'

He exhaled softly. 'He's gone off the grid, ma'am.'

'What progress have you made with your investigations?' Dade fired at Difiore and Quindica.

'Not much,' the FBI SAC answered. 'Matteo's helping us, but still—'

'You two know Grogan better than anyone else in this room, in LA in fact.'

Difiore sensed it from the chief's tight face. Her guts tightened when she heard her next words.

'Stop your work for now. You can return to it later. Find Grogan. Bring him in for questioning.'

❧ 48 ❧

Covarra brooded over Salazar's suggestion. He snapped at his protective detail over every minor irritant. He got the Forest Avenue guards to line up again, raged at them and killed one more sentry.

That didn't pacify him.

He pictured Panig Janikyan smirking at his troubles, and that made him furious.

'I told you what you should do.'

His deputy appeared in the evening, and only then did Covarra relent. He went to his bedroom and brought out the phone the attacker had given him.

'There's no bug in it. We checked,' Salazar said when he fingered it suspiciously.

The Street Front boss brought up the solitary number stored in it and, after a few moments, called it.

CUTTER WAS HALF-ASLEEP IN THE TAHOE WHEN THE PHONE buzzed.

He was parked on the Via de Las Olas, a curving strip of road in Pacific Palisades. It fronted the ocean, where steep cliffs gave way to the coastal highway down below.

There were a few other cars, most of them empty, their occupants out for a walk or taking in the natural scenery.

He jerked awake and reached for his cell. Nope, that wasn't the one that was buzzing. Alertness flooded him when he brought out the burner and checked the incoming call.

Covarra!

'Talk,' he ordered.

The Street Front boss started with a string of curses.

'Is that all you've got to say?'

He could hear the gang leader's harsh breathing as he fought to control himself.

'You don't know who you're tangling with,' Covarra whispered. 'My people are everywhere. They will find you. They will bring you to me. I'll—'

'Do you know who I am?'

No reply.

'Do you know where I am?'

'Wherever you are—'

'You don't. You know nothing about me, but I know everything about you. Fear me.'

Cutter hung up, pushed his seat back and went to sleep.

'*Puto!*' Covarra swore and threw the phone against the wall. It bounced and fell to the floor in pieces.

'What have you done?' Salazar ground at him and hurried to pick up the pieces. 'It's destroyed,' he said bitterly. 'Luis!' he called out to a guard. 'Get me a burner phone,' he ordered when the man appeared. The sentry disappeared and returned with a device that he handed over. The deputy removed its battery, replaced the SIM card with the one from the destroyed phone, and held his breath. 'The number works,' he said, with satisfaction.

He turned to his friend and waggled his finger in remonstration. 'You're letting your anger dictate to you. That man is playing with—'

'I'LL KILL HIM.'

'Do that. But first, we need to find him.'

'I WON'T CALL HIM AGAIN. IT WAS YOUR IDEA. DID YOU HEAR HOW HE SPOKE TO ME?'

'He was right. We know nothing of him. Our men have been searching for almost ten days. Have we found him? No.'

'What do you suggest?' Covarra snarled. 'You want me to ignore him? Do you know how weak that will make us look?'

'No. I am saying bring him to us.'

'How?'

'By agreeing to meet. Tell him you are ready to talk, answer whatever questions he has.'

'We'll set a trap for him.' The gang leader's eyes lit up wickedly. He rubbed his hands unconsciously. 'We'll capture him when he arrives. Why didn't you suggest this before?'

'You were too angry to listen.'

'I won't call him right away. That will only make me look weak. Fuse,' Covarra commanded his friend, 'find a place where we can meet. Somewhere secure.'

His lips curled in anticipation at the thought of capturing the attacker. Oh, the things he would do to the man.

✣ 49 ✣

Matt Lasko went to the massage parlor on Hollywood Boulevard, removed his shirt and lay down on the mattress, facedown.

He winced when the masseuse rubbed oil on his back and dug her fingers deep. He closed his eyes and drifted off as the woman pressed and ground her fingers and the heels of her palms until his body felt loose and ready. She tapped him on the shoulder when she had finished and left the room.

Only then did he get up and look at the man in the other bed.

'Cesar,' he greeted the bearded man, who was buttoning his shirt.

Lasko unpeeled several bills from his wallet and handed them over to the customer, who slipped them into his pocket.

'Tell me something useful.'

'You know about that attack in Boyle Heights?'

'Yeah. Who was behind it?'

'It's that bike rider who hit the boss's house on Hubbard Street.'

'You're sure of that? What I heard, no one knows who that man is.'

'Who else would it be? He seems to have a thing for Snake.'

'Does Covarra know who it might be?'

'No. He and Fuse have every street soldier trying to find out.'

Lasko studied Cesar as he pulled on his shirt and tucked it into his jeans. The man, a Street Front shooter, was an informant he had cultivated from his LASD days. The parlor was one of several of their meeting places.

HE HAD FOUND THE BANGER IN AN ALLEY, SHOT UP AND unable to move. The man had clutched his arm when he was about to radio for help. 'Help me,' Cesar had gasped, recognizing his uniform. 'And I'll help you. No cops.'

'I *am* a cop,' Lasko had told him.

'Take me to East LA, and I'll owe you.' The thug had given him an address.

'Why should I do that?'

'Because of who I am.'

It turned out that Cesar was high up in the Street Front, a leader who ran his own cell in Central LA. He had been a loyal banger until Covarra had come across his sister in Juarez, smuggled her back to LA and installed her as his mistress.

The relationship didn't last long. He accused her of sleeping with other men and had her killed. That turned Cesar against him.

'I killed one of the men who shot her,' he panted that night. 'But his round got me.'

'Won't Covarra suspect you were the shooter?'

'No. I was masked, and anyhow, he thinks I'm down with what happened to my sister.'

Lasko acted instinctively. He took the thug to an address, where a Hispanic doctor operated on the injured man and removed the slug from his body.

Cesar recovered, and from then on fed Lasko vital intelligence whenever he could.

. . .

'THERE'S SOMETHING HAPPENING, THOUGH.'

'What?'

'Don't know. Fuse has asked us to stay close. Stop doing business for a while.'

Lasko looked at him sharply. For a gang to stop selling product ... that had to be serious.

'No, don't look at me like that. I don't know anything more.'

'Something to do with this attacker?'

'Si, si. We're talking about nothing else these days. I think Snake is setting a trap for him.'

LASKO HURRIED BACK TO THE LAPD HQ AND TAPPED ON THE glass door to an office. He went inside when Matteo waved him in.

'That's NYPD Detective Difiore and FBI Special Agent in Charge Quindica,' the lead detective said, introducing the women to him. 'They've been working with the chief on some assignment.'

'I saw them in the boss's office yesterday.' Lasko nodded his head in greeting. 'You remember I told you about a snitch in the Street Front?'

'Yeah.' Matteo brought out a fresh toothpick and inserted it into his mouth. 'He hasn't given us any great intel.'

'That might change.' The younger detective grinned and relayed what Cesar had told him.

'That's nothing,' Cruz grunted in disgust.

'The gang's stopped dealing,' Matteo corrected him. 'I wouldn't call that insignificant. Stay on top of it and let us know what he comes back with.'

'I didn't tell you the best part—'

'Does the gang suspect who this dude is?' Estrada interrupted him.

'Nope.' His eyes flashed in excitement as he addressed the room. 'Covarra's setting a trap for him.'

❧ 50 ❧

Difiore waited until Lasko had left and turned to Matteo, who, at a warning look from her, dismissed Cruz and Estrada as well.

She got an imperceptible nod from Quindica when it was just the three of them in the office and suppressed a smile. *That's how she works. She lets me do the talking.*

'Dade's told us to suspend the task force temporarily, but we have too big a team for that. Let it continue its work. Peyton and I will focus on Grogan.'

'Works for me,' Matteo agreed. 'What do you need?'

'Access to your ALPR and traffic camera network.'

The Automated License Plate Reader was a system of street-light pole-mounted cameras and patrol car cameras that collected license plates of passing vehicles and stored them in a secure database. The technology could track a vehicle's movement over time, compare traffic to a list of stolen cars and those involved in criminal acts, and then alert officers.

The system's use was mired in controversy. Privacy and media bodies accused the police department of misusing the data, but the technology was there to stay.

'Done,' Matteo assented. 'Let's get him before he does anything worse.'

'Worse than burning a house in a residential neighborhood?' Quindica cracked.

'You know him better than me. What do you think he's capable of?'

'Grogan can pull off anything,' Difiore said soberly.

CUTTER FIGURED EVERY COP WOULD BE LOOKING FOR HIM. IT was time to get off the grid, which wasn't difficult for someone with his skills. He had a sufficient stock of burner phones. He had cloned his primary cell phone, which he had hidden in the Sycamore house, and had set up a system that allowed him to receive its calls on the device he carried.

He went to the bathroom and showered. Crushed the fake glasses he had been wearing and dumped the remains into the trash can. He inserted dark contacts into his eyes and applied a goatee. Darkened his hair with dye and applied silvery streaks. Stuck a tattoo—a large, red cross—on his neck, above his collar, and inspected himself in the mirror. He would pass random scrutiny.

LAPD will have facial recognition. They have Difiore and Quindica, who know how I operate.

He shrugged and grinned at himself. *I'll have to keep my face away from public cameras.*

He donned shades, grabbed his backpack and exited the hotel. Went to his Tahoe to check his phone. No missed calls or messages from Covarra.

He'll wait. He's driven by his ego. He won't want to show that he's being dictated to by me.

He drove to Little Armenia, aware that cameras would be capturing the Tahoe and ALPR would be running its plates against a suspect list. He wasn't worried, however. Wyatt and

Chuck paid enough city employees off to ensure their license plates were never flagged.

He parked in the same vacant space he had occupied during his previous visit and carried out a swift recon. No cruisers, no one else idling in their vehicles, no men or women lounging on benches, leaning against poles, or hanging around food trucks.

Nope. There was no LAPD surveillance at Arek Davidian's office. No bangers, either.

Cutter waited for another hour. A couple exited the broker's office, escorted to the door by the beaming man himself.

He waited a beat and got out of his vehicle.

'Mr. Davidian,' he called out before the man closed the door.

'Yeah?' the broker's smile flashed automatically.

'You were referred to me, sir, by one of your customers.'

The grin grew wider. Cutter could feel the man's interest.

'Why don't you come inside?'

That's what I want.

'Neat office,' he said appreciatively when he entered its cool interior. 'I thought you would be bigger.' He frowned as he gestured at the empty cubicles.

'Don't be taken in by fancy offices and lots of staff,' Davidian said, dismissing his competition. 'You, sir, came to me because of a recommendation. That's the service I deliver to my customers—'

He shrieked in surprise and alarm when Cutter caught his shirt and dragged him to his office.

'WHAT? WHO ARE YOU—'

'It's me. Same dude who assaulted you last time.'

The real estate agent froze. He hurried behind his desk when Cutter released him. His mouth worked several times before sound emerged.

'YOU—'

'Stop talking. Listen. I will not beat you up this time.' He tossed a phone on the desk. 'Get this to Janikyan. There's one number on it. He has to call me. As soon as he can.'

'I TOLD YOU THEN AND I AM TELLING YOU NOW.' Davidian's face turned red with fury. 'I HAVE NOTHING TO DO WITH HIM.'

'I know. But the Armenian community is tight-knit. I'm sure you can find a way to pass that phone and my message across.'

He left before the broker could protest.

'THAT PLACE ON JESSE STREET,' SALAZAR SAID, BRIEFING HIS boss. 'That empty warehouse. You remember we used to cook meth there.'

'Si.' Covarra snapped his fingers. 'We still own it?'

'We've gone legal.' His deputy smiled craftily. 'We rent it out for movie and music video shoots. You'd be surprised how much money it makes. People like that look.'

'Show me.'

Salazar brought up several pictures of it and showed it to the bangers' boss. 'It's on a street corner. We will have sentries on Rio Street and Jesse. Industrial area. No one around at night.'

'What is it?' he snapped when his deputy hesitated.

'It's safest to call him and tell him what we know. That we had nothing to do with that killing.'

Covarra controlled the burst of fury inside him. He jabbed his friend in the chest with his forefinger. 'Safe? Francisco Covarra does not do *safe*. I would have become an accountant if I wanted to live safely. No. We have had this discussion before. Don't bring it up again. This man dies at my hands. I don't want to listen to anything else. How much time do you need to make that place secure?'

'It's ours, Snake. We can set up the meeting tonight.'

'No, not so fast. Let's do it tomorrow. At night.'

CUTTER TRACKED DOWN ISAIAH LIMON AT LAX-IT AND waved at him.

'Yes, sir, you need a ride?' The driver straightened.

'Why is it that you are idling whenever I come to you? Any other cab driver would be picking rides up, dropping them off. You? You look like you don't need the business.'

Limon stared at him cautiously. 'Do I know you, sir?'

Cutter waited for him to make the connection and then slapped himself mentally on the forehead. *I am in a different disguise! How would he recognize me?*

'You got away cleanly from that crash on Sadler?'

Limon's eyes widened. He looked around fearfully. 'It's you! What are you doing here?'

'Relax, Isaiah. There are no cops around. No one knows what you did but me.'

'Why are you here?'

'I need your car.'

'No.' Limon backed off. 'That was a one-time deal. I'm not doing any crazy stunt again.'

'Isaiah, you didn't hear me. I need to borrow your car. I don't need you to do anything else.'

'Don't you have a ride of your own? Why do you—'

Cutter sighed and thrust a big bundle of bills at him. He wasn't going to go into the reasons why he needed to switch rides frequently, even if he had fake number plates. 'That's three grand there. More than you'll make today. I'll return your vehicle here. Intact. It won't be used for any criminal activity.'

'How can I be sure of that?'

'You'll know if you don't get arrested by evening.'

He laughed when the driver swallowed. 'Nothing like that will happen.'

He took the key from Limon's unresisting fingers and climbed into the car.

'Dude! I don't even know your name.'

'It's best that way.'

Cutter drove out and headed to LAPD headquarters. Parked

on Main Street in front of a long line of cars that had a row of traffic cones by their side.

It's not an official parking space, but that's where cops park when their lot is full.

He climbed out of his car, dumped his backpack in the trunk and went to the corner of Main and First, from where he could watch the building's entrance.

He was counting on Difiore and Quindica coming out to the nearest eating place for a bite. *They won't go to cafes in the building. Both of them like to get out, get some air.* Which left only two possibilities: one was a convenience store in the building, on Main Street; the other, Times Mirror Square.

Both of them are into architecture. They'll go to the LA Times building.

His hunch proved right when he spotted the couple at three pm, striding out of the main entrance. He turned away from them and spoke into his phone. Watched them from the corner of his eye and fell behind them at a safe distance.

No other cops with them, but then he hadn't expected any.

The women went to a coffee shop, ordered their food and drinks and settled on the low marble wall that ran around a thick, sculpted tree.

Cutter positioned himself behind the decorative foliage and waited patiently. He got his break when Difiore wiped her hands on a paper towel, dropped their food wrappings in a trashcan, went to a newsstand and browsed through a magazine.

She's left her bag with Quindica. Which was to the FBI agent's left, a couple of feet away from her.

He needed to create a distraction.

Using the cover of the tree, he yelled loudly. 'HEY, THAT MAN JUST SNATCHED A LITTLE GIRL FROM THAT STORE! SOMEBODY STOP HIM! HE'S GETTING AWAY.' That got everyone's attention.

'WHO WAS IT?' Several young men sprang off their chairs outside a café.

'He's wearing a white hoodie. She's in a pink dress.'

He sensed Difiore and Quindica were trying to place him from where they were, but he was well hidden by the conical topiary. The NYPD detective burst into a sprint and gave him a sideways look as she came into view. She didn't falter, however, as he kept pointing and joined the chase.

Cutter moved immediately once she was away. He went around the tree and glimpsed Quindica following Difiore. Their bags lay where they'd abandoned them on the marble surface.

He seized the opening. No one was looking at him. Several patrons in the massive hall were bunched together, excitedly discussing the incident. Many had gone into the store he had pointed at to seek out the parents of the girl.

He reached Difiore's bag and thanked his luck it was secured by magnetic clasps. He fished out a burner phone from his pocket and thrust it deep inside. Covered it with her neatly folded scarf and closed it. He hurried away just as voices approached, keeping the tree between him and them.

'There was no one there,' he heard the detective. 'No girl, either. He must have been mistaken.'

'Or drunk.' Quindica laughed. 'Did you see who it was?'

'Some dude. Greying hair. Wasn't paying attention to him.'

Cutter joined a throng of shoppers and merged with them as he exited the building. He hurried to his cab and fired it up.

Stopped at the red light at Main and First just as Quindica and Difiore stepped out on the pedestrian walkway.

He froze. Tracked them through the corner of his eyes but didn't look at them directly. Experienced operators and cops could sense the weight of a gaze. He saw Difiore's shades flash as she glanced his way. Held his breath, ready to punch through the light, but her steps didn't break as she crossed the street with her partner.

He chuckled, imagining her face when she discovered the phone.

She'll curse until the air is blue at how she was suckered.

His smile faded as he drove deeper downtown and then to East LA. Planting the device was necessary. It offered a secure comms channel to the cop.

He knew he would need it, given what he was planning.

❧ 51 ❧

'Y ou're out and about, still?' Beth Petersen mocked Cutter when he called.

He was their verbal punching bag.

'Why wouldn't I be?' he growled.

'We're following the news. We aren't dumb. What do you need?'

'GPS trackers. Soluble ones as well as small, colorless ones that can be stuck to the body.'

'When do you need them?' No surprise or shock in her voice.

'As soon as—'

'Go to West Sixth Street in two hours. It's a storage place. We'll message you the locker details.'

He stared at his phone. 'Two hours? That fast? You're in New York. Don't you have to organize—'

'We've got our caches in every major city in the country.'

He heard the murmur of voices in the background, and a man came on—Zeb Carter.

'Cutter? You need help?'

'I'm good.'

'Stay safe,' Beth piped up.

'I knew you cared for me.'

'We don't,' Meghan came on, 'but who would we mock if you got killed or arrested?'

CUTTER LOGGED INTO WERNER AND GOT IT TO SEARCH FOR the Street Front's known or suspected hangouts. Several addresses came up, all of them residential.

No, Covarra won't set up the meeting in a house. It won't be secure enough. He'll want more space. Like a warehouse or some kind of office space.

There was a building in East Hollywood, on the border with Little Armenia. The AI program had flagged it since it had come up in gang chatter on the darknet.

He brought it up on a maps and street view program and checked it out. It was a drab, two-story concrete building that showed signs of pending redevelopment: a developer's sign-board planted in its yard, a digger and earthmoving truck in its drive.

That could work. From what he could see, the ground floor was empty. *It will have several exits, and it's located where bangers can protect it.*

A recon run was necessary.

CUTTER JOINED THE LINE AT A FOOD TRUCK IN DOWNTOWN LA and ordered arepas with a filling of avocados, black beans and plantains. He ate them in his cab and wiped his hands on a paper towel. A cruiser rolled up as he was drinking from a bottle of water. A pair of cops emerged, appearing to be an experienced officer and a rookie. The woman, the senior cop, cut flat eyes in his direction but didn't break stride as she went to the counter and placed her order.

Cutter didn't linger. He didn't know if Dade had authorized a warrant for him, but he wasn't going to hang around to find out. *LAPD will be searching for me, that's for sure.* There had been several missed calls from Matteo and Cruz, calls he hadn't bothered to return.

He drove to the self-storage place that Beth referred to in her message. Circled once to find a parking space and squeezed behind a truck.

He bent his head when he spotted the cameras over the door and went inside to the locker room. Slipped his hands into flesh-colored gloves discreetly and punched the keys on the security pad.

He grabbed the backpack inside and left.

It was four pm when he went to the office building in East Hollywood and surveyed it.

Nope, he decided when he spotted the building equipment on the sidewalks. They narrowed the street and increased the risk to a clean getaway. He wouldn't set up the rendezvous in that building.

But will Covarra?

❧ 52 ❧

Matt Lasko drove his unmarked car to a car wash in Boyle Heights. He waited in the small coffee shop on the premises while two attendants hosed and waxed his ride.

He gave no sign of recognition when Cesar entered the store, went to the counter and ordered a latte. The banger returned with his drink and settled heavily into the chair next to him. There was a third customer, a woman, who left shortly when her car was ready.

'What's up? We met earlier today. Did something happen?'

'Be in this hood, tomorrow,' the thug whispered from the corner of his mouth.

'What time?'

'Will let you know as soon as I find out.'

'What's going down?'

'Fuse isn't saying. He wants the best hitters in the neighborhoods tomorrow. Snake ... I haven't seen him in some time.'

'Where's he holed up?'

'I would tell you if I knew. Both of them are on calls. Snake's in a safe house somewhere. But,' he added, shrugging his shoulders, 'I'm not senior enough. No one's told me where it is.'

'Could you find out?'

Cesar glared at him. 'Yeah. And then, Snake would cut me to pieces. Dude—'

'I get it.' Lasko motioned with his hand to get the thug to lower his voice. He got to his feet when an attendant waved at him.

'Tomorrow,' the banger reminded him as he left. 'Stay close.'

CUTTER RETURNED TO PACIFIC PALISADES AND SAT ON THE bluff to watch the sun go down. He opened the backpack when dusk was settling in and hefted the packet of GPS trackers. The soluble tag could be added to any liquid, which, after ingestion, remained active for thirty-six hours. The flesh-colored adhesive ones had the same lifespan.

Chad would love to get his hands on these, but even he doesn't sell them. The ingestible ones were based on trackers that healthcare professionals used to isolate cancerous cells. Secretive intelligence agencies around the world had adapted the technology to develop them for surveillance.

Cutter knew Zeb's Agency had access to cutting-edge devices the commercial market wasn't even aware of.

I merely asked and they delivered. No questions asked. Such was his relationship with them.

His brow furrowed when he delved deeper into the bag and brought out more gear. He whistled softly when he recognized the collapsible yagi antenna and the SMA connectors and realized what he was looking at.

A portable cell phone tower that would disguise where he was calling from.

Thank you, he messaged Beth.

Stay alive, she replied. *We would have to pick on Zeb if you disappeared, and he's no fun.*

. . .

THE CALL CAME AS HE WAS SEARCHING FOR HOTELS TO SPEND the night in.

'Mr. Grogan,' Panig Janikyan said softly. 'You are a man of many disguises.'

Cutter thought of denying it was him, then shrugged in the dark.

He's smart. He made the connection to Davidian.

'We need to meet.'

'The last time we met, you ordered me to leave.'

'I'll do that again if you come to my house uninvited.'

'Why should I agree?'

'We have a common enemy.'

53

Cutter drove to Little Armenia, took a left on Fountain Avenue and entered an unmarked alley that paralleled Serrano Avenue and Hobart Boulevard.

Narrow, just over the width of a pickup truck. Houses on each side, all of them behind metal fences. He saw heads peer out of windows when his lights lit up the neighborhood. Shadows moved in the yards; he caught the flash of cell phone screens as they were held to ears.

This is Janikyan's territory. Everyone here's likely to be in the Armenian Bros. All the occupants are like an early warning system to him.

A man came out of the alley and blocked his way when he approached a pink building to his left. He was heavily tattooed and seemed unarmed, but there was a noticeable bulge at his waist.

He rolled back a metal gate and jerked his head at Cutter as he drove into the yard.

A large house on stilted columns. On the ground level was parking. Approach to the main entrance was through metal stairs on the side. *Must have been an office that the gang converted to a safe house.*

Their footsteps clanged and echoed as they climbed the steps and entered a reception room. More hard-eyed and grim-faced thugs. All of them heavily and openly armed.

Cutter stood silently as they searched him, removed his Glock and Benchmade.

'You'll get them back when you leave,' a hood told him roughly. They took his phone, removed its battery and placed it in a tray.

He was shoved down the hallway, past more rooms and into a living room, where Panig Janikyan was seated on a couch.

'Mr. Grogan,' the Bros leader said with a humorless smile, 'so glad you could make it.'

He gestured to a couch. 'Davidian described you differently. You were in some other look at your house. Which one of those is the real you, or are they both disguises?'

Cutter had removed his disguise and was in his real self. *Let him assume whatever he wants.*

'Does it matter?'

'Not to me. I bet the cops would be interested, though.'

'Janikyan, if you wanted the LAPD here, you would have called them.'

'You said we have a common enemy. I'm intrigued, Mr. Grogan. Who do you have in mind?'

'LA Street Front.'

'That gang? Why would it be my enemy? I'm just a businessman.'

'A businessman who's surrounded by gunmen.'

'For my protection. Wealthy people are kidnapping targets. There have been attempts on my life from people who were envious of my success.'

I'll bet, Cutter smirked inwardly.

'Janikyan, save it,' he said. 'Your men searched me. I'm not wired. I'm not a cop. Let's not play games. I know you head the Armenian Bros.'

The gangster's eyes were dark pools that gave no indication of what he was thinking.

'Why are you here?'

'I want to know where the LA Street Front has its drug stash.'

'How would I know?'

'If you don't, I've wasted my time.' Cutter got to his feet and went to the door.

'Why do you want to know?' The gangster's voice stopped him.

'Because I might want to report it to the cops.'

'You think their gang bangers killed your friends? Is that what this is about?'

'My motives are none of your business.'

'I don't like it that you assume I am a thug.'

'I don't care what you think.'

A banger grunted, raised his gun in warning and lowered it immediately when Janikyan stared at him.

'Let's say, hypothetically,' said the gang leader, a thin smile playing on his lips, 'that I am who you say. If I knew where their warehouse existed, don't you think I would have taken it out?'

'Your outfit's bigger than theirs. You have more business activities than selling product on the street. There could be any number of reasons why you wouldn't hit it. I'm not interested in what you might or might not do. All I want is an address, if you have one.'

The air conditioner hummed as the distant wail of a cruiser came to them. Janikyan kept watching him, lizard-like. Silent, motionless, blinking occasionally until he finally stirred.

'Zohrab,' he ordered the banger who had grunted. 'Take him away.'

Looks like I'll get nothing from him.

He held his palm up to stop the approaching bodyguard.

'Were your men involved in a shootout with Street Front in Beverly Hills?'

'I have no idea what you're talking about, Mr. Grogan.' Janikyan's smile was silky. 'Shooting is bad for my business. I told you that before. Zohrab.' He cocked his head at his man, who came forward.

Cutter followed the banger out of the room. They reached the outer reception area, where another heavy handed him his gun, knife and cell phone.

'You're his bodyguard?' he asked Zohrab. He had noticed how the hood stood closest to Janikyan. The hood's only response was to jerk his head toward the door.

Cutter shook his head at himself. It looked like his charm and looks wouldn't work on the Armenians.

He followed the man out and down the stairs. Slipped on one of the metal steps, exclaimed in surprise and grabbed the hitter —who swore, turned around and helped him regain his balance.

'Sorry.' Cutter held his hands up in embarrassment. 'It's dark, and these steps are slippery.'

Zohrab didn't seem to be a man of many words. He turned around and continued down the steps to ground level, where more sentries stood guard. He stepped aside for Cutter to go to his cab.

'I would say it's a pleasure meeting you, but I would be lying.'

Nope, none of them rolled on the ground, holding their bellies, laughing.

'You are hard men,' he sighed. 'No wonder Janikyan keeps you around him. But this place ... really? You realize how easy it is to trap you inside? All the cops have to do is seal both ends of the alley. Sure, you might have gunmen in all the other houses, but what're they going to do when the LAPD come in hard with choppers and SWAT teams? Those stairs? They're not made for a quick getaway. This house isn't safe. You'd better move him somewhere else.'

'No?' he asked when no one reacted to his advice. 'I'll get going, then.'

'Mid-City. Third house on the left on Apple Street.'

Cutter stopped climbing into his car and stared at Zohrab, who had rattled off the address.

'That's where they have a store? Why didn't you hit it?'

'We discovered it just two days ago.'

'Don't do anything to it. Were you there at that Beverly Hills house?'

Zohrab looked at him impassively.

'Thank you.'

Cutter sighed theatrically when the banger kept his stoic silence. Manners were lost on some people.

He drove out of the parking space, aware of their eyes boring into him. Went down the alley and hung a left on Fountain Avenue. He stopped at the nearest clear space he found on the street and brought out his phone. Fingered an app and fist-pumped silently when he saw the green dot.

It was the signal from the adhesive tracker that he had planted on Zohrab's jacket, when he had stumbled on the stairs.

If he's Janikyan's bodyguard, he'll be around the man always.

That was as good as planting a tracker on the gang leader.

He had gotten lucky with its location as well. He had caught the man's jacket just beneath his armpit and had stuck the tracker there. It wouldn't be easily noticed, and if he were lucky, wouldn't be detected at all.

Mid-City. He recollected the address the bodyguard had given.

A plan began to form in his mind.

❧ 54 ❧

Covarra inspected the warehouse on Jesse Street with Salazar in attendance. Several Street Front shooters ranged outside the premises.

Nine pm at night. No traffic in the industrial area. The occasional drivers in passing cars took one look at the grim-faced men and floored their accelerators.

'It used to be a factory. Lots of machinery,' the deputy briefed his boss.

'Uh-huh.' The gang leader checked out the bare floor, the aluminum sheets lining the walls and the ceiling, which gave an old-style workshop look to the place. Tube lighting tied on bamboo poles that crisscrossed the roof completed the image. 'People really rent this for movies?'

'And music videos. There's a certain atmosphere to the place.'

Covarra nodded at that. *Atmosphere*. He liked that. He could imagine cutting the attacker's flesh to ribbons as he knelt on the floor.

'This is it.'

'Snake,' his friend said, taking a reasonable tone, 'why do you want to call him here? Tell him what he wants to know and he'll go away.'

'You're sure of that?' Covarra snapped. 'How do you know he'll disappear to wherever he came from?'

'We had nothing to do with killing those women.'

'This has moved beyond that. The moment he attacked me, it became personal.'

He shoved his hand into his pocket and brought out the stranger's phone. Dialed the number on it and put it on speaker.

CUTTER WAS NOSING THE CAB INTO A VACANT SPOT IN LAX-IT when the call came. He saw Limon approaching and waved the man away.

'Yeah?'

'You be ready tomorrow,' Covarra hissed.

'I'm always ready. Where do I need to be? What time?'

'Be in Boyle Heights.'

'What time?' he repeated.

'It will be night. I'll tell you when. Come alone. If my men see any cops, we'll—'

'Your men did nothing to protect you, or your places. Why do you think they'll get lucky tomorrow?'

He grinned when he heard Covarra's harsh breathing. *He's got a short temper. I can use that. He won't be thinking properly if he's that angry.*

'If you want your answers,' the gang leader snarled, 'you'd better be alone.'

'Why don't you tell me now and save us both the trouble? Who killed those women in Beverly Hills? Who's the shooter, who was their shot-caller and why?'

'Come tomorrow. You'll find out everything. Stay close to your phone.'

. . .

COVARRA ENDED THE CALL AND CARESSED IT ABSENTLY WITH his thumb. 'He's not a fool. He knows how I feel about him. He didn't say anything, however. He's going to turn up just like that?'

Salazar shifted his feet uneasily. 'We have increased security at all our warehouses. They're safe. Our people are checking the streets, the skies, everything. No stranger has come close to them. We've stopped our street operations as well. We know he hasn't captured any of our men and questioned them. He doesn't know our safe houses.'

Covarra jammed his hands in his pockets and brooded for a moment. 'Could he be working with Janikyan?'

'He seems to be working alone.'

'Is he? What about those cars that crashed into us on Sadler? Those drivers—'

'Janikyan would have stormed the house on Hubbard. Ernesto said he was alone.'

'Why would a single man come and meet me, knowing that I will kill him?'

HOW CAN I GET AWAY ALIVE? THERE'S NO WAY COVARRA WILL LET me leave. He'll want to torture and kill me slowly.

Cutter pondered this as he caught a cab from LAX-it and headed to where he had stowed his Durango.

No ideas had come to him when he reached his ride. He got the driver to go past it while he checked out the surroundings in downtown LA. No cruisers or cars with anyone inside.

He paid off the cab and hotfooted to his vehicle. Drove to Mid-City and checked out Cloverdale Avenue. Yet another residential street, but it was apparent, from the men hanging out in front of cars or inside their vehicles, that it was well patrolled by the Street Front.

They're smart. There are just enough of them, spaced out, to have eyes on Apple Street, Cloverdale and Bangor. But not so many that residents will be alarmed or might call the cops.

He passed the target house and saw a few hoods smoking in the front yard. He couldn't afford to slow down or look for too long. That would attract attention.

No way I can attack that house, he thought despondently, as he headed to West Hollywood and checked into a hotel.

He tossed and turned on his bed as he attacked the two problems mentally. How could he apply leverage on Covarra if he couldn't damage the warehouse? How could he escape from the meeting?

No answers came to him.

'HE WAS HERE,' JANIKYAN SPOKE INTO HIS PHONE. 'I GOT Zohrab to give up the Cloverdale house.'

'How did you know about that?' the caller asked.

'Luck. Some of my people were following some Street Front's bangers when Grogan burned down that house. They went to that place in Mid-City immediately. We staked it out, but had to move when Snake increased security.'

'We don't know if Grogan was that attacker.'

'Who else would it be?'

'We think it's him, but there's no proof.'

'You need proof. I don't.'

'Does he suspect anything?

The gang leader took a coffee mug from Zohrab and sipped the beverage. 'No. He wouldn't be here if he did.'

'Don't take him lightly.'

'I am not, but he's done nothing to my gang. Best case, he takes out that warehouse and he and Snake kill each other.'

'If that doesn't happen?'

Panig Janikyan gave a blood-curdling smile.

'In that case, I will kill him.'

55

Matt Lasko was woken by his phone chirping. He yawned, ignored it, checked the time and went to shower. Returned to find the missed call from Cesar.

'You've been up early,' he said when he called the banger back.

'Snake and Fuse have put us on sentry duty in Boyle Heights. I haven't slept.'

'Whereabouts?'

'Nowhere in particular. We've been driving up and down East LA all night, looking out for any single man, elder-looking, wearing glasses ... anyone who looks like the attacker.'

'That's why you called? To tell me about it?'

'No.' Cesar lowered his voice. 'Get to Boyle Heights in the evening. South of Pico Gardens. Close to the river.'

'You've got to be more specific. That's a lot of ground to cover.'

'That's all I know.'

'Any idea when?'

'Whatever's going to go down, will happen only late at night. That's how Snake works.'

'I'll be there.'

CUTTER DROVE TO MID-CITY AND CHECKED OUT THE HOUSE in the daylight. The bangers were conspicuous because they were doing nothing. Talking to one another, smoking joints, playing beats loudly in their rides.

Neighbors probably suspect who they are but feel intimidated.

He was in the silver-streaked hair and goatee disguise and looked away hastily when a heavy eyed him. He heard the man chuckle as he drove past and went on Apple Street.

He returned to Pacific Palisades and, on a remote bluff overlooking the ocean, opened the Durango's trunk and inspected the gear he had.

He could snipe with the Barrett ... his hand paused as he picked up the drone.

I can do a drive-by. Lob grenades through their windows.

It wouldn't matter if they didn't even shatter the windows or his aim was off. Two or three grenades in the yard, close to the house, would damage it significantly, which was his goal.

Cops will arrive and clear the bangers. I wouldn't even need to stop or show myself for the attack. He pictured it in his mind. Slowing down on Cloverdale, his left arm tossing one grenade after another ... *it'll work.*

That still left the question of how he could get away from Covarra. His eyes swept over the array of weapons, and as they lingered on the various explosives, a faint idea came to him.

'HE'S USING MULTIPLE VEHICLES AND DISGUISES.' DIFIORE tapped a pen against her teeth as she browsed through the stream of photographs on her screen.

'Yeah, and when he's on foot, he probably keeps his head down,' Quindica agreed.

They had asked their team to write programs that would

isolate the Land Cruiser and run facial recognition on anyone who matched Cutter's build. They got a dizzying number of images, none of which was their man.

Neither was disheartened. They knew identifying him from a population of twelve million would be difficult. His expertise with disguises and experience of living in the shadows added to the challenge.

'Why don't we do this another way? Go after who he knows here? He would have made contact ... you know how he is. He stays in touch with his friends.'

'He knows the chief.'

Difiore and Quindica looked at each other and had the same thought. 'We don't know who else he knows here!'

They went to Dade's office, knocked and entered.

'Ma'am, who else does Cutter know here?'

'In the department?'

'Yeah, and in the city.'

Dade removed her reading glasses and polished them with a piece of silk. 'He knows me and Jerry, of course. You think he might have told them something? His other friends in the city?'

'Yes, ma'am.' Difiore grinned at the chief's guess. *She didn't get to head LAPD for nothing. She's smart.*

'Terry.' Dade snapped her fingers.

'Who, ma'am?'

'Director of Special Ops.' The chief picked up her phone and made a brief call.

TERRY VARGAS KNOCKED ON DADE'S DOOR AND ENTERED. HE checked out her guests from habit. Law enforcement, he guessed. Their postures, the way they assessed him, it gave them away.

'You might have heard of Detective Difiore and FBI SAC Peyton Quindica by now.' The chief addressed him with a small smile.

That's who they are.

'Yes, ma'am.'

'They are helping us find Cutter Grogan.'

Vargas didn't conceal his shock. 'You're looking for Cutter, ma'am? Why?'

'We think he's behind the attacks in the city. On Covarra and on the Street Front's warehouses.' The FBI agent's eyes hadn't left Vargas's face. 'You couldn't have missed the reports on TV.'

'Cutter's behind them?' He turned to the chief. 'Why?'

'We *think* he's involved, but we've no proof,' Dade replied. 'You might have heard of the two women killed in Beverly Hills. They were his friends. He's on a vengeance mission.'

'Have you tried his phone, ma'am?'

The NYPD detective's eyes flashed before the chief answered. 'This isn't our first gig, Vargas.'

He ignored her and directed his reply at Dade. 'I'm guessing you called me to check if we met. Sure, we did. About two weeks ago, in the LA Times building.'

'He say why he was in town?'

'Yeah, about those killings. I think Matteo or Cruz told him about them. He caught the next flight from New York.'

'He say how long he would be in town? What he would be doing?'

'No, ma'am.'

'Terry ...' The chief's voice was silky smooth. 'You wouldn't be holding anything from me, would you?'

'No, ma'am,' he lied smoothly. *The chief was his friend, but so was Cutter.*

'Who else does he know in town?'

Vargas hesitated. *Should I tell her about Chad? Duh!* He berated himself. *She knows him, too. No point in holding back his name.*

'Chad Liu, ma'am. He—'

'Of course,' Dade straightened. She turned to Difiore and Quindica. 'Liu and Terry were in Delta. That's how they know Cutter. Our paths crossed in Afghanistan. The four of us stayed in touch. We used to meet for dinner at my place whenever he was in town.'

Vargas could have sworn there was a wistful look in the chief's eyes.

'Chad.' The LAPD boss nodded at the women. 'He might know something.'

'Why's that, ma'am?' Difiore asked.

'He's a weapons dealer.'

CUTTER HUNCHED OVER THE WORK TABLE AS HE CUT STRIPS OF C4, shaped the explosive and inserted them into the loops on a makeshift coat. He straightened after a while and wiped sweat off his forehead. Took a swig of water and returned to his painstaking work. A timer, detonating cord, a deadman switch lay strewn nearby, ready to be assembled.

He squinted at his phone when it buzzed. A number he didn't recognize. He ignored it, but it kept ringing.

He sighed, wiped his hands and took the call.

'Yeah?' he barked.

'You know who I am. Don't say my name.'

'Gotcha,' he replied, recognizing Terry's voice. 'What's up?'

'Cops suspect you. Stay loose.' And with that he hung up.

Cutter put the phone back on the table and rubbed his eyes. *Nothing's changed. I knew LAPD would come for me.*

He surveyed the table, looked at the gear he had laid out and got back to work.

He had found the engineering workshop in Reseda after making several calls. It was ideal for his purpose: a for-hire place, rented by the hour, and well-equipped with wood and metal-working machinery.

All he needed was a soldering iron, a big table, good lighting and privacy, which the workshop had.

Three hours later, he groaned and stretched. Winced as his back muscles protested. He brought out a cold wrapped lunch and ate in silence. Checked his phone. No messages from Covarra. He looked up Zohrab's location. The banger was at the same safe house in Little Armenia. *Looks like Janikyan feels secure there.*

He burned the food wrappings and wiped down all traces of his presence. Carefully lifted the device he had manufactured, locked the workshop and went to his Durango.

A thin smile played on his lips as he drove back to Central LA.

He had his get-out-of-jail-free card.

It was in the vehicle's trunk.

A suicide vest.

❧ 56 ❧

D ifiore folded her shades as she and Quindica walked
up to the reception desk of Chad Liu's gun range in
Culver City.

The front office was a box-like room, with a woman behind
the counter. She beamed at the arrivals as she checked their
suits. 'Let me guess, it's not the range you're looking for ... not
dressed like that.'

'We're here for Mr. Liu.' Difiore didn't return her smile.

'You have an appointment, ma'am?'

'No.'

'You'll need to make one.' Beaming Woman's cheerfulness
didn't fade. It looked like she was used to stone-faced visitors.

'We won't.' Difiore flashed her badge. 'He'll see us.'

'Help yourself to coffee, snacks.' The receptionist pointed to
a side table on which was a flask and a plate of biscuits. 'I'll
check with Chad.'

She disappeared to an inner office and returned shortly.
'Follow me.'

She led them around the counter to a small hallway and
opened the door.

Chad Liu, short, bald, was inspecting a gun when they entered the store.

'What's this about?' he asked when Difiore did the introductions.

'Cutter Grogan. Where is he?'

'Cutter? I've no idea. Why? What's he done?'

'Mr. Liu—'

'Chad, please,' the former Delta operator said with a smile.

'Mr. Liu,' Difiore repeated, ignoring his suggestion. 'We know he met you. We know you and he are close. Where is he? The LAPD's looking for him. It would help if you cooperated.'

The grin faded from Liu's face. He put the weapon back in a glass case, locked it and turned to his guests.

'I met him, yeah, about twelve, thirteen days ago. He was in town. Some friend of his died and he was here to attend to those formalities.'

'You met him just that one time?'

'Yeah.'

'Mr. Liu, lying to the cops—'

'Detective Difiore, don't patronize me. I know what the LAPD can or cannot do. I met Cutter once, that's all. I don't know anything else about him.'

'Aren't you two close?'

'We are.'

'Don't friends meet more than once? Especially if one of them is out of town?'

'I met him just once.' Liu folded his arms across his chest.

Difiore narrowed her eyes at that and saw Quindica's almost imperceptible nod. That's a defensive gesture. *He knows more than he's letting on.*

'This is your store, Mr. Liu?' Quindica slipped into good, conversational cop mode as she went around the shop, inspecting weapons mounted on the walls or in their glass cases. Each gun was tagged with make, model, price tag, and mounted-on attachments.

'Yeah.'

'Where's the gun range?'

'Through a door from the reception area.'

'You sell just about everything here. Rifles, hunting weapons, handguns, knives.'

'We carry a wide variety of gear.'

Difiore suppressed a grin when Quindica frowned. It was an act that came naturally to them. The detective went into badass mode while the FBI agent took a softer approach.

'This is everything you sell?'

'Yes ma'am.'

'Any other showrooms?'

'This is the only one for business. I have a smaller one at my home, but those weapons aren't for sale.'

'Where are the drones?'

'Drones?' Liu blinked. 'I don't sell them. I sell guns and knives, nothing else.'

'What about grenades? Smoke bombs, ANM14s ... I'm sure you know what they are.'

'Ma'am, I don't know what you're talking about. I sell guns. I have a gun range. That's all I do. Oh, yeah, I sell houses too, on the side.' His eyes crinkled with amusement as he gave them a searching glance. 'I've got showings on a three-bedroom house in the Santa Monica Mountains. It'll fit the budget of an LEO. Interested?'

'He knows much more than he's letting on,' Difiore snarled when they returned to their unmarked vehicle.

'Uh-huh,' Quindica replied.

'We should bring him in for questioning.'

'He won't say anything more.'

'We should tap his phone, get a warrant—'

'You think he and Cutter wouldn't have thought of all that? They would have taken precautions. These dudes were in the deep black business for a long time. They know every little trick.'

'You seem to be taking it well. Cutter's out there—'

'Your face.' Quindica burst into a laugh. 'You should have seen yourself when he offered to show us that house! Admit it, the good cop/bad cop routine didn't work on him.'

Difiore glared at her as she drove out angrily and then smiled reluctantly.

'I bet Vargas knows more than he told us, too.'

'Yeah.'

'Dade, too?'

'No. Cutter wouldn't compromise her.'

'He's got loyal friends.'

❧ 57 ❧

The vengeance business was best suited for solitary people. It fit Cutter to a T. He was the sole operator in his Fixing business in New York. Arnedra Jones had been his partner, but she looked after the commercial side of it.

He drove to Venice Beach on a whim as he awaited Covarra's call and people-watched. Fitness enthusiasts on Muscle Beach, kids playing in the sand, indulgent parents keeping an eye on them, couples content with each other's company.

He shoved back memories of Riley, ordered an ice cream and savored it slowly as the Earth continued rotating and revolving and people went about their business until the call came at seven pm.

'Get to Boyle Heights,' Covarra hissed.

There must be some school out there that teaches gangbangers to talk like that. Menacingly.

'What's there?' he mumbled as he licked his spoon clean. A young kid looked back at his cup longingly as his mom tugged him past. 'Nope, I'm not sharing,' he called out.

'What?' the gangster snarled.

'What's in Boyle Heights?'

'Don't you want to meet?'

'Oh, yeah, that. What time?' He was deliberately flippant, to make the Street Front boss feel unsettled, which could get him to make mistakes.

'Ten pm.'

'You bangers realize you could get a lot more done in the daytime? It'll attract less attention.'

'WHAT ARE YOU TALKING ABOUT?'

Cutter winced and grinned as he held the phone away from his ear. 'Whereabouts in Boyle Heights? Will someone be holding a sign?'

'Be near the river. I'll call again.'

'HE WAS MAKING FUN OF ME.' COVARRA LOOKED UP IN disbelief at Salazar. 'As if it were a joke to him.'

His deputy stroked his chin as he thought about it. 'He might come with the cops.'

'No.' The leader shook his head decisively. 'I spoke to Santangel. Cops suspect this puto, Cutter Grogan. They think he's carrying out all these attacks. He was one of those women's friends.'

'One man is doing all this?'

'Si, he was a soldier. Some kind of special forces. That's why he was so good at those previous attacks. Grogan won't be with the cops. They are looking for him, too. He won't be with Janikyan's men. I checked with Toros. The Armenians have no involvement at all. He's alone.'

'What kind of name is that? Cutter!'

'Forget the name. When I'm done with him,' Covarra said darkly, 'he won't have a face.'

CUTTER SWITCHED TO THE DURANGO, LOADED ALL HIS GEAR in it and drove to Boyle Heights. *Near the river, he said. That's a big stretch of neighborhood from Aliso Village to Soto Street Junction in the south.*

He cruised the area—residences, offices, industrial units, parks ... Covarra's rendezvous could be anywhere.

He parked underneath a tree and watched a couple gather kids' toys from their front yard and go inside their house. He brought out his laptop and logged into Werner. Got it to search for industrial units and warehouses.

The program threw up many.

Can't search them all.

He got it to eliminate those whose ownership was clear. The list shortened. Those that were currently empty. The number of names shrank. However, he knew that figure wouldn't be accurate. A well-organized gang would show activity at their units.

He shut down his screen and yawned. He was near the Arts District, facing the river, Aliso Village to his right.

Cutter decided to go left.

I'll go to the neighborhood's boundaries and turn back.

MATT LASKO FINISHED HIS DINNER AT A FOOD TRUCK, WIPED his hands and got into his unmarked vehicle at Soto Street Junction. He had no plan in mind. He intended to drive around until Cesar called. Matteo had instructed him to alert the task force the moment he knew what was going down.

It might be nothing, he grumbled as he fired up his vehicle and drove up the river.

CUTTER'S PHONE RANG AT EIGHT PM.

'Yeah?' He didn't recognize the number.

'I had two visitors today.'

Chad. He recognized the voice.

'LAPD?'

'Nope. Detective—'

'Difiore and Quindica?' he guessed.

'Yeah. You know them?'

'Yeah. Friends, though the detective would deny that.'

'Friends?' Chad snorted. 'They seem to be out to nail you. They wanted to know if I knew where you were, if I sold you anything—'

'They might be monitoring your calls.'

'I'm using a burner, and I'm nowhere close to home. I turned righteously indignant,' he chuckled. 'Told them I sold guns, nothing more.'

'They won't believe you.'

'I don't care. They can get a search warrant and they'll still find nothing. I emptied my garage the moment you burned that house. I moved my stock to another location.'

'Be careful.'

'*You* do that.'

Friends. Cutter shook his head. He was grateful for having them in his life. *Looks like Difiore hasn't discovered the phone I planted.*

It didn't surprise him. He had noticed her bag was stuffed with her belongings and the scarf hadn't shown signs of recent use. *She'll find it only if she digs deep.* Few people emptied their bags out regularly. *A busy cop? Not a chance,* he smiled to himself.

CUTTER WAS ON THE OLYMPIC VIADUCT, ON THE RAIL TRACKS, looking at the river flowing along its paved bed.

Fifteen minutes to ten.

He watched the lights play out on the water as the smells of debris and human waste assailed him.

He was walking back to his Durango when Covarra called.

'There's a unit on Jesse and Rio Street. Be there. Alone.'

Cutter hung up and stuffed the phone into his pocket.

I'm less than ten minutes away.

Matt Lasko was in Aliso Village when Cesar called.

'Jesse Street and Rio. An industrial unit at the intersection,' the snitch told him softly. 'Ten pm. Word is, Snake will be there himself.'

'Why?'

'I don't know. I'm on the outside perimeter, on the street. All I've been told is to look out for cops or the Armenian Bros.'

'I'll get there.'

'You can't come in a cruiser.'

'I'm not in one.'

Lasko picked up his radio and made to call Matteo. Held back. *I don't know what's happening. Let me get closer, have a look, and then I'll call.*

COVARRA WENT OUT ON THE STREET AND STOOD AT THE intersection. He looked up and down in the night. His men were spread out, dark shadows under the street lights. No vehicle could approach without their knowing.

His escape was well-planned, in case cops or the Armenians showed up. A convoy of vehicles would race down Jesse Street, toward Whittier, and draw pursuit.

That would be the decoy.

He, Salazar and his guards would run towards the river, wade through it, get to Sixth Street, where getaway vehicles would be waiting.

It was an escape route he had used before and was confident would work.

It's Grogan who won't be escaping.

58

Cutter parked his Durango on Clarence Street, between two refrigerated trucks. He used the cover to outfit himself. The Glock went into a holster at his waist, the Benchmade into a thigh-strapped sheath. Spare magazines in his pockets.

He fastened the suicide vest around himself carefully and held the wired button in his left palm. Depressed it with his thumb and applied tape over it to seal it in position.

He was in the same sideburns look he had used when he had attacked Covarra on his bike. *He won't recognize me in any other disguise.*

He removed his phone, wallet, every other belonging, and dropped them in the Durango. He locked the vehicle and walked towards the rendezvous.

He felt empty, the way he always did when he was in or heading toward action. He knew there were only two possible outcomes to the night.

I'll either be dead, or I'll know what happened that night in Beverly Hills.

Cutter saw the first sentry when he entered Rio Street from Seventh. The entire neighborhood was an industrial area.

Packing companies, cold-storage outfits for meats, warehouses, workshops, automotive bodyshops.

The guard stood arrogantly in the center of the street as he approached, holding an AR-15 in full view of whoever passed. There was no one else but Cutter on the road, however.

'Stop,' the banger commanded. 'Spread your hands out.'

Covarra's here, Cutter thought in satisfaction. *Street Front wouldn't have this kind of security if he wasn't.*

He drew his Glock with blinding speed and lunged forward to jam it against the stunned hood's mouth.

'Stand back,' he snarled. 'No one touches me until I am in front of your boss.'

'But—'

'Call him. Tell him that's my condition. Otherwise, I walk away.'

Covarra wants me as badly as I want to meet him. He won't let go of this opportunity.

The shooter stood undecided for a moment before he cursed, turned his head away and made a call.

'Go,' he ordered and stood aside. 'No tricks. I'll be watching you.'

Cutter walked past him as another banger came up from behind a car and watched him balefully. More shooters appeared, lounging, alerted by his presence. None of them accosted him. He kept his left hand down his body, the sleeve of his jacket covering his palm. He would reveal his trump card only at the last moment.

LASKO SLAMMED HIS PALM AGAINST THE WHEEL AND CURSED IN frustration as the truck in front of him reversed for a U-turn.

'THERE'S NOT ENOUGH ROOM!' he yelled out of his window and got the driver's upraised middle finger.

He thought of backing up and taking a different route and shook his head when he saw the long line of vehicles behind him, many of whom had the same idea. There was no point in leaving one congested street to go to another.

He waited, conscious of the time passing. Hoped that Covarra would hang around till he got there and called the cavalry.

CUTTER GOT TO THE INTERSECTION AND SPOTTED THE rendezvous immediately. A bunch of armed gangsters stood in front of an open door. Graffiti on the outside walls that he couldn't read.

He stumbled inside when someone shoved him. Took in the industrial look of the warehouse automatically. Shooters lined against the aluminum-sheeted walls. Tube lighting above. The smell of sweat and body odors. Two men, about twenty feet away from him, one of whom was grinning triumphantly.

Covarra and Salazar.

𝑅 59 𝑅

'Grogan.' The gang leader's voice promised violence.

Cutter felt a jolt of surprise but didn't show it. *How does he know my name? LAPD didn't disclose it.*

'Search him,' the Street Front boss ordered his people.

Two bangers stepped forward. One trained his assault rifle on him while the other searched him. The hood removed the Glock, which was visible, and tossed it to the floor. He reached down to the knife and brought it out. Whistled softly as it caught the air and waved it for show.

'DON'T PLAY AROUND. SEARCH HIM,' Covarra screeched. 'Check if he's wearing a wire.'

The hood patted him roughly. He raised his head sharply when he felt the uneven shapes beneath the jacket. He unzipped it and spread it open. He sucked his breath sharply as he stared uncomprehendingly at the suicide vest.

'HE'S GOT A—'

'A suicide vest.' Cutter shoved him away and got closer to Covarra and Salazar. He ignored the raised rifles and the angry voices that burst out.

'KILL HIM!' Covarra yelled as he shrank back.

'That would be a mistake.' He held his left hand up and

pushed back the sleeve for his audience to get a better view. 'See my thumb? Dead Man Switch. You kill me and the explosives go off. I have packed enough to kill everyone in a fifty-foot radius. DON'T MOVE!' he used his command voice to stop the gang leader, who was inching backwards. 'I'LL BLOW EVERYONE UP RIGHT NOW!'

Covarra stopped. His eyes glittered with rage and hate.

'It won't work,' Salazar said. 'He's taped it to the switch. It will stay in that position even if we kill him. He's bluffing.'

'Shoot me and see what happens.' Cutter laughed scornfully. 'The tape's not tight. The switch will activate at the slightest change in pressure. But have you seen this?' He pointed to a fabric sensor attached to his wrist, from which wires ran to the suicide vest. 'That will detect my pulse. The moment I stop breathing, the belt goes off. It's a backup trigger.'

Voices burst out in anger and panic.

'STOP!' Covarra yelled.

His men stopped talking.

'What do you want?' the gang leader asked coldly, having regained control of himself.

'I've told you a few times. Who killed the women in Beverly Hills? Who ordered the hit?'

'I told you on Sadler Avenue when you asked.' The gangster's voice dropped. 'That was you on the bike, wasn't it? I DIDN'T KILL THEM.'

'Your AR-15s, the ones you and Salazar used, were traced to the scene. One of those guns' rounds were in the women.'

'I DIDN'T KILL THEM. I DON'T KNOW WHAT YOU'RE TALKING ABOUT.'

'If you didn't, then who? Which of your men—'

'HOW MANY TIMES DO I HAVE TO TELL YOU. NONE OF MY MEN WERE THERE.' Spittle flew out of Covarra's mouth and showered Salazar, who ignored it.

'Street Front and Armenian Bros had a shootout at that house,' Cutter argued. 'Cops know that.'

'Si,' the Street Front leader replied savagely, 'my men found them dealing there. They attacked, but there were too many of those putos. My people escaped, but they got away as well.'

As Cutter stared at him, he tried to see past the hatred in Covarra's eyes. 'You could have called me and told me all this.'

'No,' the gangster smiled evilly. 'I wanted to see you. I wanted to grab your neck and plunge my knife in you. I wanted you to know what happens when you attack Francisco Covarra. They call me Snake because of my bite. I wanted you to feel it. Look at you.' He laughed scornfully. 'You look like a terrorist with those bombs. Police are hunting you like a dog. You did all this over two bitch—'

The roaring filled Cutter's ears as the warehouse faded, and all that remained was the gangster's sneering face and laugh. He charged forward without conscious thought, covered the distance separating them so quickly that none of the thugs could react. He bodyslammed into the Front's leader and sent him sprawling to the floor. He held his left hand high, dimly aware that he had to keep the trigger intact as he repeatedly head-butted Covarra, breaking his nose, splitting his lips, as he growled in rage.

'GET HIM!' someone shouted.

He was bodily lifted and separated from the gangster. Someone hit him in the side, a wicked blow that stung. Another banger kicked him in the thigh, where his wound was. He heard Covarra yelling, and then the leader was in front of him, punching him repeatedly in the neck and legs while his men held him.

'Hold that trigger hand.' 'Don't let it drop.' 'Be careful.' 'Don't let the tape fall off.' 'Don't hit the explosives.' 'Don't let him die.'

The phrases merged into a stream of sound, joined by the gangster's cursing as he slammed his fists into his prisoner.

'BOSS!'

The loud shout stopped everyone.

Cutter fell to his knees when the bangers holding him released their grip. He blinked away his sweat and raised his head slowly.

Two men had entered the warehouse. One was a thug who had jammed his gun into the other's side.

'I found him at the back, boss. He was trying to look through an opening.' The banger smiled triumphantly. 'He came down the street, hiding in the shadows. He thought he wasn't noticed, but I saw him a long way away.'

'Was he alone?' Covarra asked sharply as he gestured for the hood to come forward.

Cutter licked his lips and shook his head to get himself to focus on the here and the now. To ignore the pounding his body had taken and the agony that filled him.

He didn't recognize the prisoner.

'Yes, boss. I got several men to check out Rio and Jesse. No one else was with him.'

'Did you search him?'

'No, boss. I brought him here as soon as I found him.'

'SEARCH HIM, THEN. DO I HAVE TO TELL YOU EVERYTHING?'

The banger slung his rifle back and patted his captive down. Found a gun in a waist holster and tossed it to the floor. He searched his pockets, threw his phone to the floor and came out with a wallet. Riffled through it and froze.

'BOSS!' he yelled.

'What?' Covarra ground his teeth. 'I'm right here.'

'HE'S A COP. THIS IS HIS CARD.'

The gang leader went to him and snatched the identification. Read it and compared the photograph to the prisoner. 'Matt Lasko. Detective,' he snarled and slapped his man across the face. 'YOU BROUGHT A COP HERE.'

'I didn't know—'

'YOU ACCUSE ME OF KILLING THOSE BEVERLY HILLS WOMEN.'

Covarra hit him.

'YOU TALK ABOUT MY AND FUSE'S RIFLES FOUND THERE—'

'Their rounds were found—' Cutter groaned when another punch landed in his belly.

'AND THEN YOU BRING THE COPS HERE! I TOLD YOU TO COME ALONE.'

'I don't know anything about him.'

'STOP TALKING.' Covarra hit him repeatedly in the chest and stomach and sent him sprawling to the floor. Covarra breathed noisily as he paced the floor.

Cutter gritted his teeth and got to his knees. He tried to get up all the way but was shoved back by a banger. He met the cop's eyes, whose lips moved.

Is he trying to say something?

His body throbbed from the beating he had taken. Breathing was difficult. He knew his thigh wound had opened up again from the blows. He forced himself to ignore all that and focused on Lasko's lips.

I am alone. Didn't get to call in.

Cutter met his eyes in shock.

Why the hell did he come on his own? Why didn't he get backup?

His thoughts were interrupted by Covarra's grunt.

'He can't be alone,' the gangster raged. 'Cops don't come to our places on their own. We've got to get away. I wanted to kill Grogan, slowly, I wanted to see his eyes dim ...' He grabbed Cutter's hair and raised his head. 'But I know what to do. I will destroy your life.'

And with that he rushed to where his Glock lay on the floor, raised it and shot three times in Lasko's chest.

'NO!' Cutter screamed and scrabbled forward. He fell to the side when someone kicked him in the side and passed out.

. . .

HE RETURNED TO CONSCIOUSNESS TO THE SMELL OF DIRT AND the feel of the cold floor on his cheek. He snapped his head up when awareness flooded him and groaned at the sudden movement.

He was alone.

No, he wasn't.

Lasko lay several feet away.

Cutter dove at him, ignoring the sudden stabbing pain in his body.

The detective's eyes were open. Glazed and dull. They flickered slowly when he came into view.

'Hold on,' he urged. 'I'll call for help.' He searched the floor and dived to the phone. Lunged back and unlocked the device with Lasko's forefinger and dialed 911.

'A COP'S BEEN SHOT ON RIO STREET,' he said, having the presence of mind to disguise his voice. 'HE'S IN CRITICAL CONDITION. HURRY.'

He hung up and checked out Lasko quickly. His chest wounds looked ugly. His face had turned pale and the light in his eyes was fading.

'Hang on,' he told the cop. 'EMTs will be here soon.'

The detective seemed to hear him and his hand moved as if to beckon.

'Yeah? What is it?'

'Go ...' the word came out slowly, drawn out.

'Nope, I'll be right here, buddy.'

'Your ... gun ... your ... prints.'

Cutter froze at that. Scanned the floor and didn't find his Glock, but his right-hand glove lay several feet away. He went to it, pocketed it and returned to the cop. 'Covarra got me to hold it? When I was out?'

'Yes ... go ...'

'I won't.'

Lasko's eyes blazed momentarily. His hand twitched, grabbed Cutter's and squeezed with all his strength. 'GO,' he whispered harshly. 'Phone ...' his head rolled back and his breath started to fade. 'Cesar ...'

'Lasko.' Cutter crouched over him urgently. 'LASKO!' the detective's head rolled limply and the light in his eyes faded even as he watched.

'No!' he swore. He held his cheek against the man's face and felt a whisper of breath. Heard a siren wailing in the distance.

Cesar. What did he mean by that?

He grabbed the detective's cell phone nevertheless, placed his forefinger against it to unlock it, changed the password and slipped it into his pocket. Got to his feet unsteadily, removed his jacket and draped it over Lasko's chest.

He stood over the cop, torn, as the sirens grew closer. The detective seemed to be barely alive. *Would it help if I stayed with him till the first responders arrived?*

I'm already the prime suspect for the attacks on Covarra. Cops will arrest me even if they believe I didn't shoot Lasko.

He made his mind up and staggered out of the warehouse and into the night, conscious that everything had changed.

Covarra had outsmarted him.

He has my Glock, and if he delivers it to the LAPD somehow, I'll be wanted.

Every cop in Los Angeles will be hunting me.

𝕷 60 𝕽

Cutter almost blacked out as he stumbled his way to his ride. He leaned against a wall, behind a refrigerated truck, and drew breath hoarsely as the darkness faded in his mind.

Cops and EMTs had arrived at the warehouse, judging by the volume of sirens and the voices that carried in the night. Thankfully, no officers had come his way.

Not yet.

He gritted his teeth, resumed his half-trot and reached the Durango. Fired it up and hoped the sound wouldn't be heard by the cops.

He drove out with his lights turned off, went down to Fourth Street, where he hung a left, and crossed the river. He drove past the Fashion District and turned into a store's parking lot and stopped. He removed the tape on his thumb and shrugged out of the suicide vest.

He hadn't rigged it to blow. The explosives were real, as were the Dead Man Switch and the Pulse Trigger. However, he had wired them only for show. He had been counting on Covarra not having any explosives expert with him. On being fooled by the appearance of the vest.

I was right about that.

The thought gave him no consolation.

'I need help,' he said when he called Kozlov.

'Come over. I'm still up, writing up some notes.'

'It's not that straightforward. LAPD wants me. I am a suspect in a shooting.'

He prayed it wasn't a killing, that Lasko had survived. *He'll be able to tell what went down and he'll clear me. If he lives.*

'Come over.' There was no change in Kozlov's voice.

'Did you hear what I said?' Cutter raged at him. 'Do you want to get involved—'

'I got involved the day you flew me out of Moscow.'

'You were alone, then. You have a family now.'

'You think Marta doesn't know what you used to do?' Kozlov snorted. 'Or that I don't help you or the other operators? There are no secrets between us. She would open me up with a scalpel, without anesthesia, if she knew I turned you away.'

'Cops—'

'Screw them,' Kozlov said dismissively. 'Come over. Right now.' His voice grew concerned. 'Can you drive?'

'Yeah, I can manage that much.'

KOZLOV WAS WAITING FOR HIM WHEN HE ROLLED UP IN THEIR driveway. The Russian helped him get inside his operating room and to the bed.

'Have you thought of changing professions?' he asked as he snipped Cutter's clothing and examined his wounds. 'Accounting. That's a good one. Ever heard of an accountant getting beaten up as regularly as you do?'

Cutter groaned when his friend jabbed him in the thigh, near his wound. 'What happened to tender, loving care?' he gasped.

'That's only for my paying customers.'

· · ·

'YOU'LL LIVE. YOU'LL EVEN WALK.' KOZLOV WASHED HIS hands an hour later. 'Your body ... it can take a lot of punishment. That's why you have gotten away with just bruises, sore ribs and some cuts. That gunshot wound has opened again, but I've tended to it.'

'I need to be mobile,' Cutter warned him. 'I can't limp.'

'Painkillers in there,' his friend replied, nodding at medications wrapped in a baggie. 'But rest is what you need. Not going about whatever you are intent on doing.'

Cutter reached for the fresh set of clothing on a chair and dressed. His body hurt all over, but it was a dull throbbing that he could push to the recesses of his mind.

'There's news of something that went down in Boyle Heights,' Kozlov said casually. 'An officer was found shot.'

'Is he dead?'

'I turned off the news.' The Russian cocked his head at a small TV set. 'Shall I switch that on?'

'No.'

He hugged his friend hard and limped to the door. Climbed into the Durango and drove out.

Kozlov grew smaller in his rearview mirror and then disappeared when he turned into the street.

That might be the last time I see him.

CUTTER ROLLED DOWN THE WINDOW AND LET THE NIGHT AIR blow in, along with the sounds and smells of LA. It wasn't midnight yet and the traffic was still heavy. He drove to the house where Arnedra and Vienna were killed, on a whim.

A few traffic cones and police tape were still in place, but no cruisers on the street. He drove past without slowing and stopping, didn't see any patrol cars in any neighboring driveways, but decided not to risk going into the house. *What would it achieve?* He thought bitterly.

He went past the studios and entered the north-western part

of the city. Reseda and Northridge, beyond. He rented a house in Sylmar via a booking app, backed into its driveway and changed the plates under the cover of darkness.

He staggered into the residence with all his belongings, locked it and threw himself on the bed.

The world could wait.

He needed rest.

❧ 61 ❧

Difiore got the call at eleven-forty-five pm. A terse exchange with Dade that had her rolling out of bed, hustling into her suit. Quindica, who had overheard, was ready before she had finished.

'What happened?' her partner asked.

'Shooting in Boyle Heights,' she replied. She paused a beat, trying to find the right words, and then shrugged. There was no easy way to say it. 'Lasko's been shot.'

'Chief,' she greeted the LAPD head when they arrived at the scene. Dade nodded wordlessly. Her eyes were narrowed; the skin was drawn tight over her bones.

'He was shot three times.' She turned to them and, with her back to the rest of the cops, let emotion show in her eyes. 'He's critical. Was barely alive when the medics arrived.' She drew a shuddering breath, got hold of herself and straightened her shoulders. The LAPD boss was back.

'Do they know?' Difiore bobbed her head at Matteo, Cruz and Estrada, who were some distance away, conferring with cops.

'About my relationship with Lasko? No.'

'Who were the shooters?' Quindica checked out the warehouse, walked down the intersection of Rio and Jesse, squinted both ways and returned.

'Street Front, possibly, but this part of the city, at this time of the night, was deserted. No witnesses. Vance's got his task force checking out public cameras and also those mounted on buildings. We'll know more in the morning.'

'What was Lasko doing here?'

'He was chasing down a lead.' Matteo came over, wooden-faced. Only the rapid rolling of the toothpick in his mouth indicated his anger. 'He has a snitch in the gang. He called me in the evening and told me he had received word that something was going down. He was going to check it out and alert us.'

'Going down? What? A drug deal?' Quindica asked sharply.

'Your guess is as good as mine,' the detective said, shrugging. 'He didn't say. I was busy with Cruz and Estrada, chasing down another lead. I should have told him to take backup. I thought nothing about it when he didn't call. I should've ...' he trailed off bitterly when Dade squeezed his shoulder.

'He and I were in the LASD. However, I found out only recently that he was one of my informers in the Blue Brothers. I cut him a lot of slack. I figured if he could survive dirty cops, he could handle himself. I should have got more cops to go with—'

'Stop!' the LAPD chief told him firmly. 'There's no point beating yourself up.'

Matteo raised his head when a shout came to them. He hurried to where a group of cops and technicians was bunched around a pickup truck.

'What is it?' Difiore breathed out when she, Quindica and Dade joined him.

'We found a gun,' said the detective, whose eyes glittered when he addressed them. 'It was beneath that vehicle. A Glock.'

❧ 62 ❧

Difiore sensed the undercurrent of tension when she and Quindica entered Dade's office. She glanced at the FBI agent, who nodded imperceptibly.

She felt it too.

Matteo, Cruz, Estrada, several other officers from the task force, facing the chief.

'Covarra was in that warehouse,' the lead detective briefed them in a clipped voice when they occupied their seats. 'We got that from some of our informers. We've also got some camera sightings from a neighboring unit. Images are blurry, but there's no mistaking the gangster as he ran to his ride.'

'What was happening in that place?' Difiore asked. *He and his team must have been up all night. Dade dismissed us around two am, but she, Matteo and the others were still at the scene when we left.*

'They must have captured Lasko somehow and brought him inside that warehouse.' Matteo acted as if he hadn't heard her. He nodded to one of his officers, who fiddled with his screen and projected a blank screen on the wall.

'That's the footage from CCTV.' Matteo grunted as a video began playing.

Several figures ran out of the warehouse and headed to vehicles.

'That—' the lead detective used a laser to circle one man when his officer paused the footage, '—is Covarra. The man behind him is Salazar.'

The video resumed to show the bangers' rides disappearing out of the screen. Just when Difiore thought that was all to the footage, a shadow emerged from the warehouse and went out of sight.

'Male,' Matteo said, 'that's all we could make out. He had his head bent and used the cover of vehicles to conceal himself. We don't have a good view of him.'

'Didn't the cameras capture anything of the gangsters' arrival?' Quindica asked when the footage ended.

'Nope. Those cameras are programmed to swivel periodically and cover the front and side yards of their unit. They must have been facing a different direction when the bangers, Lasko or that mystery man came.'

He uncapped a water bottle and drank deeply. Wiped his mouth with the back of his hand and resumed his briefing.

'Lasko was found with a jacket draped over him. Technicians are still working on DNA traces, but it doesn't look like there are any. The wearer was probably wearing gloves. We played around with the timeline,' he continued. 'It looks like Mystery Man was the one who called 911. He seemed to be the last person in the warehouse, with Lasko.'

A man's voice came on when the officer played an audio clip.

'A COP'S BEEN SHOT ON RIO STREET. HE'S IN CRIT-ICAL CONDITION. HURRY.'

Difiore looked at Quindica, who shrugged. It wasn't a voice they recognized. She turned to Matteo and was struck by his body language.

He knows something.

'That Glock we found,' the cop paused dramatically, 'was fired into Lasko. Our lab's been up all night, our technicians liaised with the hospital ... there's no doubt. Whoever pulled the trigger, shot our detective with that weapon.'

'Any suspicions who that shooter is?' Dade asked tautly.

'No suspicions, ma'am. We *know* who it is. The Glock had prints on it that we traced easily. It was Cutter Grogan.'

❧ 63 ❧

'**W**HAT?' Difiore couldn't control her shout.

She felt Quindica's nails dig into her thigh and got hold of herself. She swallowed and put on her game face. 'Are you sure?'

'Yeah.' Matteo looked at her impassively. 'His prints are in the system. The Glock had a clear set on it. There's no doubt. On top of that, the 911 caller, we ran audio recognition software on it. That was Grogan. He disguised it; that's why none of us could place it when we heard him.'

'He shot Lasko and then called for help?' Difiore asked in disbelief.

'Looks like it. If I was a betting man, I would say that jacket on Lasko is his, too.'

'Tell them about that, too,' Cruz reminded the senior detective.

'Tell us what?' Dade questioned Matteo sharply.

'Ma'am, that jacket had traces of C4 on its inside.'

A murmur of voices swept through the room and died away when Dade raised her hand.

The police chief's voice was controlled when she addressed Matteo. 'Find Grogan and arrest him.' She dismissed the meeting with a shake of her head and indicated with her eyes for Difiore and Quindica to stay back.

'DO YOU BELIEVE IT?' SHE ASKED WHEN THEY WERE ALONE.

Her eyes were bottomless pools of unreadable emotion when Difiore looked at her. *Did her voice tremble just then?*

'That the Glock fired into Lasko, yes, ma'am. That Cutter shot him ...' She laughed scornfully. 'Cutter Grogan is a vigilante. He doesn't play by the rules. Nothing would give me greater pleasure than to send his ass to jail—'

'Spoken like a friend.' Dade's smile had no humor in it.

'Ma'am,' Difiore said quietly, taking no offense at the chief's interruption. *I know how I come across, as if I hate Cutter.* 'There's nothing Peyton or I wouldn't do to help him if he was in trouble. Cutter shooting a cop? No. He didn't do it. There has to be another explanation. Lasko—'

'Isn't in any condition to talk. He was operated on last night, but remains intubated. He's living on machines,' Dade said bitterly.

'You believe it?' Quindica asked her cautiously. 'That Cutter shot him?'

'No.' The chief shook her head firmly. 'But we can't look past the evidence, and I can't grant him any favors.' She squared her shoulders and gave them a steely look. 'Go, get him. Help Vance arrest him.'

'Yes, ma'am.' Difiore got to her feet and hesitated. 'That C4, ma'am ...'

'I know.' The chief rubbed her eyes wearily. 'I don't know what he's gotten himself into. Cutter has a gift for getting out of tight spots. I don't know how he can extricate himself this time.'

. . .

IT WAS ELEVEN AM WHEN CUTTER WOKE UP FROM HIS dreamless sleep. He lay on the bed for several moments as the events of the night returned to him.

His body still ached, still felt as if a champion boxer had used it as a punching bag.

That's just what happened, he snorted grimly. He didn't know how many bangers had hit him. *I bet all of them in that room took a hand.*

He got up gingerly and took a few steps. He didn't black out. He washed his face and showered carefully, and after filling his empty belly with a cold breakfast, felt human.

It was time to address what had happened the previous night and work out his next moves.

He went to the TV and turned it on to find that Lasko was in the hospital—still alive, but barely. The host said Cutter Grogan, New York resident, was wanted in connection with the shooting of the cop.

They found the Glock!

The journalist went into his background, why he had been in the city, said that the cops were also hunting for Covarra and speculated that Cutter had some kind of showdown with the Street Front and had shot Lasko. He turned off the screen when a talking head came on the air and offered more theories.

There was nothing he could do about the arrest warrant. Only the Street Front bangers or Lasko could clear him; the former wouldn't want to, and the latter couldn't.

Deal with it, he told himself bleakly.

He dealt with it by pushing it to the back of his mind.

What about Covarra? He said he didn't kill Arnedra and Vienna. Can I believe him?

Cutter closed his eyes and recollected the gang leader's face. The hate in it as he stood in front of his captive.

He was angry. He was surprised when I asked him on Sadler Avenue, too. He meant it.

He swore loudly in the house as his frustration surfaced. *I've been in LA just over two weeks and I've got nothing to show for it.*

If Street Front didn't kill them, who did? Can't be the Armenians. Covarra said his men chased those gangsters away. And Arnedra and Vienna weren't around during their shootout. He didn't mention their presence.

I've been going after the wrong suspects all along.

❧ 64 ❧

Zeb Carter looked up when Beth and Meghan joined him on the Malibu hotel's manicured lawn.

'You know about Cutter,' the younger twin stated flatly as her eyes flickered over the newspaper he had been reading.

'Nothing else on TV but him and that cop's shooting. Has he made contact?'

'Nope.' Meghan shook her head. 'He called us two days ago, wanted GPS trackers. We arranged those for him, along with a portable cell tower.'

'He knows we're in town?'

'He thinks we're in New York.'

He sipped his tea and placed the cup back in its elegant saucer.

They had needed to get away from their home city, to decompress after their last mission. LA had been an easy choice to make. It would place them close to Cutter, whom they could help if he needed it.

The Fixer wasn't with the Agency. However, he was a very close friend and there had been more than one occasion when they had rescued him from tight spots. *Not that he knows about our intervention,* Zeb thought while smiling absently.

His mirth faded when the newspaper headlines caught his eye.

'Any news?' he asked the sisters, who caught on immediately.

'Lasko's in the same condition,' Beth answered. 'Unable to talk, unable to clear Cutter.'

That their friend had shot the cop wasn't something they had even needed to debate. They knew him very well, were confident he hadn't done it.

'Where's he right now?'

'He's gone off the grid.'

'Stay close to your phones. He'll—'

Beth's phone buzzed. Her eyes widened when she picked it up and turned the screen to them. 'Someone calling from Romania,' she murmured. 'It's him.'

'Cutter,' she said, putting the call on speaker, 'how's the fugitive life treating you?'

CUTTER COULDN'T HELP GRINNING.

He was wanted by the cops. Street Front bangers would be searching for him. His body was a mass of bruises and hurt, yet Beth's voice cheered him up.

'I take it you heard,' he replied drily.

'You're hard to ignore when every TV channel is showing your photograph and narrating your backstory.'

'Cutter, what went down?'

That's Zeb. Looks like he's with the twins.

'So, it's not Covarra?' Meghan broke the silence when he finished briefing them.

'Nope. Which is why I called. Can you check if LAPD has made any progress on their investigation?'

'Hold on.'

He heard keys clacking, the soft murmur of the sisters talking to each other.

'Still the same,' the elder twin announced. 'Street Front's the main suspect. Nothing much has changed. Oh, yeah, they found Vienna's car, burned, in a parking lot in Laguna Beach. They don't know how it got there. No prints, no blood, no DNA, nothing recoverable from it. That's the most recent update. We'll message you if they've made any progress.'

He thanked them and hung up before they could offer any help.

He searched the house and found a notepad in a drawer. Drew a timeline on it.

Vienna and Arnedra's phones' last ping to the cell towers.

Reports of a shooting in the Beverly Hills house.

Their vehicles fleeing.

Time of death.

If they weren't in the house during the bangers' shootout, where were they?

Who killed them?

He had to start his investigation all over again, with fresh eyes.

And, stay alive and evade arrest as well.

❧ 65 ❧

Cutter was in the kitchen, washing dishes, when he heard a dog bark loudly. He paid it no attention initially. Probably a neighbor's animal.

It barked again, accompanied by a startled exclamation.

He peered through the window that overlooked the backyard. The rental property was on the corner of Gavina Avenue and Tibbetts Street in Sylmar, the northernmost neighborhood of the city. Situated in the foothills of the San Gabriel Mountains, the sparsely populated community was once home to olive farms, which had given way to residential construction. It was a popular destination for hikers and horse riders.

There!

He could see past the wooden fence into the neighbor's driveway, where an elderly man faced the avenue. The owner shushed his dog when it barked again and hurried inside his house.

What was that about?

Cutter wiped his hands on his jeans and went to the front of the house. He looked out of a side window, from which he could see the street, and spotted a helmeted, uniformed figure cautiously coming up the street.

Cops!

He moved even before his brain had translated what his eyes had seen.

He grabbed his backpack and swept the contents of the table into it. Zipped it up and slung it over his back. Picked up the gym bag that contained his weapons and his jacket, and ran to the bedroom. Checked that there was nothing in it and then broke out of the rear door and into the yard. Hurled himself over the fence just as he heard shouts from the front of the house.

Cutter landed on the rear neighbor's driveway. Sensed movement to his right and saw two cops less than ten feet away.

Their weapons were rising when he flung the gym bag at them and followed with a dive. One of them got out a startled yell before the heavy bag hit him and then Cutter was on them, lying bodily across them, smashing their helmets on the ground.

Can't kill them, can't shoot them.

He got to his feet, picked up the bag and raced toward the neighbor's garage. Darted into the narrow passage alongside it and toward another fence. He scaled it and ran into another backyard.

They'll trap me in this neighborhood. Not many homes here.

He ran between houses and saw a few startled faces when he leapt over fences and hedges as he heard the growing clamor of shouting and sirens wailing on Gavina Avenue.

Sweat was pouring from him when he reached Graber Avenue. Smack in front of an approaching patrol car, which swerved to a squealing stop.

Cutter didn't pause, didn't slow, didn't take time to think.

He yanked the driver's door open, grabbed the cop behind the wheel and sent him sprawling into the street.

'KEEP OFF THAT RADIO,' he yelled to the second cop in the passenger seat as he threw his gym bag in the rear, half-seated himself, floored the gas and U-turned wickedly, narrowly missing the officer on the ground.

'GET OUT,' he told the cop with him.

He risked a quick glance when the officer didn't respond.

He seems to be a rookie. He's terrified.

He leaned across to unlock the door and flung it open. 'ROLL WHEN YOU LAND! IT'LL HURT LESS,' he yelled as he pushed the cop out unceremoniously and sped away.

He hung an immediate right on Rajah Street and then on Tucker Avenue, searched desperately for an empty driveway, uttered a prayer when he found a deep one.

He drove into it, parked and switched off the engine. Climbed out, grabbed his gym bag and ran to the end of the street, where a white fence separated the neighborhood from the rocky wildness beyond.

Dense chaparral to his left, several yards away, and in the distance the looming foothills.

He turned on his heel and sprinted toward the cover. The ground was uneven, rocky, patches of grass. He was used to that kind of terrain, however. He neared the safety of the vegetation, expecting choppers to appear in the sky and bullhorns to sound, urging his surrender.

No helicopter arrived, and neither did any patrol cars.

He went deep into the thicket and stopped. Breathed shallowly to hear above his pounding heartbeat.

The sirens were still wailing, and when he peered cautiously, he caught the shine of several police vehicles on Tibbetts Street. *They'll discover the abandoned cruiser soon enough, will find I'm not in the neighborhood. They'll organize a manhunt, but not quickly.*

Word would have gotten out that he was former Delta Forces, a sniper of some repute, in addition to his other deadly skills.

They'll know I can take out several cops with a long gun. They'll organize dogs, choppers with thermal imaging, cut off my re-entry into Sylmar and hunt me.

I got lucky, he thought bitterly. *That dog warned me. That cop must have been at the forefront on Gavina. I got out before they could trap me in the house, before they positioned more officers on Tibbets.*

But how had they found him? He had disabled the Durango's LoJack. His phones were untraceable.

Phone! He dug into his pocket and came out with Lasko's device. Turned it on and sighed in relief when it showed no signal.

That's how they found me. I had removed its battery at night, but had powered it on in the morning.

The rental house had poor network coverage and a signal had registered only when he brought the device to the living room, earlier in the day.

He set up a Bluetooth connection between his phone and Lasko's and transferred all its contacts. Removed the SIM card and pocketed it.

Cesar. That's either a person or a place name. Cutter hoped the phone would offer a clue. *And that helps me,* he thought grimly.

But first, he had to get away.

❧ 66 ❧

'How did you let him get away?' Dade exploded at Matteo, as she surveyed the house. 'You had his location when he turned Lasko's phone on. You had SWAT, you had cops, this isn't a big neighborhood for him to escape through ... it should have been dead easy to capture Cutter.'

'We didn't know it was him, ma'am. Anyone could have taken his phone. It was only when we called the rental company,' the detective nodded at the house, 'that we figured it was Grogan.'

'We think the neighbor's dog gave us away.' Greg Wells, the SWAT commander, tall and hulking in his combat outfit, said, grimacing. 'My officers were approaching; we were not in position. He reacted instantly.'

He would. He was Delta! Difiore kept the thought to herself as she and Quindica observed quietly from a distance.

They had abandoned their lunch when the chief called them, just after one pm. They had joined her in her vehicle and sat quietly while Dade, stony-faced, took calls and answered monosyllabically.

Matteo, Cruz and Estrada were on the scene when they arrived, along with the SWAT commander and his officers.

Cops had mounted a perimeter to keep the curious residents away.

'Nothing in the house.' The task force's lead detective's shades caught the sun as he glanced at them. 'He escaped through the back and ran through several backyards. Those two,'—he nodded at two cops who were being attended to by EMTs— 'nearly got him.'

'Those were the two in the cruiser?'

'Yes, ma'am, Officers Phelan and Joachim. The latter's a rookie.'

Difiore and Quindica followed the chief when she crossed the street and went to the cops.

'How did it go down?' she asked them after perfunctory introductions.

'He came out of nowhere, ma'am.' The senior officer straightened against the side of the emergency vehicle. 'Chris and I were patrolling the back streets, like we were told to. He came over a fence and ran right at us.'

'Did he hold a gun to you?' Difiore asked him.

'No. He moved so fast I couldn't react. He pulled me out and climbed in and—'

'He told me to roll when I fell.'

'What?' Dade squinted her eyes at him.

'Ma'am.' The rookie swallowed nervously. 'He pushed me out and said I should roll. To absorb the impact.'

'That's what he said?'

'Yes, ma'am. He didn't threaten us.'

Difiore bit her lips to suppress a smile when she heard the chief curse. *What was that she said? Something about him being a saint.*

'We've gone door to door, ma'am.' Matteo joined them. 'If he's in Sylmar, we'll find him. We've told residents to report any stolen cars—'

'Vance,' Dade cut him off. 'If you knew Grogan as well as I do, you would know he isn't here. He's gotten away.'

The detective removed his shades and ran his fingers over his head. He spat out his toothpick and sighed wearily. 'Where could he have gone? We have roadblocks, checkpoints, his face is plastered all over the news—'

'There.' Difiore pointed at the San Gabriel foothills. 'He's in the mountains.'

CUTTER DIDN'T HANG AROUND.

He used the chaparral as cover to ease back into the rocky open area, following the dips and curves of the land to shield himself from the cops. He hustled parallel to Pacoima Canyon Road, going up into the hills until he was high enough to view Pacoima Reservoir.

He heard the first chopper as he was cutting through the mountains toward Cougar Canyon, where he crossed the dry river bed and climbed again.

He was sweating, hungry; all the bruises in his body were complaining, but he couldn't afford to stop.

It was when he crossed Wildlife Waystation that he came across two motorcycles parked on Little Tujunga Canyon Road. The winding, curving trail was a biker's paradise that carved over three summits.

Cutter crouched in a shallow beside the road and checked out the vehicles. No riders in sight. Nothing but the endless blue sky above and the rolling green of the mountains. He ran to the nearest bike and opened its canvas saddlebag. Fist-pumped mentally when he found water bottles and protein bars. He grabbed them, stuffed in a bunch of dollar bills and resumed his getaway.

He kept away from known hiking trails, went through thick brush and trees, ghosting through the mountains as if he had lived in them all his life.

That's pretty much what I did in Afghanistan, he reminisced when he stopped for a water break and drank deeply.

He shrank into the woods when he heard voices. Nope, not cops. A hiking party.

His trail took him through La Tuna Canyon, through the park. It was eight pm when he approached the outskirts of Burbank.

He was grimy, sweaty, and was sure the wetness of his thigh meant the gunshot wound had opened up again. He didn't dare to feel it, however. *Not until I find a place to hole up.*

He searched for motels on his burner phone and found one in Glendale that, according to reviews, took cash.

Forty minutes later, he had completed his check-in with a pimply-faced youth who hadn't looked up from whatever was playing on his screen.

Cutter trudged to his room and couldn't help but moan with delight at the sight of the white sheets on the bed.

He dumped his bags and went to the shower and let the warm water wash away his weariness.

He dressed his thigh with a bandage and over his dinner, protein bars and a bottle of water, he took stock.

The Durango's gone. Cops will have it. They'll find my prints on it and in the house, but nothing else.

That left the Land Cruiser and the Tahoe that he had parked in strategic locations in the city, in long-term parking lots.

He didn't want to risk going to those, however.

'Isaiah,' he called Limon, 'do you want some easy money?'

'HE GOT AWAY.' DADE CAME TO DIFIORE AND QUINDICA'S office and stood in the doorway. 'We got several birds in the air, but the mountains were thick with hikers. There was no way of knowing where Cutter was.'

'We might get lucky.' Quindica shrugged. 'He might leave town.'

'Hey!' she protested when two pairs of eyes stared at her balefully. 'It was just a thought.'

'He's the last man to bail out of any situation. That's not his style,' Difiore said. 'Ma'am, Vienna's house and the one he stayed in, on Sycamore, those were searched?'

'Yeah, we got nothing there.'

'Mind if we check them out as well?'

'Be my guest.'

Difiore watched her walk away and then grabbed her jacket.

'Come on,' she told her partner. 'I have an idea.'

❦ 67 ❦

It was a random idea.

Cutter wrestled with it as long as he could, but gave in finally.

Heck, I need to check it out. See if my hunch is right.

He drove out of the motel in Limon's cab, grinned when he recollected the driver's raised eyebrows at his sideburns disguise.

'Is that you?'

'Forget me.' He had flashed the wad of notes. '*This* is what you're interested in.'

Cutter entered North Heliotrope Drive and passed Vienna's house without slowing down. There was a cruiser parked in the front with two cops inside. Both looked bored and were chatting idly when he went past.

Can't stop there.

He went to Santa Monica Boulevard and nosed into Berendo Street, which was parallel to Vienna's street, but the houses on it would be behind hers.

No patrol cars here.

He pictured the neighborhood in his mind and placed Vienna's house. A bakery would have its backyard neighboring hers. *Can't go through that. It'll have cameras.* The house to the right was large, with several cars in its driveway. *Not that either. But the one to the left is dark. No one home?*

There was only one way to find out.

He parked the cab down the street and returned on foot. Opened the gate and walked down the concrete path as if he belonged. No dogs barked, no lights came on, no shouts of alarm. Along the side of the house ran the driveway, with a car parked on it. He ducked beneath the line of windows and approached the vehicle. Went to the concrete wall that separated Vienna's backyard from the property he was in.

That's seven feet high. He jumped high, caught a glimpse of his friend's residence and decided to break in.

He climbed over the hood of the vehicle and vaulted over the wall. Landed nimbly on his feet, his Glock coming up in his hand automatically.

He holstered the gun when he wasn't challenged by anyone.

Looks like cops are maintaining a casual surveillance.

He darted to the rear of the house and peered through a window. It was dark. Went to the side door, through which he had escaped when Covarra's thugs had attacked.

He unlocked it, turned the handle and pushed it open gently.

A strip of white wedged in the door jamb caught his attention.

A note.

He picked it up, went to a corner of the backyard and smoothed it out. Turned on the flashlight of his burner phone and played it over the piece of paper.

YOU FOOL.

He recognized Difiore's strong scrawl and couldn't help chuckling aloud.

YOU STUPID FOOL.

She repeated in a second line, as if the first one wasn't enough indication of how she felt.

TURN YOURSELF IN.

YOUR WAY WILL END WITH YOUR GETTING KILLED.

He could count on her to fill him with hope and cheer.

He smiled, folded the note and stuffed it in his pocket. His guess had been right. She had known he would come to the house sooner or later and had placed the note there. He had hoped for more information from her and Quindica, on where their investigation was, but understood their position.

They can't compromise themselves. Do they think I shot Lasko? The thought made him frown. He hoped his friends knew him well enough ... *but they're cops as well. They've seen how people act in rage.*

He returned the way he had arrived, back to his cab. Fired it up and drove out of the city on the I-15 and turned off the road when he came to Apple Valley. He drove over rocky, uneven ground, and under the stars, he mounted his yagi antenna and set up his portable GSM tower that would disguise his location.

He scrolled through Lasko's contacts and found the one named Cesar.

'Yeah?' a voice answered roughly.

'Cesar?' he disguised his voice.

'Who's this?' the man replied cautiously.

'A friend of Matt Lasko.'

A shooting star sped across the sky and faded into the vast nothingness above.

'YOU'RE HIM!' Cesar growled. 'You're the one who shot him. Cutter Grogan. Cops are looking for you. How did you get my number?'

'Why do you think I'm him?'

'Puto!' Cesar spat. 'No one else has this number. Only him. The only way you would have got it is if you shot—'

'He gave me his phone. I didn't shoot him. He asked me to contact you.'

'LIES! Lasko never told anyone about me. Even his boss didn't know my name.'

Boss? That's Matteo. Why wouldn't he know of Cesar? Why the secrecy?

It came to him immediately

'You're Lasko's snitch!' he exclaimed. 'You're in the Street Front! That's why he was there, at the warehouse.'

'I'm hanging up.'

'WAIT,' Cutter yelled. 'We've got to meet.'

'I'm not meeting Lasko's killer.'

'Is he dead?' Cutter asked. *I've been busy running through the mountains*, he thought bitterly. *I didn't look up how Lasko was doing.*

'No, puto, but he is serious. His chances of survival are low.'

'Let me guess. Lasko offered you a way out of the gang, or some kind of favor—'

'You know nothing about me,' Cesar rebutted angrily, 'and my relationship with him.'

'I don't, but with him in the hospital, what's your future? If he dies, what will happen to you? I am sure Covarra doesn't let any banger leave the gang. Not alive. How will you quit that life?'

'You're offering me a way out?' the gangster said, laughing scornfully.

'Yeah.'

'How? You're wanted by the cops yourself. What can—'

'I know Lisa Dade, the Chief of Police. She and I go a long way back. I didn't shoot Lasko. If I can clear myself, I can get her to give you witness protection.'

'That's a lot of ifs, puto. How will you achieve that?'

'Were you at the warehouse?'

'I was outside, on the streets,' the snitch said reluctantly.

Which is why he didn't see what went down and thinks I'm the shooter.

'I thought Lasko would call for backup. I didn't know he would come on his own ... why am I telling you all this? This call is over.'

'Hold on,' Cutter pleaded. 'What have you got to lose? You and I are stuck ... we need to find our ways out.'

'I am not helping you, puto!'

'Lasko gave me your name. He told me to take his phone. He knew we could help each other.'

'I'll kill you the minute I see you.'

'Meet me, in that case. You'll get your opportunity.'

'How can I reach you?'

Cutter's shoulders slumped in relief at the banger's words.

'My number should have come up on your screen. Use that.'

'That's a foreign number.'

'It will work.'

'Si, I'll tell you where to come. And, be prepared to die.'

❧ 68 ❧

Cutter thought long and hard about the next call. *Heck, I know what she thinks of me. That's not going to change. But at least I'll have put my side forward.*

He dialed the number and heard it ring. Imagined Difiore waking up, reaching for her phone and frowning at the caller ID.

'There are only two ways you'll come out of this,' the detective answered the call harshly. No surprise in her voice. 'You'll be killed in a showdown with cops or you'll go to prison.'

'How did you know it was me?'

'Grogan,' she sneered, 'I'm the best detective the NYPD has. You think I wouldn't connect a Moscow area code number to you?'

Beth and Meg set that up for me. They got Werner to assign random numbers to my phone.

'Cutter,' he heard Quindica say, 'you've got to turn yourself in.'

'Why should I? It was—'

'No,' Difiore interrupted him roughly. 'We don't want to hear your excuses. You want to tell your story? Surrender and give your statement to the cops.'

'That's what I'm—'

'Matteo's leading your investigation as well. Go to him.'

'Cutter,' the FBI agent asked softly when he made no response to Difiore's comment, 'how are you?'

'I'm fine,' he replied. *Other than the gazillion injuries I'm trying to heal from, and the aching in my feet from the mountain escape.*

'How did you get away from Sylmar?' Difiore, her voice, flat, cold.

'I took to the hills. The cops—'

'That's what I guessed. That was a SWAT team you got away from.'

'They should have blocked escape to the hills.'

'Why did you call us?'

'Huh? You wanted me to call!'

'Are you high?' she snapped. 'When did I do that?'

'You left that note in Vienna's house. That was as sure an invitation to make contact as any.'

'He got you there.' Quindica chuckled softly.

'We're listening,' Difiore said flatly. 'What do you want to say?'

'I was set up.'

'Yeah? That bike rider who attacked Covarra, that zip line dude who burned a house in Boyle Heights ... you were set up then, too?'

He grinned in the darkness. *Can't admit to them that was me.*

'I don't know what you're talking about,' he said as innocently as he could.

Her loud snort made him chuckle.

'Grogan,' she said savagely, 'this call is over—'

'Covarra knew my name. Ask yourself how,' he said quickly and hung up.

'IT WAS GROGAN,' MATTEO BEGAN WHEN DIFIORE AND Quindica joined the briefing in Dade's office. 'We got his prints from his house, the SUV. He left nothing behind, however.

Phelan and Joachim reported he was carrying two bags. One was large and another was a backpack. We're guessing those had his weapons.'

'Any progress at the warehouse?' Dade asked him.

'No, ma'am. Our street informers have gone to ground. We aren't getting any intel from them.'

'Do you have any good news, Vance?'

'I have a theory, ma'am,' he said reluctantly.

'Let's hear it out.'

'We know Grogan attacked those Street Front warehouses.' He shrugged at the look on her face. 'We can't prove it, ma'am, but it was him, no one else.'

'Get on with it,' she rapped.

'The gang lost a lot of product in those attacks. What if Grogan stole some of it and was in the warehouse to make a deal with Covarra. Lasko stumbled on them and, before he could alert us, Grogan shot him.'

Difiore would have lunged forward to protest if Quindica hadn't squeezed her forearm, hard.

She turned her blazing eyes on her partner, who mouthed: *Not here.*

'Find him, prove it, make your case,' Dade said emotionlessly and dismissed him.

'MA'AM,' DIFIORE BURST OUT WHEN SHE AND QUINDICA WERE with the chief. 'Cutter dealing drugs?'

'I know.' The LAPD's boss was her usual immaculate, composed self. Only the skin stretched tight over her cheekbones and the faintest shadows beneath her eyes spoke of the stress she was under. 'However, it is Vance's case. Let him go with it. I'm sure he will find nothing.'

'He called us last night,' Quindica murmured softly.

Dade's eyes opened wide at that. She checked that the door

was closed and turned down the blinds in her office to give them more privacy.

'Cutter? What did he say?'

'About being set up,' Difiore said. 'We asked him to turn himself in.'

'What went down in the warehouse?'

'I didn't let him speak.'

The detective held her breath when the chief stared at her in astonishment. It gave way to a speculative look, which yielded to a small smile.

'You needled him. That will make him more determined to clear himself.'

'Yes, ma'am.' she grinned. *Lucky for me she worked it out, or else she would have chewed me out.*

'He said something else, ma'am.' Her smile disappeared. 'He said Covarra knew his name.'

'It's all over the news ...' Dade trailed off when the implications struck her. 'That's *now*. Not when he met the gangster.'

'Yes, ma'am, and you can bet he would have used a disguise.'

'No one other than the task force knows we suspect Cutter for all those attacks.' The chief's lips pressed tight.

'And even then, only a handful of officers know. Matteo, Cruz, Estrada, Lasko, five or six others, all very senior.'

'We've got a leak,' Dade whispered harshly. 'Vance, Cruz, Estrada, it can't be any of them. They go through security checks.' She leaned forward and commanded, 'Drop this hunt for Cutter. Find the snitch.'

Covarra muted the TV when Salazar entered the living room.

'What's up, Snake?' His deputy frowned at the rage on his boss's face.

'He's alive. Both of them!'

'Who? Grogan? Yeah, I saw that on the news, he got away from Sylmar—'

'NOT JUST HIM!' Covarra shrieked. 'THAT COP IS ALSO ALIVE. IN THE HOSPITAL.'

'He's in serious condition, boss. He could die any moment.'

'What if he regains consciousness?'

He nodded when he saw realization flare in Salazar's eyes, too. 'LAPD will be even more determined to get me once they know I shot him. They might offer a reward. That might influence some of our men. That cannot happen. Get some men to check out that hospital. We need to kill that cop.'

'Wait.' He stopped Salazar as his deputy was leaving. 'Tell our men to look out for Grogan. He knows what happened in that warehouse. He needs to die, too.'

'COME TO THAT SAME PLACE, TONIGHT,' CESAR SAID ON THE call that woke Cutter from his doze in Limon's cab in Venice.

'Which place?' He sat up, rubbed his eyes and waggled his fingers at a kid who was licking an ice cream as he went past on the sidewalk.

'That warehouse where you shot Lasko.'

'I didn't—' he began automatically and then blinked. 'You want us to meet there? Cops will be around. It's a crime scene in case you've forgotten.'

'That's the only place I'll meet. At eleven pm.'

What's with these bangers and their nightly meets, he grumbled to himself.

'I'll be there,' he confirmed.

'You'd better be alone.'

'You, too,' he snapped and hung up.

'NOTHING HAS CHANGED TO MY BENEFIT.' JANIKYAN PRESSED Zohrab's shoulder briefly in thanks when the bodyguard brought him a drink. He dismissed his man and leaned back on the couch as he crossed his legs. 'Grogan is still alive. That cop is also alive. Covarra is out there, still in business. How is any of that good for me?'

'I thought Covarra and Grogan would kill each other, or at least one of them would be dead.'

'Why don't you leave the thinking to me?' he told him coldly and ignored the man's sharply drawn breath. He didn't care if his caller felt offended. 'Grogan is smart. I told you how he reached me. Went through a real estate agent. See how he took out the Street Front's places? As for that cop in the hospital—'

'Lasko.'

'Yeah, him. You said he was smart. That you couldn't risk having him around you for long.'

'He's in the hospital. He's not a risk for now.'

'We'll need to take care of Grogan,' Janikyan mused. 'No, don't talk,' he said sharply when the caller made to speak. 'I'll set a trap for Mr. Grogan. One he won't walk out of.'

CUTTER EXCHANGED LIMON'S CAB FOR THE TAHOE FOR THE rendezvous with Cesar. He couldn't risk the red taxi getting noticed in the industrial area.

He parked the ride in the same spot on Clarence Street and tried many of the trucks parked on the road. He climbed into one whose rear doors opened and slept until it fell dark.

He yawned and stretched when his inner clock woke him up at seven pm. Got to his feet, peered out cautiously and jumped out when he saw no threat.

The long bouts of sleep had helped his recovery. His body protested less, though the aches were still there. *Can't complain. I could have been dead.*

He circled the neighborhood on foot, with a ballcap pulled low over his head and his jacket collar high on his neck.

There were cruisers at the warehouse, and even from a

distance he could see uniformed officers moving under the portable floodlights.

How does Cesar think we can meet here? Maybe he's testing me, too, to see whether I'm going to turn up alone.

He checked out the street with his NVGs, night vision goggles, from underneath a truck. *That unit over there has the best view of the warehouse. I can't go there, though. Cops will see me.*

The building was opposite the warehouse, a tall, white structure. *Looks like it has a flat roof.*

That gave him an idea.

Despite the heightened police presence, there was still traffic through both streets. Tail lights flared as cars slowed down to look at the warehouse, and from a distance, he could hear voices as people talked to the cops.

Cutter hugged the walls of buildings, filtering from shadow to shadow, until he came to the structure he had checked out.

It seemed to be a loading terminal for trucks. Two semis were backed into it, their front cabs gleaming in the night. He went into its large yard and checked out the L-shaped side of the building. Shuttered doors on the short leg where trucks backed up. The other side had a sheer, high wall and nothing else.

Pipes! There were four of them running down the side. *Concrete*, he found out when he felt one of them.

Cutter didn't waste time. He fastened the gymbag securely around his waist and started climbing. The tubular construction held its position despite the weight on it. He went up swiftly, aware that he was a dark, man-sized beetle on the wall. Any passing vehicle could spot him if they looked high enough.

No one stopped him, however.

He hauled himself over the roof, which was flat, with air-conditioning equipment and pipes running across.

He crouched low and ran to the front of the roof and lay prone on it. Inched forward carefully until he could see over its edge.

Officers, police tape, cruisers with their lights flashing. No civilians that he could spot through his binos. He had discovered the scene of his rendezvous with Covarra was a movie-shoot location. *Street Front owns it, I bet.* He reminded himself to message its location to Difiore after meeting Cesar.

'Puto,' Cesar called him at eleven pm. 'Where are you?'

A banger who's punctual! He grinned in the dark and checked out the shadows on the intersection of the streets.

'I'm stuck in traffic,' he lied. 'Are you there?'

'Why else would I call you?'

'Wait for a few—'

'WAIT! THERE ARE COPS HERE.'

Is that him? Cutter trained the binos on a shadow lurking at the mouth of an unmarked passage on Jesse, away from the presence of the cops.

The man was leaning against a dark pickup truck, motionless except for his hand motions.

'You picked this spot,' he retorted. 'You should have known—'

'WHEN WILL YOU GET HERE?'

'I can't show up just like that. Have you forgotten I'm a wanted man?'

'And I'm a banger, *ese*. The risk is the same for both of us.'

'How will I recognize you?'

'Me? Don't worry about that. I know what you look like. I'll recognize you.'

That's him, against that vehicle. His hand gestures match his words.

'Come to the river. You can cut through the buildings on Mission Street. I'll be there, next to the rails.'

'Puto.' Cesar straightened and swore. 'You never planned to come here, did you? Meeting's off. I am not going anywhere.'

'Don't you want to know what went down in that place? How Lasko got shot?'

'I know how. You shot him. Everyone in the Street Front's talking about nothing else.'

Everyone? There were several bangers in that place. They saw what went down.

Cutter's brow cleared when the explanation came to him. *Covarra's ordered everyone who saw it to stick to the story that I shot Lasko.*

'With Lasko out, I'm the only one who can help you.'

'You? A criminal? I can find another cop.'

'Do that.'

'Ten minutes,' Cesar replied savagely after a while. 'Be there, or I'll be gone. You picked a good spot, *ese*—I'm gonna kill you and throw your body in the river.'

❧ 69 ❧

Cutter followed him with his binos until Cesar turned the corner on Mission Road.

He seems to be alone.

He got to his feet and hustled to the edge of the roof. Maneuvered himself to hold the pipe and slithered down fast.

He slowed to a walk when he came to Jesse and ghosted across the street. *Lucky no cops looking for me here.*

He spotted Cesar's silhouette on Mission and crossed to the other side of the street to follow him. The banger moved quickly, without looking back, and crawled through a hole in a wire fence into an open plot.

That will go to the river.

Cutter gave him time to vanish from sight and followed him.

THE STINK OF STALE WATER AND URINE. LIGHT GLEAMING dully off the rails that ran along the bank of the river. Debris on the paved surface of the river bed.

And Cesar, a tall shadow, hunched over his phone, fifty feet away.

As he got closer, the banger sensed his presence, turned and started drawing his gun out with an oath.

Cutter dived at him and brought him down, let the weight of his body and luggage rest on the hitter, who jabbed and punched but was ineffectual.

'I could have killed you if I wanted to, when you were on Jesse, against that car.'

The thug's mouth gaped at that. 'You were watching me?'

'Yeah, and I had my gun on you as well.'

He snatched Cesar's weapon and got to his feet. Unstrapped his gym bag and laid it on the ground, all the while keeping a cautious eye on the hood.

'You really didn't shoot Lasko?' the thug studied him.

'No.' He sized up the banger in return. Swarthy, thick beard, glittering eyes, loose shirt over low-hanging riders.

What do I have to lose?

He told Cesar what had gone down at the rendezvous and couldn't help chuckling at the man's rounded eyes and gawping stare.

'You wrapped a suicide belt around yourself, *ese?*'

'Yeah.' He wasn't going to admit that there was no way the explosives would have gone off. 'What's the deal between you and Lasko?'

'He saved me.'

Cutter listened quietly as the banger told him his backstory and about his vengeance mission.

'What will you do if Lasko dies?'

Cesar side-eyed him. 'You said you could help me.'

'I will do everything I can.'

'You'd better come through good.'

'Uh-huh.' *I told him about Dade ... but I'll probably have to go through Difiore and Quindica. They'll be able to arrange Federal Witsec for him.*

'Lasko said my name?' the thug asked after a while.

'Yeah. Why do you think he did that? I can't make out the connection.'

'You asked Snake about his and Fuse's rifles.'

'Yes, but Lasko wasn't there then—' Cutter stopped abruptly as he recollected Covarra yelling and punching at him. 'He was there, though, when your boss repeated that and hit me.'

'That's it.' The banger snapped his fingers.

'What?'

'He knew what I did with the rifles.'

'What did you do?' Cutter asked him, feeling stupid that he wasn't connecting the dots.

'I sold Snake and Fuse's rifles.'

70

'What do you mean, you sold them?' Cutter stared at him.

'Just that, *ese*,' Cesar said impatiently. 'Keep up with me. Both of them used AR-15s, but as the gang grew, it wasn't right they went around with the rifles. They are leaders. Bosses don't need those weapons. There was no need for them to carry those. Fuse ordered me to get rid of them. I sold them to a dealer.'

'After they killed the women?'

'No!' the banger scowled at him angrily. 'Snake told the truth there. We didn't kill them.'

'How do you know?'

'I was there, *ese*, at that house. I was shooting back at those Armenian putos. All of us escaped. There were no women, no one else at that house.'

'You didn't return to that house? No other banger?'

'No.'

'Did you search the house?'

'Why would we do that, *ese*? Those bangers were in the yard. We attacked them as soon as we saw them.'

Vienna and Arnedra could have been hiding inside. They could have seen what went down. Were they killed because of that?

He growled at himself in frustration. He had questions but very few answers. Every time he thought he had made progress, like going after Covarra and getting him to talk, he had setbacks.

'Who did you sell those weapons to?'

Got to find the men who fired those.

'A dealer. He buys and sells from gangs. He supplies all of us, Armenian putos as well. He's neutral, doesn't take sides.'

'Where can I find him?'

'He doesn't have a store, *ese*,' Cesar sneered, 'he meets you on the street, somewhere away from the cops. He won't see you. He only does business with people he knows.'

'Set up a meeting for me. Say you want to buy some weapons.'

'He may not have them anymore.'

'He doesn't,' Cutter grated, 'unless he's the killer himself. He sold them to someone else.'

'He may not remember. All this happened last year.'

'Do you want to help? Do you want to get out of the gang? All you seem to be doing is making excuses.'

'If Snake finds out—'

'You wanted to buy a gun. What's unusual about that?'

Cesar nodded after a while and brought out his phone. 'Barrel doesn't take calls. He works on messages only.'

'Barrel?'

'That's what we call him. Tomas Cabal.'

The thug fired off a message and pocketed his phone. 'We should go,' he said. 'He may not get back to me right away. I'll let you know when he does.'

Cesar laughed humorlessly as they walked down the tracks.

'What?'

'This.' The banger gestured at the two of them. 'We both are wanted by the cops. Here we are, working together.'

Cabal responded when they reached Fourth Street.

'Compton Avenue, near Nickerson Gardens.' Cesar showed him the dealer's text. 'You know where it is?'

'Yeah, housing project in Watts.'

'Tomorrow night.'

'I'll be there. Is there some secret code or something?'

'You see too many movies, *ese*.' The banger's teeth flashed. 'He drives a Hummer. Black. It'll be parked on that road. You can't miss it. He'll roll down the window when I turn up. Like I said, he deals only with known customers.'

'But you won't be there.'

'Not my problem, *ese*.' Cesar shrugged. 'I fixed the meeting for you.'

'Give me his number and forward all his messages to me.'

'How will you approach him?' the thug asked after sharing the details.

'Like you said, that's my problem.'

71

That warehouse is owned by the Street Front.

Cutter assembled the GSM tower and fired off the text the next day, then went to shower in a motel in Central Alameda.

Difiore's reply was waiting for him when he returned.

We know. Don't message me again.

How's Lasko?

Still critical. Thanks to you.

He grimaced at that, thought of calling her, but what could he say?

He logged in to Werner and checked out Tomas Cabal. Found several men of that name. *I need to know what LAPD has on him.* Which meant he had to call Beth or Meghan.

He braced himself for more sarcasm and ribbing and dialed the younger sister's number.

'How are you?'

He blinked at her question. *No,* he told himself firmly. *That's not concern in her voice.*

'Cops haven't found me yet,' he told her. A thought struck him. 'I should stop calling you. You'll get incriminated—'

'Why don't you leave that to us?' Meghan drawled. 'We are aware of the risks.'

'But—'

'Cutter,' she sighed, 'get to it. We have work to do. What do you want?'

'Tomas Cabal, aka Barrel. What does the LAPD have on him?'

'Who is he?'

'A gun dealer.'

'Cabal, yeah, cops have a file on him,' Beth told him. 'Thirty-five years of age. Said to live in South LA, but when the cops checked it out a few months ago, the place was empty. Suspected gun dealer. Did time for illegal weapons possession. Three years in the county jail. Got into numerous fights while in prison. Goes around with three associates: Juan Noboa, Ramon Ferranto, Luz Arnal. All three are dangerous. Check your phone; I've sent their photographs.'

The gun dealer was a large man, bulky with muscle, a shaven head, a walrus mustache and eyes that looked mean even in the file image that Beth sent across. His men were unassuming looking, all of them dark-haired, dark-eyed, with tattoos on their bodies.

'Good luck hunting them.' Beth wished him and hung up.

CUTTER WAS AT NICKERSON GARDENS AT FIVE PM, A COUPLE of hours ahead of Cabal's arrival. It was the largest housing project west of the Mississippi, with yellow-colored multifamily buildings laid out in a horseshoe shape that opened into Compton Avenue.

Kids played in patches of grass. A few young men bounced a ball against a hoop in a yard, many of them giving him hard stares as he strolled past.

He didn't look like his photographs on TV. He had changed

his contacts to brown, had painted a scar on his cheek and had inserted a pad in his mouth to give his lips a twisted shape.

He had gone for a shoulder holster for his Glock, beneath his loose jacket, while his knife was in a sheath around his right calf. His jeans were dirty, sneakers were scuffed, while his upper clothing had tears and streaks of food residue on them.

He didn't attract any attention.

Cabal could be based in any of these houses and the cops wouldn't know. Cutter was intimately familiar with such neighborhoods. One of his foster families had lived in such a project in New York. Gangs, fights, the invisible jungle-drum-like alarm system that warned its residents of the cops' arrival ... *I know how these places work.* He fingered his belly unconsciously where a thug's knife had punctured him when he was young.

Compton Avenue was a long stretch of concrete with residential buildings on both sides. Commercial establishments were few: a donut shop, a pawn dealer, a car wash. Cutter checked the street, saw no sign of the Hummer, and gave in to the tempting aroma coming from the food joint.

He carried the donuts in a brown bag and leaned against the metal fence of a house. Ate them slowly as he bobbed his head to the beat playing in his earpiece.

That sound got drowned out by the loud music blasting from the Hummer when it arrived promptly at seven pm.

❦ 72 ❦

Cutter didn't move from his position, didn't look up when Cabal's ride rolled to a stop in front of the housing project's office. Cars and pedestrians gave it a wide berth, as if the residents knew who was inside the vehicle.

Fifty feet from me, on my left. Two shapes in the front. Can't make out who they are.

The passenger door opened as he watched from the corner of his eye, and a man jumped out. He circled the Hummer, kicked its tires, said something to the driver and climbed back inside.

That looked like Ferranto.

Cutter crushed the paper bag and licked his fingers as he straightened. He wiped his hands on his jacket and hummed tunelessly as he shuffled down the sidewalk towards the Hummer.

Felt the driver's and passenger's eyes scan him as he grew closer.

That's Cabal in the front, Arnal's behind the wheel.

The dealer made a comment, at which his man laughed. Neither looked like they felt threatened by the approaching man.

Cutter felt loose and ready as he grew closer. Four men inside the vehicle, all of them likely to be armed. *But they're inside, they're boxed in.* He lost his balance when he was at Cabal's window, which was darkened, and slammed against the Hummer.

He backed off and raised his hands to show he was harmless and showed his blackened teeth in a grin. He whistled as he made a show of checking out the vehicle and tapped the window.

No response.

He punched it with his fist.

The glass lowered to reveal a scowling Cabal.

'What do you—'

Cutter drew his Glock and smashed its barrel into his mouth. Punched him in the throat with his left hand, leaned inside and shot Arnal in the side, trained his gun on the men in the rear, who were reacting, hands lowering to weapons at their feet. His one-two shots in their chests and legs left them immobile.

He checked his surroundings as he removed zip-ties from his pockets and cuffed Cabal's wrists. The dealer was still dazed and offered little resistance, but Cutter took no chances. He smashed his gun in the man's temple and knocked him out and then secured his legs as well.

He unlocked the passenger door cautiously, but Ferranto and Noboa didn't attack. He had placed his shots deliberately, shooting high on their left chest and in their thighs, and it looked like his rounds had taken out the fight in them. He secured them as well and went to the driver's side, where he dealt with Arnal similarly.

He grunted with effort as he shoved the driver in between the seats and to the back and climbed inside, behind the wheel.

He flashed the indicator to indicate he was moving out, checked his mirror and slid behind a passing car on Compton Avenue. Just over five minutes had elapsed since he had knocked on the window.

No one heard my shots above the music. Even if they did, people mind their own business in a neighborhood like this.

He turned down the radio's volume and switched to a news channel as he drove southwest.

The gun dealer returned to consciousness when he entered Redondo. He groaned and swiveled his head. Did a double-take when he took in who the driver was.

'WHO ARE YOU? WHERE'S ARNAL?' he screamed and attempted to free himself. He cursed and swore when he found his wrists were not only tied together but also taped to his seat.

'Look behind you.'

He twisted his body and stiffened when he saw his men lying in the rear, slumped and bleeding on the seats, moaning softly.

'Who sent you?' Cabal hissed. 'Which gang? I've delivered all the guns—'

'I'm not with any gang.'

'Who are you, then?' The dealer showed no fear. 'You want to take over my business? Where are you taking us?'

Cutter drove to a remote bluff overlooking Redondo Beach and parked under the night sky. He turned off the Hummer's lights, then checked the men in the back and found they had lost consciousness. He examined their wounds, which didn't look life-threatening to him.

He went to Cabal and cut the tape, freeing his wrists from the seat. He dodged the man's headbutt, grabbed him by the collar and pulled him out of the vehicle.

'You want to attack me? Wait a minute, you'll get your chance.' He slashed the ties that held the man's hands and legs and stepped back as Cabal charged at him with a growl of rage.

The dealer's yell turned to a grunt of agony when Cutter punched him in the belly and followed it up with a chop to the throat.

'Who ... are ... you ...?' Cabal wheezed as he fought to suck air. 'What ... do ... you ... want?'

'Cesar from the Street Front sold two AR-15s to you last year. What happened to them?'

'I don't know any—' the dealer began automatically and screamed when Cutter yanked his ear savagely.

'I can cut you to shreds and leave you to die here,' he told the dealer emotionlessly. He had no pity, no remorse for the criminal. *His business results in hundreds of deaths each year.*

'Why do you want to know?' Cabal gasped when he had recovered his breath.

'Wrong answer,' Cutter told him coldly and tripped him when the dealer charged at him with an angry yell. He hauled the man up and fisted his hand to deliver a punch.

'I don't have them,' the dealer yelled.

He's not denying he bought them.

'What did you do with them?'

The dealer reared up suddenly and headbutted him with a snarl. He punched furiously when Cutter lost his balance as he backtracked, and landed on his chest with a feral grin.

'You—' The dealer hit him. 'Thought.' He punched again. 'It would be this easy?'

Cutter brought his hands up to deflect the next blow, followed up with a blurring move that applied a lock on the dealer's incoming fist and snapped his wrist savagely.

Cabal's shriek was lost on the vastness of the bluff.

Got to finish this fast, before we draw attention.

He jabbed his knuckles in the dealer's sternum, a blow that punched the air out of the man. He shoved him to the ground, drew his knife and buried it deep in his flesh, just below his right shoulder.

Cabal screamed and writhed.

Cutter jabbed him in the thigh and looked down at him coldly.

'I asked you a question. What did you do with those rifles?'

The dealer shrank when he made a threatening move. He held his hands up weakly.

'I sold them,' he sobbed.

'To whom?'

'Armenian Bros.'

73

Cutter thought he hadn't heard right.

'Armenian Bros?' he repeated.

'Yeah. They were looking for AR-15s. I sold these two, along with several more.'

'You're lying.' He dropped to his knees and raised the knife.

'NO! I MAINTAIN RECORDS. I CAN SHOW THEM TO YOU. EVERY GUN, EVERY TRADE, I WRITE IT DOWN.'

'How do you remember this particular sale?'

'Because of who sold them and who bought them.'

'Who were those?'

'Cesar, from Street Front. He was a first-time seller. It's usually Fuse who comes with other bangers. They sent Cesar for this deal.'

'How did you know it was him?'

Cabal managed to throw him a contemptuous look despite his agony. 'I called Fuse and verified him. I don't do business with strangers.'

'Who bought them?'

'Zohrab, he's—'

'I know who he is.'

Cutter felt as if he had been punched in the gut as he considered the dealer's confession. Armenian Bros. *They had the guns all along.*

'Do you know if they still have them?'

'How would I know?' The dealer cradled his broken wrist. 'They haven't been sold back to me.'

'Where do you keep your records?'

Cabal twisted his head to look at him. He licked his lips when he saw the blood-stained knife in Cutter's hand.

'I can punch more holes in you.'

'Why do you want to know?'

'I ask the questions. You answer. That's how this is played.'

'Wait!' he scrambled back on the ground when his attacker loomed over him. 'It's in the Hummer. Under my seat. A notebook.'

'You keep it there? In the vehicle?' Cutter asked him, astonished. He went to the ride and opened the door. Lifted the front seat, and there it was, a worn, well-thumbed book, filled with pages of handwriting.

'It's the safest place,' the dealer moaned softly. 'It's secure— it's where I spend most of my time.'

'Show me the page,' Cutter ordered. The criminal took the notebook with shaking fingers, riffled through the pages until he came to one dated the previous year.

'That's the one.'

'Only the date makes sense to me.'

'I write in code. What did you think?' Cabal's spirited reply faded into a groan when he gingerly felt his thigh.

'Translate it for me.'

'Replace each letter with the corresponding one, backwards in the alphabet.'

Cutter snatched the records from him and ran his finger down the list of entries. 'Z instead of *A, Y* for *B?*'

'Yeah.' The criminal curled his body tight and rocked on the ground.

'That's not very difficult to crack.'

'I sell guns,' Cabal gasped. 'I'm not a crypto ... whatever they are called. Aren't you going to get us to a hospital? We'll die here.'

'No loss to the world if that happens.' He grunted softly when he found the sale. Ten AR-15s for two thousand dollars each, eight new, two used, the latter being the Street Front weapons.

'That's a good price.' He raised his eyebrows. *Those go for around a thousand bucks on the street.*

'My guns are untraceable. I am trusted. I don't snitch on my customers.' Cabal raised his head to reply proudly. 'Gangs pay a premium for that.'

'You got the same price for the Street Front's guns too, even though they were used.'

The dealer hesitated and moistened his lips when Cutter drilled him with his eyes. 'Zohrab wanted ten guns; I had only eight new ones in stock. I told him I had two used ones. He wanted to know who had owned them before. I don't normally tell my customers where I have bought my guns from, but the Armenians buy a lot from me. He got interested when I told him. He made a call and said he would buy those, too. I sold them at the same price. It's about demand.'

'Do you know who he called?'

'No. He spoke in their language.'

'You're lying.' Cutter kicked him in the thigh. 'No one remembers those kinds of details after so long.'

Cabal's shriek pierced the night and trailed off into a sobbing moan. 'I am not,' he uttered through trembling lips. 'I have a good memory ... and ... I told you. This sale stood out.'

Can I believe him?

Yeah. It's in his voice and eyes. He's telling the truth.

He wiped his knife on the dealer's clothing and sheathed it. Went to the Hummer and checked the other men. They were alive, but still out.

I can't leave them here. Once Cabal recovers, he'll remember it was Cesar who set the meeting up. He'll expose the banger.

'I need some help.' He turned away from the dealer, walked several paces towards the bluff's edge and pulled out his phone.

'Tell us,' Beth answered his call. 'You're on speaker.'

'I have four bodies. Alive, but injured. Three of them have gunshot wounds in their chests—'

'How serious?' Meghan asked him.

'Right side, on the chest. Rounds don't seem to have damaged anything vital. Their breathing is strong. They have leg wounds, too. The fourth man has a broken wrist, knife cuts in his body.'

'Who are they?'

That's Zeb. 'Tomas Cabal, an arms dealer, and his men.'

'You want them to be picked up and held?'

'Yeah,' Cutter admitted. 'I'm in a bind. I don't know what to do with them.'

'Where are you?'

'On a bluff in Redondo.' He read out the location coordinates.

'Leave the men there,' Beth commanded. 'We'll arrange for them to be picked up.'

'How?' he argued. 'You folks are in New York.'

'He wants to know how we work,' Meghan announced sarcastically. 'As if we're going to tell him. Cutter, if you want our help, do as we say. Leave, now! Those dudes will be collected in half an hour, or even less. They'll still be alive by then, won't they?'

'We'll get them collected even if they aren't,' her sister said flatly.

'You can't be seen, can't be anywhere nearby when the help arrives,' Zeb told him firmly. 'You got a ride?'

'Yeah, I'll use Cabal's. I'll dispose of it when I return to the city.'

They didn't ask for details, didn't turn me down. They must have a network all over the country, people who can do this kind of work at very short notice.

'How can I thank you?'

'We'll think of something,' Beth said with a smile in her voice.

He returned to Cabal when the call ended and secured his legs and hands with plastic ties. The dealer yelped when the binding cut into his injured wrist and cursed at his attacker.

Cutter went to the vehicle, dragged out the guards individually and dumped them next to their boss. He surveyed them critically and decided the men would survive for half an hour. He taped their mouths, searched their bodies and pocketed their wallets and phones.

He searched the ride and found a blanket, which he draped over them.

'Someone will come for you,' he told Cabal. 'They'll get your wounds treated and hold you.'

'Hold us?' the dealer shouted. 'I'll kill you—'

'Try to stay alive until they arrive.'

He climbed inside the Hummer and drove away without a second glance. He rolled down the window when he hit Torrance Boulevard and let the wind clear his mind.

He drove automatically, paying little attention to the traffic, with just one thought in his mind.

Panig Janikyan played me.

❧ 74 ❧

Zeb and his team rolled to the bluff in two SUVs in just over half an hour.

He jumped out of his ride and spotted the mass of bodies immediately in the glow of the headlights.

Cutter picked a good spot for interrogation. No one comes here, since the ground is rocky.

'What kind of ride does Cabal have?'

'Hummer.' Beth guessed his thoughts. 'It can drive here.'

'Uh-huh,' he grunted as he removed the blanket covering the men. He inspected the wounds of the bangers and nodded to himself. They weren't serious but needed attention.

Bear bent over Cabal and ripped the tape from his mouth, who yelled in anger.

'WHO ARE YOU?'

Bwana joined them—tall, dark, his face all angles and edges. 'What did he want?'

'WHAT DID WHO WANT? WHO ARE YOU?'

'The man who did this to you. What was he after?'

'What's that to you?' Cabal raged. 'He said someone would take us to a hospital. Is that you?'

'We will,' Bwana promised solemnly, 'as soon as you tell us.'

'Can't you see we're dying?'

'You surely will if you don't spill.'

'Who are you?'

'We?' Bwana chuckled humorlessly. 'That dude who did this to you ... we're ten times worse than him.'

'JANIKYAN SET CUTTER UP,' MEGHAN SAID QUIETLY AS SHE drove the lead SUV back to the city.

'Yeah.' Zeb looked out of the window, at the passing traffic and flashing billboards, though none of it registered. He was thinking of his friend, who was out there, alone, wanted.

'He'll go after the Armenians. They're bigger, more ruthless than the Street Front,' Beth chimed from behind.

'I know.'

'We've got to help him.'

'We will,' he promised. 'Not yet, though. Let him complete his investigation.'

'He may not have time on his side. Have you forgotten cops and Covarra's bangers are hunting him?'

'Cutter Grogan is a survivor,' Zeb said confidently. 'LAPD, all those thugs, they have the wrong idea about him. They think they have him cornered in this city. They don't know that's when he's most dangerous.'

❧ 75 ❧

'Tell me about the hospital,' Covarra demanded when Salazar entered the living room.

'I got some of our men to check it out,' his deputy responded. 'Lasko is on the fifth floor, in an intensive care room. Two cops outside, in the hallway, in shifts.' He found a piece of paper and drew on it with a pen. 'Two cops here, where the elevators open.' He made a cross in the lane that marked the corridor. 'They're about a hundred feet away. Lasko's room is at the end of the hallway. Windows on the wall that look over the parking lot.'

'Only four men on that floor?'

'Four are enough, Snake. All of them are armed. Our men say they're alert.'

'There must be stairs as well, and a service elevator.'

'Stairs are next to the main elevators. Service one is down the hallway.' He made another cross to indicate it. 'What are you thinking?'

'What about cops on the ground floor?'

'Yeah, five of them in the lobby. Two cruisers outside.'

'Are they checking identities?'

'They were doing that on Lasko's floor the first night, but the medics protested. They said it was holding up the entire floor, the surgical staff and operations. They quit, after that.'

'Access doors?'

'Those are controlled by the cards the staff have. The ones they have around their necks.'

'Send two of our best shooters. Don't send more. They'll stand out. Get passes for them. Kill two nurses if you have to. That hospital is large. It will have its own security, but it's so busy no one will check the card and compare it to the face.'

'How will they get out, Snake? The minute there are shots, the entire hospital will be alerted.'

'A getaway car in the parking lot. Filled with our men.'

'Yeah, but how do they get to the ground?'

'They go out of that window in the hallway. I bet there will be pipes that go down.'

'Boss, our men are not special forces kind of—'

Covarra gripped his shoulder and squeezed lightly.

'Killing Lasko is important,' he said softly. 'It doesn't matter if our men die.'

'Cops will know those are our men.'

'Yes.' Covarra's eyes blazed. 'I want them to know. I want Grogan to know, wherever he's hiding.'

'LAPD will wonder why we killed the cop.'

'Let them. With Lasko dead, there will be no witness to what happened.'

'Our best shooters, boss? Those are Munoz and Rodrigo. You want to sacrifice them?'

'They're smart, they'll get away. And if they don't,' Covarra shrugged, 'we have other men who are just as good. We get new recruits every day.'

'Do it tonight,' he ordered and dismissed his deputy with a flick of his fingers.

· · ·

CUTTER'S PHONE BUZZED WHEN HE WAS IN THE SHOWER. HE turned off the water and cocked his head. Yeah, that was his device vibrating on the table. He toweled himself hastily, went to the living room and checked the number.

'Cesar?' he asked cautiously as he looked through the window of the Laguna Beach motel room he had rented the previous night.

'I have heard talk,' the banger whispered. 'You've got to go to the hospital tonight.'

'Which hospital?' *Is he talking about Cabal and his men? No, that can't be. Beth said she would get those men collected last night.*

'Where Lasko is,' Cesar hissed angrily.

'Why?' he straightened abruptly. 'What's going down?'

'Snake has ordered a hit. It will happen tonight.'

'Are you sure?' Cutter turned cold.

'Of course, *ese*, why would I call you otherwise?' the hitter exclaimed irritably. 'Munoz and Rodrigo are the shooters. They're good, very good. I and other bangers will be in the parking lot, to get them away after the hit.'

'How will they get inside the hospital?'

'I don't know. They're planning it themselves. Fuse told us to be in the getaway car.'

'What time will you be there?'

'He said to be there at nine pm.'

CUTTER DRESSED AS HIS THOUGHTS RACED. HE REACHED FOR his phone to send a warning text to Difiore. *What about Covarra's informer in the LAPD?*

His fingers paused. *She and Quindica will tell Dade; the snitch will come to know soon enough. That might get Covarra to act sooner.*

No, he couldn't take the risk.

How could he stop the hit, though? He was alone, and every cop would be looking out for him.

I'll have to try.

He put his personal mission behind him as he applied his disguise. He had slept well and his body was almost back to peak physical shape. Janikyan ... his eyes narrowed as he recollected Cabal's revelations the previous night. *He isn't going anywhere,* he decided. *Lasko comes first.*

IT WAS MIDDAY WHEN HE TOOK THE LAND CRUISER TO BOYLE Heights. The choice between Limon's cab and the SUV had been easy to make. *Chuck's armored this one up. I'll need its protection in case I have to make a fast getaway with cops firing at me.*

Not just the cops. He grinned sardonically. *Street Front, too.*

The hospital was on Chavez Avenue and occupied an entire block. Brown and cream-colored walls, a small parking lot in the front, a bigger one at the back.

He parked his ride in the rear and helped a couple wheel their elderly relative from their van. He accompanied them, making small talk, looking like he was part of the family.

He drifted away when they entered the lobby and went to the coffee machine. Poured himself a drink, stood in a corner and took everything in.

Marble floor, high ceiling, large seating area, busy reception desk, at which uniformed staff directed visitors and patients. He spotted five cops, three of them alert, watchful, while the other two were lounging on couches, checking their phones.

He kept his eye on them, but none of the officers moved from their positions. *They're the perimeter; there will be more throughout the building and on Lasko's floor.*

His attention went to a wall-mounted TV where a news bulletin was playing. His photograph came up briefly as a journalist explained why he was wanted.

Cutter put on a disinterested look, briefly. He looked nothing like his real self and hadn't attracted the attention of the officers in the lobby.

He threw his coffee cup into a trashbin and went down the hallway behind a cleaning attendant.

'Buddy.' He tapped the man on his shoulder and dropped his voice conspiratorially. 'This is where that cop is? Lasko?'

'Yeah,' the attendant said wearily, 'fifth floor. He's just a cop, you know? Not some Hollywood actor.'

'Thanks, bud.' Cutter gave him a big smile. 'You just won me ten bucks. I had a bet with my friend.'

He watched the attendant go down the hallway and through a door. Returned to the lobby and watched the elevators. *I'll need a swipe card ... what about the stairs?*

They were behind large double doors that opened automatically when he neared them. He climbed swiftly, keeping his head down, and on the fifth floor pulled out his phone and talked with an imaginary caller.

'Sis,' he said loudly as he entered the corridor. 'The operation went well. Mom's in her room now ... yeah, intensive care. I'll hang around all day. You'll be coming in the evening?' He passed two cops, aware that they were sizing him up, and went to the water dispenser. 'Yeah, bring those cookies. I don't think she'll be able to eat, but she sure can smell them.'

He poured himself a cup and drank it deeply. He yawned and stretched as he turned around and took in the entire hallway.

Rooms on each side. Chairs for visitors. The two cops who had watched him, a distance away, in front of the elevators, next to which were the stairs. Doctors and nurses hustling, attendants rolling in oxygen tanks, equipment to various rooms.

He went past more rooms, a coffee machine and snack dispenser, then spotted two more officers lounging against the wall, outside a room.

Cutter scrolled through his phone as he approached them, snorted and chuckled as if he had read a joke.

'Sir?' One of them barred his way.

'Yeah?'

'Are you a patient? Visiting someone?'

'My mom's in a room down there.' He jerked his head down the corridor. 'I'm just stretching my legs. Something up?' he asked curiously.

'You can't come any further, sir. Security. Please turn back.'

'Some VIP in that room? Who is it?'

'Sir.' The officer used his command voice. 'Please leave.'

Cutter gave them a grouchy look and turned back. He occupied an empty chair and played with his phone idly as he mounted watch. He spotted Munoz and Rodrigo when they arrived through the elevators and went to the coffee machine, but nothing about them pinged his radar.

'You see them?' Rodrigo barely moved his lips as the machine filled his cup.

'Yeah.' Munoz bobbed his head in thanks as he took the drink. 'Two cops just behind us, two more down the hallway.'

'That's where Lasko is.'

They made a show of laughing at a joke and went as close as they could to the injured officer's room. They stood in front of a wall-mounted bulletin board and read through the posters and leaflets pinned to it.

'Cameras, cops, how will we do this, *ese*?' Rodrigo whispered.

'We'll have to shoot them and Lasko. No other way. Go down the stairs and join the crowd running outta here. This is bad. For us. Snake and Fuse aren't giving us enough time to plan.'

'It's all risky. You saw the cops in the lobby. They'll come rushing at the first sound of shots.'

'Snake and Fuse don't care, do they?' Munoz said bitterly. He took a deep breath and straightened his shoulders. 'We may not live through this.'

'*Ese*.' Rodrigo laughed humorlessly. 'We kill people for a living. We are bangers. You really thought you would live a long life?'

'So, we got a plan?'

'Yeah. Shoot the cops and Lasko. Go down the stairs and, hopefully, we will get to the getaway ride.'

'It would be better if we were disguised as doctors.'

'Let's kill two of them, take their coats and ID.'

CUTTER TOOK IN THE MEN AT THE BOARD AND ASSESSED THEM automatically. *They seem to be good friends.* He waited and observed, became part of the furniture, didn't attract any attention.

The shift change happened at four pm. The elevator doors opened and two officers replaced the hallway cops, after a short discussion. Two other uniformed officers took over on Lasko's detail.

Cutter saw one of them nod his head in his direction. *He's telling the arrivals about me.*

He got to his feet after half an hour and pretended to wince as if his knees hurt from the prolonged sitting. Anything to give the impression that he wasn't a threat.

He went down the stairs as he thought of the setup. *That hallway has just two exits, the elevators and the stairways. Both can be easily blocked.*

There was no easy way to hit Lasko and escape. Not unless the shooters were prepared to die.

Bangers are not suicide killers, he thought. *Shoot indiscriminately and get away. That's what they might do.*

How do I get away if I stop them?

He would be caught on cameras and the entire hospital would be alerted by the shots. *Nope, can't go down the elevators or the stairs.*

He went into the lobby and out, spotted the two men who were heading to their ride. Thought nothing of them as he circled the building and went to its side, where there was more parking. He squinted up and counted windows. *That fifth one, that's where Lasko's room is.* He could crash out through it, but there were no drain pipes, no support for him to come down. There were ledges, however, at the bottom of each window.

His eyes lingered on them, and he nodded to himself.

That would be his escape route.

🌿 76 🌿

Cutter returned at six pm. Armor over his chest, loose shirt, jacket on top, several spare magazines in his cargo pants pockets.

He nodded to the Elevator Cops and went outside a room that had no visitors. Waved at the patient through the window and grinned widely. 'I'll be here, all night,' he told the elderly woman who smiled uncertainly as she tried to place him.

He occupied a chair, pulled out his phone and briefed his nonexistent sister that he had returned with his takeout meal.

Room Cops were close to a hundred feet away, to his right. The elevator and stairs were at his ten-o'clock. No sign of bangers. Nothing on the floor to indicate that a hit was impending.

Two nurses came out of Lasko's room after a while, pushing a trolley of equipment and medicines.

'Yeah, he did that to me, too.'

Cutter's ears pricked.

'He clutched my hand. I don't think he saw me. His eyes had that wild look, you know. *He didn't come.* That's what he said. I told Choudhary about it.'

'He did the same to me, too,' the other nurse nodded. 'Shame he had a relapse. Doc said he wasn't going to tell the cops. Not yet. He thinks they will crowd around him and get him to talk. That won't be good in his current condition.'

Lasko talked? How? Wasn't he intubated?

He followed the nurses to the service elevator but didn't get anything more from them. He checked the news on his phone. No change to the cop's condition.

He must have recovered briefly. That nurse said he'd gone back to critical condition.

He returned to his seat and thought about Lasko's words. They didn't make any sense to him. *They don't have to. People say things when they are in that state.*

He read various news articles to see if there was any mention of Lasko's family. Didn't find any references.

Fired off a text to Beth.

Does Lasko have parents? Siblings?

No response.

She or Meghan are quick to respond usually. He shrugged. *They weren't there to do his bidding.*

'*Ese*,' Cesar called at eight pm. 'We are here.'

'Where?'

'In the parking lot at the back.'

'What about the shooters?'

'I don't know where they are. They said we should be ready to roll as soon as they turn up.'

'Are you alone?'

'No, *ese*,' the banger whispered, 'there are many in my ride. All of us are armed. Did you alert the cops?'

'How can I? I'm a criminal in their eyes. What do Munoz and Rodrigo look like? Will they be in disguise?'

'I've got to go,' Cesar said hurriedly, 'someone's calling me.'

. . .

A WHITE-COATED DOCTOR ARRIVED AT EIGHT-THIRTY PM WITH the same two nurses in attendance. He spoke briefly with the Room Cops and went inside Lasko's care unit.

He emerged fifteen minutes later and shook his head at the officers.

That means what, no change? He looks Asian. He could be Choud-hary, the one the nurses were talking about.

The medical team passed him, speaking too softly for him to overhear, and entered the elevator.

Cutter got to his feet and paced to the end of the hallway. Nodded at Elevator Cops and at the patient, and on his return, the elevator's doors opened and two doctors entered the corridor with their backs to him.

He went to the water dispenser and drank. Looked casually to his right, where the Room Cops were, where the medics were heading.

That's strange. Lasko just had a doctor's examination.

He tossed his cup blindly at the trashbin. Took two steps forward when one of the coated men looked at the other and laughed, giving Cutter a profile view.

That's them! Bulletin board men.

They have to be Munoz and Rodrigo.

77

Cutter grew alert as his right hand crept to his chest, ready for an easy draw.

The Room Cops straightened and faced the approaching doctors.

Their hands ... I can see only their left. They're hiding something in their right, beneath their coats.

Something dark and metallic flashed in the right man's hand.

That looks like a gun!

'HEY!' he yelled; his hand close to his Glock. He had to be sure the men were armed.

Left Banger fired at the cops without looking at him. Right Banger spun on his feet to face him.

Cutter took it in instantly. A Hispanic-looking man, cold, dark eyes, a folded-stock weapon in his hand that was rising.

He dived to the floor as his Glock came out in a smooth draw. Landed on the hard floor just as bullets burned the air over his head. Right Man didn't react at the missed shots. He started to correct his aim as screams burst out in the hallway and people fled for cover.

Cutter heard shouts and groans behind him but couldn't risk looking back. He took his time to aim. Eye to Trijicon Sights that framed Right Banger. He fired three times and knew they were good shots from the way the shooter jerked and rolled desperately to seek cover behind the water dispensing machine, as Left Banger turned.

He blanked out the panicked sounds and groans of the injured as the surviving hitter sent a flurry of rounds in his direction that struck his protective cover and the wall. A few ricocheted off the floor.

He'll come shooting. My cover's not big enough.

He timed it in his mind. Felt the floor shudder as the shooter started running. Ignored the chips of tile, plastic and concrete that flew from the impact of the rounds. Jammed his Glock between his teeth, straightened to grab the water canister, yanked it free with a savage pull and, crouching low, hurled it blindly in the direction of the approaching banger.

Left Banger in his vision, fury and startled alarm on his face as he ducked to escape the flying water container. The shooter kept firing wildly as Cutter crouched low in the hallway. Something slammed into his chest and sent him staggering back a step. A round blew past his cheek, but he held his ground, brought his Glock up and emptied his magazine at Right Banger.

Cutter fast-reloaded his Clock as he crabwalked cautiously forward and kicked the shooter's gun, an HK416, out of the way. The hitter was alive. He fired into the man's legs and shoulders to immobilize him and hurried to Right Banger.

He's dead. What about the cops?

He bent over them, felt one of them move, just as shouting reached him. He looked up to see armed cops burst into the hallway.

'STOP. THROW YOUR GUN DOWN.'

Cutter exploded in a run as guns blazed. He threw himself at the window at the end of the hallway as another round hit his armor. Glass shattered from the impact of his body. He tossed his Glock into the night, reached out desperately with his hands and grunted in relief as his fingers found the ledge and halted his fall.

He let go immediately and dropped to the lower window, caught the sill, took a fraction of a second to regain his breath and repeated his maneuver until he reached the ground.

He hunted for his Glock for a moment and then gave up. *I have spares.* He shrugged out of his jacket and hurried deeper into the parking lot. *Cops haven't cordoned it off yet.* He couldn't blame them. *They don't have enough intel ... it happened so fast.*

He ran to his Land Cruiser and climbed into it. Stuffed his jacket beneath the seat and threw his shoulder holster in the back, fired up the vehicle and joined the throng of escaping rides.

'I heard shots,' he shouted in panic at two patrol cops who were directing the vehicles. 'I was planning to visit my sister but ... what happened? Is there an active shooter? Is he firing?'

'Keep moving, sir,' the cop told him.

Cutter did as ordered and drove out of the hospital into the city. Several cruisers and command vehicles passed him as he headed to Reseda, and when he tuned to a news channel, the first reports of the incident were coming in.

'Active shooters opened fire in a hospital, injuring several people. At least four officers were among them.'

Those cops survived?

He hadn't checked the Elevator Cops to see if they had taken any rounds. There had been no time for that.

Did Cesar escape?

His phone buzzed at eleven pm.

'Did you get away, *ese?*'

'Yeah, you?'

'We didn't wait for Munoz and Rodrigo. We got away as soon as the shooting started.'

'What happened to them?'

'You didn't follow the news, *ese?*'

'Nope,' Cutter replied, tiredly.

'They died. How did you survive that? They were two of our best hitters. News says you jumped through the window.'

Sheer luck.

He recalled the glimpse he had of the intensive care room as he had raced down the hallway. The LAPD detective on his bed, pale, with tubes and machines hooked to him.

'Did Lasko say anything about family? A girlfriend? Wife?'

'We never spoke of personal matters, *ese.*'

He showered and broke out another Glock. Loaded it and put it on the night table. He didn't know if the cop would survive long enough to clear him.

It doesn't matter, he shrugged to himself. *I have questions. Panig Janikyan has the answers.*

❧ 78 ❧

Difiore and Quindica listened quietly as Matteo briefed Dade at the hospital.

They had still been in the LAPD HQ when reports of the shooting arrived.

'Eleven people injured,' the task force lead said grimly, 'of which four are our cops.'

'How seriously?' the chief rapped out.

'One, Jeff Muller, is critical. Rounds in his belly and chest. The others will survive. They were shot in the shoulder or legs. We're sweeping the hospital, but it looks like it's clean.'

'What about the third shooter?'

'Early reports were confusing, ma'am. It looks like he was firing *at* the gunmen.'

'Who were Street Front?'

'Yes, ma'am. Munoz and Rodrigo. We have extensive files on them.'

'Why were they there?'

'It's possible Covarra sent them, ma'am. To kill Lasko.'

'But why?'

'No way of knowing, ma'am.'

'This third shooter—'

'Was Cutter Grogan,' Difiore broke in. 'He must have found out somehow that Lasko was going to be killed.'

'Grogan?' Matteo whirled on her in astonishment. 'That man looked nothing like him.'

'Disguise. He's expert at them. Who else would it be? Why else would a stranger open fire on Street Front shooters?'

'There could be many reasons,' Cruz said heatedly.

'Yeah? Such as?'

'It was Grogan,' she asserted when none of the cops had an answer. 'You've got camera footage of what went down?'

'Yeah,' Matteo nodded.

'Let Quindica and me go through it as well. We'll—'

'Vance!' A cop hurried over, holding a gun in a baggie. 'We found this beneath a vehicle in the parking lot to that side. Where that shooter jumped out.'

Difiore leaned in to look at the weapon. 'Glock,' she noted. 'That's Grogan's preferred gun. I'm sure you'll find his prints on it when you dust it. He must have thrown it out when he jumped.'

Matteo looked at her, at the weapon and then at Dade. 'What I said the other day,' he said, rubbing his chin thoughtfully, 'about Grogan having some kind of a deal with Covarra ... what if Lasko was in on it, too? That would be why the Street Front wanted to kill him. Grogan got some—'

'Vance,' Dade cut him off. 'More evidence and fewer theories, please.'

'Yes, ma'am.' He nodded to Cruz and Estrada and led them away.

'That isn't true,' Difiore protested as she checked out the chief's expressionless face.

'I know.' Dade turned to her. 'Vance's got the wrong idea about both of them. He won't find any proof to back it up. Then, he'll start digging and come up with the right answers.'

'Ma'am, how did Cutter know the hit would happen?'

'Ask him when he calls.'

❦ 79 ❧

C utter saw Beth's text when he was checking the news the next day.

Lasko doesn't have anyone. His folks died young. No special person in his life, from what we can see. He's a loner.

He shrugged after considering it for a moment. He couldn't make sense of the detective's words. *They might not be significant.*

LAPD suspects you, she continued, *but haven't disclosed it to the public. Those shooters are Munoz and Rodrigo. Street Front Killers.*

He nodded to himself. He knew their identities.

He turned on the TV and followed the news for a while. *Security beefed up at the hospital. Suspected gang shooting. One cop in serious condition.*

He grimaced at that. *Could I have done anything more? Should I have shot them in their backs?*

They could have been doctors, he argued with himself. *I had to be sure.*

His phone buzzed as if on cue. Another text from Beth.

Matteo's updated the case file. He suspects you, Covarra and Lasko had some kind of arrangement. Drug dealing.

He read it in disbelief and called her immediately.

'Yeah,' she replied, as if she had been talking to him. 'He

thinks you took Street Front drugs from his warehouses. That meeting on Jesse Street was to strike a deal with him. Lasko was dirty, too. You had some kind of disagreement with both of them, shot the cop and got away.'

'That's what Matteo thinks?' he asked, stunned.

'Looks like his task force is considering that angle. You gotta admit, it makes sense from their perspective.'

'Anyone who knows me—'

'Dade knows you, but why would she overrule her best detective? She'll want to see proof. As of now, this is just speculation on Matteo's part.'

Makes sense. It changes nothing for me. LAPD was already hunting me.

'What about Lasko?'

'He's been disciplined several times. Suspended as well. There are rumors he's a racist. He's not the most reputable cop in the city. He could be dirty.'

What if that was an act? To gain the trust of snitches he was developing?

Only the detective could answer his questions, and he was in the hospital.

'Think of the upside,' she urged. 'You can walk into any gang now and they'll accept you.'

She hung up on that positive note.

He smiled ruefully, thought for several moments and then shrugged.

There wasn't anything he could do to clear himself, other than hope Lasko recovered.

No point in going to Difiore and Quindica. They might believe me, but my word won't be enough.

Got to get back to my mission.

He brought up the GPS tracking app and checked the green dot on it. *Zohrab's still in Little Armenia.*

He washed his breakfast dishes and dressed swiftly. Carried his gymbag and backpack out and considered which ride he would take. He still had the Tahoe, Limon's cab and the Land Cruiser.

I'll take the Toyota. It's built well and Chuck's beefed it up. It's sturdy enough for what I'm planning.

Cutter drove to Little Armenia and looped around Janikyan's alley in a wide circle. Fountain Avenue, Sunset Boulevard, and back. *Where should I station myself? Does it even matter?* He argued with himself. *As long as Zohrab's got the patch, I can follow him anywhere.*

He parked behind a food truck on Serrano Avenue and began the wait. It turned out not to be a long one.

The green dot moved at lunchtime, and judging by its speed, the bodyguard was in a vehicle.

He's heading to Hobart. Cutter squeezed into a narrow gap in the traffic, waved apologetically when an angry honk sounded, and sped through traffic. He drove fast, got on Fountain and took the left to Serrano, flicking his eyes between his phone and the traffic in front.

'There!' he said aloud when the green dot turned out to be a Tahoe with darkened windows. He followed it as it joined Sunset Boulevard and headed to Hollywood.

He got confirmation at a red light that Zohrab wasn't alone. *I can make out three heads inside.* He crossed his fingers and hoped one of the men was Janikyan.

He unzipped his backpack, which was on the passenger seat, searched through it and brought out the soluble trackers. He applied them liberally to his right palm and drove with his left hand.

What he planned was called PIT, Pursuit Intervention Technique, aka TVI, Tactical Vehicle Intervention, a maneuver widely used by cops and military forces to stop a fleeing vehicle.

Cutter got the opening to implement it once they had crossed Van Ness. Traffic had cleared up all the way to the next set of lights, some distance away.

He floored the gas and closed the distance to the Tahoe.

Came up on its left and swerved into it abruptly just ahead of its rear wheel.

The Tahoe skidded with an audible squeal of tires. It spun in a slow arc with rubber burning as the driver fought to control it and came to a shuddering stop almost a hundred and eighty degrees, facing the way it had come.

Cutter steered his ride to the right lane and stopped. He had to act fast, while the Tahoe's passengers were jolted and in shock from the collision.

And before cops arrive.

He jumped out with his Glock in his left hand and a hammer in his right and shattered the front and rear windows of the SUV. Zohrab, blinking in shock in the driver's seat, struggled to free his seat belt.

Cutter knocked him out with the hammer and switched the instrument and gun between hands as he took in Panig Janikyan in the rear seat. Bleeding from a cut in his forehead, clawing for the door handle, no seat belt around him. A third man by his side, who had recovered the quickest and had brought up an assault rifle.

He shot the man in the face as someone screamed in the distance. He didn't look up, didn't panic and let his surroundings fade into grey. He was nothing but controlled motion and cold, calculated action as he yanked the door open and dragged the gang leader out with his left hand. It was an awkward hold because of the hammer, and the Armenian leader punched him weakly.

Cutter took it on his chest, then crushed the gangster's lips with a savage slam of his right palm.

'You knew all along,' he growled. 'You knew those women were killed with your guns. Who was it? Did you shoot them?'

Janikyan wasn't the head of a vicious gang for nothing. He lunged forward with a roar, blood streaming from his cut lips. His fingers came up as claws to scratch and gouge.

Cutter slammed the hammer on his temple and caught his collar to drag him to his vehicle.

'Who killed them?' he yelled as he yanked his captive savagely.

The round slammed into concrete at the base of his feet.

He acted instantly and brought Janikyan in front of him as cover. Curled his left elbow around the man's throat and squeezed hard to throttle his struggling.

A vehicle was coming up fast on Sunset, with bangers hanging out of it. One of them fired wildly as he took in what was happening.

I can take Janikyan, but they'll chase me. A shootout in LA's crowded streets wouldn't go down in his favor. *They won't care who they kill, but I can't risk civilians.*

He released Janikyan and kicked him on the butt forcefully, to send him staggering at the oncoming vehicle. He fired a burst of rounds at it as it swerved and the shooters ducked inside.

'This isn't over,' he threatened Janikyan and dashed to the Land Cruiser. Fired it up in an instant and raced down Sunset. He cut through the red light, narrowly avoiding a crash with a tour bus, hung a right on Gower, twisted and turned through alleys and streets, conscious that his ride would be reported to the cops by civilians.

Got to move fast and dump it somewhere.

The journalist on the radio channel burst into excited chatter as he reported the shooting. 'They turned Sunset into the Wild West!' he exclaimed. 'Initial reports that it was a movie shoot were wrong. These were criminals—'

Cutter turned down the volume and headed into the Holly-wood Hills. Took Fern Dell Drive up into the hills and turned into The Trails, a café in the midst of Griffith Park. He parked between two SUVs and climbed out. Donned his shades and looked about casually. Hikers and families. No cops, no one looking at him suspiciously. He checked that the neighboring vehicles were empty and swiftly changed his ride's plates with spare ones he carried.

He shouldered his backpack and gymbag and hit a hiking trail.

'Camping overnight?' another traveler asked him.

'Dunno,' he grumbled. 'Some friends were supposed to join me but they're running late. Can't raise their phones.'

'Yeah, signals here suck.'

Cutter drifted off the main trail and went high up the side of the hill until he could look down on Griffith Observatory.

Got to stay here till it gets dark.

He checked his phone and smiled grimly when he saw the green dot for Zohrab had returned to Little Armenia. There was a fainter signal next to it. *That's Janikyan. He ingested a little of the soluble on my palm. That signal will fade.*

It didn't matter. He had drawn first blood.

I'll keep going after him, like I did with Covarra, until he gives in.

❦ 80 ❧

'He struck me,' Janikyan said wonderingly as a doctor cleaned up the cuts to his temple and lips. 'No one has come close to me in years, but Grogan ...' he shook his head in disbelief. 'One man could do this to me,' he waved his hand peremptorily to dismiss the medic.

'But—' the doctor protested.

'Go!'

The Armenian boss surveyed his men in the room. Zohrab, with a large, purplish bruise on his forehead, was to his side. The men from the second ride were ranged in front of him.

'Vartan was with us for a long time. He and Zohrab, the three of us, founded our gang. Now, he's dead. Killed by one man you couldn't stop.'

He held his hand out to Zohrab, who placed a dashuyn, a dagger, in his palm. It was a ceremonial weapon with an ornate handle and jewel-encrusted case. The blade gleamed when he extracted it and caught the light.

'You know the rules,' he told the assembled men. 'One of you must die for letting him get to me. Who will it be?'

None of them moved.

'Garbis?' He eyed a bushy-eyebrowed man. 'You talk a lot of

how strong and brave you are, that you would die for me. Why aren't you coming forward? Artoun, you have killed many people. You are one of the most ferocious men we have ... you are scared of death?'

He taunted each of the five men in turn, none of whom looked him in the eye.

He spun on his heel suddenly. The dagger rose in his hand and plunged into Garbis's chest.

'You ... failed ... me,' he panted as he extracted it and jabbed repeatedly as the man groaned and fell to his feet and blood splashed on his hands and face, but no one stopped him.

It was the Armenian Bros' code.

'Take him away,' Zohrab ordered when Garbis's body stopped twitching, 'and clean the floor.' He snapped his fingers and a flunky ran up with a large container of water, a jug and a fluffy towel.

Janikyan raised his arms as his bodyguard undressed him in full view of anyone in the house and then bathed, dried and dressed him in new clothes.

'Are you all right?' he asked Zohrab.

'Yes, boss. I'm sorry I couldn't—'

'We'll get him.' The gang leader dismissed his apology. Garbis's killing had given his rage an outlet. He was back in control of himself, but the fury remained in his glittering eyes.

'How did he know where we would be?'

'We sweep the house every day, boss. There are no listening devices. We check our vehicles; they're clean. He must have been watching the alley and followed us.'

Janikyan nodded absently and then snapped his fingers.

'Call him.'

'Our friend?'

'Yes.'

Zohrab dialed a number and brought the phone to his boss.

'You can't call me on this number,' the voice hissed in anger. 'Not this time of day. You know where I'll be.'

'I don't care,' Janikyan told him. 'You heard about the attack on Sunset?'

'Where do you think I am?' the speaker's voice rose.

'It was Grogan.'

'Grogan? Are you sure?'

'Yes,' Janikyan snapped. 'I know who attacked me. It was him. No disguise. Meet me tonight. Usual place.'

'I'm in the middle of an investigation.'

'Do I care? Have you forgotten our arrangement?'

JANIKYAN WAS FACEDOWN, BEING POUNDED BY A MASSEUSE, when the man arrived. They were at a spa in Little Armenia wholly owned by his gang. It closed to customers whenever he was present. Every member of staff was vetted and searched, and the entire establishment was checked for weapons and surveillance devices whenever he visited.

'What have you found out?'

'Grogan disappeared,' the man grunted while another masseuse worked on him.

'How can he vanish like that?' Janikyan asked calmly. He didn't need to raise his voice. He was aware his visitor knew how dangerous he was.

'We identified the vehicle he drove, a Land Cruiser, but that's one of the most common SUVs in the city. No vehicle thefts of that make have been reported—'

'He'll use false plates.'

'I am aware. We have found nothing, however. We stopped several drivers and all we got was angry citizens.'

'LAPD, with all its resources, has nothing?'

'Give it time.'

'Time,' Janikyan snorted. 'Was it him in the hospital? Why was he there?'

'To protect Lasko.'

'The man you want dead.'

'Yeah. I don't trust him.'

'He's not talking, in any case,' Janikyan said callously.

'We'll get Grogan. He can't escape forever. He's just one man.'

'I'll get him,' the Armenian said, bunching his fists. 'I know what to do.'

'What's that?'

'You'll know when you see Grogan's body.'

❧ 81 ❧

How *is that other cop?* Cutter messaged Difiore. *The one who got shot in the hospital.*

Did you shoot him?

No!

Why do you care, then?

I was there to save Lasko!

How did you know it would go down?

I can't tell you.

Why should I believe anything you say?

Because, he replied spiritedly, *I seem to be the only one who's doing something!*

Why don't you get back to doing something, in that case, she texted sarcastically, *instead of wasting my time.*

He had no reply to that and checked the green dots on his screen. Both Zohrab and Janikyan were still in their locations.

I can't repeat yesterday's move. They'll be alert to it. Is there an Armenian Bros cache that I can strike and force him to talk to me?

He sucked his breath sharply when the call came. *Number withheld. That could be Covarra or Janikyan.*

'That was some move yesterday,' the Armenian Bros leader

said coldly. 'No one has ever touched me, other than my own men—'

'I didn't touch you,' Cutter reminded him. 'I hit you. I should have buried the claws of that hammer in you.'

'There won't be a next time for you. There will be for me, however. I'll dangle you from a meat hook, upside-down, and rip your body—'

'That's what Covarra said he'd do to me, too. Do you two compare notes? He threatened a lot, and what happened? He lost a lot of his drugs and men. I'm still free, but he—'

'This is not Iraq or Afghanistan or Cameroon,' Janikyan swore. 'This is my city. My people have eyes and ears everywhere. You can't escape, you can't hide—'

'Did you kill my friends?'

'I'll watch you bleed—'

'Did you shoot them? Did you rape them?'

'You don't know what you've got yourself mixed up in. You should have left the city after the funeral.'

'You,' Cutter fought to control his rage, 'are a gangster. A small one. You are nothing but a sewer rat—'

'Enjoy your freedom, Grogan. It won't last. The next time we speak it will be—'

'Did you kill them?'

'You'll have to meet me to know that,' and with that the Armenian hung up.

Cutter brooded for a moment before jamming the phone in his pocket. The call had given him an idea. *There's someone who might know where the Bros operations are.*

He had to gear up appropriately for that, however.

'I NEED A VAN,' HE TOLD BETH AND MEGHAN WHEN HE GOT them on a call.

'You can steal one. Why do you need us for that?' the elder sister asked.

'This one is different. It has to be a gas company van.'

'You want to go as a gas technician?' Meghan mocked him. 'You've been reading too many pulp thrillers—'

'It's the third house on the left on Apple Street, in Mid-City,' he interrupted, before she or Beth started ribbing him. 'It's used by Street Front as a store.'

'You know this, how?' Beth commanded. He could hear keys clicking in the background.

'Not important.'

'Got it,' she said softly, almost to herself. He could picture her and Meg in their New York office, intense concentration on their faces as they brought up satellite images of the street.

'SoCalGas is the energy supplier to that house,' the older twin informed him. 'You'll need their van, or one that looks like theirs, their uniform ...' she trailed off.

'We'll need to log him in their system,' Beth told her, both of them talking as if he didn't exist.

'Yeah, we can do that. We can hack into it—you can't be alone. Their technicians rarely go out on their own.'

Who can I take with me? Cutter frowned as he thought hard and smiled to himself when it came to him.

'You can get uniforms for me and another person? He'll be about an inch shorter than me, about the same build.'

'We can get you an Abrams tank.'

They probably mean it, too.

'Give us three hours,' Meghan told him. 'We'll text you where you can find the van, the uniforms, the equipment inside, everything you'll need.'

'How are you able to organize this stuff when you're not in the city?'

'You'll never know that.'

'Why are you folks helping me this much?'

'We want you alive long enough for Difiore to slap cuffs on you.'

They chortled when he had no comeback to that and hung up.

'No!' Isaiah Limon shook his head firmly. 'I have no idea who you are, what crazy stuff you're up to. You got me to crash into a car on Sadler, I did that for you. I gave you my cab—'

'And you got paid well for that.' Cutter fanned himself with bills. 'These bennys,' he added, looking pointedly at the hundred-dollar notes in his hand, 'are yours. You need to drive a van for me. That's all.'

'Nope. Nada. Read my lips. Where's my car?'

'I see you got a new one. Why do you need another?'

'Go.' The driver gesticulated angrily and took a breath when that got the attention of a few travelers at LAX-it. 'I don't want to see you anymore.'

'My heart's broken,' Cutter told him solemnly. 'I thought you and I had a thing going on.'

Limon looked at him as if he had lost his senses.

'You've earned more money by helping me than by driving people around.'

'I'm alive, I'm not arrested. That matters to me,' the cab driver retorted.

'You'll be all of that, and richer, if you come with me.'

'Come where?'

'To Mid-City.'

'And do what?'

'Nothing,' Cutter told him innocently. 'You just need to sit in a van and look official.'

'Official? Like what?'

'Like a gas technician.'

❦ 82 ❧

'I don't want to see you again,' Limon grouched as he drove his new cab to a big-box store on Sepulveda Boulevard. 'When this is over, you get out of my life and never return.'

'You don't know what I really look like,' Cutter reasoned with him. 'How would you know if I came to you in a disguise?'

The driver looked at him suspiciously and turned back to the street when a car honked behind him.

'Ever since I met you—'

'You've made more money than ever before. Go to the back,' Cutter instructed him when they reached the store.

He fist-pumped inwardly when he saw the white panel SoCalGas van parked in a corner, with no other vehicle near it.

'Is this stolen?' Limon eyed the vehicle warily when he got out.

I don't know.

'No,' he replied confidently. He went to the rear wheel well and ran his hand along its arch. Grunted in satisfaction when he found the key attached magnetically.

He unlocked the vehicle and opened the rear doors. Cast his eyes appreciatively over the racks of equipment inside. He brought out his phone when it buzzed. A text from Beth.

You'll need to carry the tool bag, which is to your right, on the lower shelf. The scheduler is above it. You'll have to get the occupant's signature on it. If you get any questions, get them to call the number printed on it.

'What's that?' Limon demanded. 'Who's messaging you?'

'Nothing to do with you,' Cutter pocketed the phone and picked up the scheduler. It had SoCalGas's logo on it, a telephone number and a stylus for writing on the screen or taking signatures. He pressed a button on the screen and a job number came up, assigned to Roy Pollock. *That's me.*

'Here,' he handed the driver a uniform, 'change into this.'

He went to his backpack while Limon changed and inspected the equipment he would need. Explosives, remote-controlled detonators, cables—yeah, he had everything he needed.

'You look smart,' he told the driver when he emerged. 'Here,' he tossed him a set of cheek pads and a false nose. 'Apply these, too.'

'Why?'

'You want anyone to describe Isaiah Limon?'

'I HAVE NEVER EVER DONE THIS,' THE DRIVER SWORE SOFTLY AS he navigated the van expertly to Mid-City.

'You have never earned ten grand for doing nothing, either.' Cutter pushed his seat back and closed his eyes.

'If we get caught—'

'We won't. Drive, look as if you belong behind that wheel, say you're Brice Lanza, employee of SoCalGas, show them your identity card. Relax, you're cool.'

'Easy for you to say,' Limon grumbled. 'You do this for a living.'

'How do you know that?'

'Have you looked at yourself, dude? This comes so easy to you.'

'Wake me up when we get there.'

. . .

Cutter was conscious of eyes on him when he opened the gate to the Apple Street house and went up the walkway. *Can't see anyone, but I can feel them watching from inside.*

He went to the door and knocked firmly. Repeated it when there was no response. Was raising his fist when a burly man opened it.

'Yeah?' the man asked rudely.

Tats all over his arms and on his neck. His right hand's behind his body, probably holding a gun.

'SoCalGas,' Cutter tapped his uniform. 'I need to inspect your meter, the water heater and run a few checks. We're getting faulty readings from several houses in Mid-City.'

The banger looked at him and then at the van on the street in which Limon sat. He shifted his weight as he breathed noisily.

I bet he's never had to deal with a gas technician.

'YO!' he half-turned and bellowed. 'Someone's here.'

A lean man came to him, eyes watchful, face still.

He's likely to be the shot-caller on the street. Tasked with protecting the product inside.

'Yeah?' the arrival asked him.

'Got to inspect your meter and equipment,' Cutter repeated his story.

'No one told us about that.'

'No one will. You don't get calls beforehand. We are checking every house in Mid-City; yours is next on my run. Here,' he opened the electronic scheduler and turned it around for the bangers to see. 'Roy Pollock, that's me.'

'We're in the middle of something,' the shot- caller said, giving him a false smile. 'Come back later.'

'No can do,' Cutter shook his head. 'We've got several complaints already, and if I don't fix this today, my boss will have my ass. Look, this won't take long. About half an hour at the most.'

'We've never had a gas—'

'Sir, please call my office and speak to them. They'll confirm what I said.'

'All right.' The shot-caller glared at him and checked out the SoCalGas van on the street. 'Meter's outside. Felipe will take you to the water heater when you're done.'

'Keep an eye on him,' he told the hitter in Spanish in what he thought was a low tone, but Cutter heard and understood him.

'CAN YOU GIVE ME SOME ROOM?' HE LOOKED BACK IN irritation when Felipe crowded behind him at the meter. 'This is gas. It can be dangerous. Step away, please.'

'I've got to—'

'You can go to the front and stay in the yard. Safety regulations, sir. There's shade there.' He dropped his voice.

Felipe looked at him as he wiped his sweat and nodded.

Cutter turned to the meter swiftly when the banger had disappeared around the corner. He molded C4 and applied it to the rear of the equipment. Inserted a detonator, rigged up the remote receiver and used electrical tape to cover the assembly.

He went to the front and nodded to Felipe. 'Need to go inside, to the water heater.'

The banger wheezed as he climbed the porch and entered the house. 'Toy gun,' he laughed uneasily when Cutter eyed the AK47 that was propped against a wall. 'I and several friends are renting this place.' He nodded when another man appeared in a hallway, looked at them and went inside a room. 'We were fooling around when you came.'

I bet you were.

Felipe took him to the utility room at the back and pointed to a wall-mounted water heater.

'Need to work alone, buddy,' Cutter told him softly, waited for the hitter to leave and was turning to the heater when he heard the murmur of voices outside.

He unscrewed its panel and repeated the procedure, with one

difference. He jammed a tiny wireless camera into the explosive and programmed it to broadcast images to his phone. The device was linked to a satellite signal, with a battery that lasted for a week.

I won't need that long.

'All done.' He wiped his hands on a paper towel as he joined Felipe in the living room. 'I might have to return if we still get wrong readings. Sign here, please,' he thrust the scheduler at the hitter, who looked indecisive and then picked up the stylus and scribbled on the pad.

'WHAT DID HE DO?' ESTEBAN ASKED FELIPE WHEN THE GAS technician had departed.

'He fixed something, applied tape.' He shrugged his shoulders. 'I wasn't watching all the time.'

'Fixed something?' The shot-caller frowned. 'I thought he was going to inspect the meter, that's all.'

'I don't know what technicians do,' the banger said defensively.

'Show me.'

Felipe took him outside and pointed at the meter. 'He did something there and covered it in tape.'

Esteban crouched over the piping as he tried to figure out what lay beneath the covering. He prodded it with his fingers and felt some give.

'What about at the water heater?'

'I didn't stay around to watch,' the hitter said when they entered the utility room. 'I heard him remove the cover. Don't know what he did afterwards.'

'Screwdriver,' Esteban commanded.

'Why're you so uptight about this? He's a gas technician!'

'Because,' the shot-caller snarled, 'in all these years, no technician has ever come to this place.'

'You should have called the office and checked it out then.'

'I DID! THEY DID SEND POLLOCK OUT—' Esteban bellowed.

'Then what's the big deal?'

'Get me a screwdriver.'

Felipe huffed and went away reluctantly and returned with several.

The thug's boss inspected them and chose one. He turned to the heater and unscrewed the front panel.

'What's this?' he peered at the tiny lens that was stuck in what seemed to be a similar assembly to what was at the meter. 'Is that a camera?'

He sucked his breath sharply as he worked out the meaning of the wires that could be seen beneath the tape.

'IT'S A BOMB!'

He raced out of the room with Felipe on his heels and dashed for the door. His feet faltered when he reached the exit.

'What?' the thug asked him. 'We have to get away.' More bangers joined them in a chorus of voices and angry yells.

'Quiet!' Esteban snapped. 'Why would he put a camera on it?'

'What are you doing?' Felipe yelled at him angrily when he returned to the room.

The shot-caller paid no heed and inspected the explosive again. He peered behind it and exclaimed in surprise when he saw the card that had fallen.

It had a single line of writing on it.

TELL COVARRA TO CALL ME.

83

'What is it?'

Covarra held his finger up to silence Salazar as he took in Esteban's excited chatter.

'That's all on that card? No name, no number?'

'No, boss. I called SoCalGas and they confirmed a technician's visit had been scheduled.'

'You're sure it's a bomb?'

'No, but I won't know until I remove the tape—'

'Don't touch it!'

'I won't, boss,' Esteban said with feeling. 'What do we do?'

'Stay there. Don't allow anyone to come to the house. No technicians, no building inspectors, no one. Am I clear?'

'Si, but what about the bomb?'

'DON'T YOU THINK IT WOULD HAVE GONE OFF BY NOW, IF IT WAS MEANT TO?' Covarra exploded and hung up angrily.

'I have to do all the thinking here,' he complained, glaring at the only other person in the room, Salazar. 'I am surrounded by fools.'

'What happened, Snake? There's a bomb?'

'DIDN'T YOU HEAR?' Covarra shouted at him, forgetting

that only he could hear Esteban's call. 'SOME ONE CAME TO OUR APPLE STREET HIDEOUT AND PLANTED TWO BOMBS THERE.'

Salazar stared at him in disbelief. 'Bombs? Two of them?'

'SI. AND THAT MAN LEFT A NOTE THAT I SHOULD CALL HIM.'

'The bomber? He left a number? How do you know—'

'DON'T YOU GET IT?' Covarra grabbed his friend's shirt and shook him physically. 'ONLY ONE MAN COULD HAVE DONE THIS.' He grunted with effort. 'ONE MAN WHO HAS BEEN AFTER ME. IT'S GROGAN.'

EVENING.

Cutter was in the van, his seat reclined as far back as it would go, sipping coffee from a takeout joint.

He had paid Limon off after their return from Apple Street. The driver had waggled his finger at him and warned him never to call or approach him again.

He moved his gear to the SoCalGas vehicle after his accomplice's departure, figuring the ride was safe enough to use for a while.

Beth and Meg would have ensured its plates will be legit. The company's logo will arouse no suspicion.

He broke a cookie and stuffed half of it in his mouth. Stopped chewing when it brought back a memory.

Arnedra loved Lin Shun's desserts. The Chinese American owned a bodega in New York, along with her husband and another business partner. It was her baking that attracted customers from all over the city, however. *Those cookies that Beth and Meg gave us ... she was into them, too.*

Her loss was like a hole in his heart, a vast emptiness that he knew from experience wouldn't ever be filled. He squeezed his eyes shut, and when he opened them, his detached self was back.

He was wiping his fingers on his jeans when his phone buzzed.

'Yeah?' he answered, without checking the screen. He knew who was calling.

'I'LL KILL YOU—'

'Don't you think that's repetitive?' He cut off Covarra's low hiss. 'You live in LA, the center of the entertainment world. Movies are made here. You can't come up with some better lines?'

He grinned when he heard the gangster grinding his teeth. 'You won't kill me,' he told the Street Front leader coldly. 'You don't know where I am ... heck, for all you know I might be looking down at you through a scope.'

He chuckled when he heard the gangster draw a sharp breath.

'Relax. I don't want to kill you. Not yet. I want something from you.'

'What?'

'First, those bombs. If you or your men touch them, or bring someone, they'll go off. I can see and hear everything through that camera. I'll know if you try to tamper with them. You know what will happen if they go boom. You've got product there, don't you? Imagine those baggies burning. Say, how're you getting on with the Juarez Cartel? Have you managed to pay them—'

'WHAT DO YOU WANT?'

Cutter winced at Covarra's scream and held the phone away from his ear.

'Where do the Armenian Bros keep their product?'

✺ 84 ✺

'Why do you need that?' Covarra stiffened in surprise, momentarily forgetting his rage.

'That's not your business. I'm sure you know where Janikyan has his warehouses. You and he have been attacking each other's gangs for years.'

'If I knew, don't you think we would have taken them over?'

'I don't care what you do or don't do. It's six pm. I'll give you four hours. Your next call had better be about a location.'

Covarra swore when Grogan hung up. He ran his fingers through his short hair as he paced the room.

'What did he want?'

'Where the Bros have their product,' he told Salazar bitterly. 'As if we know!'

'We would have attacked if we did.'

'That's what I told him, but he wasn't listening. If he destroys that house, we're done. We'll be as good as wiped out. I have told the Mexicans to be patient ... but how long will they keep quiet? If we don't have product to sell, how will we make money?'

'Why's he interested in Janikyan?'

'How would I know?'

348

'Why don't you ask him?'

'I just spoke to him. Weren't you listening?'

'I mean Panig Janikyan.'

THE ARMENIAN BROS LEADER DIDN'T PACE HIS LIVING ROOM the way Covarra did. He was still, staring into space, as Zohrab dealt with the gang's business.

He stirred when his bodyguard brought him a beverage. 'Everything going okay?'

'Yes, boss.'

'Grogan?'

'He's in the wind, boss.' The banger made a face. 'We've got men looking for him ...'

'We won't find him. He's too good for that.'

He sipped his drink appreciatively and licked his lips. 'Where's Toros?'

'I can get him, boss. Should I?'

'Yeah. Covarra doesn't suspect that we know he's a snitch?'

'No, boss. We've deliberately been feeding him low-level information. Why do you need him, boss?'

'It's time to meet Covarra.'

THE BANGER ARRIVED AT EIGHT PM AND STOOD NERVOUSLY IN the Little Armenia house.

'Toros,' Janikyan said, smiling briefly, 'it's the first time I have met you. I hear a lot about you.'

'It's an honor to be here, boss.' The thug bobbed his head in a jerky bow.

'We know you're Snake's snitch.'

The hood's eyes widened in terror. His face turned pale. 'I ... no ...'

'It's all right,' Janikyan said, soothingly. 'I've known about it for a long time. You're still alive for a reason. I've been using you. Whatever you've told Snake has been approved by me.'

'I ... don't ... understand.'

'You don't need to,' Janikyan told him sharply. 'Make contact with Snake. Tell him I want to meet him.'

'He wants to meet with you too, boss.'

The gang leader looked at him in surprise.

'I got the message as I was coming here, boss. Snake wants me to set up a meeting.'

THEY MET IN THE BROS-OWNED MASSAGE PARLOR IN LITTLE Armenia.

Covarra had been reluctant to meet there initially but had given in when Janikyan threatened to call it off.

'My people will be there. If you try anything, there will be shooting,' he had warned.

Janikyan greeted the Street Front boss as if they were close friends when the leader arrived at eight pm.

'Your men and my men will be in the outside room. This place is secure. We check it every day for surveillance devices; every employee is hand-picked; you don't have to fear anything.' He led the gangster inside, stripped and lay down on his belly for the masseuse to work on him.

'How can I be sure you won't cut my throat here?'

'Have you seen this place?' Janikyan barked at him. 'I won't spill your blood here. I'll kill you somewhere else if I have to do that. Relax, Covarra,' he said impatiently. 'There will only be talking here. No fighting.'

He hid a grin when Covarra lay down on the bed reluctantly and winced when his masseuse began pounding him with the sides of her hands.

'You go first,' he told the Street Front boss.

'I have an enemy, Grogan,' the man gasped.

'I've heard of him. He's all over TV.'

'He's hunting for you, too.'

Janikyan pretended to look surprised and stared at him.

'Me? Why?'

'I don't know. He planted two bombs in my warehouse. If I don't give up one of your stores, he says he'll blow my place up.'

'How does this concern me? It's your problem.'

'Are you following the news? Grogan was some kind of hotshot special forces soldier. He has destroyed two of my warehouses already. If he's hunting you, it's only a matter of time before he gets you. Don't be overconfident.'

'Why should I give up my location to save you?'

'I'm not asking you to do that. But, together, we can set a trap for him. I have to call him in a couple of hours.'

'Call him tomorrow, to Warner Boulevard. In the evening.'

'Why there?'

'Tell him you'll give him the address, but in person. He has to show himself.'

'He won't agree to that.'

'He will. He needs that address desperately. He wouldn't go to the trouble of planting bombs if he didn't.'

'I'm not sure—'

'Tell him you'll be there, too.'

'Why should I risk myself?'

'You want Grogan taken out? Yeah? In that case, do it like I say. Both of you, on Warner Boulevard, tomorrow evening. I'll take care of the rest.'

'How do I know you won't kill me, too?'

Janikyan looked at him contemptuously. 'I could kill you here, right now. Your men wouldn't know it. Why would I wait till tomorrow? You've got to trust me.'

'How will it go down tomorrow?'

'You call me and point out which vehicle Grogan is in.'

'What's on Warner Boulevard?'

'Grogan's grave.'

85

'Why can't you tell me right now?' Cutter seethed when the Street Leader called him. 'Should I blow up your warehouse? I'll do that—'

'STOP!' Covarra yelled. 'How can I trust you?' Covarra exhaled harshly. 'I can give you the location, but you still might go ahead and explode those bombs.'

'You can't, just as I know you will double-cross me.'

'That's why I'm proposing this,' the gang leader said triumphantly. 'Let's meet in Burbank. Warner Boulevard.'

'What's there?' he asked suspiciously. *Film studios over there, not much else.* 'You producing a movie? Life and times of Francisco Covarra, a biopic?'

His sarcasm was lost on the gangster, who told him coldly, 'Be there. Alone. We'll meet face to face—'

'Like last time, when you planned to kill me?'

'Puto, I still want to do that. I still want to bury my knife in you. But that will have to wait. Come there. I will tell you where Armenian Bros warehouse is when I see you.'

'Tell me here and now.'

'No. Go ahead. Blow that warehouse. We'll survive.'

'You won't. Juarez Cartel will send hitters after you.'

'Snake does not fear anyone,' Covarra said proudly. 'You want your address, come to Warner Boulevard today.'

Cutter scratched his forehead as he considered the gangster's call. *What's he up to? Why does he want me there?* He was sure Street Front would set a trap for him ... but where? *That's an open street. There'll be traffic, tour buses.*

He shook his head and gave up trying to figure out Covarra's motives. *It'll work in my favor, too. He won't be able to take me out in the open.*

He needed a foil, however. Some way he wouldn't be recognized immediately even if Street Front filled the street with its bangers.

He drove to LAX-it.

'DID YOU SET IT UP?' JANIKYAN ASKED WHEN COVARRA CALLED him. The two men had set up a protocol for communication. Burner phones, which were replaced after every interaction, both knowing that the truce between the two gangs was temporary.

'Si. He'll come. How will we take him out, though? There will be many people there.'

'Meet him on the corner of Cordova Street and the boulevard. There's an incomplete building there. Developer ran out of funds and got into trouble with the city. We'll kill him there.'

'No.' LIMON BACKED OFF WHEN CUTTER APPROACHED HIM.

'How do you know I'm not a passenger?'

'Dude,' the driver said, laughing, 'that beard, that silver hair, those sideburns ... they don't fool me. Only one person has come to me here. You!'

'Yeah? About that, why is it you are never with passengers?'

'It's my break. You know how I work.'

'If you do this last job for me, you'll never have to work again. I'll give you twenty ks.'

'What use is money if I'm dead?'

'Did anyone come after you when we were on Apple Street yesterday? You gotta trust me.'

'Trust you!' Limon scoffed and shook his head in disbelief. 'You've never shown me who you really are and you—'

'Isaiah, that's for your safety. I need you for this job.'

'What do I have to do?' the driver growled.

'Be my passenger.'

CUTTER DROVE TO WARNER BOULEVARD WITH ISAIAH LIMON in the rear seat. He checked his mirrors when he entered the street from Riverside Drive and scanned vehicles and passersby as he went up slowly.

'Who are you looking for?' the driver asked from the rear.

Should I tell him?

'Some of those men from Apple Street might be here.'

'Hey! You said they wouldn't come after us.'

'That's not what I said, but in any case, they won't recognize you. Those cheek pads you have and those streaks in your hair ... they make you different.'

'I'm going to haunt you if I die.'

'You won't. Keep watching the street and let me know if you spot anyone suspicious.'

Limon grumbled and cursed but watched out of the windows.

Cutter drove past Avon Street and hung a right on Cordova. Didn't see bangers or Covarra. A tour bus rolled past with cameras flashing in its windows. People came out of offices, got into their street-parked cars and headed for home. *It'll get quiet in another half an hour.*

He joined Olive Avenue, turned on Riverside Drive and entered Warner Boulevard for a second pass.

His phone buzzed when he passed an unmarked alley on his right.

'Yeah?' He turned on the speaker.

'Puto,' Covarra's voice filled the cab. 'Where are you?'

He saw Limon jerk in surprise in the rearview mirror. He held his finger up to silence his question and checked out both sides of the street as he inched forward slowly.

No vehicles behind him. No one approaching them on foot. The parked cars on the street were empty. *Only snipers from high above can take me out, but these are office buildings on both sides. Covarra's got juice, but not so much that his shooters can infiltrate them.*

No, he shook his head. He's planning something else. *If he's here.*

'Show yourself,' he ordered. 'Otherwise I'm leaving and you can forget about your meth and oxy.'

'Are you on the Boulevard, puto?'

'I'm entering it,' he lied.

'Come inside. You'll see me. In a Suburban.'

Another unmarked alley. More people unlocking their vehicles and driving away to homes, friends, dinners and families.

No Covarra. No Salazar. No SUV in sight.

Something flashed in the distance. Light reflecting off a windscreen.

That vehicle, in that unmarked alley that joins Avon. Is it Covarra?

He squinted as he tried to make out the ride, but the glare was intense.

'Isaiah,' he told his passenger abruptly. 'You see that tour bus parked on our left, just ahead?'

'Yeah, what about it—'

'Get out when we're passing it. From the left door. Take that gym bag with you.'

'What? Why? That's heavy, dude—'

'Isaiah, do it,' he used his command voice. 'This is going to get nasty. You don't want to be here when the shooting starts.'

'But—'

'GO, NOW!'

Limon hesitated for a moment and then ducked and grunted as he grabbed the bag. Flung open the passenger door and slid out.

'What will I do with this?'

'I'll find you at your usual place.'

Cutter sped up a fraction when he saw the driver duck and disappear swiftly, using the bus as cover.

Eyes back to the front. To the vehicle that was inching out of that alley on his right, up ahead.

It was a Suburban. Black. Dark windows.

He held the wheel with his left hand and brought his right to his chest. Close to his Glock. He had enough magazines in his cargo pants and more weapons and equipment on his pack strapped to his back.

He drove forward.

'DO YOU SEE HIM?' JANIKYAN ASKED.

'No. There are just a few other vehicles here. An empty cab—'

'That's him.'

'No. I can see the driver. He doesn't look like Grogan—'

'Covarra, he'll be in disguise. He's not stupid. Identify yourself, see what he does.'

'What if he shoots at me?'

'YOU'VE GOT MORE MEN THAN HIM,' Janikyan exploded. 'Confirm that it's him. I'll handle the rest.'

The Street Front leader stiffened in anger at the Armenian's yell. He lowered his window, nevertheless, enough for his face to be seen.

. . .

CUTTER SAW THE DARK PANE SLIDE DOWN. A FACE APPEARED in the frame. Dark hair, savage face, hostile eyes staring right at him.

That's Covarra.

'I see you,' he told the gangster.

'Is that you in the cab?'

'Yeah.'

'Keep going.'

'That's not what we agreed. Give me the address. When I've confirmed it's a Bros warehouse, I'll defuse the bomb.'

'Drive! I need to see you're alone. That you haven't brought cops.'

'Cops?' Cutter laughed scornfully as he kept going. Covarra was at his two-o'clock, his head cocked sideways. *Is he talking to someone else?* 'Have you watched the news? I'm as wanted as you are.'

'IT'S HIM,' COVARRA WHISPERED LOUDLY IN THE SECOND phone that a banger held up for him.

'Keep talking to him,' Janikyan ordered. 'He'll be distracted. You drive out in the opposite direction once he's passed you.'

'WHO ARE YOU TALKING TO?' CUTTER ASKED, LOCKING EYES with the banger as he drew abreast.

'My men. I'm telling them how I'll enjoy killing you.'

'Enough games. Where's the location?'

'In a moment.'

'Why? What are you waiting for?' His eyes went to the rearview mirror as the Suburban came up on it. He frowned when it entered the boulevard and turned towards Riverside Drive. 'Where are you going? Where's that address?'

'Puto, I wish it was me—'

Cutter sensed the movement. He swiveled his head and

watched in horror as the cement truck lurched out of Avon Street and headed right at him.

'HEY!' he yelled at the driver.

Another SUV ahead, on the street, to his right, which hadn't been there on his previous run. A man grinning at him from the passenger window.

Janikyan!

'I told you I would come for you,' the gangster shouted.

The truck crashed into Cutter's cab.

❧ 86 ❧

The force of the impact buckled the passenger door and crumpled the side of the cab. The truck shoved the vehicle to the sidewalk on Cutter's left. It kept coming, its engine whining as the taxi offered temporary resistance.

He freed his seatbelt and fired wildly at the truck's windscreen. Felt rather than saw his rounds punch holes in the glass.

His ride slid jerkily on concrete. A wire mesh fence approached that separated an under-construction building from the sidewalk. He sensed thugs spilling out of Janikyan's SUV.

Cutter kicked his door open and squeezed out of his cab just as it slammed into the fence and brought it crashing down. He fired over its roof, long bursts at the approaching thugs, and sent them diving and ducking for cover.

They didn't shoot back. Janikyan wants me alive.

That bought him some time.

He leapt over the fallen wire mesh and went deeper into the incomplete building. Realized instantly that he was trapped. High walls around it to protect the surrounding neighborhood from the construction. *No way I can scale that.*

He heard shouts and yells and thought he heard Janikyan issuing orders.

No other traffic. No screams. Did he block off the roads?

He would worry about it later.

Cutter ran up dust-laden stairs, leapt over iron bars and concrete blocks, surveyed open space that was the second floor. Spotted a tree in the distance just as he heard footsteps pounding below.

He rushed to the edge of the floor and saw that the tree was on a neighboring alley, a dead end, with branches that hung deep over the road.

He fired several rounds as the first head came up over the stairs. Saw it disappear. More shouts came to him.

Cutter took several steps back and ran full tilt to the edge of the floor. He threw himself into the air with outstretched arms.

Did I get it wrong?

A branch slapped his face and then his fingers had gripped a tree limb and he hauled himself through its leaves, gasping as sticks and shoots raked his cheeks and neck.

The tree held. It took his weight and had enough sturdy limbs to let him crawl swiftly deeper inside. He paused for a moment and looked behind him. Several thugs stood at the open edge of the floor, gesticulating in his direction. More hitters entered the dead-end alley and ran towards the tree.

It wasn't time to linger.

He got to the high wall that bordered the studio and jumped over it. Fell several feet and landed awkwardly on concrete.

He was in a studio complex. Safe.

But, from the sound of raised voices, he wouldn't be for long.

❧ 87 ❧

Cutter got to his feet and oriented himself quickly. Wide streets and large buildings around him. An electric vehicle passed him, with its occupants giving him a curious look.

Covarra sold me out, he thought bitterly. *He and Janikyan have gotten together, somehow, to nail me.*

He had to escape, go south. *The LA River is that way. I can get away from there.*

He hustled quickly as he felt his face and arms. It looked like he had numerous small cuts from the branches, which stung, but none seemed to be bleeding much. He went along the side of a tall building, rounded the corner into an alley—and came across three men.

Bros!

He recognized them instantly from their manner—the narrowed eyes, the hands reaching beneath their shirts.

Can't risk shooting and drawing more people.

He went at them with a roar, leapt high and crashed into them. His right leg smashed wickedly into the farthest banger's face. He chopped with the edge of his palm and caught the nose of the hitter on the left. They went down, him on top, kicking, gouging, using his elbows, body weight and temporary advantage to knock them out.

The hitter in the middle punched up and caught him in the neck, then reared up with his body and dislodged him. Leaned over him, drew his fist back and hit Cutter repeatedly in the chest and face.

The red mist descended on Cutter. He felt the gangster beneath him moving, trying to extricate himself. He elbowed the Armenian savagely in the temple just as he took another blow on the neck. His vision was dimming; his world had constricted. He saw only the leering face of his attacker above him.

He trapped the incoming fist with both hands and twisted his body to pull the attacker's arm down, to smash his hand on the ground. The shock of the blow sent a shudder through the banger, who groaned. Cutter jabbed his chin sharply, making his jaws snap and his head roll back, which exposed the man's throat enough for him to deliver a killing blow.

He got to his feet drunkenly, shook off an arm that weakly tried to stop him and kicked that thug in the groin for good measure.

He lurched into a run down the alley, sucking lungfuls of air, drawing in oxygen to clear his mind. Reached an intersection and heard a vehicle coming on his right.

Janikyan in his SUV, his head leaning out with a victorious grin.

Cutter didn't have a choice.

He drew his Glock and fired a long burst at the vehicle, making it swerve. Men shouted from within it as another banger's vehicle drove up.

He didn't linger.

He darted across the street into a narrow passage. Low-slung construction to his left that resembled a European village. *That's what it is. A movie set.* He heard shouts from behind and saw several thugs racing down the alley, following him. *Can't outrun them, not in my condition. Can't shoot them down, either.*

The eave of a house caught his eye, and before his mind could translate it into action, he jumped high, grabbed its edge and swung himself up on top of the house. He crouched low and ran over the uneven surface of the roof.

It was a make-believe house, not a full-fledged construction. He hoped it would take his weight.

It did.

The set had several such residences, closely grouped, with narrow alleys in between. Cutter leapt from roof to roof, heard scrambling behind him and, when he turned to look, saw bangers giving chase.

He burst into full speed, running heedlessly in the general direction of the river, making good progress. *They won't shoot. Janikyan wants me alive.* That was to his advantage.

The flimsy roof collapsed. He went down, along with a swath of tarpaulin that cushioned his fall. His head glanced off a beam, and he stumbled as he got to his feet.

Four men were facing him when he straightened.

Cutter had no choice.

He drew faster than they could and shot the two on the left in the chest. Trained his Glock on the last man, who was reacting faster, when the banger in the middle charged at him with a ferocious yell.

Cutter stepped aside nimbly, tripped him and sent him sprawling. The fourth man stooped and grabbed a loose wedge of construction material and slashed at him wildly. The first blow struck him in the ribs; the second missed his face by an inch. He backed up, stumbled over the fallen man and shot his attacker just before he lost his balance.

The thug on the ground got an elbow around his neck.

'GOT HIM!' he yelled and squeezed.

Cutter shifted his body as much as he could, pointed his Glock downwards and shot the hitter in the thigh. He rolled free when the grip around his throat eased and knocked the gangster out with his barrel.

The increased volume of shouts somewhere in the distance warned him it wasn't just Janikyan's men who had been alerted.

He resumed his stumbling run, struggling to ignore the punishment his body had taken. He reached the edge of the village and peered out cautiously. An open space ahead, beyond which was what looked like several storage buildings and a line of trucks. No one behind him, but he thought he saw shadows bobbing in the distance.

He ran across the empty road and took cover by the side of the nearest building. Darted to the nearest truck and peered around its rear. More trucks, forklifts and cranes, neatly parked.

That's the compound wall behind them. It was high, smooth and looked forbidding. *Can't risk the time to scale it, not with thugs following me.*

The vehicles gave him an idea. He climbed to the roof of the truck closest to the wall and threw himself across the ten-foot gap.

He pulled himself up to the narrow top of the wall when his fingers caught and held. Below him was the steep drop of the wall and the concrete artificial river bed.

He sat on the edge and let himself fall, hugging the wall as closely as he could to try to slow his fall.

He groaned with the impact and instinctively rolled to absorb as much of the shock as he could.

Move! he ordered himself. Janikyan would get his men to position themselves on a bridge to spot him. He had to put distance behind him.

He jogged west, grimacing with every step, as his body made him aware of the numerous blows it had taken. The smell of grass and children's yells came to him.

Buena Vista Park, he thought groggily. *Can rest there.*

He searched for a section of wall that was lower than the rest.

No luck. He would have to do it the hard way.

He went back to the edge of the river, which was no more

than a few feet wide in that part of LA, a stream. He sprinted to the wall, planted his left foot as high as it could go, which gave him lift-off, and vaulted over the top.

He fell heavily on grass and drew startled gasps from a bunch of kids playing nearby.

'It's all right,' he mumbled at them. 'I'm a Hollywood stuntman.'

He didn't know if they believed him and didn't stay to find out. He went to the deeper part of the park and fell to the ground amid a thick growth of bushes.

He uncapped his bottle of water from his backpack and drank from it wearily. The sky was darkening ... *No, it isn't,* he thought woozily. *It's me. I'm fading.*

Scenes flashed. Janikyan in his SUV on Warner Boulevard. Then, inside the complex.

He didn't come.

No, he didn't say that.

Who did?

Don't remember.

What did Janikyan say?

Something about coming for me.

Why did I think he wouldn't come?

This isn't Cameroon.

Yeah, I know that.

Darkness fell over him.

❧ 88 ❧

The sound of a mower woke Cutter up.

He blinked his eyes and sat up.

Sunlight filtered through the trees and bushes around him. He peered through the foliage and watched a county employee drive his machine across the grassy surface of the park.

I was out for ten hours.

He waited for the mower to disappear out of sight before coming out of his cover, then headed back east. He fired up his phone when he reached a business center and ordered a cab, which took him to a Glendale motel, where he checked in.

He stood for a long time in the warm spray of the shower, taking stock of his body. His ribs hurt and his neck had angry bruises, but no bones were broken. The wound in his thigh had healed and hadn't opened up again.

The strange thoughts of the previous night came to him.

Why was I thinking of Lasko and what he said in the hospital? Why did I even think of Cameroon?

He didn't have an answer for himself.

He shrugged. His mind had brought up random thoughts as he was losing consciousness.

Yeah, but why those? He frowned.

There was no connection between Lasko and Janikyan, and even what they had said wasn't the same.

Cesar was Lasko's snitch. The detective didn't have an informer in the Armenian Bros. Not that he knew of.

It's nothing, he told himself firmly. *No one knows about Cameroon, anyhow.*

He froze. He stared at the wall as water sluiced down his face.

That was it.

Lake Chad Basin centered on the lake that shared borders with Chad, Nigeria, Niger and Cameroon. He had been in Cameroon while in Delta, on a covert mission to track down terrorists.

No civilian knows about Cameroon. That operation is in my military file, which requires security clearances to be accessed.

How did Janikyan know about it?

That's what his subconscious mind had been telling him.

The Armenian Bros not only had a mole in the LAPD, it had a very senior one.

Cutter felt fear at his subsequent thought.

No ... can it be him?

'HE GOT AWAY,' JANIKYAN TOLD THE CALLER. 'WE GOT through inside the studio, we even cornered him a few times, but Grogan escaped,' he said bitterly.

'He'll know you and Covarra are working together.'

'Let him. What can he do?'

'We need to find another way to trap him.'

'What about you?' the gangster snarled. 'I or Covarra seem to be doing all the dirty work. How far have you gotten to getting him?'

'You know my constraints,' the caller said stiffly. 'I can't work as freely as you do.'

'Yeah, but you enjoy the benefits, don't you?'

'Are you making some point?'

'GET GROGAN!' Janikyan yelled. 'He can bring everything crashing down on us.'

'He can't. He doesn't know about you and me.'

'Yeah? How long do you think it'll take him to figure it out?'

'I DON'T WANT TO SEE YOU EVER AGAIN,' ISAIAH LIMON looked nervously around him when Cutter approached him. 'Dude, I saw what went down, that crash ... how did you escape?'

'I got lucky.'

He grinned when the driver's eyes bulged in astonishment.

'Lucky? I saw those men going after you! Who were they?'

'You don't need to know that. Where's my bag?'

'Take it,' Limon brought it out of the trunk and grunted with effort as he dragged it toward him.

'Whose car is this?'

'I borrowed it. I need wheels to make my living.'

'Living?' Cutter snorted. 'All you seem to do is hang around here and smoke. You tried to peek inside the bag?'

'How could I? It's locked.'

'That stopped you?' Cutter grinned at him and brought out a bundle of money. 'That's the twenty grand we agreed on. Use it well. Make a new life—'

'Women and Vegas, baby. That's what I've got in mind.' Limon's smile faded. 'Relax. Isaiah Limon will walk the straight and narrow.'

'You'd better, or else I'll turn up wherever you are—'

'Nope.' The driver held up his hands defensively, 'I've had enough of you. That bag was heavy, you know. It clanked ... as if it had guns.'

'You'll never know what's in it.' Cutter bumped fists with him and walked away.

'Dude,' Limon called after him, 'I'd better not read about you in the newspapers.'

'If you do, how will you know it's me?'

'You got me there.'

Cutter brought out his phone when he was in the back of a cab, heading downtown.

'We need to meet,' he told Cesar. 'No,' he interrupted the banger, 'this can't be done over a call.'

'THIS IS WHERE LASKO AND I USED TO MEET.' CESAR REMOVED his shirt and draped it on a hook.

'A massage parlor?' Cutter took it in. 'In the heart of the city?'

'Who'll suspect this place, *ese?*' the banger said, grinning, and sighed when the attendant poured warm oil on his back. 'What is it? Why did you want to meet?'

Can I trust these masseuses?

'You can.' The thug read his mind. 'I know them very well.'

'I think LAPD has a mole. Someone on a gang's payroll.'

'You think?' the banger scoffed. 'I know Snake's got his informer there. Why wouldn't other gangs have their snitches? What's so special about this rat you're after?'

He set me up. He and Janikyan.

'I need to flush him out.' He avoided the banger's question. 'I need your help.'

'Me? How? Have you forgotten I'm a Street Front hitter?'

'You helped Lasko.'

'He's in the hospital.'

'You can go to the cops with a story.'

'Why would they listen to me?'

'Tell them you know what went down in that warehouse. You know what happened to Lasko.'

'They'll arrest me.'

'Not if you do it my way.'

Cutter waited until the masseuses had finished with them and left the room. He reached for his Tee, put it on and tucked it into his jeans.

'Those bruises look recent, *ese*,' Cesar commented.

'Uh-huh.'

'You've been in many wars.'

I have.

He brought out a new phone from his backpack and broke it out of its wrapping. 'Use this.' He handed it to the banger. 'To call the Gangs and Narcotics Task Force. Their number is on the LAPD website.'

'What do I tell them?'

'That you were Lasko's informer and you were there, that night. That's sure to get their attention.'

'*Ese*, this is too dangerous—'

'Don't show up. Arrange to meet them in person, whoever takes the call. You can decide where to meet. Let me know where and when, and don't turn up. Destroy the phone after they agree to the meeting.'

'How will that help you? Won't everyone in the task force come?'

'Not everyone.'

'You think this will work, *ese*?' Cesar looked at him doubtfully.

'Yeah, along with something else I have in mind.'

'Tell me everything,' Janikyan growled at Covarra.

The two men were at his parlor again, though this time, they had passed on the opportunity to be attended to.

'Everything from the time Grogan arrived in LA.'

'How would I know about that?' the Street Front boss scowled at him. 'I only heard about him when he started attacking us.'

'Nothing unusual happened before that? From the day those women died in Beverly Hills?'

Covarra rubbed his jaw as he frowned thoughtfully. 'Moe and Dime,' he said after a while. 'They were shot in Moe's house. His woman disappeared. I think it was Grogan who killed them, but there's no way of knowing.'

'Is she with him?'

'Moe's woman? I don't know. My men searched for her but didn't find a trace.'

'Where was Moe's house?'

'Oregon Street, in Boyle Heights. But you won't find anything—'

'My people will,' Janikyan said confidently. 'If she's in LA, we'll find her. She might know where Grogan is hanging out.'

'You think we haven't tried?'

'I think your gang is lazy, overconfident. Watch how we find her and Grogan and kill them both.'

CESAR DIDN'T WASTE ANY TIME. HE LOOKED UP THE TASK force's number on the burner Grogan had provided and went to the nearest pay phone on Hollywood Boulevard. He dialed the number.

'I need to talk to a detective,' he said when a woman came on.

'What's this about, sir?' she asked politely.

'I can't tell you that—'

'Sir, this is a busy line. If you have any information on gangs or narcotics dealing, please let me know or else hang up.'

Cesar closed his eyes and scratched his forehead. How would Grogan play this? Would he take the direct approach?

'I know how that detective was shot,' he said. 'I was there at the Jesse Street warehouse that night.'

'Which detective, sir?' she asked after a moment.

'Matt Lasko. I know what went down that night.'

'Sir, who are you? How do we know you're telling the truth?' Cesar glanced at the phone as a man's voice came on. *She must have called a superior.*

'I got no reason to lie.'

'Sir, we get many crank calls—'

'I'm not one of them. I know what happened,' he insisted.

'Go on then, tell us,' the cop replied, shortly.

'No. It will be in person. At a place and time of my choosing.'

'That won't happen, sir. If you've got any useful information, please spill it now.'

'I was Matt Lasko's snitch in the Street Front,' Cesar said angrily. He didn't have to fake the emotion, it came naturally, the result of his bottled-up frustration. 'I can help bring down who shot him.'

'How do we know you're telling the truth?'

The informer blinked at that. I should have worked my story with Grogan before making the call, he swore at himself, as he thought desperately for a way to identify himself.

'You didn't find Lasko's phone, did you?' he said and grinned at the ensuing silence. 'I will tell what I know, to detectives, tomorrow, in person.'

CUTTER HAD GOTTEN THE IDEA WHEN HE HANDED THE BURNER to Cesar.

Can you find out who Lasko called or messaged before he was shot?

Don't you have his phone? Beth's reply to his text came back immediately.

Yeah, but there's nothing in his logs.

Why're you asking, in that case?

He might have erased his logs. He was close to that warehouse and there was a risk he could be caught. He might have taken precautions.

He carried his identification with him but wiped out his call and message history?

Calm down, hotshot, she messaged when he didn't respond. *You might be onto something. You're improving.*

Improving, how?

Our smarts are rubbing off on you.

He grinned as he pictured her chortling and pocketed his phone.

CESAR CALLED HIM IN THE EVENING WHEN HE WAS HAVING HIS solitary dinner.

'It's done.' There was a smile in the informer's voice. 'I almost messed it up. The cops wanted some proof that I was the snitch. Then, I remembered you had taken Lasko's phone.'

'Good thinking,' Cutter congratulated him. 'They'll meet in person?'

'Yeah. Tomorrow, lunchtime, at the Blue Goose. That's on—'

'On Virgil and Santa Monica. I know it. Do you know who will come?'

'They didn't say. They wanted me to describe myself.'

'I hope you didn't do that.'

'No.' Cesar chortled. 'I told them I would approach the cops when I was sure it wasn't a trap. I would know who they were in the bar. I can smell cops a mile away, even if they aren't in uniform."

He chose that bar well. Street Front bangers go there. That will reinforce his story.

'Crush that burner I gave you and stay low.'

Cutter ate silently and went outside the motel after he had finished.

He brought out his phone and brought up the camera feed from the Street Front's house on Apple Street. He could see no one in the room.

He looked up at the night sky, which was dark and cloudy, an air of stillness about it.

I'll bring some thunder and lightning.

'A bomb will go off on Apple Street at any moment,' he said in a call to 911. 'You should clear the houses.'

He blew up Covarra's safe house ninety minutes later.

❧ 89 ❧

Zohrab led the search for Moe's woman personally.

He had found that her name was Brae. No second name. His men had gotten a description by asking neighbors and the neighborhood convenience store clerk.

'She's either dead, lying low, or has left the city,' he briefed Janikyan. 'There's no other way to disappear like that.'

'She won't leave the city. Her entire life was here,' the gang leader asserted. 'No, he's hidden her somewhere. You've got her photograph?'

'Yeah, boss, from Moe's house.'

'Take it to our hackers. They'll find a way to track her down.'

CUTTER PUT ON THE SOCALGAS TECHNICIAN'S DISGUISE, TOOK the van and drove it to the Blue Goose. He found a parking spot on Virgil Avenue that gave him a good view of the front entrance.

He unfolded a newspaper, rested it on the wheel and pretended to read.

. . .

'THAT HOUSE ON APPLE STREET THAT THE BOMB BLEW UP,' Vance Matteo briefed Dade, 'was a storage place for Street Front. We found traces of oxy and meth. Nothing much is left of it … it's turned to rubble. No bodies, ma'am, no one injured, no other houses were damaged. Patrol cops vacated the street when we got that warning call.'

'Was it Grogan's doing?' The chief raised an eyebrow.

'We ran voice analysis on the 911 call. It was inconclusive. But,' he added, shrugging, 'he's got the motive. Looks like he's taking out their warehouses.'

'You've made no progress in finding him,' she pointed out.

'No, ma'am,' he admitted. 'But we are putting every effort toward it. We might have a lead on why Lasko was on Jesse Street.' He smiled briefly at the chief's interest. 'We got a call on the toll-free number. A man who said he was Lasko's snitch. He was there, that night.'

If that banger's telling the truth, he'll know who shot Lasko. He could clear Cutter. Difiore put on an expressionless face but couldn't help leaning forward an inch to take in what Matteo was saying.

'We get lots of fake calls, Vance. Why is this different?'

'He knew that Lasko's phone was missing.'

Whoa! Matteo kept that out of all the reports. Only someone who was there would know.

'What else did he say?'

'He wants to meet.' He flicked back the cuff of his suit and glanced at his watch. 'At lunchtime.'

'Who are you taking?'

'Diego and me. No one else.'

'Why are you still here? Go.'

'MA'AM,' DIFIORE ASKED TENTATIVELY WHEN THEY WERE alone.

'Yeah,' Dade broke off from her brooding silence and looked at them.

'Permission to be there?'

'Where? At Vance's meeting with this informer? No. It's his investigation.'

'Not with him, ma'am. Peyton and I will hang around outside.'

'Why?'

'Matt didn't tell anyone who this informer was.'

'That's normal. I'm sure you protect your snitches back home. What are you getting at?'

'The timing doesn't sound off to you, ma'am? Why is this man coming forward now? He could have called us immediately after the shooting.'

'Go,' Dade commanded, her eyes flinty.

ZOHRAB BROUGHT COFFEE TO HIS BOSS AND STOOD respectfully by his side while Janikyan sipped.

'You've got something. I can sense it in you.'

'Yeah.' The bodyguard's lips creased in a brief smile. 'Our men hacked into traffic cameras. They found the woman, Brae. She got into a car with some other man.'

'Excellent. You traced its plates?'

'They were fake, boss. But,' his grin grew wider, 'We spotted her at another set of cameras. At the Lintock Foundation. She's hiding there.'

CUTTER KEPT WATCH FROM HIS RIDE. CUSTOMERS ENTERED the bar and left it, but he didn't leave his vehicle. He lowered his chi, his inner energy, as he waited patiently. He became one with the environment, as Los Angeles flowed past around him.

DIFIORE DROVE THEIR UNMARKED CAR EXPERTLY THROUGH the traffic as Quindica read their task force reports.

'Nothing,' the SAC sighed in disgust. 'Cutter's dropped off the radar. He's able to move freely in the city, set bombs off, but no cop is able to find him.'

'He's no rookie.'

'We made no progress on the original investigation and have no movement in finding him.'

'Matteo's people are canvassing Apple Street. Someone might have spotted Cutter, his ride ...'

'You think so?'

'No,' Difiore sighed. 'Dade might fire us, and she would be right to do so.'

'You're worried about that?'

'I've never been sacked. It won't look good on my record.'

'Good to know you've got your priorities right,' Quindica said sarcastically.

Difiore grinned and parked on Virgil, behind a van.

She stretched and cracked her knuckles. 'Let's check if Matteo is here.'

WHY ARE THEY HERE? THEY HAVE NOTHING TO DO WITH THE GND *Task Force.*

Cutter watched as the car eased into the space behind his vehicle. He recognized Difiore immediately from the way she moved, the way she flicked her hair back.

He flipped a page on his newspaper as the detective and the FBI agent came out of their ride and went to the bar. He tracked them through his peripheral vision as they circled Blue Goose and returned to their ride.

'HIS CAR ISN'T HERE.' DIFIORE TOOK IN THE SOCALGAS VAN and its driver, who was munching on a piece of fruit and reading a newspaper. 'Nice to have the day to yourself,' she muttered.

'Who?' Quindica asked, bewildered.

'Him.' She jerked a thumb at the gas technician.

'He must be on his break. Cut him some slack. Anyhow, why're we talking about him?'

'You're right.' The detective waved a hand in apology and climbed behind the wheel. 'Let's wait out here,' she told her partner. 'We can't risk going inside.'

VANCE MATTEO ARRIVED JUST BEFORE LUNCHTIME. HE parked his ride in the lot behind Blue Goose and straightened his clothing as Cruz joined him. Both were dressed casually, in loose shirts and slacks, nothing to show that they were cops.

'Let's hear what he has to say,' he told the detective, 'then we can decide what to do.'

He led the way to the front of the bar as he checked out the surrounding vehicles. None of them roused his suspicion, and he entered the bar without breaking a step.

CUTTER FELT NO EMOTION AS HE WATCHED THEM DISAPPEAR inside the bar.

Matteo and Cruz.

They could have sent other cops in the task force, but they turned up themselves.

It doesn't mean anything, he argued to himself. *They lead the investigation. They would be here.*

Nope, it's them. They could get access to my military file. He knew the Chad operation was mentioned by location, while the rest of its details were redacted.

They're colluding with Janikyan. They must have been there with him when Vienna and Arnedra were tortured, raped and killed.

He picked his phone up when it buzzed. Unlocked it and stared at the string of messages from Beth.

This is the first text from Lasko.

'Covarra's here at a warehouse on Rio and Jesse Street. Come down with backup. We can get him.'

This one was sent fifteen minutes later.

'Are you coming?'

That was followed by a call.

All of those, within an hour of his getting shot.

He called Matteo.

THAT'S PROOF. CUTTER DROPPED THE PHONE ONTO THE SEAT. *That's what Lasko meant by 'he didn't come.'*

He sat motionless for what felt like hours as the rage inside him swirled and eddied. He wiped his palms on his jeans when he had banked his fury to a cold simmer. It would fuel him for what he needed to do.

Bring them down.

❄ 90 ❄

Cutter watched Matteo and Cruz emerge from Blue Goose after ninety minutes. The lead detective scanned the streets as he donned his shades and left for the parking lot, with his partner behind him. His movement was jerky, his shoulders squared, as if he was angry.

He checked out Difiore in his side mirror. She and Quindica had slid down their seats when the cops arrived. They sat up straight and appeared to be conferring with each other when the men drove away.

Cutter assembled the GSM tower swiftly as he kept an eye on them and fired off a text message.

Trust no one but Lisa and Terry.

DIFIORE SUCKED HER BREATH SHARPLY WHEN SHE READ THE message and showed it to Quindica.

'That's ... from Cutter?' the SAC frowned.

'Yeah.' She stared down Santa Monica as if she could still see Matteo's vehicle through the traffic. She signaled with her flasher and joined the traffic. Paid no attention to the gas technician she drove past. She swallowed the bile that rose in her throat and looked at Quindica briefly.

'You're thinking the same as me?'

'Yeah, Matteo! Possibly Cruz and Estrada, too. If they're dirty,' the SAC said bitterly, 'it explains a lot. Why we made no progress in our LAPD investigation. Matteo knew everything that we were doing. He—'

She broke off and looked out of the window blindly. Her voice was quiet when she spoke again.

'He could be as corrupt as the Blue Brothers. His seniority and reputation ... those would be enough for him to recruit dirty cops. He would know how to massage the reports so that nothing looked off. He knew the mistakes those deputies made. He wouldn't repeat them. But,' she drew a long breath. 'We can't prove it.'

'We don't need to,' Difiore said softly.

'Cutter?'

'Yeah.'

'Gina Difiore needing his help. That's something.'

I NEED AN APP THAT WILL DIAL A NUMBER, KEEP THE CALL GOING and simultaneously record an ongoing conversation. All this, without being visible on the screen. No notifications of any kind, either.

Beth snapped her fingers, which brought the rest of the operatives crowding around her. They were in the hotel's game room, playing pool, when her phone buzzed.

'That from Cutter?' Zeb guessed.

'Yeah. We've got an app like that. I'll message him installation instructions.'

Her eyes gleamed when they met his. 'I'll program it so that we can listen in to whatever he does. Even when he's not making calls.'

'And that app,' Meghan grinned, 'will give us his location at any time.'

Zeb nodded as he fingered the cue stick idly. 'He's planning something.'

'High time.' Bear fist-bumped Bwana. 'We were getting bored.'

ZOHRAB WENT TO THE RECEPTION DESK IN THE LINTOCK Foundation's building and put on a concerned face. 'I'm Brae's friend, from Amarillo. Where she's from.'

The woman looked at him and then back at her screen. 'Brae, sir? We don't have anyone by that name here.'

'Damn,' Zohrab slammed his palm on the wooden counter in frustration. 'I've been searching every women's shelter in town. Her sister is seriously ill.'

'I'm sorry, sir. We have no one by that name here.'

He thanked her, jerked his head at the banger who had accompanied him and headed out. He smiled coldly when the receptionist, whom he could see in the glass door's reflection, made a call.

'She's here,' he told his man. 'She'll come down to get our description. That's when we'll grab her.'

91

C utter raced back to his motel, where he had parked his Land Cruiser. He dumped the SoCalGas van a block away and ran to his room. He removed the Glock he had hidden beneath the dresser and stuffed it in his backpack and went out.

Climbed into the SUV, checked that his weapons bag was in the rear and drove away. He wouldn't be returning to the motel again.

He floored the gas, his lips tight, as he navigated the afternoon traffic. *Matteo will try calling Cesar. He'll find the number's dead. He'll check with the task force and see if the snitch made contact. That's when he'll wonder if he was set up.* Which would get the detective to reach out to Janikyan.

The two will decide to set a trap for me.

He had to get ahead of the curve. Be prepared for that eventuality.

CUTTER REACHED BEVERLY GROVE DRIVE AND TURNED INTO A dirt clearing midway up the hill where several other vehicles were parked. Hikers left their rides at this spot when they hit the trail. He shouldered his backpack and lifted the gymbag with his left hand. Locked the SUV and walked up the road, looking like any other traveler.

He didn't look at the murder house when he reached the hairpin bend. He kept going, instead, picturing the neighborhood in his mind, knowing precisely where he wanted to be.

He cut through dense foliage between two houses when he emerged. All considered, he was high enough now. He made for a good vantage point on the side of the hill.

There. He could see the kill site. He checked his six. No one near him. The nearest residence was to his left, over a hundred yards away. It was hidden by trees and bushes, however, and all he could see was patches of white wall through the foliage.

He dropped to his belly and crawled forward beneath a bush. He ignored the branches that scratched him as he moved forward cautiously, until he could take in the house fully.

He brought out his binos and trained them on the building. The patio leapt out in his lenses, its concrete floor, partial roof and the glass and concrete wall that jutted out from the cliff. He checked out the windows of the house and could detect no movement.

He went to his messages and read the instructions Beth had sent him for the app. He clicked on the download link, installed it and familiarized himself with its features when it came on screen. He stored Difiore's number in it and exited the application.

He double-pressed the volume button, waited a beat and double-pressed it again.

He opened the app and nodded in satisfaction when he saw it had called the detective. The second set of presses had ended the outgoing ring.

He placed his phone on the ground and waited.

· · ·

MATTEO NODDED TO CRUZ DISCREETLY AND LED THE WAY TO their office in the LAPD headquarters.

'That informer didn't call.' His deputy shut the door and turned to him. 'I checked with our officers. His number's been disconnected. It can't be tracked.'

The lead detective's stubble rasped against his fingers when he rubbed his cheek. 'He never intended to show up,' he growled. 'We've been made.'

'By him?' Cruz jammed his hands in his pockets.

'No. There's only one person who could think of that.'

'Grogan.'

'Yeah. He has Lasko's phone. He must have got the informer's number from it.'

'But how would he suspect us?'

'I don't know.' Matteo waved impatiently. 'The *how* doesn't matter. I bet he was there, at the bar, watching us—'

'He wasn't. We checked out the—'

'Diego,' the detective hissed. 'He wasn't inside. He must have been parked outside. We didn't run any license plates, did we?'

'So what if he saw us? We were there to meet an informer.'

'No.' Matteo shook his head decisively. 'Grogan knows about us.'

'Lasko's text messages to you,' Cruz said, straightening, 'he must have read those. We were thinking that Lasko deleted them.'

'Possibly. Come on.' The senior cop headed out of the office. 'We need to make a call.'

PANIG JANIKYAN WAS STABBING ONE OF HIS MEN IN HIS LIVING room when the phone rang.

He slashed the banger across the throat with his dashuyn and gave the bloodied weapon to one of his men. He wiped his hands on a towel that a flunky gave him.

'Let that be a lesson,' he said, eyeing the watching men

coldly. 'That's what will happen to anyone who steals from us. He thought he could pocket some product and I wouldn't know it. I am Pain. I know everything that happens in our gang. Take his body away.'

He reached for the phone, glanced at the number and held it to his ear. 'What?'

'I think Grogan's onto us,' Matteo told him.

Janikyan listened when the detective laid it out for him.

'I warned you,' the cop's voice rose, 'there was no need for those women to be tortured or raped.'

'We had to know what they were doing there.'

'They told us when you slapped them. They were watching the sunset. And then they hid, when Covarra's and your men turned up.'

'They saw you with us, when you arrived after the shooting.'

'They didn't recognize me or Cruz.'

'You both are highly visible. You give interviews ... they could have seen you on TV and identified you. We both have invested a lot in our relationship. I couldn't risk that.'

'You could have just shot them. There was no need to go to that extent.'

'Zohrab needed to play with them. You know how he gets.'

'His actions and yours have brought us to this. We had—'

'A nice deal. I know. You benefited, not just from turning a blind eye, but even more by actively helping us in our operations. Now,' he sneered, 'you're scared that you'll be found out.'

'Grogan made it personal,' Matteo spat, 'when he knew how the women were treated. If they had been shot, he would have accepted our explanation that they were caught in a gang shootout.'

'ENOUGH!' Janikyan roared. A thug hurried into the room to check on his boss and disappeared when the gang leader glared at him. 'Don't forget I made you,' he told the cop.

'Don't forget that without my help, you wouldn't have gotten to where you are.'

The Armenian controlled himself with effort. He knew Matteo was right.

'I was planning to set a trap for him,' he told the cop.

'How?'

He chuckled mirthlessly. 'I'll offer you to him.'

'He might not fall for that.'

Janikyan looked up when Zohrab burst into the room with a woman whose mouth was taped, hands bound and eyes wide with fright.

The gang leader smiled slowly at the sight. 'I know just how to convince him,' he told the detective.

MATTEO POCKETED HIS PHONE WHEN THE CALL ENDED, AND brooded.

Their relationship had started when the detective joined the LAPD. Matteo stumbled onto Janikyan by accident. He had been returning to the precinct, alone in his vehicle, when he spotted movement in a dark alley in East Hollywood.

He had crept up on the men on foot and identified Janikyan immediately when he trained his flashlight on them. The Armenian was with two hitters, cartons of oxy baggies at their feet.

He had been reaching for his comms unit to call for backup when the gang leader smirked at him.

'You can arrest me now and get a promotion. Or, you can arrest these men, let me go, get a promotion, and be rich for the rest of your life.'

The detective didn't need any convincing. He had admired the Blue Brothers even while he was helping to bring down the deputies' gang. He had envied their culture, their willingness to break the law.

He recognized the opportunity Janikyan presented and grabbed it. He was smarter than the LASD deputies, however.

He made the deal with the Armenian that night, and his fortunes changed.

From being a newcomer in the LAPD, he rapidly rose to being its smartest detective. His closure rate, helped by Janikyan's tips on his rivals, was the highest in the department.

The Armenian Bros had made him wealthier than he had ever imagined. He not only got paid for dropping cases, letting criminals walk, turning a blind eye, but also got bonuses for targeting rival gangs based on their tips.

He hand-picked the cops to join his gang. He didn't make the mistakes the Blue Brothers had made. No tattoos, no secret handshakes, no identification to give them away. All of them believed in white superiority, but they didn't act in any way that would reveal that.

That's why Dade was unsuccessful, he thought proudly. *She couldn't find any signal that we existed as a gang. And those women she brought, Difiore and Quindica, they couldn't find anything. We don't work in any obvious way.*

Cruz had been his first recruit, and the two of them grew their secret outfit to thirty members, a mix of detectives and patrol officers.

He had learned just who Matt Lasko was when he spotted the cop meeting Dade in the headquarters' parking lot, late one night. That had aroused his suspicions, and he had dug up everything he could on the detective. He hit paydirt when he visited Dallas, interviewed the Lasko family's neighbors and discovered the chief's relationship with the cop. He didn't let on that he knew about it, and when he discovered that it was the cop who had fed him inside information on the Blue Brothers, he knew what he had to do.

Lasko had to be killed. He was smart, tenacious and a risk to Matteo and his gang.

He got lucky when the detective found out about Covarra's presence on Jesse Street. He ignored the officer's messages, figuring the Street Front would take him out.

It went down like I hoped, he thought in satisfaction. *It doesn't look like he'll recover. He's still hooked up to tubes. Even if he does, there's nothing he can do. I'll say I was busy on another investigation if he accuses me of not providing backup. Dade won't think anything of it. She thinks I'm her best detective.*

As for Grogan. His hands curled into fists. *He won't be a threat for long. I'll be there when Janikyan kills him.*

92

Cutter's phone buzzed at nine pm.

He swallowed the protein bar he was eating and washed it down with a gulp of water. He checked the house with his night-vision binos and thumbed the call.

'Yeah?'

'Grogan,' Janikyan gloated. 'How does it feel to be the most hunted man in the city?'

'No different from how you feel every day and night.'

'I'm still a free man.'

'So am I.'

No one at the house. Doesn't look like he's sent his thugs there.

He checked his phone for the GPS trackers he had planted. Zohrab was in the Little Armenia house, but there was no other green dot in that location. *That soluble's signal has died.*

'We should meet,' the Armenian declared.

'So you can kill me?'

'I don't need to. I'll give you what you want.'

'What's that?'

'The people who shot your friends.'

'You know who it is?'

'I'll present them to you. In person.'

391

'Tell me who they are.'

'No, we have to meet for that.'

'You're setting me up.'

Just like you did all along.

'Why would I do that?'

'Because you know how much of a threat I am.'

'Enough talk. Do you want the killers or not?'

'You know I want them,' he growled. 'But I don't trust you. We'll meet at a place of my choice.'

'No—'

'No meeting in that case.'

'Wait,' Janikyan asked him quickly. 'Where did you have in mind?'

'That same house in Beverly Hills where they were killed. Tomorrow. Nine pm.'

'There?' the gang leader burst out in surprise. 'Why not some other place?'

'I want to kill them on the same spot they murdered my friends.'

'You're not afraid I'll kill you?'

'You, killing me?' he snorted. 'Janikyan, count how many chances you had to capture me. Now, count how many times you succeeded. It's you who should be afraid of meeting me.'

'Pain does not fear any man.'

'We have a date, in that case. Tomorrow. That house.'

'IT WILL BE TOMORROW,' JANIKYAN TOLD MATTEO, 'IN THAT same house.'

'Beverly Hills?' The detective stared into the darkness of the night. 'Why did you agree to meet there?'

'He asked for it. He wasn't ready to meet anywhere else.'

'How did he sound?'

'How does that matter?' the Armenian asked in exasperation. 'We'll finish him tomorrow and get back to our business.'

'Was he worried? Scared?'

'Grogan? No expression in his voice.'

'It's a trap.' Matteo stood up and paced the room.

'Trap?' Janikyan asked angrily. 'How's that possible? He can't get the cops there. You're looking for him.'

'And I would know if he approached the chief.'

'Exactly.'

'We suspect he was wearing some kind of suicide belt at Covarra's meeting. That's how he stayed alive.'

'Let him wear whatever he wants,' Janikyan said. 'We got a trump card. The woman he rescued.'

'Which woman?'

'Brae. She used to be a Street Front banger's girlfriend.'

Matteo's brow cleared as he remembered the incident. 'Moe,' he breathed softly.

'Yeah. Grogan can set whatever trap he wants. We'll be ready for him.'

❧ 93 ❧

C utter went down the hill swiftly, sprinting when he was between houses and slowing to a casual walk when he was passing in front of them.

He approached the hairpin turn cautiously and spotted no traffic, no parked cars, no dog walkers or joggers.

He held his breath as he vaulted over the metal gates to the house and exhaled in relief when no alarm or lights went off.

He checked the outside yard to see if the cops had mounted any security cameras but didn't spot any.

He checked the lawn at the front of the house, the gate and the adjoining wall. He tested the front door and found it locked.

He went to the side window where he had entered the previous time. Nothing seemed to have changed. The same stale air, the smell of an unused house. He checked all the rooms and went out to the patio, which was partially shaded by roof. His face turned grim when he took in the dark patches on the concrete. *No one bothered to clean the blood stains.*

He went to the front of the house and headed to the garage at the side. Cut its lock with the bolt-cutters he had brought along and inspected the contents.

He found what he was looking for, neatly arranged on a shelf on the wall. Neutral-colored duct tape, cans of paint in various colors, a bag of cement and, hanging on the wall, a shovel. A bunch of floor tiles, strips of ceiling molding, rolls of lawn turf and sacks of soil were a bonus.

CUTTER WENT TO THE LAWN AND DROPPED THE WEAPONS BAG and backpack to the ground. Rolled up his sleeves and got to work.

He dug several holes strategically in the lawn and at the base of the wall. Assembled C4 slabs with detonators and timers. He rocked back on his heels and wiped sweat from his forehead.

When do I need the first one to go off?

Forty-five minutes from my arrival?

He thought about it and nodded. Adjusted the timer on the first bomb and buried it in the first hole, near the gates. He set the other explosives to go off at random intervals thereafter and buried them, too.

He covered the holes with soil and turf where needed, got to his feet and surveyed his work critically. He adjusted a patch of grass here, raked soil there with his fingers, until he was finally satisfied the front yard and lawn would pass muster.

They won't be looking for explosives.

He was confident about that.

CUTTER WENT INSIDE THE HOUSE AND CUT MOLDING FROM THE ceilings of several rooms and planted more explosives behind them. He went around the house testing for loose tiles. Dug them out carefully when he found them, and buried bombs in the holes he made beneath them.

Sweat streamed down his face by the time he went to the patio. *It's concrete. I don't have the equipment to dig it out.*

His took in the large flower pots in the corners, long since dried out. *Those will do.* He removed their soil, planted his explosives and covered them with a fresh layer. The low wall that hung over the bluff had two ornate light poles in the corners. He turned them into bombs by inserting C4 into their hollows, then wiped his hands on his camo pants.

He went inside the house and duct-taped scabbards to the back sides of the legs of several chairs. He inserted four-inch knives in them and painted over them, a color to match the wood. He dragged a glass coffee table to the patio as the emulsion dried.

He checked out the chairs when he returned inside. A close look would show the tape and the bottom of the hilt. *It'll have to do*, he thought, shrugging. He drew the knives out to check they moved freely in their sheaths and dropped them back in place.

He brought out the chairs and arranged them around the table, with a couple to each side of the sliding door.

Janikyan and Matteo will come to the house and go out to the patio when they see the furniture.

It was war strategy that he had learned in Delta. Draw the enemy into the field of his setting.

He leaned over the low wall and let the breeze cool his face as he took in the panorama of the city spread out below him.

It might be the last time I get to see LA like this, he thought grimly. *Alive.*

❧ 94 ❧

'**G**rogan,' Janikyan gloated. '*How does it feel to be the most hunted man in the city?*'

Zeb listened along with his team while Beth played the recording on her phone.

They were in his hotel room, playing cards, watching TV or reading, when she had snapped her fingers to draw their attention to the call.

'This was last night?' he turned off the recording when it ended.

'Yeah, nine pm.'

'What's he planning?' Chloe asked, a pinched look in her eyes. 'He can't go in there alone. They'll kill him.'

'I'm sure he knows that.' Bear reached for the fruit basket, inspected an apple critically, polished it against his shirt and crunched into it heartily. 'He'll have planned his getaway.'

'How?' his girlfriend challenged him.

'How would I know?' he replied with a helpless shrug. 'I can't read his mind.'

'We'll be there,' Bwana said—a statement, not a question.

'Yeah.' Zeb smiled briefly. 'But we won't show ourselves. Will we be able to hear—'

'That phone's recording everything.' Beth's ponytail bounced as she nodded her head. 'Anything he does, anyone speaks near it, we'll hear it.'

'Where's he now?'

'In Beverly Hills,' Meghan answered. She turned her phone to show them Cutter's location, a red dot on the side of the hill. 'He spent the night there. Alone.'

That's what I would do, too. Zeb gazed at the screen and pictured the hill where his friend was. *I would be out there, above the house, watching, waiting, preparing myself for the showdown.*

CUTTER WOKE AT THE BREAK OF DAWN, CHECKED THE HOUSE with his binos and found no trace of visitors.

He worked out for an hour and stripped to his waist to let the breeze cool his body.

He broke open a protein bar and ate it slowly. Followed that with a piece of fruit and drank water. He wiped his hands on his trousers and turned on his phone.

I came to LA twenty-five days ago, he began recording. *To claim the bodies of my friends and find out who had killed them.*

He narrated every incident since his arrival succinctly and finished half an hour later. He composed an email to Difiore and attached the audio file to it. Set it to be delivered the next day. Finally, he uploaded the recording to his cloud storage account.

He strapped on two custom-made Velcro strips, one on each wrist. They had magnetic loops that stretched to accommodate whatever was inserted in them.

He thrust the hilt of his Benchmade in them and tested that they gripped the blade tightly. They did.

He emptied his mind and returned to watching.

CHLOE SUCKED HER BREATH SHARPLY WHEN MEGHAN PLAYED the audio file an hour later. No one else displayed any emotion.

They listened quietly in Zeb's room, and when the recording ended, Bwana got to his feet, stretched, cracked his knuckles and started cleaning his Glock.

CUTTER WATCHED THE TWO SUVS ARRIVE AT EIGHT PM. He made Janikyan, who was hustled inside the house by several hitters. *Was Zohrab among the men?*

He checked his phone and found no green dot on the app. *Tracker's died or he's discovered and destroyed it.*

Did that change anything? He considered it for a moment and then shook his head.

No, it didn't. *I must have missed spotting him. He'll be there with Janikyan. The gang leader doesn't go anywhere without him.*

He saw movement inside the house through the windows. *They'll search the house to make sure it's empty.* He hoped they wouldn't discover the knives or the explosives.

The vehicles drove away when the last of the bangers had gone inside and quiet returned to the street.

Cutter went down the hill at eight-forty-five pm.

☙ 95 ❧

He left his backpack and the weapons bag on the hill, pushed deep inside a thicket, locked.

He had his Glock, several spare magazines and his knife on him. No disguise. There was no longer any need for that. No armor, either. *They'll search me and remove it.*

He went down like a wraith, slipping through the shadows of the trees and then onto the street. A tall, lean figure who used the darkness of the night to his advantage as he got closer to the house.

He felt empty, relaxed; he knew he was at his most lethal in that state.

How I feel doesn't matter. I'll either come out of this alive, or I'll be dead.

He knocked on the metal gate at nine pm.

TEN MILES TO THE EAST, MATT LASKO OPENED HIS EYES.

· · ·

TOROS MADE THE CALL AT THE SAME TIME. HE KNEW JANIKYAN would kill him if the gang leader found out, but, what the hell! Covarra paid well for his information.

'There's a meeting going down in Beverly Hills,' he told Salazar. 'Right now. Janikyan and Grogan.'

The deputy ran to his boss as soon as he hung up. 'I know where Grogan will be,' he burst out.

Fifteen minutes later, Covarra and Salazar rolled out of their safe house, along with several hitters.

ZEB CHECKED BEVERLY GROVE DRIVE UP AND DOWN. NO traffic. The two SUVs in which they had arrived were deep inside the driveways of two adjacent, empty houses.

'You expect trouble?' Meghan joined him and looked up the hill. The hairpin bend was barely visible in the night, but the house was unmistakable.

'I've got that feeling.'

'Beth and I'll go down the hill,' she said. His inner radar was known to them. 'We'll check out approaching vehicles and warn you if we spot anything suspicious.'

'And,' added Chloe, who had come up to them, 'Bear and I will go up and check out cars that are coming down.'

'HE'S HERE,' A BANGER YELLED TOWARD THE HOUSE, AS HE opened the gate and checked Cutter.

❧ 96 ☙

Cutter double-pressed the volume button on his phone, raised both hands high and stepped inside.

The gates rolled shut behind him as a banger pushed him towards the house.

He checked out the yard from the corners of his eyes as he went up the walkway. *Nothing appears disturbed. Doesn't look like they've found the explosives.*

He climbed up the porch and went through the front entryway.

'Go on,' a hitter growled behind him.

He continued deeper into the house, through darkened rooms, until he stepped onto the patio.

Janikyan was seated on a chair, flanked by two bangers, his back to the low wall over the cliff.

'I was wondering if you would come.' The Armenian flashed a smile, but his eyes remained cold.

Cutter took in the assembled men casually and stopped counting after he got to six.

Where's Zohrab? He isn't here.

'Why wouldn't I? I told you, I want answers.' He raised his hands higher when a banger searched him and removed his

Glock, knife and all his magazines. The hitter felt his pockets and came out with his phone. He checked that it was turned off and placed it on top of the weapons that were on the floor, to the side.

DIFIORE WAS WITH QUINDICA IN DADE'S OFFICE WHEN HER phone buzzed. *Nope, don't recognize that number. I don't take calls from strangers.*

Something stopped her from declining it, however. She recognized Cutter's voice instantly when she accepted it and heard his *Why wouldn't I.* She turned on the speaker, placed the device on the chief's desk and motioned for silence.

'YOU'RE SOMETHING,' JANIKYAN SAID ADMIRINGLY. 'YOU ARE alone, surrounded by my men, and yet here you are. You don't look scared. Any other person wouldn't have come.'

'You know why I'm here.' Cutter took a step closer. Another stride and he would be at the table.

He sensed movement and glanced back to see two bangers inch nearer to him. They had hands on their assault rifles, alert for any move he made.

Janikyan snapped his fingers, as if he had forgotten. 'You want to know who killed your friends.'

Footsteps approached before Cutter could respond. Matteo and Cruz entered the patio, followed by more shooters.

'It was you all along,' he said, addressing the lead detective contemptuously. 'You misled me from the start. Heck,' he spat coldly, 'I was at the same spot. Here, over those blood splotches, when you, Cruz and Estrada found me. You lied to me. Told me there was a gang shootout—'

'I didn't lie,' Matteo's face and voice were expressionless. 'There *was*—'

'Where's Estrada?'

'He isn't involved.'

'How does it feel to be a traitor? Why, Matteo? Why did the two of you throw in with Janikyan? You both are two of the best cops in the LAPD. Why did you cross the line?'

'How did you figure it out?' the lead detective ignored his question.

'You made mistakes. You should have checked on Lasko. He recovered briefly … enough for the medics to remove his tubes. He told the nurses you didn't come.'

'How do you know that?'

'I overheard them talking. That shootout in the hospital, that was me, in case you didn't work that out.'

'That was enough for you?' Matteo asked expressionlessly. 'Just those words?'

'Your friend,' Cutter said sarcastically, as he nodded at Janikyan, 'let slip that LA wasn't like Cameroon.'

The detective closed his eyes momentarily, disgusted at himself. 'That was in your military file.'

'Yeah. I knew then that he had someone in the LAPD. That's when I set the trap for you.'

'He's clean?' Matteo turned to Janikyan, who was following the conversation with a thin smile.

'Yeah.' Janikyan's eyes danced. The gang leader was clearly enjoying the moment. 'No wire, he's got no backup. No suicide belt, no weapons.'

'Kill him. Let's finish this.'

'Who killed my friends?'

Cutter's belly tightened when two more people came onto the patio.

Brae, her mouth taped, her hands tied behind her, a look of terror on her face—and behind her, Zohrab, a wicked grin on his face.

'Let her go,' Cutter said hollowly as he turned to Janikyan. 'She's got nothing to do with this.'

'She's insurance,' the gangster said, grinning. 'We know you by now. You wouldn't have come here on your own without an exit. With her here,' he chuckled savagely, 'it's over, Grogan. Here's where you die.'

Brae made unintelligible noises behind her gag and shook her head furiously.

'What's she saying?' Janikyan asked irritatedly.

'I DON'T KNOW WHO HE IS. PLEASE LET ME GO. I WON'T TELL ANYONE ANYTHING,' she burst out when Zohrab ripped the tape off her mouth.

The gang leader looked at her strangely for a moment and then smiled knowingly. 'Of course.' He nodded. 'Grogan, you never showed your real face to her, did you? That's why she doesn't recognize you.'

'He was the one who killed your boyfriend,' he told her sneeringly. 'And took you to the Lintock Center. He thought you would be safe there. Safe from us!' he snorted.

'Shut her up,' he ordered coldly before Brae could speak.

Zohrab slapped her casually, applied the tape on her mouth and shoved her on a chair.

Cutter looked away when she fell heavily. *That look on her face ... I've got to save her, whatever happens to me.*

'She's your insurance?' he shrugged contemptuously. 'Kill her and then you lose any leverage you have over me. Did you think about that?'

From the looks Matteo, Cruz and Janikyan exchanged, they hadn't.

'I came here for answers,' Cutter said, 'not to save anyone's life. Who killed Arnedra and Vienna?'

Janikyan was startled by his uncaring response for a moment. He recovered and sneered. 'Haven't you figured that out by now?'

He paused dramatically for a moment. 'It was Zohrab and me. With the rifles the men behind you are holding.'

❧ 97 ❦

'They're at that Beverly Hills house,' Difiore's head looked up from the phone on which their attention was riveted.

'Your task force.' Dade rose abruptly and put on her jacket. 'Can they handle this?'

The NYPD detective took a moment to absorb her meaning. *She doesn't trust Matteo's team. We don't know who else is dirty there.*

'Yeah,' she replied.

'Let's roll.'

IT WAS ZOHRAB AND ME.

Janikyan's declaration seemed to reverberate in the night.

Cutter was conscious of the small details.

The tic on Matteo's cheek, his dark gaze. A shoe squeaked as someone shifted his weight behind him. A moth flew past the corner light and vanished in the night. The wail of a distant siren.

Something settled in him.

'Why did you have to kill them?'

'They saw me and Cruz,' Matteo answered, 'with Janikyan.'

'Why were they here?'

'They came to watch the sunset.'

'They hid when all the shooters arrived,' Cutter guessed, 'but then you came and—'

'They had to die.' Janikyan's eyes glowed with an unholy light.

'Why did you torture them?'

'That was Zohrab's doing.'

'Why?'

'I like it.' The bodyguard shrugged. 'I like to watch people suffer.'

'And you?' Cutter challenged Matteo. 'You were there? You watched it all?'

The detective's lips tightened. He looked away from the intense gaze on him. 'I told Janikyan to shoot them. Torture and rape were unnecessary.'

'No one tells me or my people what to do,' the gangster declared.

'You killed them,' Cutter said bitterly, 'just because they were there. To watch the sun go down.'

HE WAS HALF-TURNED TO JANIKYAN, WHO WAS STILL SEATED, towards his left. A stride away. Matteo and Cruz by the gang leader's right shoulder.

Zohrab's to my right, several paces away. Many more bangers behind me, and Brae. She's not in the line of any shooting.

Attack was the best defense.

Cutter lashed at the glass table with his right leg and shattered its surface. He hopped back on his left, as the bangers and cops ducked from the flying glass. He pivoted smoothly, spun-kicked the hitter behind him in the head and sent him crashing into his neighbor.

'DON'T SHOOT HIM,' Janikyan yelled. 'I WANT HIM ALIVE.'

A banger slammed into Cutter and punched him furiously.

Another hitter kicked him, while a third shooter crashed the butt of his rifle in his belly.

He staggered and fell over Brae's chair with his back to the hitters. He braced his left hand against its arm and slid his right, deep down. He felt the hidden knife's butt instinctively and jammed the Velcro strip's magnetic loop over it.

'Stay tight,' he whispered to Brae just before he was yanked back savagely. He caught the cuff of his right sleeve by his fingers, dragged it over the blade, turned around to face whoever had pulled him and doubled up in agony when a fist landed in his belly.

'STAY BACK,' Zohrab shouted at his men. 'HE'S MINE!'

'Kill him,' Matteo yelled angrily. 'Kill her as well. Let's not waste time.'

'No!' the bodyguard shouted. 'I'll do this my way.'

He grabbed Cutter's hair and raised his head savagely.

'You didn't ask one question,' he snarled. 'You didn't ask who raped them. I did. Now, I'll rape that woman, Brae, in front of you. I'll kill her and then it will be your turn.'

Covarra was in the first vehicle with Salazar beside him. He and his deputy, the driver and two more bangers, with a second SUV behind them.

'Go faster,' he urged as their ride started climbing Beverly Grove Drive. 'I want to get to Grogan before Janikyan does anything.'

'We'll have to shoot it out with them.'

'I'm looking forward to that, Fuse,' he snarled through gritted teeth. 'Those Armenians ... we can finish them at that house.'

He hefted his assault rifle and was peering down its sight when a dark SUV came out from a driveway and rammed into them. The force of the impact sent them careening off the road to crash into a lamp post.

Covarra sat dazed and in shock as steam rose from beneath the hood. Something dripped from his forehead onto his hand. Blood. He stared at it uncomprehendingly for a moment and then realized his head must have slammed into his weapon.

He raised his head when he sensed movement.

Ghosts was his first thought about the shadows that came out of the night and through the steam.

'FUSE!' he screamed when he spotted the weapons in the intruders' hands. He shook Salazar and looked back to find that the second vehicle had been T-boned by another SUV.

He whirled around when his ride shuddered and saw a large man, his skin like dark coal, his eyes white, his teeth drawn in a feral snarl, had climbed on the buckled hood and, as he watched, poured a stream of lead through the windscreen that took out the driver and Fuse.

'NO!' Covarra raged as he heard the chatter of assault rifles and raised his gun.

He didn't get to fire.

Something shattered his window and a barrel broke his teeth.

'Tell me,' a voice asked softly. When he looked at the speaker, a lean man with fathomless eyes, he saw death. 'Who shot Matt Lasko?'

CUTTER LET HIMSELF BE HAULED UP BY ZOHRAB'S PULL ON HIS hair. He felt the bodyguard punch him and groaned.

'I enjoyed it,' the Armenian gloated. 'The look on their eyes when they realized what I was going to do.'

He was transported to Afghanistan.

ZEB AND HIM, BARE-CHESTED, BENEATH THE BLAZING SUN IN THE *Hindu Kush mountain range. His friend had been teaching Cutter and his team knife-fighting tactics.*

'*No.*' *His friend danced away easily from his charge.* '*You're doing this wrong.*'

'*In what way?*' *Cutter panted as he swiveled to face his friend.*

'*It's not your technique. That's fine. You're thinking about it wrong. That knife.*' *Zeb pointed to the blade in Cutter's hand.* '*You're still thinking of it as your weapon.*'

'*Huh? It is!*'

'*The weapon is you!*'

CUTTER LUNGED FORWARD WITH THE MEMORY PLAYING IN HIS mind. The concealed blade slipped into his palm as if it were an extension of his body. He bodyslammed into Zohrab before the Armenian could evade him and jammed the knife deep into his chest.

The bodyguard staggered back from the force of the crash, towards the low wall overlooking the cliff. Cutter stabbed him two more times in the chest before the man recovered enough to yell at the bangers: 'NO! I DON'T NEED HELP.'

Zohrab wrapped his arms around his attacker and crushed him in a bear hug, as if the wounds—which were bleeding his shirt red—were nothing.

It was just the hold Cutter needed. He ignored the arms wrapped around him like steel bands, squeezing his ribs, making breathing difficult. He dismissed the shouts and yells of the Armenians behind them. Zohrab leered at him, his eyes tight with anger.

I enjoyed it.

The bodyguard's words came back to Cutter. He stabbed again, right over the thug's chest. And again, and again, robotically, as he recalled the times he had spent with Vienna and Arnedra, their joyous laughter. His arm kept moving mechanically while his breath stuttered from the punishing squeeze around him.

They were flush against the low wall, beyond and below them the lights of downtown LA, beckoning invitingly.

Cutter groaned as Zohrab kept applying his monstrous crush. His hand felt sluggish as he withdrew the knife from the body-guard's flesh with a horrific sucking sound. He shook his head to clear his vision and, as the Armenian's hold loosened, stabbed him in the throat.

The thug's groan echoed. His arms slackened.

Cutter kneed him in the testicles with all his strength, which got Zohrab to drop his hands.

Now!

There was room for him to maneuver.

He stabbed the thug in his right eye, withdrew the knife and plunged it into his left.

He crouched to get his shoulders against the bodyguard's chest, as the man shrieked.

Cutter wrapped his left hand around Zohrab's body, and with a roar of effort straightened to pick up the Armenian in a fire-man's lift. He took a step to the wall and, with a tremendous heave, threw him over the bluff.

He whirled to face Janikyan, who looked shocked at the speed with which it had all happened, as if expecting his body-guard to miraculously reappear over the top of the wall.

Cutter was still outnumbered and facing well-armed thugs. All he had going for him was the fractional moment of surprise.

And the explosives.

'KILL HIM,' Matteo yelled in rage.

The explosives at the gate went off before anyone could react. The house shook and a window shattered inside.

Everyone froze.

'Go ahead,' Cutter taunted Janikyan. 'Shoot me. I've wired the entire house. Only I know where the bombs are. How will you get out if you kill me?'

'HE'S LYING,' Matteo shouted. 'KILL HIM. LET'S FINISH THIS.'

A chunk of concrete fell as another explosive went off. More bombs went off inside the house in quick succession.

The bangers stood uncertainly, looking to take their cue from Janikyan. The gang leader's face twisted in rage as he raised his hand to command them to fire.

I tried. I can't shoot them all. Cutter braced himself for the impact of rounds. He met Brae's eyes helplessly. *I can't save her.*

The light post behind Janikyan exploded and blew out a section of the wall.

❧ 98 ☙

'THE HOUSE IS FALLING,' Cruz yelled as concrete and tile chips showered them. He grabbed Matteo's elbow and pulled him towards the exit.

His warning and the pronounced tilting of the patio floor started the stampede.

The Armenian bangers forgot about shooting Cutter. They followed the detectives as they rushed to the sliding door and struggled to get through as the remaining bombs went off in the house.

'Not you!' Cutter lunged at Janikyan, who was racing to the exit, grabbed him by the shirt and brought him to the floor. He turned his head and caught the gang leader's kick on the side of his neck, a blow that sent his gun skittering across the floor.

'GET HIM!' the Bros boss commanded just as the second light pole exploded and shrouded them in darkness.

None of his men listened. They followed their instinct for self-preservation in a panicked getaway.

Cutter punched Janikyan in the belly and rolled towards Brae as the patio floor tipped farther, the unstable edge of the cliff beneath it shifting after the explosions. He ripped the tape from her mouth and shoved her towards the patio doors.

'Go,' he whispered at her. 'No one will stop you. Cops will be outside. They'll keep you safe.' *I'm not sure of that. Difiore might have ignored my call.* But she didn't need to know that.

He whirled to see the Armenian leader get to his feet and launched himself again at the gangster. His momentum sent them crashing through the door, just in time, as the patio shuddered and yawed at an unnatural angle.

The Armenian snarled in rage and beat at him with his fists. Cutter tried to duck and evade as he attempted to pin down the Bros leader, but the man was wiry and quick.

Got to finish him before the house collapses. He could hear the roof falling as more detonations sounded. He gritted his teeth, got his hands around the man's neck and squeezed.

Janikyan grunted. His eyes narrowed in rage. His hands clawed the floor desperately, and one of them found an abandoned assault rifle. He couldn't straighten it and instead used it as a battering ram.

Cutter took the blow on his temple. His head reeled and he nearly lost his grip, but he kept on squeezing. The Armenian cursed and swore, hit him repeatedly on the head and the side of his body, but he held on.

'You,' he raged, 'killed them.' He dug his thumbs into Janikyan's windpipe as he felt a rib crack from the rifle's impact. The gangster thrashed as his face turned red. He gasped and kept smashing the rifle against Cutter as the house began to tremble.

Cutter felt himself losing consciousness from the pounding, but he didn't let up. He heard someone yelling at him and looked up dazedly. No one but them in the collapsing house.

'CUTTER GROGAN!'

Stone and masonry fell near them and enveloped them in a cloud of dust. He choked and heard Janikyan plead. His forehead split and blood ran down his face when the butt of the rifle cut his skin. He clamped his knees tight against Janikyan's chest and forced himself to squeeze the breath out of the gangster.

'CUTTER. COME OUT!'

That wasn't his imagination. Someone from outside was calling his name. It didn't sound like Matteo, Cruz or anyone else he knew.

I'm not leaving until Janikyan is dead, he thought blearily.

He looked up when something rumbled overhead and saw a crack forming in the partial roof over the patio.

'We ... both ... will ... die,' Janikyan panted weakly.

'I'm good with that,' he grunted with the effort of speaking.

The gangster heaved up with all his might, but Cutter held on. The Bros leader hit him with the rifle with his remaining strength, but he didn't let up. A block of concrete landed a foot away. He looked up again and saw another large chunk loosening right on top of them.

He freed his hands and made to dive, but Janikyan reared up and grabbed him with both hands.

'No ...' His teeth gleamed. 'I ... won't ... let ... you ... escape.'

Cutter headbutted him frantically, sensed the incoming rush of air, slammed his elbow in Janikyan's throat and lunged away desperately just as the roof caved in.

❊ 99 ❊

'Call him again,' Difiore snapped as the house collapsed in front of them. The opaque cloud of dust and concrete was lit up eerily from the flashlights LAPD officers had trained on the building.

The cop looked at her as if to object, but took in her expression and that of the police chief. He raised his bullhorn and called out again.

'He would have gotten away,' Difiore whispered as she strained her eyes to look through the debris. She felt Quindica clasp her elbow reassuringly and blinked hard to fight back the bitterness that welled in her.

Her heart caught in her throat when something moved in the haze.

'THERE!' she heard herself yell when the gloom parted to reveal Cutter, bruised, bleeding, but alive.

He staggered through the wreckage of the gates as cops rushed to help him. Turned their way when he heard her yell and grinned tiredly.

'Difiore,' he swayed on his feet. 'That was just like Hollywood, wasn't it? Me coming through that dirt cloud.'

Don't cry, she told herself. Why should she? It's not as if she liked Cutter. He was a vigilante. He was a rule breaker.

She went to him and punched him hard in his belly.

'All this,' she glared at him, 'just so that you could have a dramatic escape?'

'Think how it'll look on TV. I'm going to be flooded with interviews. I'll name-drop if you wish—'

'I don't want to be associated with you.'

'You'll be famous.'

'That's what you get for being famous?' she surveyed his wounds quizzically.

He made a *peace* gesture and drank deeply from a bottle of water a cop offered. He waved away an approaching medic and looked at her. 'You came.'

I almost ignored your call.

'You heard everything?'

'Yeah,' she nodded. 'Recorded it as well. Matteo and Cruz—' she nodded in the direction of cops and police vehicles that crowded the street '—are in custody. Along with all the Armenian hitters who escaped.'

'SWAT would have entered the house,' Dade joined them. 'But they didn't figure the house was safe.'

Why's she looking like that? Difiore took in the chief's tight lips and narrowed eyes and her stomach churned. *Isn't she glad Cutter came out, safe?*

'There was a woman … Brae, her hands were bound—'

'She's safe,' the LAPD head answered. 'Where's Janikyan?'

'Between a slab of concrete and the floor.'

'Cutter.'

Difiore's head snapped up at the tone in her voice.

'Ma'am?' she asked disbelievingly when Dade placed a hand on his arm and directed him to a patrol car. 'What are you doing?'

'Gina,' Quindica spoke softly and laid a restraining arm on her shoulder. 'The chief's right.'

She looked at the LAPD head, who stared back expressionlessly, and then at Cutter, who winked.

'You've always wanted to see me arrested.'

She watched dully as he was driven away and turned to Dade. 'Lasko?'

'Yes. He's still the prime suspect for Matt's shooting.'

❦ 100 ❦

Two Days Later

CUTTER INSPECTED HIMSELF CRITICALLY AFTER HIS SHOWER. He poked a nasty-looking bruise on his chest with a finger and winced at the flare of pain.

It will heal. That broken rib, too.

He dressed in a Tee and jeans, squinted at his armor and shook his head. He wouldn't be needing it anymore. He drove his Land Cruiser out of Heliotrope and headed to Lasko's hospital in Boyle Heights. His whistling stopped abruptly when he found Difiore, Quindica and Dade by the cop's bed.

'Come in.' The chief beckoned him with a warm smile. 'I won't be arresting you again.'

'I'm not complaining,' he grinned. 'You made Difiore's dream come true.'

'What would have made me happier,' the NYPD detective scoffed, 'is if you hadn't been released.'

'It's my fault,' Lasko said weakly from his bed. 'He's out because of me.'

Cutter's grin faded as he sized up the injured cop. *He's still in bad shape but looks like he'll pull through.*

THE DETECTIVE HAD REGAINED CONSCIOUSNESS THE NIGHT OF the showdown in Beverly Hills but had been unable to speak until the following morning. His statement had exonerated Cutter, who was released swiftly from his detention in the Hollywood Area Jail.

Difiore and Quindica were on the sidewalk on Wilcox Avenue to greet him. The FBI agent hugged him tight and even Difiore had dropped her façade to grin and bump a fist with him. Dade was present too, in a discreetly parked SUV. 'I had to take you in,' she told him, looking deeply into his eyes. 'You understand?'

'Yeah,' he reassured her. 'We're good.'

'I SHOULDN'T HAVE LEFT YOU,' HE TOLD THE WOUNDED COP.

Lasko reached out and squeezed his arm. 'City's safer now. Covarra and Janikyan are gone.'

'What about Cesar?'

'Quindica pulled strings. My deal with him will be honored.'

'Federal witness protection program,' the FBI agent replied when Cutter looked at her quizzically. 'There's still a threat to him, even though Street Front's leadership is gone.'

'Matteo and Cruz?'

'They're singing,' the chief filled him in. 'Confessing everything, hoping they get a lighter sentence.'

'You agreed to that?'

'No. They aren't getting any leniency.' Her jaw hardened. 'I knew we had some bad cops, but didn't think it would be them.'

'They've given us a list of names,' Quindica said when Dade

lapsed into silence. 'Everyone in their gang. They were so good that no Internal Affairs investigation, none of the chief's task forces, identified them.'

'Vance and Diego fooled me, too,' Lasko added bitterly. 'They found out I was close to the chief and hoped Covarra would kill me that night, on Jesse Street. They accused me of being in with Covarra.'

'They figured you were colluding with Street Front, too,' Dade said tightly when Cutter looked bemused. 'Vance's theory was that's why you and Lasko had turned dirty.'

Will she take a political hit? Matteo was a star cop. Will the mayor sack her?

Nothing will happen to her, Quindica guessed his thoughts and lipped at him.

'Cutter.' Dade sensed they were talking about her and turned to them. 'You'll be leaving soon? Leaving LA?'

'You want me gone?' he chuckled.

'Who wouldn't?' Difiore retorted. 'The amount of destruction you have caused—'

'Who, me?' he pointed at himself with an innocent look.

'Yeah, you. A bike shooting—'

'That wasn't me.'

'That house on Alice Street? You razed it to the ground.'

'I'm an upstanding citizen,' he said indignantly. 'I don't go about shooting people or destroying property.'

'Save it,' Difiore sneered. 'What's keeping you here?'

'Vienna's house.'

'Which is yours, now.'

'Yeah, but I'm giving it away to the Lintock Foundation. Judith will put it to good use.'

'Janikyan's got a team of hackers in East Hollywood,' Dade informed him. 'The bangers who got out before you brought the house down spilled everything. We made several arrests in the last forty-eight hours. Those criminals broke into the traffic camera system and tracked your and Brae's escape from that banger's house. They traced her to Judith's house. Zohrab snatched her from there, when she came out to go shopping.'

'She needs to be protected as well.'

'Judith's taking care of it. I've recommended a good security firm to her. She'll be safe.'

'CUTTER,' DADE STOPPED HIM AS HE WAS HEADING TO HIS RIDE an hour later.

'Yeah?' he turned to face her. Difiore and Quindica, flanking her, looked on with unreadable expressions.

'You know Covarra's dead, don't you?'

'I saw it on TV, yeah. Salazar, him, a few bangers—'

'A few?' the NYPD detective snorted. 'There were two SUVs filled with hitters. All of them were killed.'

'I heard that,' he said mildly.

That was Zeb's doing. Beth, Meg and he played me, too. They were in LA all along. He had figured it out when he heard the news. *That app they got me to install ... I bet they could hear everything that happened at my end. They could track me, which is how they could cut Covarra off. I'll have to ask them how they knew that gang would be coming.*

'Who killed them?'

'Beats me, Lisa. I was inside that house. On TV they said it was likely to be Armenian Bros.'

'That's what we put out as our suspect. We're still investigating, however.'

You won't find anything. Not when Zeb's involved.

'He knows,' Difiore accused him. 'It's just like that vigilante in New York.'

'Vigilante?' Dade's eyes narrowed. 'Who was that?'

'We never found him, or her.' The detective briefed the chief on the mystery sniper who had saved them from a white supremacist gang.

'If it hadn't been for him, or her,' Cutter said, shrugging and putting on an innocent look, 'none of us would have been alive.'

'It's the same pattern here, too.' Difiore's eyes didn't leave him. 'Unknown shooters save his ass. If Covarra and his men had come to that house—'

'They would have shot it out with the Armenians.'

'Yeah, but sure as heck your trick with the bombs wouldn't have worked. Street Front wanted you dead. Covarra was impulsive. He would have shot you.'

'This shooting wasn't the work of one person. Two vehicles were involved, several guns.'

Cutter shifted uneasily when Dade stared at him, too.

'I don't know anything about them,' he protested.

'They're good. We couldn't find any prints. Spent brass is untraceable. Security cameras at the scene were knocked out.'

Her green eyes had a knowing light, while a small smile played on her lips. Difiore and Quindica had similar looks.

Chloe! She was in the 82nd too and toured Afghanistan. Dade must have known her. The chief would have stayed in touch with the Agency operative. *With her contacts, it wouldn't have been hard for her to work out they're my friends, and that they're in town.*

'If you do find them,' he declared, 'give them my thanks.'

'Those shooters recorded Covarra's confession. That he was the one who shot Lasko.'

He looked up, startled, at the chief.

'Those shooters emailed me that audio file from a dummy account. It wasn't needed, since Matt had given his statement by then. That's not all. A gun dealer was found outside the headquarters, in his Hummer. His hands were tied to the wheel, his legs bound and his mouth taped.'

That's Cabal. Beth and Meg must have discovered where I dumped his vehicle and recovered it.

'There was a notebook with him with many entries, all in code. We cracked it. A list of all his transactions. Who he bought weapons from, sold to ... we have already busted several bangers from that information.'

'Nothing to do with me.' Cutter raised his hands. 'I don't know any gun dealers.'

He climbed into his Land Cruiser and fired it up. Lowered the window when Dade tapped on it.

'You really thought we wouldn't work it out?'

'Work what out?' he played dumb.

'Tell Beth and Meghan Petersen,' Difiore said with a smug smile, 'and Zeb Carter, we said hello.'

He drove away without a word and grinned to himself when he saw them in the mirror staring after him.

Those cops. He couldn't pull a fast one on them.

MORE BOOKS

Check out Hangfire, the next Cutter Grogan thriller

Check out Tightrope, the next Zeb Carter thriller

Join Ty Patterson's group of readers, on Facebook

BONUS CHAPTER FROM HANGFIRE

Cutter was in Los Angeles, at a crematorium on Santa Monica Boulevard, when the freak thunderstorm struck.

It was the death of two friends, killed in gang violence, that had brought him to the city. On arrival, he had discovered they were victims of a deep-rooted conspiracy. His hunt for the perpetrators had brought him up against vicious gangs and traitors.

I barely survived. He looked up at the grey sky, streaked with flashes of lightning, as people took cover from the sudden downpour. *It's over, finally.*

He had taken shelter under a palm tree, but its fronds offered little cover from the rain, which dripped on his head and face. He inched closer to its trunk.

His friends' last rites had been performed at the crematorium, and he had returned now, on the eve of his departure for home, for some time alone.

Its grounds were an oasis of green in the city, offering calm and solitude to those seeking it. The deluge of rain and dark sky suited his somber mood.

He blinked raindrops from his eyelids and chuckled at

departing mourners fleeing for the shelter of their cars. *Angelinos,* he scoffed inwardly. *They can't handle a few drops of rain.*

He patted his pocket when his phone buzzed. Brought it out and frowned. *Who could that be?* Only a handful of trusted friends had his number.

'Yeah,' he barked.

'Cutter Grogan?'

'Yes, ma'am.' He straightened instinctively in response to the refined, elderly voice.

'I got your number from Zeb Carter.'

'He's a good friend, ma'am.'

'He was recommended to me by someone I know ... but when I approached him, he mentioned your name. He said you were more suited ...'

Suited for what, he wondered when she trailed off. There was no background noise at her end. No other voices, no sirens, car honks. Just a deep silence.

'You've had some issues with the LAPD, Mr. Grogan.'

He blinked at that, wiped his face and rubbed his wet palm against his jeans. *She's done her research on me.*

'I'm not a criminal, ma'am,' he replied automatically.

'I know. I wouldn't have called you if you were.'

Why did you call me? Who are you?

'Forgive my manners, Mr. Grogan.' Her voice dropped. 'I'm Amy Breland.'

Why's that name familiar?

Breland? Amy Breland? Her?

'You're the—'

'Yes, Mr. Grogan.' There was a smile in her reply. 'Some people know me as the Speaker of the House.'

I bet it was President Morgan who recommended Zeb to her.

'Mr. Grogan, are you there?'

'Yes, ma'am.' He swallowed. It was not as if he often got calls from one of the most recognized and powerful people in the country. 'I respond better to Cutter, ma'am.'

'Cutter? That's an unusual name.'

'Yes, ma'am.'

'You're called the Fixer, in New York.'

He shuffled his feet in embarrassment. It was a title he had given himself when he had acquired a degree of fame. The name had stuck and gotten him several new clients.

She's gauging my responses, assessing me ... that's why she's drawing this out.

'Yes, ma'am; it sounds good on TV.'

'I'm not judging you, Cutter.' She took a deep breath. 'I have a problem. I'm wondering if you can help me with it.'

'What's that, ma'am?'

'It's my grand-daughter. Lauren Breland.'

The same name as her?

'Long story,' she read his silence correctly. 'My daughter and son-in-law died in a car accident. She was their only child. I took on caring for her and she took my last name. She's a freelance journalist, well-regarded. She's missing.'

'The cops—'

'She was investigating a sex-trafficking ring in DC when she disappeared about a week ago.'

'You should go to the cops, ma'am. They can help better than me.'

'I can't. They're involved in that ring.'

AUTHOR'S MESSAGE

৩১৯

Thank you for taking the time to read *Powder Burn*. If you enjoyed it, please consider telling your friends and posting a short review.

Sign up to Ty Patterson's mailing list and get The Watcher, a Zeb Carter novella, exclusive to newsletter subscribers. Join Ty Patterson's Facebook Readers Group.

ABOUT THE AUTHOR

Ty has been a trench digger, loose tea vendor, leather goods salesman, marine lubricants salesman, diesel engine mechanic, and is now an action thriller author.

Ty feels privileged that thriller readers love his books. 'Unputdownable,' 'Turbocharged,' 'Ty sets the standard in thriller writing,' are some of the reviews for his books.

Ty lives with his wife and son, who humor his ridiculous belief that he's in charge.

Made in the USA
Middletown, DE
24 January 2021